Justin Newland was born in Essex, Eng1953. His love of literature began soon aft pirates and tales of adventure.

His taste in literature is eclectic from lite fiction, with a special mention for the magi Along the way, he was wooed by the muses of .... and modern, and then got happily lost in the labyrinths of mythology, religion and philosophy.

Undeterred by the award of a Doctorate in Mathematics from Imperial College, London, he found his way back to the creative keyboard and conceived his debut novel, *The Genes of Isis* (Matador, 2018), an epic fantasy set under Ancient Egyptian skies. *The Old Dragon's Head* (Matador, 2018) is his second novel. *The Coronation* (Matador, 2019) is his third.

His stories add a touch of the supernatural to history and deal with the themes of war, religion, evolution and the human's place in the universe.

He lives with his partner in plain sight of the Mendip Hills in Somerset, England.

Reviews of *The Old Dragon's Head*

"A stand out novel that ticks all the boxes – murder, mystery, treason, glorious villains, reluctant heroes and more than a touch of the supernatural."
DISCOVERING DIAMONDS.

"The author is an excellent storyteller."
BRITISH FANTASY SOCIETY.

"History meets magic, culture meets supernatural… I would recommend this story to anyone who enjoys historical fiction with a twist."
BOOKS BEYOND THE STORY.

"This is an exceptionally well-written book which takes one back to the China of 1400."
THAT'S BOOKS AND ENTERTAINMENT

"I absolutely loved the mix of fantasy elements well-rooted in Chinese history."
JESSICA BELMONT

"I enjoyed the different perspectives and the magical realism."
ROSIE CAWKWELL

"This book was part murder mystery and part fantasy with some fabulous villains and heroes."
OVER THE RAINBOW

"This isn't your typical coming of age story – it's filled with tough choices, unexpected surprises, and a destiny that's bigger than anyone can imagine."
THE FAERIE REVIEW

"This epic story has it all – adventure, mystery, villains, the supernatural, and at its heart a true coming of age journey."
BOOKS AND EMMA

"This is a book of historical fantasy, but in terms of the fantasy, it is subtle, and firmly rooted in cultural beliefs and superstitions within the time period covered in the book."
BOOK MAD JO

"This is not just a fantasy book, this is a fantasy with history, murder, mystery, legend, myth and of course the supernatural. There are villains and heroes and action and adventure."
BOOKMARKS AND STAGES

THE
OLD
DRAGON'S
HEAD

JUSTIN NEWLAND

Matador
9 Priory Business Park,
Wistow Road, Kibworth Beauchamp,
Leicestershire. LE8 0RX
Tel: 0116 279 2299
Email: books@troubador.co.uk
Web: www.troubador.co.uk/matador
Twitter: @matadorbooks

ISBN 978 1789015 829

British Library Cataloguing in Publication Data.
A catalogue record for this book is available from the British Library.

Printed and bound in Great Britain by 4edge Limited

Matador is an imprint of Troubador Publishing Ltd

Nanjing, China.
In the Chinese Year of the Goat, 23rd January, 1368.

I, Zhu Yuanzhang, have expelled the Mongol invader. For too many winters, we have suffered at the hands of the barbarian. I will restore the greatness of China both in Heaven and on earth.

While my followers exhorted me to grasp the Mandate of Heaven, I dared not do so without a propitious sign.

Five days ago, on a cold, snowy day, I erected an altar of worship to the Supreme Cosmic Deity. I prayed that if the Lord on High approved of my new ruling house, then the appointed day of my enthronement – 23rd of January, 1368 – would be a bright day.

Today is that day and, miracle of miracles, the warm rays of the sun pierce the gloom and have melted the frozen earth. The Lord on High has heard my supplication. The Yang exerts itself upon the Yin. The order of the Tao is restored. Thus, I take my seat on the Dragon Throne.

As a bright day in Heaven means a bright day on earth, I name this the Ming – the Bright – Dynasty.

Zhu Yuanzhang, the Hongwu Emperor.
THE GREAT MING CODE

CHAPTER 1

The Fortress of Shanhaiguan

Shanhaiguan, the Eastern End of the Great Wall of China.
In the Second Year of the Reign of the Jianwen Emperor.
The Penultimate Day of the Year of the Rabbit, 1st February, 1400.

Bolin swooned and propped himself up against the metal railings. He rubbed his temples, hoping it would ease the shooting pains in his head. It didn't. His vision was as blurred as the mists that rolled off the sea.

"Are you fit for work?" Wen railed at him. That was his new superior.

"Why, yes, Master Wen," he said, adding an obsequious bow.

"Do you want to fail on your first day?" Wen snapped.

"N-no, of course not," Bolin stammered. Behind them, one of the donkeys brayed and let out a huge fart, bringing smirks to the lips of the assembled apprentices, all except Bolin. This headache was more than a pain.

Wen scowled and said, "This is the most eastern end of the Great Wall of Ten Thousand Li and, in this province, I am its maintainer." He puffed out his chest and crossed his arms. "This section, in the neck of land between the mountains and the sea, was built twenty years ago. Tomorrow is a special occasion and I want you to return it to its pristine condition."

The apprentices made approving noises as he went on, "The Great Wall is made of more than stone and packed earth. Woe betide anyone I hear say otherwise! It is host to a living, breathing entity, the Old Dragon Laolong, and we are standing on the Old Dragon's Head, the Laolongtou. Below us, this end section of the wall protrudes right into the sea. The old dragon is taking a cooling drink. Make sure you pay him the respect he deserves."

That was Wen, the famous Master Builder. Folk said he breathed fire when raised to anger. Bolin wasn't sure whether they were referring to Wen or the Laolong.

1

Wen bent his neck and glowered at them from beneath his brow, taking them in one by one.

"Other than me and the Laolong, the wall belongs to the military, the monks and the Great Wall Mummers. For you new conscripts, it's the first time you've ever trodden its hallowed soil, so be warned. If you're tempted to sneak your family up here for a quick view of the land of the barbarians, I will haul you before the county magistrate, who'll parade you around in a tight-fitting cangue. You wouldn't want to suffer that shame, now would you?"

While the workers hung their heads, Bolin wished he could appreciate the great honour of his newfound position. His headache was thumping like a gong in a Buddhist temple. Never before had he suffered like this.

He patted the donkey. On the cart were buckets, carrying poles, wheelbarrows, rakes, spades, tampers, rammers, as well as bags of lime and sand and gourds of muddy water; all the paraphernalia of repair and construction. The donkey was ready for work – Bolin was not.

A clutch of guards was clearing the twigs and leaves scattered over the road that ran along the length and breadth of the Great Wall, while another group furiously swept away the puddles deposited by the overnight storm. Some of the conscripts were gathering bits of wood and various belongings that lay strewn over the road, while others set about re-building the guards' makeshift huts.

It was bitterly cold and Bolin rubbed his hands. The sea mists swirled across the fortress in huge curtains of moisture. The garrison commandant eyed their group with an air of studied suspicion and asked, "What brings you onto the wall road today, Master Wen?"

"Instructing more apprentices, Commandant Tung," he replied with a curt bow.

"They've much to learn to match your dedication," the commandant suggested. "Every day, you inspect the wall and its fortifications."

"Thank you. I have to ensure that our defences against the Mongol horde are strong and impenetrable."

"Hah!" Tung declared. "We sent those barbarians scampering back to the land of the Blue Wolf and that's where they can stay."

"Aye to that," Wen nodded. "Today we are preparing the Great Wall for the New Year festivities."

"Indeed. The Year of the Dragon promises to be a splendid year."

"It would be even better if this work is finished today," Wen added sardonically. Turning to the apprentices, he said, "Yesterday's tempest tore into the cladding of the wall. The lights from tomorrow night's fireworks will show up the tiniest cracks and holes. I want the blemishes smoothed, the crevices filled, the lichen and moss removed. Everything must be as auspicious as possible, with the stronger yang and weaker yin in their rightful places. Now, get to it."

Wen and Tung set off at pace. Bolin hurried at a respectful distance behind them, his feet slipping and sliding on the moist surface. It was curious, because as soon as he left the Laolongtou and ventured onto the main land-based part of the wall, his headache lifted. What a relief!

For years, he'd lived in the shadow of the wall and now, for the first time ever, he was going to enjoy a panoramic view of the sheer scale of the fortifications. From the vantage point of the wall road, he could see the pale winter sun glistening in the cold, grey waters of the moat surrounding the square fortress. Next to that, walls as tall as trees and thicker than ten men standing side by side, as well as a frightening series of watchtowers, ramps and gates, protected the army and citizens of Shan-hai-guan, the 'Mountain-sea-pass'. Rows of billets housed thousands of soldiers and enormous warehouses stocked supplies of food and armaments with which to send them to war. Fine stables for the cavalry horses sat next to the more rudimentary housing for the hundreds of oxen, donkeys and mules yoked to the supply wagons.

A guard on the battlements of the east gate interrupted his awe.

"Hi! Hi!" His cry resounded along the wall. He was pointing across the plain, where a rider raced along the coast road towards them. Bolin watched the horseman pull up on the edge of the moat, his horse panting as if chased by the hounds of hell. A small flag bearing the yellow-red emblem of the Prince of Yan protruded from his saddle.

"The rider comes from our fief lord. Lower the drawbridge," the commandant ordered.

The soldiers clambered into the wheelhouse and the wooden drawbridge creaked open. Bolin leaned over the parapet to get a better view. The rider was soon over the drawbridge and through the outer gate. The sound of his horse's hooves echoed around the arched tunnel that ran under the gate tower. Leaping off the horse and with barely a break in his stride, the rider knelt down on one knee, bowed low before the commandant and handed him a scroll.

"A message from our prince," the commandant's voice boomed around the courtyard. "He'll pass through the garrison with fifteen thousand victorious troops. Tomorrow."

The news was greeted with the customary waving of hands. That was a large army and Bolin had witnessed many troop movements in and out of the fortress, even more so since the death two years ago of Zhu Yuanzhang, the Hongwu Emperor. The prince consort had died, so Zhu had bequeathed the throne to his grandson, the Jianwen Emperor. Soon after, the new Emperor's uncle, the Prince of Yan, had rebelled, precipitating a bitter war of succession.

Bolin raised an eyebrow on hearing of the prince's manoeuvre. Up to now, the battles between the prince and his nephew had taken place on home soil, so why was he picking another fight with the Mongols?

He turned to his new friend, Cui. He would know.

The old soldier screwed up his face into a frown and whispered, "With a civil war in full flow, the Mongols eye an opportunity to invade our borders and re-instate their reign of terror. The rumour is that the Emperor himself has urged the Mongols to harass our northern frontier – against our own prince. We've recently removed the barbarians and our new Emperor's making them an ally." His expression was suitably sour. "Our fief lord was having none of that, so he took an army up there to deal them a killer blow. Sounds like he's succeeded." Cui grinned revealing the blackened remains of his teeth.

Master Wen added his own brand of chastisement. "With the prince arriving, there's another reason to make the wall look its finest. I want teams of eight, each working on adjoining segments. Jump to it. No slacking, you hear?"

Cui was in charge of Bolin's group, which was stationed in the shadows of the Yanshan Mountains. They spent the rest of the day clearing debris from the wall road and cleaning its vertical faces. Both he and Cui descended on rickety bamboo cradles, roped onto the crenellated battlements. Hanging at precarious angles, they shovelled a lime mix into every crack and fissure they could find. Holes restricted the flow of ch'i through the wall and that was inauspicious. When the cold wings of dusk drew in, he and Cui made their way back to the east – the Zhendong – gate.

Cui wandered off to the White Mulberry Inn. He went there so often, it was almost as if he was drinking to forget something from his past. Bolin hurried through the market place, where he joined the stall holders and shoppers scuttling off home before the dusk watch announced the locking of the city gates for the night.

Swathed in the long afternoon shadows, he glanced back up at the wall, towering above him like the face of a cliff rising up to Heaven.

That was when it happened – again.

His temples started pounding. His eyes misted over. This time, there was more than the intense discomfort of before. Vivid images marched through his mind like soldiers in a line, forcing him to witness…

Bamboo scaffolding reached from the earth to the great height of the wall road, entwined with the turrets like embracing lovers. Workers swarmed like ants over every part of it, lifting buckets, hauling tools and carrying hods of earth. He recognised the stone cladding on the wall. This was the Shanhaiguan Fortress under construction, twenty years before.

It was early morning, the sun had risen and a little boy stood on the ground, bathed in the giant shadow cast by the Great Wall. Up above him on the east gate wall road, a worker was walking backwards towards an unguarded edge. The boy seemed to recognise him. With a smile like a spring flower, he shouted and waved up to the man, but his cry was lost amidst the clash of the hammers and the pounding of the earth works.

The man cradled a plank of wood like he was nursing a child. Oblivious to his imminent danger, he took another step back.

The boy yelled at the man, this time anxious, pleading.

Too late. The man slipped and fell backwards. His scream rent the air. Everyone heard it. The little boy heard it. In his vision, Bolin heard it.

In the air, the man turned a slow, elegant spiral, rather like those fireworks that Bolin had seen on New Year's Day that whizzed round and round before fizzling into nothing, a light carried before being consumed by the darkness.

On the ground, the boy stared up at the macabre sight of this man, this aerial apparition, plunging towards him. The air was disgorging the man and he was going to land on top of him.

Get out of the way! Bolin screamed.

But the boy's feet had grown roots.

Perhaps the gods would descend from their jade pagodas and reverse the irrevocable march of time. Perhaps karma would change the course of events.

Neither of these things occurred.

At the last moment, the flight of the man twisted in mid-air and he slammed into the cold, unforgiving earth. His head screwed round and faced the wrong way, staring obliquely up at the boy.

The wall was silent. The earth drew breath. Even the gods missed a heartbeat.

His eyes wide in terror, the boy mouthed a word as old as the human race. "Father."

CHAPTER 2

The Blue Wolf

The Blue Wolf was born with a destiny from Heaven above.
THE SECRET HISTORY OF THE MONGOLS

The next day, Bolin forced himself to return to duty. Still marooned on the shore of his terrible vision, it was the last thing he wanted to do but as a new conscript, he knew absence was not tolerated. Scared and anxious, he made his way to the wall. It was karma, because he and Cui were assigned to work near the market which now occupied the place where the man had fallen to his death. Bolin shuddered to think about it. He was even stood in the shadows cast by the Great Wall, exactly where the boy had been. There was no escaping the dream. What had he done to deserve this awful fate? He grabbed a broom and swept away the fallen leaves with unbridled fury. If only he could sweep away his vision of the fallen.

"What's the matter?" Cui asked.

"Is it that obvious?"

"My ladle wouldn't prise open your furrowed brow. Come on, out with it."

When he told him about it, Cui scoffed, "Now you're seeing visions?"

"I honestly don't know if that's what they are." Bolin shook his head. His bones ached as if he had walked the length of the Great Wall. He had never had headaches or visions before. He hoped he never had them again.

"Listen," Cui said. "To see a ghost, the old women claim you need yin-yang eyes. Soothsayers have them. Clairvoyants have them. Priests have them. But you're a fisherman's son. How did you get yin-yang eyes? You can't buy them in the market, you know?" Cui added with a guffaw.

Bolin felt hurt and confused. After a moment, he said, "I don't know much about these yin-yang eyes. Anyway, it was more than just a vision."

"What was it then?" Cui asked.

Bolin took a deep breath. "The event I saw really happened."

"How do you know?"

Cui glared at him like he was mad. He wasn't. He was certain about this. With pinched lips, Bolin said, "I know who the man was. It was Heng. And the little boy was his son, Ru."

Cui's mouth dropped open. "What? Luli's family? Are you sure?"

Bolin gritted his teeth and nodded. "The family are our neighbours in Shanhai village. Ru is my friend. He was five when it happened. Me, I was suckling at my mother's breast, so I have no memories of it. The incident so traumatised him that he's barely spoken since. Now it's haunting me."

While they carried on clearing the debris from the area in front of the Zhendong Gate, Bolin was preoccupied. He kept seeing a forlorn little boy standing in the long, dark shadow of the wall, watching as his father plunged out of the air and spread-eagled in front of him.

Bolin shook his head; maybe that would make the vision go away. And what about the yin-yang eyes? By a strange coincidence, Luli, Ru's mother, was a seer and a healer. She had them. But he, Bolin, could never have them. Then why had he 'seen' such a gruesome slice of history? Was it karma? Did he have too much yang, or too little yin? Either way, he must have erred from the path of the Tao, the true way to Heaven. The vision must be a mistake, an aberration. It wouldn't happen again to him.

Before either of them could speak again, the guards on the upper battlements raised a hue and cry, waving the yellow and red emblem of the House of Yan. The vanguard of the prince's army had appeared on the horizon. Bolin was stationed within the fortress' confines, so couldn't see the column. That was about to change when a runner called for him and Cui to report to Major Renshu, the commandant's adjutant.

The major was inspecting troops at the entrance to the tunnel beneath the Zhendong Gate. He and Cui gave him their best salute. The major said, "You two, come with me."

What had he done wrong now? Was this karma? Bolin feared the worst.

The major shouted orders at them. "I want you to form an honour guard of twenty soldiers and escort the monks out to meet the prince's column."

Cui nodded with enthusiasm. "Yes, Major."

What a relief and a privilege, Bolin thought. Curious though – the major's voice had a Mongolian twang. Then again, many Mongols had settled in China – or the Zhongguo as it was also called – and were loyal citizens.

The welcome drums raised a clamour. The major scampered off to greet the vanguard, which was already marching into the fortress with heads held high.

7

Their halberds prodding the sky, they led the riders into the huge square by the Bell and Drum Tower amidst loud cheers. The riders carried tattered Mongol banners and broken flagpoles. Many sported spears abutted by a severed head.

As they passed nearby, Bolin frowned. "I expected more trophies after a major campaign. Where are the chains of prisoners, heads bowed in shameful defeat? Where are the rich spoils of war?"

Cui smirked.

"Come on, Cui. What's going on?"

"Well, I bumped into a friend in the White Mulberry last night."

Cui knew everyone who frequented the well-known inn, especially its controversial proprietor, One Hand Zhou.

"Tell me, who was it this time – the constable, the camel master, or the assistant salt commissioner? You seem to know a lot of important people."

"I do, but it was none of those," Cui said with a wicked smile. "It was the rider who brought the news of the prince's arrival yesterday."

That got Bolin's attention.

With an air of calm authority, Cui explained, "It concerns the Great Ming Code and its new rules for dealing with barbarian peoples. The Hongwu Emperor wrote them before he died. You see, we live in the land of the Yellow Dragon. We are a civilised, cultured and sedentary people. The Mongols on the other hand inhabit the land of the Blue Wolf. They're wild, migratory and barbaric. So it's important that no prisoners or banners contaminate the sacred land of the Zhongguo. In tonight's New Year celebrations, the prince will throw the captured flags into the cleansing fires."

"Well, that's reassuring," Bolin murmured.

"It is but listen; the victory came with a heavy price." Cui glanced over his shoulder and whispered, "During the campaign, the prince lost his most able commander, General Shimei."

Before he could reply, the major returned and ushered them into line with the honour guard and the monks. They followed the major into the tunnel. At the far end of it, the drawbridge had already been lowered over the moat. The prince's column had halted about one li – about three hundred paces – from the Zhendong Gate, their horses pawing the dirt, oozing sweat into the chill morning air. Six abreast and dressed in battle attire, the cavalry waved back at the tumultuous welcome from the massed soldiers on the wall. Many hung down from the parapet on ropes, ladders and cradles to gain a brilliant, if unconventional, view of the victorious army.

He and Cui set off amidst a guard leading eight Taoist monks, including Dong the Abbot. Banging drums, clashing symbols and shaking rattles, the monks were making enough noise to scare every stray ghost between the mountains and the sea. Bolin revelled in the rich and heady atmosphere of the occasion. Every step took him nearer to the prince. His mother and father would be so proud of him. Well, if this was karma, his fortunes were riding the dragon clouds.

The rising sun shone on the prince's magnificent black stallion. With a regal wave, he acknowledged the rousing welcome echoing along the battlements. Standing near to the prince, an equerry held the reins of a riderless horse, its armour bedecked in the red and gold livery of a commanding officer. That must be the dead general's.

Bolin could smell the sweat of the two horses and see their mud-caked hooves. But his headache returned, accompanied by an incessant ringing in his ears. An eerie feeling crept over him like an early morning mist over the moors.

The prince's steed seemed unnerved as well, because it pawed the ground, kicking up spurts of the damp earth, which agitated the riderless horse. The prince hauled on his reins, but it resisted, snorting loudly.

The riderless mount bucked its head, throwing off the dead general's armour, which clattered onto the unyielding earth. The equerry patted him on the back while pulling on its tether. Instead of calming the beast, its nostrils flared and its eyes opened wide as if in terror.

Amidst cries of alarm, all Bolin could hear was heavy thrumming against his temples. The air in front of him seemed cloudy, full of swirling strands of ch'i. The ch'i currents whirled around the cavalry, who seemed unaware of its invisible presence. Three paces in front of the prince's horse, an ethereal figure emerged from the spectral mists. Bolin inhaled sharply. *Who or what is that?*

The spectral figure menaced the prince's horse, which neighed and kicked its hooves wildly. Straining every sinew, the prince hung on to his reins for dear life.

Bolin noticed thick crimson streaks running like the tracks of a wagon wheel across the man's chest. A dried stream of blood that had flowed from a missing ear now caked the warrior's neck and shoulder. In his hand, the man clutched a tattered, blood-speckled parchment. The spectral figure was wearing silk of gold and red – a general's uniform.

The ghostly figure struck fear into the dead general's horse, which reared up, snorting. Unable to handle it, the equerry let go the reins, slipped and fell. The horse's whirling hooves crashed on his head, splitting it like an egg, splattering brains and gore over the prince's silken uniform.

The world stopped. The prince stared at the blood on his damask tunic. The column held its collective breath. A pall of silence descended on the ramparts, the initial playful welcoming atmosphere suffocated by a moment of horror. In that hiatus, Bolin seemed the only one still awake and aware. He could see what was happening. Why couldn't they? In that suspended moment, he felt as if some demon, some errant spirit, occupied his being, as if – he was possessed. The weird, eerie feeling passed almost as quickly as it had come, releasing his voice to shout as loud as he could, "A ghost! There! Look!"

He stabbed his finger at the spectre.

His words broke the spell that shackled the world. Fright and loathing replaced the cheers from the battlements and all mayhem broke loose. Horses reared, throwing riders onto the ground. Soldiers rushed around like frantic geese, spreading chaos. The dead general's horse ran off by the side of the moat. Riders from the column gave chase. Commotion surrounded the prince, who clung to the reins for dear life. A military physician ran across the drawbridge to care for the injured.

Cui's cries of alarm rent the air. "Who? What are you talking about?" The old soldier yelled.

"It's General Shimei. Can't you—?"

"I don't see anything," Cui interrupted him. "Besides, I told you that he's dead!"

"I know. It's a ghost. He's there!" Bolin felt like his face was about to explode with rage.

A voice of authority calmed the dispute. "I see him. Leave this to me." It was Dong, the Abbot of the local temple. In moments, the Taoist monks struck up a clamour on their drums and cymbals, unnerving the general's ghost. As Dong led them towards the spectre, it shimmered around the edges, lost its human form and gradually melted back into the clouds of ch'i like a man sucked into quicksand.

Once the ghost had gone, a semblance of order was restored. The riders brought back the run-away horse. The prince's equerry patted his horse. Whispering in its ear, he brought it under control. The prince's entourage gathered around him. The officers harangued the column back into line.

The other equerry lay in a crimson pool, his brains leaking onto the cold ground. Even Bolin could see that the man was on his way to Heaven – or hell.

As soon as Shimei's ghost had disappeared, Bolin's headache went too. What a relief that was. He could move. He could think about what had just happened. Why was he 'seeing' a dead general? Why had the equerry had his brains scattered over the ground like seed? And how close was the horse to killing the prince?

With frantic intent, he turned these events over in his mind.

Dong came over and, to his surprise, greeted him with a low bow, denoting respect. "Good work," the Abbot said. "I hadn't spotted the ghost. But you had. I didn't know you had yin-yang eyes. Anyway, once I knew where it was, the monks could exorcise it. You did very well."

"I did? Thank you, Abbot," Bolin said, flushing with embarrassment.

Dong hadn't finished and explained, "Dead soldiers are a terrible burden on the living. Their ghosts march alongside the column, sit on the supply wagons and hang around the camp fires. What you did was brave and demonstrated your loyalty to your fief lord."

"I didn't know," Bolin stammered.

"I'm sure your commanding officer will want to thank you, too," Dong said.

Bolin peered through the brightening rays of the sun as the Taoist monks marched along the length of the column, smashing their drums and cymbals, clearing the column of any lingering spectral presence. The monks must have known what they were doing, because the horses and men relaxed. Even the general's riderless horse quietened.

The column reformed. The prince's bodyguards lined up alongside him, halberds pointing up and frowns pointing down. To a subdued welcome, Bolin, Cui, Dong and his monks led the Prince of Yan and his huge army over the drawbridge, through the tunnel and into the square by the Drum and Bell Tower.

The prince greeted the awaiting crowd with a regal wave. As his equerry corralled his horse, he descended like a god, an apotheosis to grace his minions on earth. Was he really the future Son of Heaven? Everyone must have believed so, because they threw themselves onto the ground in full reverence.

Bolin hated kow-towing. It was a humiliating and undignified way for one human to show respect to another. Everyone was so compliant, timid and unquestioning, that he had to keep those rebellious thoughts to himself. He lay face down on the bald earth, growing numb with cold. His nose was snared on a stray twig and his hand rested in an icy puddle.

His overactive mind drifted back to the spectres haunting his life.

Yin-yang eyes, for the second time. Meaning the first was no aberration. What good are they anyway? To 'see' a friend's father die a gruesome death and a general's ghost with a severed ear? But wait, that vision helped save the prince. Even Dong praised me. So, there was some good karma in it. I don't know. It's confusing. I'm afraid of the next headache. Afraid of what I'll see next.

CHAPTER 3

End and Beginning

Iron will erode, rocks will decay.
Only the spirit never wears away.
CHINESE SAYING

After the prince disappeared into his quarters, everyone hauled themselves off the ground, brushed the dirt and leaves from mud-stained robes. Throughout the rest of the day, Bolin and Cui helped the fortress troops find billets for the arriving prince's army. Bolin didn't know what to think about them. Yes, they were conquering heroes, but they were rebels too, fighting against kith and kin.

As dusk fell and the last remnants of the cavalry units trudged over the drawbridge, Bolin tripped over a lip in the pavement, just managing to keep his balance. If that wasn't a warning to tread with more care in his life, what was? He couldn't shake the nagging feeling that he was at odds with himself and the world.

The ghost of an army general had struck terror in him and sowed panic amongst the prince's battle-hardened warriors. In a state of war, how could he be at peace with the Tao? The fabric of the world was out of joint, like a clown becoming an Emperor, or an Emperor becoming a clown.

Tonight was the turn of the tide, the eve of the New Year, the eve of the new – the dark – moon. When the darkness of yin was full, the light-giving yang returned and the Heavenly cycle recommenced. On the crest of a propitious wave, he resolved to make a new start.

When dusk fell, Bolin came off duty and went straight to meet Cui in the throng gathering in the Bell and Drum Square. Scores of lictors hurried around its perimeter lighting the torches and placing them back on their cradles. A small battalion of men was hauling planks of wood, branches and anything flammable into the centre of the square for the bonfire.

The Shanhai villagers and off-duty soldiers were swelled by officials including the magistrate, constables, commissioners, mandarins and other officials from the Yamen, as well as the tailor, carpenter and silk merchant, blacksmith and rice merchant. Peddlers touting sausages, duck and chicken vied with others selling tea, wine and rice vodka under the shadows of the Bell and Drum Tower. The traditional red lanterns swayed in the breeze blowing off the Bohai Sea. The animated crowd, the rich smell of dumplings and the boisterous activities of a troupe of acrobats and stilt walkers drew his attention away from past anxieties to present joys.

Bolin stood as near as he could to the Zhendong Gate, a formidable tower with walls thirty paces thick and crowned by another tower with two elevations. Beneath it ran an arched tunnel, with a drawbridge and moat at the outer end and heavy wooden gates at the inner end, which was where Bolin was stood. Like the rest of the crowd, he wanted to be the first to see the procession of acrobats, singers, dancers and musicians gathering at the far, moat end of the tunnel.

While they waited, folk chatted amongst themselves, exchanging gifts, greetings and well wishes. Lovers embraced. Mothers fussed over their sons and fathers hoisted their young daughters onto their shoulders.

A procession of monks entered the tunnel to clear away debris and litter. Behind a donkey cart, a monk carrying a bag of sackcloth hurried along, head bowed and a burning torch in his hand, examining the path with furious intent. Jin was the assistant to the Abbot of the Temple of the Eight Immortals. From previous years, Bolin knew what Jin was looking for and called out, "Did you find any yet?"

"Indeed I have, Master Bolin, indeed I have," Jin looked up and nodded. His round moon face shone with perspiration.

"Show me?" Bolin asked.

Jin obliged by plunging his hand into the sack and held out his palm, saying, "This is the biggest piece. I reckon it must have sheared off a passing cart."

As his head swirled and his temples pounded, Bolin let out a long, slow groan. He gazed at the piece of metal and swooned. He would have fallen over if Cui hadn't propped him up.

"What's the matter, young fella? Is it the iron this time?" Cui asked, gripping his elbow.

"I-I don't know. It must be," Bolin replied. His heart was thumping like he'd run up the spiral stairs of the Great Pagoda.

"Dear Bolin, may the healing gods look kindly on you," Jin said with due reverence. "I must pick up every last piece of iron from the path of the procession. Iron is an enemy of the spirit worlds, of the old dragon – the Laolong – and, it would appear, of you. Please excuse me, so I can remove it from your presence – and everyone else's."

As soon as Jin took the iron away, the pressure on Bolin's head eased. He could actually think again. The iron had brought on the head pains, yet the only metal he'd ever been sensitive to was silver, in the main because he never had any of it; not a single tael. When he was a child, he was friends with the son of the blacksmith and iron was strewn around his workshop. Bolin wasn't sensitive to it then, so what had changed? His life was growing deep veins of instability. What was he seeing through these yin-yang eyes? A man falling to his death? A ghost soldier? He whistled. Was he going mad?

The beginning of the festivities was heralded by a long roll from the drummers on top of the Bell and Drum Tower. The whole fortress seemed to vibrate with power and strength.

Dressed in colourful red, black and green silk robes, Dong led the monks out of the tunnel into the square. The crowd, about thirty deep, waved their hands in the traditional silent welcome. One day, when Bolin was three, he'd clapped with noisy enthusiasm at the New Year Festival, only to be reminded by his father that the way to show appreciation was to wave hands, not clap them. Behind the monks came the musicians, banging drums with bamboo sticks, blowing on flutes and strumming the lute with vigour and skill.

Then along came the dragon. It wasn't a real one. Bolin had never seen the actual Laolong, no, this was a ceremonial one made for the occasion. Amidst great noise and clamour, it meandered down the street in a cascade of motion and colour. Up and down, the dragon surged first this way, then that, miming the real beast's subtle rhythmic undulations.

Not everyone had such a sanguine view of the proceedings. Cui, for one, was nostalgic, "It's such a shame," he said.

Bolin recognised the sadness in his words. "Why's that?" he replied.

"Before my time, in the days of the ancient Sung Dynasty," Cui said, wagging his finger at him, "we could have seen the real Laolong, not some paper substitute on stilts."

Cui paused as it waltzed by them, supported on poles by scores of exuberant villagers. Their movements were sinuous and as fluid as the waves of the Bohai Sea. Despite Cui's complaints, the celebrations freshened up the garrison, a feat enhanced by the loom of buds in the flowers and trees, and their promise of a coming spring.

Cui wasn't finished. "If you've really got these yin-yang eyes," he said, "you would have been able to 'see' the great supernatural beast for yourself."

Bolin nodded. Of course, Cui was right. Even Bolin knew that ordinary folk, without the benefit of yin-yang eyes, couldn't 'see' the Heavenly realms.

But they could witness the dragon's presence, as revealed by claps of thunder and forked lightning spearing into the earth. Along the length of the Great Wall, the Laolong would appear in all its savage power, protecting the Zhongguo and keeping the Mongol scourge at bay.

And it put in a special display on New Year's Eve. At least, it used to – until twenty years ago, when the Shanhaiguan fortress and the Laolongtou was built. Ever since then, the Laolong was conspicuous by its absence. The people grew disconsolate. To satisfy their craving, the Abbot conceived the idea of a facsimile dragon made of paper, lantern and cloth, held up by cavorting citizens, on wooden sticks and poles, with fireworks to replace the pyrotechnics.

"That's all we have now," Bolin admitted with a touch of rue. Cui, evidently unimpressed, folded his arms and stared pensively at the ground.

A burgeoning crowd around him, Dong halted the procession and stood on a podium on the square by the Bell and Drum Tower. "Welcome, everyone," the Abbot cried. "I wish you all an auspicious New Year in this, the Year of the Dragon. Let the celebrations commence."

To tumultuous cheers, a dozen soldiers grabbed wicker torches from their cradles and kissed them against the piles of tinder on the bonfire in the centre of the square. In moments, the soothing warmth of the blaze suffused the gathering evening cold. The orange-gold flames licked the edge of the bonfire, lighting the night with a myriad of sparks. A dozen officers marched forward, holding aloft captured standards, showing the wolverine Mongol symbol, before throwing them onto the pyre with unabashed glee.

As the red flames consumed the blue Mongol standards, the first fireworks spiralled into the sky, lighting the stars and the dark moon with slivers of fire. The rockets were Bolin's favourite, shooting into the sky like magnificent comets. The brightness blinded him for a moment and he stumbled backwards. A man standing behind him grabbed his armpits, saying, "Watch out where you're going, lad."

It was Park, the county magistrate, enjoying the festivities with his wife and son.

"I'm sorry," Bolin said, turning and bowing with reverence. "I... I didn't mean to."

He held his breath. Laying a hand on an imperial official was a serious offence. Should he have wanted, Park could have brought Bolin up on a charge.

Park replied, "It was an accident." The magistrate smiled in that mild-mannered way of his. Bolin had known him all his life. Park had told him off as a youngster for stealing apples from his orchard and chastised him when he accidentally released a herd of camels into the market.

The firecrackers shot into the moonless night sky, bursting into a cascade of noise and light. Bolin was fascinated by the whooshing sound of firework wheels, the crackle of the bonfire and the thunder of the rockets as they broke into a million pieces and eased down to earth like fiery raindrops.

As the display ended, Cui grabbed him and said, "The major wants us again." Cui pointed a thumb in the direction of the banqueting hall.

"What have we done wrong now?" Bolin asked.

"Let's go and see," Cui said.

They found the major at the entrance to the banqueting hall. He was surrounded by runners, sending missives to – and receiving messages from – all and sundry. Even at this late hour, men were unloading food and drink from an array of wagons and carts that arrived and departed with bewildering regularity.

The major called them over and said, "Bolin, you did well to alert the monks to the ghost. As a reward, I want you two to guard the entrance to tomorrow's banquet."

"Yes, Major!" Bolin performed a brisk salute. This was a great honour, to stand guard at the prestigious New Year's Day banquet. He was walking on air. Tomorrow, he would welcome the old soldiers, retired officers and local officials. What a change of fortune! So, the yin-yang eyes had brought him good karma after all.

CHAPTER 4

The Prince's Banquet

The winner becomes king.
The loser becomes outlaw.
POPULAR CHINESE SAYING

On a cold, late-winter's day, the sun rose with characteristic indolence. Like ancient foo dogs, he and Cui had stationed themselves on either side of the banqueting hall entrance. With two hours before the banquet, scores of waiters and runners bustled around the tables, laying out a sumptuous banquet. Hundreds of people milled around the entrance to lap up the excitement of the atmosphere and gawp at arriving dignitaries.

No one was going to slip in unnoticed. During the morning, sedan chair after sedan chair disgorged very important persons, their wives and consorts. Bolin and Cui checked everyone's identity tablets and invitation – Master Wen came first, then the Honourable Salt Commissioner, the Secretary to the Board of Works, the Minister for Roads, the military physician and so on. A scribe checked their names against the guest list and a steward ushered them to their seats.

When some army officers from Cui's old battalion passed by, Bolin noticed a nostalgic glint in his friend's eye.

"Do you wish you still marched with them?" he asked. "You know, living the soldier's life."

"Not anymore," Cui said. "For a young man, the campaigning life is attractive and exciting, but I soon learnt that it's as stark and alluring as the sands of the Gobi Desert. No, at my age, I'm glad I'm out of it."

"When did you serve?" Bolin asked.

"About forty-five summers ago," Cui muttered, scratching his chin beard. "Back then, China creaked under the Mongol yoke. My village sat on the banks of the Yellow River, which suffered annual floods. During a great famine, our mothers and fathers ate grass and berries so that we children could eat. It makes me weep just to think about it. When the astrologers told us that Heaven had turned against the Mongol invaders, I joined the rebellion against them."

"Red bandannas," Bolin said, adjusting his hair bun. "Wasn't that what the rebels wore?"

Cui grunted and said with a wry grin, "I kept mine, along with a few other trophies. My favourite is that red kite, you know, the one I always fly higher than yours."

"Hah! Now you're boasting," Bolin said with mock surprise. In fairness, Cui was an expert kite-flier and Bolin had learned much from practicing with him.

The crowd was swelling by the moment to catch sight of their fief lord, who would always arrive last. In turn, that drew in a host of peddlers selling melon seeds, sweet pastries, dumplings and flasks of rice wine. Beggars and street urchins joined in, many still the worse for wear from the previous night's feasting and revelry. Two rows of soldiers kept the entrance passages clear.

Bolin could barely keep still. He kept walking over to Cui's side of the entrance and asking him questions. "This is my first time at one of these. Who's on the guest list?"

"The community elders, mandarins and senior civil servants – the prince has to follow the New Year's tradition," Cui replied.

Bolin scratched the fluff on his chin. "Why does the prince uphold some customs and ignore others?"

"What do you mean?" Cui added a cautionary shake of the head. He must have known Bolin was going to say something controversial.

"You know," Bolin said, narrowing his eyes. "We're taught to respect our parents, our fief lord and above all, the Emperor. But the Prince of Yan is his vassal. Not only that, they are closely related: the prince is the Emperor's uncle. On both counts, this rebellion is against the precepts of Heaven. What would happen if we all ignored the customs of the land? Will we defy our parents, contravene the wishes of our ancestors, build houses in inappropriate places, choose unlucky days on which to travel, or to marry, or—?"

"Stop!" Cui interrupted, eyes blazing. "Don't you know in any feud, *the winner becomes king, the loser becomes the outlaw?*"

"And that gives the prince the right to revolt against his own nephew?"

"Actually, it does," Cui nodded, as if that settled the argument. "If the prince wins the war, it will be because he has the power of Heaven on his side."

"Is that how it works?"

"It's called karma," Cui scowled.

18

"Karma works in mysterious ways," Bolin said. When Cui didn't reply, Bolin went back to his guard post.

Last minute arrivals were ushered to their seats with due haste. Major Renshu strode right past him and Cui without so much as a 'by your leave'. Next was Commandant Tung, looking proud as a peacock in his silk uniform. Bao, the assistant magistrate, sauntered in looking like a cat who'd found a dead mouse. The man was a piece of work. Bolin did not like him one bit. Accompanying him were two girls – twins – known as Black Orchid and White Orchid.

One of the last to arrive in his silk-curtained sedan chair was Magistrate Park, honoured for his many years of loyal service to the province of Yan. Bolin bowed to the magistrate, who, with kind generosity, acknowledged his greeting, which was more than most of the other Yamen officials bothered to do.

The magistrate donned his finest black silken robes of office and black hat, befitting his position as the prince's guest of honour. On one arm was the Lady Lan, his wife, her phoenix fan aflutter and on the other, Feng, his young, ambitious son. No sooner had they taken their seats at the top table than a yellow-curtained sedan chair approached the hall.

Carried by four burly porters dressed in golden robes and red turbans, and accompanied by dozens of attendants, was the Prince of Yan himself. Bolin and Cui stiffened their sinews in readiness and the crowd surged closer to their liege lord. Members of the brocade-clad Jinyiwei, the menacing Imperial secret police, patrolled the open space between prince and crowd.

The two rows of soldiers wielded spear and halberd to herd the crowd onto one side of the prince's sedan chair. The exception was a solitary beggar, who was squatting against the back wall and had somehow slipped through their cordon of steel. The porters deposited the prince's chair near to the entrance. The prince remained behind silken curtains, despite receiving a rapturous welcome from the crowd.

Bolin was even more surprised when the beggar waved in the direction of the prince. Bolin couldn't see if the prince waved back.

While everyone was trying to catch a glimpse of the prince, a member of the Jinyiwei in his embroidered uniform stood to attention by the open curtain of the sedan chair, presumably receiving princely instructions on the blind side of the crowd. The Jinyiwei sidled over to the beggar, a bearded fellow wearing a faded, tatty, black turban, where they exchanged a few words. The beggar fumbled in the folds of his grubby robe, pulled out a crimson envelope and gave it to the policeman with such care it was as if he was passing him the Dragon Pearl itself.

The policeman hurried across and handed it to the prince. The curtains snapped shut. By the time Bolin looked back, the beggar had slunk back into the crowd.

Why was the prince receiving an envelope from a beggar? Had the gods turned Heaven and earth upside down? Bolin shot a surreptitious glance at Cui, but his friend didn't appear to have witnessed the mysterious incident.

The porters carried the prince's chair into the banquet hall. The musicians' pipes, cymbals and drums announced the prince's arrival with an elaborate flourish.

Bolin and Cui turned their attention to the banqueting hall, where the servants dressed in red and yellow livery scuttled up and down, making the final adjustments to the tableware and seating. This was a noble gathering. The succulent odours of roast duck were making Bolin salivate and he found it hard to concentrate on his duties.

The prince whispered in the magistrate's ear and handed him the crimson envelope. Park tucked it in his inner sleeve and announced, "Ladies and gentlemen. Let us welcome Master Zhu Di, the venerable Prince of Yan and our own fief lord."

A thousand hands shot into the air and waved their appreciation of the prince, who waited until they stopped. He had a high forehead, broad cheekbones, a narrow, angular nose and a fine, tailored Asian Tojo moustache that drooped from his upper lips to his clavicle.

"As I speak, I am the oldest living son of my deceased father, Zhu Yuanzhang, the great Hongwu Emperor," the prince bellowed. "That is my principal claim to the Dragon Throne. My nephew's advisers are corrupt and have led him away from the true path of the Tao. Everyone can see that the Mandate of Heaven slips from his grasp. The Lord of Heaven favours my armies and that is why I am winning this war. Five days ago, in the land of the Blue Wolf, I devastated a Mongol army loyal to my nephew. The Blue Wolf is running away with its tail between its legs."

Everyone waved in approval of the prince's rhetoric, which disguised the underlying sense of shock – no, it was more like abject humiliation – that an Emperor of China would ever again trust the Mongols. Had the Jianwen Emperor forgotten the damage the Yuan Dynasty had caused during their despicable tenure?

The prince had more to say. "My father founded the Ming Dynasty. Like a dutiful son, I shall follow in his footsteps. I shall wait for divine acknowledgement to take the Mandate of Heaven. I will demonstrate to you that I hold the true claim to the Dragon Throne."

Bolin wondered how he was going to achieve that. He imagined everyone else did, too. The answer was forthcoming. "The Laolong – the Old Dragon itself – will do my bidding. That will prove that Heaven supports me and not my nephew."

A murmur of hope ran through the banqueting hall. The waiters, the runners, the stewards and the porters stopped what they were doing. The prince had made a powerful statement. Only the Dragon Master could summon the Laolong, as long as he possessed the fabled Dragon Pearl. The trouble was, the last Dragon Master, the mighty Lord Wing, had gone missing twenty years ago and had not been seen or heard of since: nor had the Laolong. The prince's words were more than a promise; they were tantamount to a bold claim to have the ear of the Lord of Heaven.

The prince's speech reached a crescendo. "I will not rest until I find the Dragon Pearl and its custodian. If that is Wing, I shall find him. If Wing is in Heaven and another holds the reins of the Laolong, I shall find that man. Either way, when the Laolong is summoned, it will appear in its serpentine glory and will serve me, the future Emperor of China. That is why I can pledge good harvests, no floods and no droughts. Then you will know that I am the true custodian of the Mandate of Heaven."

The banqueting guests were ecstatic at this remarkable promise. Bolin's heart was racing, "I'll even get to see the Laolong," he murmured to his friend.

"With your yin-yang eyes, you might be one of the fortunate ones," his friend quipped.

"Let the feast begin," Park announced and scores of waiters swarmed into the hall to serve the first course.

Magistrate Park sat down as the servant leaned over and served him a plate of roast duck in an orange sauce. The magistrate spoke with deep respect to the prince, though Bolin couldn't hear a word for the clatter of plates and porcelain dishes. As Park swallowed the first mouthful, the servant snatched away his plate from right in front of him.

Park's face was flushed. "What are you doing?" he complained. "Put it back."

"Apologies, Your Excellency," the servant said, bowing with reverence. "It's a mistake. This dish was prepared only for the prince's palate."

As the servant placed the dish before the prince, Park's face went from red, to blue to purple in quick succession.

His wife, the Lady Lan, gave him a gentle pat on the back, asking, "Are you all right, dear?"

Even Bolin could see the poor man was anything but. Park held his own throat like he was throttling a chicken. He spluttered into a 'kerchief and stood up, his free hand grasping the air, clutching at the invisible threads of life. His legs wobbled. Then, like some giant felled in battle, he toppled over head-first onto the table, splattering the duck and the sauce over the prince and Lady Lan.

In the pregnant hiatus, you could have heard tea brewing.

Bolin was horrified. He was not alone. As he stepped forward to help, everyone at the tables stood up at the same time. Then Bolin noticed the servant in question scurrying towards him and the exit, with a wild, savage look in his eye. His instinct took over and Bolin thrust his halberd out, hissing, "Where do you think you're going?" The servant stopped a hair's breadth from the tip of Bolin's halberd.

The military physician rushed to the side of the ailing magistrate. He turned Park over and took the man's three pulses at the wrist. Then, with a quiet reverence, he closed the magistrate's eyes for the last time. With a sorrowful frown, he announced, "My sincere condolences, I'm afraid he's on his way to Heaven."

"Nooo!" the Lady Lan yelled, pressing his tear-strewn face against her husband's body.

The prince seemed to know exactly what had happened and scowled, "Jinyiwei. Arrest that man!"

The black-robed policemen swarmed around the fugitive and grabbed him by the hair, arms and legs. The man struggled like a demon, kicking and yelling. Bolin gave him a kick as they dragged him out of the hall.

A Jinyiwei bustled up to the prince and said, "Your Highness, you must leave. The magistrate has eaten poisoned food that was meant for you."

The prince brushed him away and turned to the assembly, "I do not fear my nephew. See how he is poisoning our country in the same way he has poisoned our honourable magistrate. I am the only one fit to mediate for humanity between earth and Heaven, to save the Middle Kingdom of Zhongguo and lead it back to the path of the true Tao."

Surrounded by anxious Jinyiwei, the prince strode out of the hall. Bolin heard his parting command, "Treble the watch. Find this man's co-conspirators. I want them all brought to justice."

The prince disappeared behind the curtains of his sedan chair, leaving the banquet in pandemonium.

CHAPTER 5

Thousand Cuts Liu

When the wood has been burned,
We can point to the blackened charcoal.
Yet when the fire has passed on,
How do we know where it has gone?
THE BOOK OF CHUANG TZU

It was New Year's Day. Feng had accompanied his parents to the banquet, where he expected to share in his father's pride as the prince's guest of honour. Instead, he had witnessed his father's horrific murder.

Feng's head was spinning like a tornado. He stared at his father's corpse. It seemed unreal, a piece of elaborate theatre. But it was real enough. The Abbot Dong was arranging with other monks for the body to be transported back to the Yamen. It would be kept in a special room in their house for the ritual mourning period.

The banquet hall was transformed into a temple of sorrow. His mother, the Lady Lan, wore a fine silken dress, a coronet and a necklace of white water pearls – clothes more appropriate for a wedding than a funeral. Her wails and shrieks echoed around the rafters. His mother's poignant grief was a painful yet salutary reminder that some things can never be changed and how the Great Tao, the underlying fabric of the universe, can protrude into normal life.

Feng glanced around the banquet hall. The servants stood in the middle of the aisle, clutching trays of steaming food, while appetites were held in abeyance. The guests remained at their tables, eating their disappointment at the abrupt end to the banquet. A few courageous ones edged towards the entrance where they stood fingering their robes, waiting for the right moment to slip out unnoticed.

Feng choked on the enormity of what had just happened. His father was no more. His mother was a widow. He was the head of the household. The province had lost a fine magistrate.

He watched as the servants beat a hasty retreat into the kitchens and more guests slunk away, twitchy and uncomfortable around the noxious smell of murder. Death was the ultimate unknown. It frightened them. It frightened Feng. He kept glancing at his father, prostrate on the table. He half-expected him to wake up and start discussing some arcane legal matter with him. It didn't happen. It was never going to happen. All he could hear was his mother's grieving sobs and Dong's guttural intonation of a Taoist prayer.

A mangy cat scuttled under one of the tables in search of scraps. A few friends and work officials of Park paid their respects and excused themselves. Only Bao, the assistant magistrate, hung around like a vulture waiting to pick at the carcass. The servants re-entered the hall and started scoffing the uneaten food strewn across the tables, their hunger overriding their sense of decency.

"Stop that!" Feng railed at them. "At least wait until they've taken my father away. Show some respect!"

Bequeathing him a scowl and a rebuke, they shuffled back to their empty lives and grumbling stomachs. This was really how people regarded his father, who was in truth an honourable man who had tried his utmost in a dishonourable job, who had punished himself to punish people. For all his supreme efforts, what had Heaven bestowed on him – an unwanted dose of poison and a hollow commendation for saving his prince's life? A premature end, more like, and where was the honour in that? It was not his father, but the prince, who should have chewed on that poisoned duck meat.

The late afternoon shadows enhanced the profound sense of melancholy that pervaded the hall. His mother was surrounded by a knot of sisters, aunts and servants, wailing and beating their chests. Outside this coterie of sorrow, Feng found himself making a low growling sound, like a prowling wolf. Was that how he grieved for his father? Or was he sinking into the abyss? He had to find a way out.

Someone tapped him on the shoulder. It felt like the cold finger of death.

"Who's that?" he snapped. "Oh, Bao, it's you. I nearly jumped out of my skin."

"Have you got it?" the man asked, as bitter as bile.

As far as Feng was concerned, Bao was one of those creatures who slithered along the ground, reared up and bit you when you least expected it, often followed by an injection of poison. While Bao had been assistant magistrate to his father, Feng had tolerated him. Now his father was gone, why maintain the pretence?

"Got what? My father's been murdered," Feng spluttered. "This had better be important."

Bao re-tied his hair bun and adjusted his robes of office. The man was ingratiating.

"It is. The crimson envelope – the prince should have given it to your father."

"Oh, the envelope; yes, my father has it," he stammered. How could he have forgotten? New Year's Day was the day of the prince's clemency. Inside the crimson envelope was a list of prisoners who were to be pardoned. Should the prince's wishes not be executed, the subtle balance of yin and yang and Heaven and earth would be upset and that would be deeply inauspicious.

"I'll get it then," Bao said and moved towards his father's corpse.

"No!" Feng shouted, barring his way. "Get away from him!"

Feng reached into his father's inner pocket and felt for the papers. The body was still warm. And he'd touched it! Yuck! Afraid, he pulled his hand away.

"It doesn't bite," Bao scowled. "Here, let me."

"No!" Feng insisted. "I said don't touch him." Feng reached into his father's inner pocket, pulled out a wedge of papers, amongst which was the crimson envelope.

Bao grabbed at it.

Feng pulled his hand away, saying, "On second thoughts, I'll take it to the jail myself. I've accompanied my father there before. I'll read the list."

"That's not possible," Bao complained. "Now your father has gone, I am the acting magistrate and will perform his duties."

"Until the prince announces his replacement; I think that will be me."

"You?" Bao rolled his eyes. "You couldn't read the Emperor's calendar, let alone step into the magistrate's shoes!"

His fists clenched, Feng felt a flash of anger before remembering where he was. Taking a deep breath, he replied, "Fine. Then come with me."

He was surprised when Bao agreed. After taking leave of his mother, he set off with Bao for the jail in the comfort of his father's official sedan chair.

At this time of early evening, the Yamen administrative district was full of officials going home, porters pulling carts, wagons trundling along with supplies of wine and rice, and clandestine meetings between soldiers and their lovers.

Tonight, it was as quiet and deserted as the snowy peaks of the Yanshan Mountains. Everyone had gone home, shocked at the magistrate's tragic murder. The ugly filaments of the civil war had intruded into their lives and they were afraid.

The stark image of his father's bulging, terrified eyes, as his noble spirit squeezed out of his every pore, drenched his mind. His head swirled with thoughts of missed opportunities. How had he failed to foresee it? Why did his father accept the honour of hosting the prince, meaning he would sit next to him at a table, exposing himself to this awful family feuding?

Feng knew they were approaching the prison – not so much from his familiarity with the locale, more from the toxic mix of sulphur and fear which smacked his nostrils. He had smelled it many times, because a narrow alley separated the prison cells from his father's magistrate's chambers, where he was a frequent visitor. As a boy, the noxious odour had given him a belly-full. Not anymore: since then, he had acquired a taste for it. The fat guard at the prison cells' door woke up and grabbed a lantern from its cradle, shedding light into the gloomy alley.

"It's you, Master Feng." The guard stifled a yawn. "Sorry to hear of your father's…"

"Yes, it's me," Feng scowled. "Wake up and let me in."

The guard looked aggrieved and hustled to unlock the door, the key clanging in the cold lock.

"Did you bring…?" the guard murmured.

"Of course, I did; why do you think I'm here?" Feng waved the crimson envelope in front of him.

"It's just… the prisoners were asking," the guard added.

Bao led him down some steps to the cells. Another long corridor stretched out in front of them, dark in the evening shadows, hiding the prisoners' faces as they huddled together in a cell no bigger than a broom cupboard.

Bao stopped in front of a row of cells that housed the worst offenders and motioned for the guard to unlock the door. In anticipation, the prisoners stood up; at least, those who could. Many wore heavy, bulky cangues, rendering their lives only a little better than a centipede's.

"One of you is amongst the lucky ones," Feng said.

"Is it me?" One of them chimed.

"You, Suitong?" Bao guffawed. "We'd sooner release your worst nightmares into Heaven than let you walk amongst the innocent people of the Zhongguo."

"It must be me," cried another. "The magistrate promised." His voice sounded like he didn't fully believe it himself. Feng certainly didn't. Even at his tender age, he'd heard it all before.

As Feng announced the name of the first man to be pardoned, he was drowned out by a loud, prolonged scream that seemed to rise up out of the bowels of the earth. It came from the 'underworld', the vault where they were applying legal strictures to his father's killer. The sound of the scream was like a delightful blessing to Feng.

"Here," he said, shoving the crimson envelope into Bao's hand. "This is what you wanted. You announce the names."

"Where are you going?" Bao asked.

"To follow the screams," he said, as another horrific yell pitched into the world, terrifying even the devils in Yama. Feng grabbed a lantern. Never was the descent into the underworld so satisfying, a path he knew from his visits with his father. Soon he was lowering his head beneath the lintel of the torture chamber, where he made a bow of reverence to Thousand Cuts Liu, the undisputed king of the underworld.

Liu was a torturer, a very successful one. So successful that other jailors came from as far as Beiping to study his methods at first hand. He had perfected a gruesome ability to bleed the victim dry yet keep him alive for prodigious lengths of time, all the while extracting layer on layer of confession.

By the time Feng arrived, Liu had ushered his victim halfway to hell.

His father's murderer was sitting in a high-backed wooden chair, his hands and legs bound tight to the armrest and chair legs. The chair was perched on a plinth the height of a man's hand, so the murderer's legs rested on thin air. The murderer was covered by a loin-cloth and an ample coating of sweat and fear.

Major Renshu was also present, a cruel satisfaction in his eyes. There were a few wicker torches cradled along the walls. The vault was bathed in shadows and the stench of human excrement, which didn't deter Liu, who on the contrary seemed to thrive on it. Feng sighed. This was a wretched place, but there was nowhere else he would rather be.

"Your name?" Liu hissed, wielding a scythe-like instrument. While waiting for a reply, he made small nicks in the murderer's skin; on his arm, torso and forehead and, most excruciating of all, on the base of his feet. Each nick joined the scores of others that sat like neat stitches in the tapestry he was weaving on the man's torso.

"Shun," the man yelled. Liu made it sound like an eerie confession.

Shun squirmed on his throne, twisting his head from side to side, trying any which way to blot out the slow, deadly, accumulation of suffering.

"And who sent you?"

"I told you," Shun replied. The timbre of his voice betrayed his agonising pain. The man was a whisker from surrendering. Soon he'd be glad to spill his darkest secrets and, if necessary, condemn the whole lineage of his ancestors.

"Tell me again," Liu snarled, as he extracted every last morsel of fear and loathing from the man.

"The Emperor!" Shun shouted, as Liu traced the blade across Shun's bloodstained skin.

So, the prince was right. As Liu bent over him, Shun spat with defiance in his face. A huge man, Liu was not given to taking spittle from anyone. Liu had once been a blacksmith's assistant and broken the neck of a donkey that had inadvertently kicked him. In hauling his scythe across the nerves at the base of Shun's left foot, Liu showed admirable restraint. Shun displayed none whatsoever and screamed the walls down. He should have known that in the underworld, no one would come to his rescue.

As the echoes died, along with yet another part of the man's soul, Liu was back in Shun's face. "A snail leaves a distinctive sign of its slow progress, just like you did. It's inconceivable that you executed this plan alone. I want the names of your associates and I want them all now," Liu growled.

"I-I worked alone," Shun stammered, his eyes flickering open and closed with the pain.

"I don't believe you," Liu said, adding more crimson threads to his loom.

Shun's eyes closed and his head lolled to one side. He had fainted. Despite Liu's guileful and inventive persuasions, he failed to rouse him. Liu crossed his legs and confessed to his one weakness, "I have to piss. But don't go away, I'll be back."

Sweat pouring off his forehead, Renshu licked his lips. "We're almost out of water. Feng, will you fetch some for us?"

"All right," Feng replied. "But he's a murderer. Watch him."

"Of course," Renshu said.

Feng made his way to the well head, lifted the iron casing and dowsed his face in water. That felt good. Liu joined him, having finished his latest trip to the latrine.

"Nearly there?" Feng asked, excited by witnessing a master craftsman at work.

"See for yourself," Liu grunted, his eyes bright with the light of success. "This man won't leave the chamber until he's coughed up every last morsel of information, I guarantee you that."

A loud scream escaped from the chamber.

"That was the major," Feng snapped. "Something's wrong. Quick!"

Liu moved like a lithe dragon, Feng not far behind him as they raced back.

Shun was sitting on his throne, his head was slumped to one side. Liu grabbed his hair knot and yanked his head back. Shun's skin was purple, his eyes bulging. His mouth frothed crimson bubbles.

"What the hell has gone on here?" Feng snapped.

"He's dead!" Renshu cried, his face a picture of contortion.

"I can see that!" Liu yelled.

"How? What do you think happened?" Renshu snarled, shaking his head.

"I-I don't know," Feng said, clasping his head in his hands.

"I was so close to breaking him into little pieces," Liu hissed. "Now we'll never know his associates."

CHAPTER 6

Audience with the Prince

You can't get anywhere without the trust of others.
A cart without a linchpin in its yoke bar –
How can you get it to go anywhere?
THE ANALECTS OF CONFUCIUS

As Feng settled into the back of his father's sedan chair, the first night watch sounded across the fortress. Had he been that long in the underworld? Back on earth, a bitter northerly wind was gusting from the mountains, coating everything in a carpet of white. Undaunted, the pinnacles and spindles on the top of the pagodas and towers forever reached upwards. It was so cold that even the beggars had sought refuge in the corners and doorways of Shanhaiguan.

Feng pulled the flaps of his cap over his ears. Peering out of the curtains, he noticed abandoned kites and sodden lanterns protruding in ungainly fashion out of the thin layer of snow, forgotten vestiges of the New Year's celebrations.

He was as cold as he was disappointed. Could Renshu have done more to save Shun's life? In the end, they would never know the truth. Either way, the murderer's premature death could prove costly in the sordid fight against the Emperor.

It was a short trip from the prison. The sedan chair paused at the entrance gate to the outer courtyard of his home. Qitong, the house boy, was squatting, head in hands.

"Master," Qitong said, wiping away the tears from his eyes with the sleeves of his gown. "Father's body is in a coffin in the annex. Dead. Murdered." His little body was heaving with sobs and despite being an orphan, Qitong still thought of himself as a fully-fledged family member.

"There, there," Feng sighed. "I know. Be a good boy and fetch me some clean clothes." The boy scampered off. Feng waited for him to return behind the lattice that gave way onto the inner rooms. He could hear his mother talking to another woman, whose voice he didn't recognise straight away. Who had called on her so soon after his father's death and in the middle of a snowstorm?

His mother was saying, "His murder has been a great shock, more than I could ever have imagined." How weary, how frail, she sounded.

"I do understand. I also lost my husband," the other woman replied.

"Of course, you did. I'm sorry, how could I forget that tragic accident?" his mother replied, full of sympathy.

Qitong returned and Feng changed his gown. He was about to enter the room, when he heard footsteps behind him.

"What are you doing here, Master Feng? Listening in on your own mother?" It was Precious, his mother's maid. That was ironic – often he found her crouching in the shadows behind a lattice or a slightly-ajar door.

"I'm not eavesdropping," he insisted as she breezed by him into the room with a tray of tea and sweet pastries.

He followed sheepishly.

"Luli!" The name blurted from his lips. "What a surprise!" She was the local astrologer, geomancer and seer. What was she doing speaking to his mother in her private chambers?

"Master Feng," Luli said, bowing with respect.

"My son," his mother called out. "Come, join us." The maid lit more lanterns.

"Thank you, Mother," he said.

Her voice swollen with grief and pride, his mother spoke to Luli, "My husband was the head of the Yamen, the most important figure in the civil administration of any province. His funeral must befit that importance. It must be held on a lucky day. You've brought the imperial calendar and your almanac. Please, be so kind to advise us."

Luli opened the tables and moved her dainty fingers along the rows and columns, pausing at one glyph then careering onto another. Feng was impressed. She was a woman in the midst of her art and her art was in the midst of her life, which was more than he could say about most people he encountered. Aside from his father, most people were full of thunder and blunder in equal measure. When the storm had passed, all that remained was an empty vessel. Not even rain – just a flood of chagrin and the bitter taste of almonds.

No one spoke, only the wind howled around the alleys of the Yamen.

Luli glanced up and said, "The pre-eminent alignment is in twelve days."

"Two days before the end of the Lantern Festival," Feng replied.

"Yes and on that day," Luli said, turning to Lan, "your husband's spirit will find no impediment on its way to Heaven."

"That's a relief," his mother said, visibly relaxing.

The second night watch sounded and Luli said, "It's late, I must leave."

"It's freezing outside. As a token of our thanks," Feng persuaded her, "let my porters take you home in the warmth and comfort of the magistrate's sedan chair."

"Are you sure it's appropriate?" Luli asked. "Have you now been assigned the post of county magistrate?"

"Not yet, but I will be," Feng snapped. It went without saying that he was going to occupy his father's shoes. "In the meantime, please, accept my hospitality."

Feng saw her to the front gate, where he found Qitong asleep amidst a tranche of blankets.

"Wake up!" he thundered. "Look, the laundry wagon is here. See to it."

Qitong rubbed the sleep from his eyes and scampered off to help the men load the dirty linen.

Feng saw Luli off in the magistrate's sedan chair and then made his way to the shrine of the house to pay his respects at his father's coffin. His mother had laid out fruit, pastries and other offerings to his father's spirit. He prayed with fervour and burned incense to help cleanse his father's way to Heaven.

At the fourth night watch, he was heading for bed when a thunderous knock sounded at the outer door, waking the whole house. Moments later, Qitong came running to him, crying, "Master, master. A messenger... at the gate."

"What does he want at this late hour?" Feng asked.

"He says he must pass his message to you and to you alone."

"Mmm," Feng said, guessing that it came from the prince. "Bring him to the study."

The man lurched into the room, his breath reeking of stale rice wine. "The prince is s-sorry to interrupt your mourning," he slurred. "He requests your presence at the Hall of Ancestors."

"What, now?"

"Yes, s-sir," the messenger said, swaying from side to side. "The p-prince is leaving with the army at the dawn watch."

"I shall attend," Feng said, with a dismissive wave of his hand.

His porters had already returned from Luli's with the magistrate's sedan chair, so he travelled in comfort and style. Along the way, the streets were lined with yawning soldiers stomping their feet on the snow-laden ground, cavalry with their horses chomping at the bit and supply wagons, their donkeys munching on their early morning feed. Hundreds of lanterns lit their dawn preparations. The magistrate's chair was given priority. On arrival, one of the prince's eunuchs ushered him into an antechamber. Bao was already there.

"What are you doing here?" Feng asked, with deliberate contempt.

"I might ask you the same thing," Bao replied, with that ingratiating leer of his.

"It's obvious the prince will confirm my appointment," Feng said, surrendering to the desire to boast. "I am a fitting replacement for my father."

"We'll see about that," Bao said. Feng had heard his bluffs before.

The eunuch called them in to see the prince, who was discussing tactics with his generals and Commandant Tung. When Feng entered the room, he broke off and said to him, "I am shocked at the tragic loss of a great servant of the Empire. I held your father in the highest esteem."

"Thank you, Your Highness," he replied. That was all he could think to say. He was more accustomed to talking to convicts than addressing royalty.

The prince turned to the commandant. With his mouth turning down at the edges into a practiced snarl, he said, "Decapitate that dog's head Shun and impale his head on the railings of the Yamen. I want to strike fear into the hearts of the enemies of the Prince of Yan. Then find his co-conspirators. Turn the fortress upside down. Look in every wagon. Look in Beggar's Alley. Look in the prostitutes' quarter. Whatever you do, find them. I want justice for Magistrate Park."

"Yes, My Prince." The commandant bowed and left.

"You two," the prince said to him and Bao with a heavy sigh. "I have summoned you to let you know my decision regarding the appointment of county magistrate to Hebei Province."

Feng felt awkward, like he had stepped onto a stage and no one had told him his lines.

"I'll start with you, Master Feng," the prince said. "I once considered you a prodigious legal talent. At twenty years old, you have already passed the Jinshi, the imperial exams. Your knowledge of the Five Classics is unrivalled in Hebei Province and your fine calligraphy shows a constancy and depth of character. That's not surprising, since your father schooled you for this position for many years. If anyone deserves it, you do."

'I'm here,' Feng almost said and remembered that Confucius lauded the virtue of modesty. Despite the small slip in his mask, he felt confident and glowered at Bao.

"But," the prince thumped the table, "I have insurmountable reservations about your claim."

Surely the prince wasn't addressing him? What was going on?

"Reservations, Your Highness? What kind of... reservations?" he stammered.

"Bao tells me that last night you refused to execute my order to pardon the prisoners. This is a grave offence not only against your prince, but also against the Heavenly deities who were meant to have been placated by my act of clemency."

"I-I, don't know. I gave the list to Bao," he replied, casting a grave look at Bao. Why was the assistant magistrate looking so smug?

The prince gritted his teeth, "Second, that dog's head Shun should not have been allowed to die before yielding vital information. It was not your business to interfere in the underworld and disturb Liu's delicate work. I hold you in part responsible for that calamity."

Feng bit his lip. Bao must have whispered in the prince's ear. In this game of political chess, Feng had been in checkmate ever since he walked into the room but was only just realising it. Feng could not utter a word. It was rude to contradict a superior.

"Third," the prince went on, "you have failed to show the modesty required of a magistrate."

"Modesty? How? When?" He was squirming.

"You have abused your position. Bao tells me he saw you using the magistrate's sedan chair last night," the prince said with a snarl. "How can I trust you with the trappings of high office?"

Feng was distraught. Once again, propriety prevented him from offering any defence. His hopes and dreams dissipated by one act of kindness to Luli. It wasn't fair.

"And finally," the prince continued, "in the event of a parent's death, the Great Ming Code exhorts us to show filial respect and sacrifice to them at the appointed times. I did that with my father. You must also do that and so you must forego your imperial ambitions until the period of mourning has passed. Because your father was a loyal servant, the code allows me to waive any charges that otherwise would have been brought against you for your suspicious and compromising behaviour."

Seething inwardly, Feng bowed to his liege lord.

The prince's final words stung his ears, "I have sent runners to the capital to summon the new magistrate here. Until he arrives, Master Bao, you will act as such."

What? Bao? Acting county magistrate? Feng couldn't believe his ears. This couldn't be true. It turned out it was.

The prince addressed Bao, "While you're waiting for the new magistrate to arrive, you are to delve into the archives of the Yamen."

"What am I looking for?" Bao asked.

"I want you to investigate the mysterious disappearances of Wing, the Dragon Master, and Abbot Cheng."

"That was some twenty years ago, My Prince," Bao said, a bewildered look on his face.

"Yes, that's right," the prince said, wagging his finger. "Now as far as we know, the Laolong is trapped inside the Jade Chamber. He must be freed and brought into my service. Only the Dragon Master can do that. Find Wing and Abbot Cheng and we find the way to release the Laolong. Their fates must be intertwined."

"I see," Bao murmured.

"With the Laolong in my service," the prince confirmed, "I can command the yin and the yang of Heaven and earth. I can command the light and the dark, the firm and the yielding. This will bring good harvests, the devotion of my people and harmony between Heaven and earth. The Laolong will authenticate my claim to the Mandate of Heaven."

"I will do as you request." Bao knew how to make a grovelling reply.

Before the prince could leave, Feng plucked up courage and asked him, "What shall I do?"

The prince played with his Asian Tojo moustache and said, "Let me ask you a question: if the linchpin is missing from the yoke bar of a cart, can you expect the cart to move?"

"No, My Prince," he replied, raising his eyebrows. "Of course not."

"Then by the same token, if a man's word is untrustworthy, he is no good to me or to Heaven, let alone himself."

And with that, the prince marched out of the chamber. His equerry helped him onto his waiting horse. The dawn watch broke over the ice-laden roofs of the barracks and kissed the crimson snow clouds. Congealed with inner turmoil, Feng watched the prince lead the cavalry out of the west gate, accompanied by raucous cheers.

Feng felt like one of those icebergs that on occasion floated down the coast on the currents of the Bohai Sea – frozen, meandering and forlorn. His career was in tatters and only one person kept him in Shanhaiguan: his mother. She needed his care. He was about to sneak out of the door, when Bao grabbed his elbow and snarled, "I've got you where I want you."

"And where is that, exactly?" Feng pulled his hand away.

"Under my foot," Bao said, grating his heel into the floor for effect.

Not for the first time in his life, Feng felt like giving Bao a bloody nose. He hissed to himself. That wouldn't solve anything. He had to bide his time, so he growled back, "You are no better than a mutton-eating Mongol."

"Hah! I'm not the enemy here," Bao said, dismissing him. "But at least I have a roof over me."

"What are you talking about?" He frowned. He wasn't going to scare that easily.

"You and the remnants of your family are occupying the magistrate's official residence. Vacate it before the new magistrate arrives, otherwise I'll have you thrown out."

That, he knew, was no idle threat. And rotten timing.

CHAPTER 7

Ghosts of the Past

Past events leave their shadows behind them.
CHINESE PROVERB

Luli sat up in bed and wiped the sleep from her eyes. She'd returned late from visiting Feng and his mother. Outside, she heard a horse whinny. Hooves thudded against the frozen earth. A man shouted a rasping command.

She glanced across at Ru's bed. Empty. Her heart was racing. "Ru! Where are you?"

She found him staring through the slats in the lattice making soft, cooing noises. He did that when he was excited.

"There you are," she said.

The soldiers and cavalry filed by the window, wrapped in rudimentary winter uniforms. Reinforcements were always coming and going from the fortress, but this was a huge army and it was led by the prince himself. No wonder Ru appeared in awe of the sheer scale of the marching column. Luli grasped his hand. It was cold. It was always cold. Sometimes she wondered if he had reptilian blood.

That was how it was that chilly morning: the soldiers' yells, the horses' neighing, the creak of wagon wheels, the shouted commands of the officers and the constant chatter of hundreds of infantry, going to make war on their fellow Han Chinese. After a while, Ru looked up at her with a face like a dried prune. After twenty years, she knew the meaning of every single one of his looks. This was one of the first she had learnt.

"I know," she sighed. "I'm hungry too. But the soldiers have eaten the town out of food and burnt all the firewood. We'll have to go to the market."

A short while later, Luli led him through the west gate. He stared at the soldiers' frosty breath, the steam rising from the horses and mules. The army was leaving safety behind and moving towards danger, and Luli had that same sense about her own life. She pulled at Ru's hand. The soldiers' feet had scrunched up the snow and earth into a mud bath and Luli was tracing her steps with care around the dryer edges of the road.

As they passed the Bell and Drum Tower, Ru stared up at the roof of the huge edifice. She imagined he was trying to catch a glimpse of the drummers pounding those huge gongs, sending out the coded message that the prince was leaving. Nearby was the gate to the Yamen, around which a large but hostile crowd had gathered. They were hurling obscenities and pointing up at the railings. She went closer to see what the interest was. When she realised, she covered Ru's eyes.

"Don't look," she whispered. Ever since his tragic accident, Ru abhorred the sight of blood and gore. The crowd didn't know that. They were throwing stones at a bloody, severed head.

Someone quipped, "Who's lost his head?"

"That's Shun, or rather what's left of him," came the acerbic reply. "He's the dog who poisoned our magistrate."

She squeezed through the crowd as quickly as she could. In the market, they found little produce. Stragglers yet to join the prince's column bartered with peddlers for the dumplings, melon seeds and the remaining few sweet pastries. Others sought extra clothing to endure the last of the winter snows.

As she approached, an old woman wearing a head scarf and a long, billowy gown was handing out willow branches to the departing soldiers. It was Granny Dandan, who, together with her daughter, Precious, served at the magistrate's house. Ru stared open-mouthed at her antics.

"A willow branch for a safe journey. It's a tradition," she croaked.

Ru didn't respond. He wasn't deliberately difficult, although Luli supposed that was a distinct possibility. Older folk knew what had befallen him all those years ago.

"You're a good boy," Granny said, tousling his hair. "Here, you take one and give it to a soldier."

Ru reddened in the face and glanced at her. Luli smiled, saying, "Go on, Ru. Be brave." And he was. He gave one to a soldier with a heavy limp and a breath like a brewery.

"Thank you, lad," the soldier muttered and went on his way.

The boy smiled at her, evidently pleased with himself. In truth, he was not a boy anymore; he was taller and stronger by far than she. He had seen nearly five and twenty summers and most of them passed him by like wind against a high mountain ridge.

"I'm here with you… right now," she said, repeating the mantra by which she reassured him of her presence.

He glanced at her with those uneasy, dancing eyes and shook his head. He knew that she was sad. He didn't like that, no, he didn't like that at all.

"I'm not…" she objected and stopped mid-sentence. There was no point hiding it. The cloak of sadness was an ill fit on her. She'd grown accustomed to wearing it, ever since that unconscionable day of reckoning some twenty summers before. Ru jutted out his chin. That meant he wanted to know where they were going.

"To the market. Remember, for food and firewood?"

At least he could read her lips. Ru grunted an acknowledgement. Despite the early time of day, the crowds swirled around the stalls like fish in a shoal – merchants, guards, villagers, farmers, artisans, scholars, scribes and Yamen officials on their way to work. Ru clung to her like sticky rice. Up ahead, with the rising sun low in the sky, part of the market nestled beneath the shadow cast by the stoic facade of the Great Wall. As they moved from the sunny side into the shadow, Ru halted, stamped his foot and screamed.

"Nooo!"

In a flash, she realised what she'd done. "Oh, Ru," she said hastily. "I'm so sorry. How could I forget?"

Ru wiped an errant tear away with his sleeve. His face had gone from a brilliant sun to a shadowy moon in the time it took a sparrow to alight from a bough. A woman passing by stopped to comfort Ru, saying, "Is everything all right?" It was Zetian, Bolin's mother.

Of course, it wasn't. How could it be? The boy – well, the man – was still suffering from the trauma of witnessing his father's tragic fall. The shock had broken his little heart, retarded his natural development and stemmed his tongue. From that day on, all he could say was his name, 'yes', 'no' and a gaggle of incoherent sounds.

"There, there," Zetian said, laying a comforting hand on Ru's shoulder. "It's the shadow again, isn't it?"

Luli nodded. Whenever Ru stepped into the shadow of the wall, it reminded him of the incident and he froze. His lips turned blue. His shoulders drooped. She pulled Ru out of range of the wall's shadow and whispered in his ear, "I'm here with you… right now."

"To this day," Luli added, "I wonder how we must have upset our ancestors for such misfortune to visit my poor family."

"You must be strong," Zetian said with a thin smile. "It's karma. It has taken away from you and Ru. In the end, it must yield to your prayers and continued suffering and balance your loss. It will give you something back, you'll see."

"I hope so and thank you for your kind wishes," she replied. What a good friend.

When he had calmed down, she said to Zetian, "I was coming to your husband's fish stall and forgot that it backs onto the Great Wall. I-I am so angry with myself."

"Don't be. Look, Ru will be fine," Zetian said, with a glowing smile that lit up the dullest of winter days. "Stay here and I'll fetch some for you – and Ru."

"That's so kind," Luli said, with a bow of reverence. As Zetian disappeared into the long shadow, Luli dried Ru's tears. His body quaked. She held him close. One day, she prayed, he would overcome the shock of his father's death. But not today.

Zetian returned, accompanied by the smell of fish. "Here," she said. "It's not much. Please, have these."

"Let me pay you," Luli said. "I've never yet seen a rich fisherman."

"True enough," Zetian replied. She had narrow eyes and broad forehead, her hair tied into a bow at the top of her head, like most working women. Bolin had inherited his good looks from her. "By the same token, I've yet to see someone grow rich from the Po Office business."

Two bronze cash was all she had. She pressed it into Zetian's hand.

"Come on Ru, let's find some firewood then go home and cook these," she said.

"Bye bye, Ru," Zetian said. Ru didn't wave back. His bottom lip was trembling.

Luli was at her wits' end. After Heng, his father, had died so tragically, Ru had stopped growing up; not physically, but mentally and emotionally. That day had changed Ru's life and hers too. Eligible men avoided her, afraid the same fate as Heng would befall them. Marriage offers were as sparse as winter flowers. She had pored over books of potions and spells, in the so-far vain search for the one that would loosen the dreadful bindings wrapped tight around her son. If only he could step out of its shadow and into the light. That would make her happy beyond all else.

CHAPTER 8

The White Mulberry Inn and Wine Shop

Power can be as hot as flame.
It burns people's fingers.
Be wary of the magistrate.
Watch for his frown.
A SONG OF FAIR WOMEN

The Laolongtou was somewhere over there, a pier jutting into the cold Bohai Sea. It was concealed by the southern fortress wall so Bolin couldn't see it. But just thinking about the place made his temples throb. He felt grateful he wasn't posted to work there. Today he was on duty in the large square in the shadow of the Bell and Drum Tower, surrounded by hundreds of other conscripts rushing into line. Cui stood beside him, as calm as a sheep on the ridges of the Yanshan. How did he do it? When those around him were panicking, his friend had this uncanny ability of staying quiet, like he and he alone occupied the eye of the storm and walked the tightrope of the Tao.

Behind him stood the monumental Bell and Drum Tower, an edifice of yang strength and power, the beating heart of the Shanhaiguan Fortress. From its roof, the general orders were issued: different drum rolls for different messages, the more frenetic, the more alarm. Today was a rhythmic beating that stung the air, as the twenty drummers beat the leather in perfect synchrony.

A cold dawn hung over the fortress, as a sparkle of frost glittered like so many pieces of jewellery bestowed by the gods. The ripples of sound from the drums eased away, sending a faint echo into the mountain ridges.

On the second storey of the tower, the Percussion Master smashed his mallet against the huge nipple gong, sending out metallic waves of sound across the roofs of the houses and barracks, over the wall, up the mountains, rising high up into the frozen wastes of Heaven from where the gods awoke from their slumber and crooked their necks to see what the matter was on earth.

A fraught silence descended on the assembled troops. Bolin stamped his feet to keep them from freezing. The commandant stalked the open ground in front of him like a mountain lion.

"While we still mourn for Magistrate Park, we can bring those responsible for his terrible death to brook." Tung's voice was gruff and stern. "Shun was sent here by the Emperor but was not acting alone. The prince wants his co-conspirators found and brought to justice. Search the pagodas, the watchtowers, the temples, the inns, the drinking houses, the market, the supply depots, even Beggar Alley and the latrines. Men do not just disappear. They are hiding somewhere. Arrest anyone without a proper identity tablet around their necks. I want them found today, not tomorrow. Thousand Cuts will relieve them of their confessions. I want to see them beaten and bruised, with a cangue hanging from their necks, ready to be tried by the new magistrate when he arrives. Is... that... clear?"

Everyone bowed their head and murmured a soft but powerful agreement.

"Good. Then go to it," Tung snarled.

Bolin was with Cui and three other soldiers. Their task was to search the area around the market, starting with the White Mulberry Inn and Wine Shop, frequented by off-duty soldiers looking for an exciting time. Cui sent one man to cover the back door and led the rest of them through the front.

A single lantern in the corner sent out flickering shadows into the room. Other than the rough-hewn tables and rickety chairs and the smell of stale wine and urine, the inn was as empty as it was gloomy. A man was sweeping the floor with difficulty, gripping the broom with one hand. His other hand had been severed at the wrist.

"Master Zhou," Cui said, addressing him by his official title. Most people called him One Hand. The rumour was that he had been a young fire fighter. Caught stealing jewels from a burnt-out house, he'd suffered dismemberment in the punishment yard and then exile. Apart from the obvious, no one was quite sure about much else where One Hand was concerned.

"Early for a drink. Even for you," Zhou said, a mischievous glint in his eye.

Cui cussed and shook his head. "Not today. We're searching for the accomplices in the magistrate's murder."

"Terrible thing," Zhou said, downing a slug of wine and belching. "What's the world coming to when a magistrate can't have a bite to eat without choking to death?" Zhou then playfully throttled himself with his one good hand.

"Mind your tongue," Cui scolded him. "Tell me, you seen anyone new hanging around these parts?"

"Hah!" One Hand chortled. "You know, in my line of work, I don't ask many questions. Gets you into trouble. And Ol' One Hand don't want no trouble."

"Glad to hear it," Cui grunted. "Then show me your register of guests."

"Register of guests?" One Hand replied, with a look of feigned incredulity.

"Yes, you're obliged by the Office of Alien Affairs to register any non-Han Chinese guests – that means Mongols, Tartars, Jurchins, Koreans, all barbarians. Or have you conveniently forgotten?"

"Well," One Hand said. "I've no guests at the moment."

"Don't believe you," Cui snarled. Then, pointing to the stairs, he ordered the soldiers, "Up there. Search every room!"

One Hand barred their passage, insisting with all the charm he could muster, which wasn't much between yellow teeth and rotten gums, "You don't want to go up there."

"Out of the way," Cui shoved him aside and raced up the stairs. The first floor consisted of bedrooms either side of a corridor. Bolin worked one side, Cui the other.

One Hand was on their backs, complaining bitterly, "I tell you, leave things be. Stop there."

Who was he hiding? Bolin wondered.

All the rooms were unoccupied, until they arrived at the door at the end of the corridor. Bolin could hear voices inside: a man talking in salacious tones and a woman giggling. Another woman cried out in pain.

"I told you already," One Hand said, "leave it alone."

Someone important was occupying that room.

Cui thrust open the door. Two girls lay in various degrees of undress on top of the bed with a man. The girls pulled the bedclothes up to their necks to conceal their modesty. The man was none other than the venerable acting magistrate, and cocksure to boot.

Naked as the day he was born and clearly proud of it, Bao railed at them, "What's the meaning of this?"

"I tried to warn him but he wouldn't listen," One Hand insisted, bursting into the room.

"You're useless," Bao scowled at One Hand. Then he barked at the girls, "You two, get dressed and get out of here." Like blushing brides, Black Orchid and White Orchid took half the bedclothes with them. As they disappeared behind a modesty screen replete with phoenix motifs, Bolin noticed black and blue bruises on their backs and around their necks.

Cui stood up tall and said, "We're following the prince's orders, which is more than I can say for you."

By criticising a Yamen official, Cui had broken social etiquette and Bolin squirmed for his friend. Bao leapt from the bed and stood in the middle of the room, marshalling both his authority and his manhood, which hung from his loins like a long, flabby pipe.

"Dog's head! How dare *you* hold *my* actions to account? Who do you think you are? You're not worthy to eat my faeces. You are a pimple on the face of the gods." Bao was purple with rage.

Faced by this verbal assault, Cui took an involuntary step backwards and made an obsequious apology.

"I'm so sorry, I don't know what I was thinking…" he said, bowing and grovelling, as well he might. Did he have a death wish, challenging a senior official like that?

Bao's eyes were ablaze. "Watch your tongue or I'll have it out!" he yelled, spraying spittle into Cui's face.

Humbled by Bao's angry rebuke, Cui turned, stumbled and fell backwards, knocking over a soldier behind him, like skittles in a row. Standing nearby, Bolin had his legs whipped from under him and took a tumble. He thrust his hands out but instead of preventing his fall, he pushed Bao over and landed on top of him.

For what seemed like an eternity, Bolin lay on top of the naked Bao, struggling with all his might to remove himself not only from the room but from the inn, from Shanhaiguan and, as time and embarrassment progressed, from the earth itself.

"Get. Off. Me!" Bao yelled, pushing and shoving him.

By the time Bolin managed to extricate himself, his face was flushed red. He lay staring at the Orchid sisters, who by now had all their clothes on and were milking the soldiers' undivided attention. Fluttering fans and eyelids, they danced past gawping admirers. Bolin looked for the marks on their necks he had seen earlier, but both now wore chokers. As the girls departed, Bao's page slipped into the room. He helped his master dress and Bao exited with haste, leaving curses and disgust behind him.

Bolin still lay on the floor, vaguely aware of what was happening around him. Near him was a length of rope. As soon as he grasped it in his hand, images struck his mind with the force of a hurricane. He was battered with vivid pictures of a bedroom, dimly lit, lattice shut. A man in the black robes and cap of a scholar had his back turned to him. The scholar was standing next to a girl, who was tied on the bed. Her skin, like milky porcelain, had that dull sheen of perspiration. A trickle of crimson blood ran down her abdomen from the nipple on her pert alabaster breast. Except for the rope around her hands, feet and neck, she was naked, unless rope counted as clothing. Her modesty lay for all to see between wide open legs. She was foaming at the mouth and her facial colour was an unctuous shade of purple.

She gasped, though it was more like a gargled croak. At least the china beauty was still alive. But for how much longer? The scholar wiped a trace of saliva from her chin then, as calm as you like, tightened the noose around her neck another notch. She let out a strangled gasp, then a prolonged sigh. Bolin wanted to cradle her in his arms, save her from this despicable man. There was a noise. He drifted upwards from the deep recesses of his mind. Someone was shaking him by the shoulders and calling his name.

The dream vision returned, stronger than ever, demanding attention. The scholar was naked, his manhood erect. The girl's body lay limp on the bed, her head slumped, the noose taut. As the man prepared to mount her, he turned to face Bolin. His lips curled into a snarl. His eyes – alive with lust – seared into the caverns of his soul.

It was Bao.

Spluttering and coughing, Bolin sat up, trying to shake the horrible dream from his fevered mind. The last image before he awoke was of a modesty screen covered in phoenix motifs. Then he knew. This was the room in which the assault he had just witnessed had taken place.

"You've come back," Cui said.

"Argh," was the best he could muster.

"You all right? You've been murmuring to yourself," Cui said, offering him a helping hand.

"Have I? Yes, I suppose I have. Thanks," he replied. He reached out his hand to Cui's, only to realise that he was still clutching the length of rope.

"Where did you find that?" Cui asked.

"I don't know."

"Here, give it to me," Cui said, taking the rope and examining it.

As soon as Bolin let go of the rope, the images ceased. It was unbelievable – the rope was infused with evil foreboding. When he touched it, he saw horrific pictures in his mind's eye. He was frightened. Not by the rope but by this new-found ability, these yin-yang eyes. They'd helped him before. But not this time. What else would he 'see'? Did he have to be careful what he touched now?

He shoved his hands in his sleeves. If he confided again in Cui, his friend would scoff at him.

Bolin had to find some relief, talk to someone. Otherwise he would go mad.

CHAPTER 9

The White Flag of Mourning

O for a sight of the plain white dress.
How my heart would feel for the fatherless.
And my heart would cling to youth forlorn.
Aye, and as one with him, would mourn!
THE SHI KING (BOOK OF ODES)

Feng moved his brush-pen smoothly across the paper, making each character as distinct as a solitary cloud against a clear blue sky. This was his finest calligraphy and he was well pleased with it. He dabbed the brush on the ink slab and started the next stroke.

It was late afternoon and he'd spent the day dealing with the manifold repercussions of his father's death. He didn't mind but just when he thought he'd finished, there was another regulation to follow, another ritual to observe, another funeral practice to consider: the paper offerings, the models of the furniture, the offerings of food and drink and that was before the arrangements for both the Taoist and the Buddhist monks for the chanting, prayers and incensing.

He had written letters to his father's friends and relatives. Park had contacts in the legal profession all over Hebei Province, in Beiping and some in the south and west. There were a few in Mongolia, Korea and some as far afield as India. Thus far, he'd sent out thirty runners. He folded the paper with care and called out, "Qitong."

The house boy stumbled into his office.

"Take this to the runner waiting by the outer gate," he said. "Here, he'll need some cash for the journey," he added, handing him a string of silver.

While the boy delivered the letter, Feng wrapped his silk robes around himself and stood by the window. He couldn't see far, because the Yamen was situated near the market and being inside a military fortress, it was surrounded by high, stone walls. Often, he felt hemmed in by them. Sometimes, it felt like a prison.

His mind flashed back to the interview with the prince. Why had he refused his claim to be the next magistrate? What evil had he committed to be so shamed by him? Feng dreaded to think what lay in store. Perhaps he should see a fortune teller? Like Luli. What would she tell him? That Bao had robbed him of the magistrate's post? Yes, well, he knew that already.

He was distracted by the sound of a boy's footsteps outside. It was Qitong.

"Did you deliver the message?" he asked.

"Yes, master," Qitong replied, his breath steamy from the cold. Given the little food the boy ate, Feng wondered if he survived on air alone.

The boy loitered on the threshold. Feng asked, "Is there something else?"

"Yes, master. It's the flag, the prince's flag," Qitong replied, wringing his hands.

"What's the matter with it?"

"Master, I've just noticed; it's not been changed." Qitong bowed his head low.

"What!" He was furious. "I ordered it changed after father's murder and that was two days ago. Who's responsible? I'll beat them black and blue. No wonder the bad omens keep crossing our threshold. It's shameful. Bring me the white flag of mourning. I'll change it myself."

The boy scuttled off. Feng stormed out of the office, brushing by Precious and Granny Dandan, who were supping tea in the confines of the kitchen and scowling at him.

Feng climbed the steps of the tower leading to the flagpole. This was for father. The more he thought about it, the more shame he felt. The whole town would have wondered why the flag had remained unchanged. It was his duty as an obedient son to ensure it was done and done on time. He could hear their whispers – the tragic murder of his father and what did his shiftless son do? Nothing. It weighed on him like a heavy cangue. No wonder Precious wore that look of disdain.

The flagpole was still flying the prince's yellow and red colours. Qitong arrived clutching the white flag of mourning.

"Pull it down," he snapped. Qitong did as he was told and the prince's flag soon lay at his feet, a crumpled piece of sodden cloth. With quick hands, the boy hauled the plain white flag into place until it fluttered high in the wind, daubing the fortress in mourning.

"That's more fitting." Feng heaved a sigh of relief. At least he had redeemed himself in his father's eyes and in the eyes of his peers. Perhaps karma would bring him some relief.

From the platform on top of the Yamen, he grasped the railings and looked down on the hustle and bustle of the town. At eye level, across the way, scores of soldiers marched along the wall road. Others flooded the alleys and by-ways searching for Shun's conspirators, who had so far proved elusive. To the north, the snow-capped Yanshan Mountains, with the Taoist temple nestling in the foothills, rose into the low cloud. To the east, a light squall of rain was heading towards the Laolongtou. Gliding in the air above it was a large flock of gulls, their black and white markings hard against the sullen sky. They were circling like vultures around a carcass. Something had captured their rapt attention, although the high fortress wall about five hundred paces distant restricted his line of sight. He could only see what was unfolding above it.

There were scores of gulls, gliding through the steel-grey sky and swooping down on the Laolongtou in a black and white cloud. While gulls were often aggressive, they were never like this and never as a flock. It was as if they were possessed by a harmful spirit. One after another, they rose up to a great height and dived through the turbulent air, their wings taut against their bodies like a flying spear. It was the most bizarre aerial display he'd ever seen. After a while, the squall rolled in and swamped their acrobatics. By the time he turned to leave the tower, the flock had dispersed. From the roof of the Yamen, he glanced down and noticed Luli making her way into his residence. There would only be one reason she was here. He left the roof and went down to meet her.

Entering the inner court, he saw his mother's maid and asked her, "Precious, did I see Luli just enter the house?"

"Yes, master, she's come to see your mother," she murmured. Her voice was mellow but sad. That wasn't surprising since his mother was feeble and Precious was devoted to her.

He met Luli outside his mother's bedchamber and she said to him, "I have come to help your mother and your family heal your wounds."

"Thank you," he replied and then asked, "I wonder, did you see the gulls as you arrived? They were swarming above the fortress, flying right above me. They almost scared me."

"I did see them, Master Feng," Luli said, narrowing her eyes. "The lines of ch'i in the air above the fortress are disturbed, fragmented and that's upset the gulls. I'm afraid these are ominous times."

"Indeed, they are," he replied.

Feng accompanied Luli as she attended to his mother, who lay propped up in bed, her face drawn and tired. Oozing care and sympathy, Luli held Lan's wrist and took her three pulses. She asked her some questions, to which Lan replied in a weak, weary fashion. Luli pressed her hand in his mother's and gave her a parting smile.

Feng spoke to Luli outside the bed chamber.

"How is she?" he asked, pressing his hands together.

"Drained and depleted, I'm afraid," Luli's voice was crisp like fresh lavender. "She's grieving for your father and that's sucking out her ch'i."

"Is there something you can do…? Some herbal remedy…? Anything?" he asked in desperation.

"A poultice of herbs will only cure physical problems, like a rash or a cut," Luli said, a tinge of melancholy in her voice. "The Lady Lan is suffering from a spiritual malaise."

"You're an experienced doctor. You must be able to help her," he complained, although from Luli's furrowed brow, he could see she too was at her wits' end.

"I'll leave her some herbs for a tisane," she answered, "but what your mother needs is to be raised up by the medicines of the gods, medicines only she can provide."

Before taking her leave, she whispered, "Whatever happens, prepare yourself to make amends with your ancestors – on her behalf."

Feng felt a piercing in his heart. Not his mother. He couldn't face losing her as well. He peered back into the bedchamber. His mother let out a prolonged sigh that seemed to rise up and roam around the house like some malignant spirit.

Precious was sitting with her head on the bedclothes, comforting his mother. The light was pale through the curtains. He remembered bouncing into this room as a five-year-old, the sun streaming through the windows, his mother and father, happy and smiling. It was the same sun and the same room, only a little older, a little tawdry.

He'd lost his father to a terrible murder and his mother was shuffling towards death's door. His family had offended the spirits of the ancestors. He had to endure. Everything was wrong, incongruous, out of place, like a wooden gate, swollen by the rain, which refused to close. The natural order of things was upset. They could never be restored. Nothing was the same anymore.

CHAPTER 10

The Gulls

Near to rivers, we recognise fish.
Near to mountains, we recognise the songs of birds.
It is very important to make on-the-spot investigations.
CHINESE SAYING

As he strode along the wall road, Bolin shook his head, still trying to expunge the vestiges of his latest vision. He had not told anyone about it. How could he? Yes, Bao had a reputation as a ladies' man, but not the cruel viper he'd witnessed in his dream vision. Besides, what would Bolin say? That a length of rope had stimulated his yin-yang eyes? No. On this, he was determined to keep his own counsel. Perhaps the Baku – the dream-eaters – would gobble up his nightmare and everything would return to normal again? He could always pray.

He and Cui trudged past the commandant's centre of operations in Ninghai City Fortress.

He was still preoccupied. Yesterday's anxiety had leeched into today. Bao was not the forgiving sort and Bolin expected to see a knot of troops storming up the ramp with orders to arrest Cui. None came, but it didn't stop him looking with suspicion over his shoulder as the two of them approached the Laolongtou. It was guarded by the famous Stone Guardian, a large rectangular tablet. Back there again, his head was already pounding like a pestle grinding on mortar.

As Cui issued his unit of twenty soldiers with their orders for the day, the bottom rim of the winter sun rose above the line of the horizon. Wuzhou, Cui's eagle-eyed younger brother, was the first to spot a dark smudge on the southern horizon, an inauspicious direction according to the almanac of the day.

"What's that?" Wuzhou cried, squinting into the low-lying sun.

"A rain squall?" Cui suggested.

"No, it's moving too fast," Wuzhou said.

"Whatever it is, it's coming our way," Cui said.

The dark smudge resolved into a screech of gulls, moving inexorably towards them through the metallic-grey sky. Like everyone else, Bolin expected the mobile cloud to fly over them. The flock slowed and circled the Laolongtou – right above them.

The fascinated troops pointed up at the swarm. With a vociferous cry, a gull swooped down towards them and dived at Wuzhou like he was a prearranged target. Ducking to avoid a collision with the bird, his cap fell on the ground.

"Well, I never. That was close," he murmured.

Then the entire aerial swarm swept down on them like avatars of the wrathful Yama, the king of the demons. Battling to fight them off, Cui and Bolin waved their hands about their heads. Wuzhou prodded his halberd at the marauding birds.

Not all the troop was as brave. The gulls knocked one soldier's lance out of his hands and harassed him off the Laolongtou altogether. He ran off with a knot of gulls squawking and pecking at his head. The others, feckless brood to a man, followed him, hands gesticulating in the air.

Bolin was left alone with the two brothers and the belligerent flock.

Wuzhou was adamant, "I refuse to move for a few unruly birds!" he said.

The gulls seemed to think otherwise. That was when the guano started. At first, there was only one drop that splattered in the middle of Wuzhou's cap, which still lay forlorn on the ground. That was met with raucous protestations of defiance.

The next ariel deposit soiled Wuzhou's uniform. He shook his fist, adding a few choice expletives. Another drop landed fair and square on Cui's shoulder, dribbling down his upper arm. That earned some more ripe curses.

Then it rained guano as about thirty gulls, with dark grey mantles and black wingtips, dropped their sticky white excrement on the valiant three. They sheltered in the lee of the Stone Guardian, watching helplessly as blobs of guano splattered around them. It smelled – and looked – foul!

By the time the flock pulled away to conduct some sort of damage assessment, the three of them were covered in guano, their robes and even their faces and hair.

Bolin tried wiping it from his robes with a 'kerchief, muttering, "This is gruesome."

The brothers were plotting revenge. "I've had enough of this," Wuzhou grimaced, wielding his halberd above his head.

"Me too. Let's take some of them out." Cui unsheathed his bow and arrow.

The birds were strutting up and down the battlements, cronking and snorting with a degree of arrogance normally only witnessed in the highest grade of mandarin. Cui nocked his arrow and was about to unleash it, when a woman's voice rang out, "Stop! Don't shoot!"

Luli strode towards them, breathing fire. She planted herself right in front of Cui and pressed down on the bow until the arrow pointed to the ground.

"Luli," Wuzhou snarled. "Don't interfere. They've soiled us."

"I can see," she replied. Her benign presence seemed to calm the gulls, who perched quietly along the three sides of the battlements. "They mean no harm," she added.

"Then why were they attacking us?" Wuzhou replied.

"They want you to leave the Laolongtou," Luli pleaded, pulling at Wuzhou's sleeve.

"No," Cui said, a thread of anger in his voice. "They've humiliated us."

"Harm them and you will bring bad karma on yourselves," Luli said.

They knew she spoke the truth.

"Come, let's leave," Luli said, pulling Wuzhou by the sleeve, who reluctantly allowed her to lead him off the Laolongtou. Bolin and Cui followed, the birds staring at them like their exit was the final part of some elaborate theatrical performance.

Once the Laolongtou was vacated, the rest of the flock flew down and occupied every last morsel of space, jostling each other on the battlements and the ground. Some even settled on top of the Stone Tablet. While Wuzhou growled inconsolably, Bolin heaved a sigh of relief, since his headache had lifted. Not that it helped him explain what he was happening. Luli made an attempt.

"Birds are messengers from the spirit worlds," she said, in that soft, lilting voice of hers. "If you'd have maimed or killed one of them, we'd no longer be able to see, or hear, any messages they sent us."

"That may be, Mistress Luli," Wuzhou growled. "It seems to me the birds are possessed of a bad spirit. Look, they're strutting about the Laolongtou like they own the place."

It was true. Scores more had swollen the flock. The once brown-black mud brick promontory was a seething mass of black, white and grey feathers. The gulls owned the Laolongtou.

Bolin let out a long, slow hiss. This talk of malign spirits and messages from another world played on his already fractured mind. He couldn't hide from his condition any longer. He had to find out what was afflicting him, because it was maligning the people who were close to his heart.

CHAPTER 11

Death Bed Instructions

Human nature can be improved.
Use the Chinese way to transform barbarians.
Immerse captured Mongols in the teachings of our great sages.
Gradually, they will tread the path of righteousness and follow our ritual.
THE GREAT MING CODE

Feng lifted his head from the papers he was reading and brushed away a white moth fluttering precariously close the lantern. A moment later, it returned and headed straight for the naked flame, where it was duly scorched. Life was cheap – at least for moths. His karma might be to return to this world as a moth and perish in a similarly futile way.

He slumped back in the chair and rubbed his eyes. He was absorbing the onerous and extensive requirements in the Great Ming Code to fulfil the ritual funeral obligations. He had to satisfy his ancestors. He had spent most of the day discussing the arrangements with Abbot Dong. The prayers, the incantations, the chanting, the incense, everything had to conform to the Great Ming Code.

He must have dozed off in the chair, because he was abruptly awoken by the second night watch. The sound soon dissipated and a pall of silence descended again on Shanhaiguan. He picked up another document on his desk entitled "Daily Proceedings of the Hebei Provincial Law Court, day three, month one, in the first year of the reign of the glorious Jianwen Emperor."

Already it had an archaic feel, as if it originated from an earlier dynasty, when the Jianwen Emperor had grasped the Mandate of Heaven. Yet it was only a little more than a year ago. How quickly his life had changed. He was without a father and was the head of the household. And there were demons around every corner.

He heard footsteps and low voices in the corridor.

"Who's there?" he cried. "Strange, is that you?" Strange was always creeping around at night, mumbling to himself and bewailing the parlous standards of the 'modern world' as he called it. Feng was fed up with his moaning and needed a new manservant. That would be Qitong, as soon as the boy was old enough. The shuffling sounds grew louder and from the corridor, his mother emerged in her nightgown, dishevelled and with a wild look in her eye.

"Mother, why are you wandering around in the middle of the night? You should be asleep." He chided her gently. Half-asleep, Precious stumbled into the room after her.

"Why are *you* still awake then?" His mother wanted to know. "Studying again?" It was clear her acumen was undiminished by her grief.

He put his arm around her shoulder and endeavoured to turn her round. Despite her frailty, she resisted him. "I don't need any help," she grumbled, plonked herself down in a chair, whipped out a 'kerchief and wiped her nose. "Now, I want to know your intentions."

"Mother, listen to your son," the maid interrupted, "let me take you back to bed. The doctor told you to rest."

"I'll have plenty of time to rest where I'm going," Lan said, as waspish as ever. "Precious, let me say something to you, while I still can. Come here, girl, sit down. That's better. Now listen to me. For the most part, you've looked after me over the years. You've followed my instructions and only pilfered small items. You thought I never missed that ivory brush and comb. Remember, the ones you intentionally mislaid? I know about that and the phial of perfume of mine that you like to use. Oh, don't look so aggrieved. Don't spoil it now I'm near the end. I've said my piece to you, now let me talk to my son. Leave us alone, but first bring us some tea."

Precious blushed and scampered out of the room. "Don't talk so candidly to the servants, mother," Feng said to her.

"Why not?" Lan's voice croaked with exhaustion. "When I'm about to embark on the final journey, I can talk how I please."

He returned his mother's frown. She fixed him with staring eyes like he was a common thief in the night, then her features relaxed. She was inscrutable, or was that merely because she was a woman? Was that why he had not yet found a wife? He was only twenty, so there was still time. With the inheritance from Park, he would be rich and have his pick of the local heiresses. Precious returned with hot tea and ghosted out of the room, leaving them alone with the moths, the lantern and the night.

"What's this about?" he asked. This must be serious. Her frown returned.

"It concerns your father."

53

"You mean his funeral arrangements? Mother, everything's in hand; I have spoken to Abbot Dong at the Taoist temple as well as the Buddhist monks."

"No, I don't mean about that. I mean about this." She handed him a scroll.

"What is it?"

"Read it and you'll find out," she snapped. Her breath was shallow and laboured.

He broke the seal and read, 'Deathbed Instructions and Confessions of Magistrate Park. Being with the Tao in strength and harmony, I hereby bequeath my worldly goods, including chattels, servants and estate, as well as my library of legal books and manuscripts, to Xu Yingxu, the son of General Xu Da, courtesy name Tiande. During a dreadful purge in the eleventh year of the reign of the Hongwu Emperor, Tiande secreted his youngest son, Xu Yingxu, to Shanhaiguan. We loved him as our own son and called him Feng. Written and sealed in this, the first day of the first month of the 30th year of the reign of the Hongwu Emperor.'

Feng's world stopped spinning. He could hear its gears grind to a sudden halt. He tried to start it again, by peering at the document. He prayed it would disappear, like an apparition, or if not, that he had misread its meaning. Was there a lacuna? There often were in legal documents. Not this time. Park had written it. His father's assiduous brevity was all over it. Feng read it again. The words were the same.

He had to be certain. "Who is this Xu Yingxu?"

"Feng, you are."

"N-no," he stammered. "This isn't true. This can't be true. You're my mother, aren't you?"

Lan's face was stern and unflinching. Her expression was like a fist, smashing every word to pieces. None of it was true. All these years he had lived a gigantic lie. Something fractured in him, splintering into a thousand small pieces. It was the familial connections to the people he knew and loved. So fragile, it had dissipated in an instant. He felt hollow and empty, as if the Tao had sucked out his ch'i. He imagined this was how beggars and orphans felt, homeless, helpless. This morning, he belonged. Now he didn't.

"I wanted you to read this while I was here to answer your inevitable questions," Lan said, then coughed into her 'kerchief.

"Tiande. My father? I can't believe it," was all he could say.

"Yes, it's true. Every word of it."

"Why did the General give me to you?"

"Park referred to the Emperor's purge in his letter, but I'll tell you more. Tiande helped Zhu Yuanzhang eradicate the scourge of the barbarian Mongol from the Zhongguo. When Zhu became the Hongwu Emperor, he ordered your father to strengthen our northern defences against the Mongol hoard. With the help of Dragon Master Wing, Tiande chose this site, the neck of land between the Yanshan Mountains and the Bohai Sea, to build the Shanhaiguan fortifications.

"During that time," the Lady Lan continued, "rebels mounted insurrections against the Emperor. To quell them, the Emperor culled tens of thousands of officials up to the ninth administration grade. He was jealous of anyone exhibiting success in the imperial court which meant that Tiande, his most celebrated general, was exposed and vulnerable. When your real mother, the Lady Xie, conceived, they hid her pregnancy from the court. You were born during the time Tiande was supervising the construction of the Shanhaiguan fortress. He brought you here and approached Magistrate Park and me."

Feng puffed out his cheeks. Thoughts battled for space in his already over-crowded mind. The Lady Lan continued, "Park worked in the Imperial legal department, where he befriended your father. That's why they asked us – Park and I."

"Oh," Feng said, scratching his head. "That makes a little more sense." Not that it eased his burden. If he couldn't trust his mother and father, who could he trust?

"I realise this must be hard for you," Lan said, coughing into her 'kerchief. "Heaven never blessed us with children. We've cared for you and loved you as our own."

He felt like he was walking on quicksand. "Does Qitong know? Precious? Strange? Granny Dandan? The Yamen staff?"

Lan shook her head. With a shaky hand, she sipped her tea and wiped a dribble from her dry lips.

On most days, all the objects in the room – the ornamental table, the fine chairs, the porcelain vase of flowers, the marble statues, the bronze artefacts – wore a kind, friendly face. But today they were frowning, hard and out of reach. They had lost their sheen, their soul. They had disappeared, along with his parents, his identity, his place in society.

Nothing had changed, yet everything had changed.

"What must I do?" he asked.

"Try and fulfil Park's deathbed instructions," his mother said.

"Try?"

"Yes, your father thought they might be contested."

"How?" This was deteriorating by the moment. In the space of as many days, he had lost his father, not once, but twice, and his inheritance was heading the same way.

"Your father had a brother in Beiping, who's passed on now. When his children hear of Park's death, your cousins might want to claim the estate."

"Might? Will, more like. Legally, it's theirs. I have no claim."

"You have a legal training. You can fight the case and win. You're our son."

"In all but name! And that's what matters in the courts."

Lan lowered her head, pained by the sharp rebuke, which he instantly regretted. His mother, or rather his adoptive mother, was dying and he was acting like spoilt child. He had lost a father, but she had lost a husband and a 'son'. This conversation could not be easy for her. For him, it was a test of his character, of his life, of his integrity. The first he'd ever had to undergo.

"What happened to Tiande?" It was odd to say his name as his father.

"He died, poisoned some fifteen years ago."

"The Emperor got him in the end, then," he said, more a statement than a question.

She nodded and replied, "Your father – Park, I mean – was so proud of your acumen. He saw you as nothing less than a legal dragon scaling the heights of the profession."

"Thank you, Mo—," he stammered and couldn't say the whole word. What should he call her? She wasn't his mother, not anymore.

"There's one more thing," she added. "Tiande left you some letters."

"Where? Can I see them?"

"I don't have them. Luli does. When she visited earlier, she confirmed she still held them."

"Luli? But she only keeps letters from soul donors for their soul successors – those who later inherit their soul."

"She does, but she keeps other kinds of letters too. Tiande left them with her for a reason, so go and retrieve them."

"And what about… my new family?" he blurted out.

"You are high born and connected to royalty. One of your sisters, Xu Yihua, is married to Zhu Di, our own Prince of Yan."

"So… the prince is my brother in law?" he stammered.

"Yes, he is," Lan said. Her shoulders slumped and she added, "I'm exhausted. I'm going back to my bed." This interview had sucked as much out of her as it had from him. But she had less to give.

"Precious," he called out.

The door opened and the maid emerged into the room. Had she been eavesdropping? Ah, what did it matter? The truth would come out in the end. It always did.

Precious took his adoptive mother by the arm and helped her back to her room. If Lan was in a bad way, what about him? Talk about an upheaval. He was no longer the person he thought he was. In the time it took him to read the script on a scroll of paper, he'd changed from being the son of the local

Shanhaiguan magistrate to the son of the most feared army general in recent memory.

His situation was more than ambiguous.

On the one hand, his 'father' had been poisoned. His 'mother' was dying. He was likely to lose his inheritance and he had definitely lost the magistrate's post. On the other, he had acquired a new 'family', an elder sister and princely brother-in-law. The irony didn't escape him. Tiande had placed him in the care of Park and Lan to protect him from an Emperor terrified of rebels, yet Feng now found himself an unwitting member of a rebel family. Was he always to be a rebel?

CHAPTER 12

The Temple of the Eight Immortals

God of Thunder, clear out and kill the ghosts and send down purity.
Behead the demons, expel the evil and keep us eternally safe.
Let this command from the great Lao Tzu,
Be executed with all due haste.
TAO EXORCIST CHARM

Bolin awoke in a sweat. He sat upright in bed, staring at the cold dawn rays sneaking under the lattice. As he dressed, a voice whispered in his soul, 'Help me.'

It was the same voice that had plagued his dreams all night.

He felt like someone gripped his throat and was trying to throttle him, except there was no one in the room. Not a soul. He would not survive another night of hearing such plaintive cries. Nor could he face another day of endurance on the Laolongtou. He had reached the end of his tether. He needed help – from someone well versed in matters of the spirit worlds, of yin and yang, of mortals and immortals. Dong, the Abbot and Tao Celestial Master, would save him.

Walking across the muddy field from the village to the temple, the cold wind gusted from the north, blasting his skin. His life felt chaotic, careering towards the edge of a precipice. He had lost track of himself. He felt the urgent need to clear the way and re-discover that fine balance of the Tao in himself.

Two huge stone statues – one of a crouching tiger, the other a flying dragon, the yin and the yang – stood guard outside the Temple of the Eight Immortals. The human guard was Jin, the master stonemason who'd sculptured the Stone Guardian of Laolongtou. Even now, his hands were busy whittling a piece of pine wood.

"What are you making?" Bolin asked.

"I don't know," Jin said with a broad grin. Then, as inscrutable as ever, he added, "I'll follow the way the grain falls and see what's hidden inside the wood."

Bolin nodded. That was the natural way of the Tao.

Jin led him across the path to the main temple. Every time Bolin stepped on its hallowed ground, a tingle of spiritual ch'i snaked up and down his spine and today was no exception. Built long before the Shanhaiguan section of the Great Wall, the temple was located according to the most harmonious Feng Shui alignments, at the conjunction of lines of spiritual ch'i in the land. The legend was that the locale would one day attract and host a powerful and benevolent Heavenly influence, encapsulated in the famous phrase set above the Zhendong Gate, The First Pass under Heaven. In the distance, the Great Pagoda, tall and elegant, nestled in the shadows of the Yanshan Mountains. A Taoist grotto was set behind it in the caves of the foothills.

Bolin followed Jin through the gardens, whose only colour was provided by those three friends of winter – the plum, the bamboo and the pine. Jin led him to a stone courtyard, where the monks were praying by the cloister wall and invited him to sit cross-legged on a rush mat.

Dong greeted him with typical warmth. Bolin explained what had happened to him, from the dream-visions of Heng falling to his death on the Great Wall and of General Shimei's phantom, to the voices crying to him for help and the suffocating dreams. The Abbot spent a long time reflecting before he said, "It seems you are possessed of an errant spirit that wants release."

"Can you help?" Bolin asked.

"I can. You need an exorcism," Dong replied. "Do you want me to perform one?"

At last! Real help. Bolin felt like a man, marooned for years on a desert island, who had spotted a boat on the horizon. "Yes," he replied. "I'd like that very much."

"Wait there and we will prepare for the ceremony." Dong said.

When Dong returned, he wore an imperious-looking black gauze hat and a red and yellow silk Robe of Descent, the centre of which was decorated with images of the crane, the sacred bird on which Taoist Immortals ascended to Heaven. The border of the robe was edged with the embroidered images of the Eight Trigrams of the Book of Change, the I Ching, which made up the famous Bagua symbol.

Dong prowled around the courtyard like a mountain lion with a pine needle snared in its paw. With meticulous care, Jin arranged various items on the silken altar cloth – an ivory spirit tablet, an image depicting the Eight Immortals, a blue and white porcelain vase of holy water, a mortar and pestle and a lit candle.

Behind him, a temple servant swirled an incense burner, filling the courtyard with clouds of pungent, sweet-smelling smoke. Another monk beat a cymbal with great vigour. On the other side of the altar, a third monk chanted a mantra in a high, screeching voice.

Dong's movements were now like those of a giant tortoise. With a vacant gaze, the Celestial Master placed a blank scroll on the altar. With both hands, he then grasped the spirit tablet, an ancient symbol of wisdom and authority. Every action seemed to take an age to complete.

Bolin watched this with an air of intense curiosity, not that he had any idea what to expect.

Dong rocked from side to side, mouthing some sacred text. The presence of Heavenly ch'i aggregated in the courtyard. As the atmosphere thickened and intensified, Bolin struggled to keep his eyes open and his wits alert.

Jin planted a quill pen in Dong's hand, which he seemed to move over the blank scroll as if guided by a Heavenly presence. Dong seemed to drift in and out of a trance, writing a stroke here and there. Bolin was certain the Abbot was unaware of what he was writing, but writing he was.

When he came out of the trance, Dong peered at the characters he'd written and nodded, apparently satisfied with the outcome of the spell. The incense fumes dispersed. The monks stopped beating the cymbals and intoning the mantra. In a silent moment, Dong pointed to the writing on the scroll and said, "This Taoist Charm will exorcise your demons."

Bolin grinned. How he had yearned to hear those words.

The Tao Celestial Master cried,

"God of Thunder, clear out and kill the ghosts and send down purity.
Behead the demons, expel the evil and keep us eternally safe.
Let this command from the great Lao Tzu,
Be executed with all due haste."

Dong placed the scroll in the mortar and touched the candle flame to it. The red and yellow flames kissed the paper. In moments, the fire had consumed it to thin, blackened ashes. Then he ground the pestle into the ashes, poured them into a beaker of water.

"Drink this," he said and handed Bolin the beaker of grey-black, swirling ash.

Bolin felt a surge of relief. Finally, he would be rid of this deviant spirit. He downed the last dregs and prodded his finger into the mortar to extract the residue. The ashes tasted bitter and some lodged in his mouth. What did he care? He was going to be free. He was going to get his life back.

"How do you feel?" Dong asked.

"Err, no different," he said, darkening his brow.

"Wait a little longer. An exorcism can take a while," Dong suggested.

The charm worked its magic through every part of his body and soul. His limbs started shaking and Bolin sat down again on the rush matting. Jin packed away the paraphernalia from the altar. After a while, Dong gathered the trail of his Robe of Descent and announced with a sour grimace, "The ceremony is over."

"What's the matter? What's happened?"

"Nothing happened," Dong said, in a curt way.

"What do you mean?"

"I mean, I completed the exorcism," Dong insisted.

"Good, so the spell is working and the malign spirit is leaving me."

"Well, yes and no," Dong hissed.

"I'm confused," Bolin said.

"Don't be," Dong replied. "It's quite simple. I'm afraid the exorcism didn't work."

"What do you mean, didn't work? I thought you said you'd completed it."

"I did. But it didn't work."

"Why?" he railed.

Dong enunciated each word one at a time, "Because there was no malign spirit to exorcise."

Incredible – all this time and he wasn't possessed! Bolin puffed out his cheeks. Out of all the outcomes he had imagined, he had not expected this one. "I suppose I should feel relieved but I don't. I still have to face my bad dreams, my visions, nightmares and the voices. They're as real as my hand."

"I don't doubt that," Dong said. "But believe me; I have the ear of the gods. This robe is full of power and in all the exorcisms I have done, the charm never fails."

"I-I, don't understand," Bolin stammered. "Have you come across this kind of thing before?"

Dong let out a long, slow hiss and said, "No I haven't. But I have heard it does happen on rare occasions. I am sorry I was unable to help. Here, take this amulet, it may help."

"Thank you," Bolin said. He was confused. If he wasn't possessed, what were these visions? And what about the voices? Would the amulet quieten them?

He headed for the gate. As he stepped beyond the threshold, a sharp pang shot through his forehead, doubling him up in pain. He thrust his palms against his temples. The wind gusted amongst the reeds and the trees and a man's voice insinuated itself into the creases in his soul, whispering,

"Help me. Release me."

CHAPTER 13

The Zhongguo

Depending on the karma being planted,
we harvest the corresponding transmigration.
He who feels, corresponds; he who is the cause, becomes the effect.
This is the Law of Tao which no man can escape.
To free himself from the transmigration cycle, a man must become the Tao itself.
TAOIST SCRIPTURE

Ru was playing in their small garden while Luli sat at her writing desk. She moved her calligraphy brush over the paper. She was crafting 'Zhongguo', the two-character word for China. The Chinese character 'zhong' comprised four independent brush strokes. The character looked like an arrow hitting a target in the 'middle', from which it derived its core meaning. She added the descriptive character 'guo', meaning kingdom – hence Zhong-guo, Middle Kingdom.

Encapsulated in one word – Zhongguo – were the three ideas: that China was the kingdom in the middle of the earth, that it was a gateway between Heaven and the rest of the world, and that the Han people were a bridge between Heaven and the peoples of the world. Whenever any divine ch'i flowed from Heaven, it first appeared in the Zhongguo. Above all others, the gods favoured the Middle Kingdom and her Han people. Both were chosen to fulfil a special purpose on earth. And one day, one day soon, Luli would join that special purpose and help summon divine ch'i not only to the Zhongguo, but to the whole world.

That was a noble idea, but her attention was drawn by the jerky, uneven nature of her brush strokes. They lacked her usual subtlety and finesse. Something was wrong and it wasn't her. She decided to check the day's almanac.

She rifled through the charts, her eyes following the deft movement of her index finger, along row and column, until she found the relevant entry.

It indicated that today was a good day to receive a visitor.

Would that be Dong, she wondered? The Abbot often sent her parcels of food and bundles of firewood, but rarely visited himself. Perhaps her neighbour Bolin? But he never came to see her, because when he did call, it was for Ru. Of late, Bolin had joined the conscripts working on the wall, so she hadn't seen much of him.

So long as it wasn't that vile Bao. The man was dangerous and always abusing his senior position. She'd heard about his dreadful antics at the White Mulberry Inn the other day. She wasn't surprised. She was a widow and even if she admitted it herself, she was still pretty – not youthful pretty, but elegant pretty. Bao would often pester her for a kiss and a cuddle and sometimes more. She was having none of that! What a gross apology for a man.

Then it must be Feng. Twice, she had called on his house in the Yamen. The Lady Lan had asked her about some letters for him. He would be along to collect them sooner or later.

She pulled the lapels of her robe and rubbed her hands together. In a cup, she fingered a dozen bronze cash and a silver tael. Her finances were good. The Po Office business brought her a steady if unspectacular income. While it was over thirty years since the Hongwu Emperor had thrown the Mongols out, people were wary of the uneasy peace with them. Villagers in a border fortress like Shanhaiguan lived in daily fear that the blue wolves would swarm out of the northern steppes and re-occupy the Zhongguo. In the shadows of an uncertain future, people were cautious, but that failed to deter them from abiding by the traditional belief in soul transmigration.

Since the Song Dynasty, donors had left Po or soul envelopes for their successors and even passed on IOUs. Of late, the Great Ming Code had confirmed that financial debts *were* transferable in that way, so a soul donor could pass on their financial debt to the person who inherited their soul, a debt the latter would be liable to pay in full. Luli earned a fee from everyone who left a Po envelope with her, providing her with a profitable livelihood.

She put away her cup of money, tidied her writing desk and wandered into the herb garden. There she was pleased to find a few brave shoots nudging up through the cold earth. When they flowered, she'd need them to treat her growing list of patients.

"Yay!" Ru let out a muted shriek of pleasure from the end of the garden.

What had he found now? A snail? A dead bird? She rushed down the garden path to share her son's delight. He was playing with sand and gravel. He loved making towers and battlements, like the Shanhaiguan fortifications, and then knocking them down.

The boundary of their property was marked by a low stone wall. It was made of the same stone as the fascia of the Shanhaiguan section of the Great Wall and constructed in a similar manner. Ru was kneeling next to the wall and was moving his finger along the folds of a near-vertical crack in the stone.

He was trying to show her something.

"What is it?" she asked, tousling his hair.

She looked again, this time, with a wide angle in her eye, out of her whites.

"Yes," she shouted with glee. "I see it. I see her."

It was there.

The profile of a face.

Ru ran his finger up and down the seam in the stone, highlighting the woman's profile. How many times had she glanced at the wall and not seen that profile? A young woman's face: proud forehead, puckered lips and dainty chin. It was there, in front of her, if she'd only had the eyes to see. Hah. And she was meant to have yin-yang eyes. Did Ru have them as well now?

She patted him on the back, "Thank you for showing me."

He flashed a quizzical look.

"No," she replied, "I don't know who the woman is or was, or how her profile became embedded in the stone."

He hadn't finished. He ran the flat of his palm along the vertical part of the boundary wall, from left to right and then looked up at her with a broad beaming smile. He repeated the action, moving his flat palm over the wall's vertical surface in the same direction as the last time, removing it and then beginning again at the same place. He was stroking the wall, as if he was smoothing the coat of a dog or cat.

Wait a moment. Then she realised what he was doing.

When she was a callow apprentice, she remembered how Jin had shown her how stonemasons built a wall by finding and using the Tao patterns in the stone, a feat they achieved by matching blocks hewn from the same part of the quarry. This in turn allowed them to align the same blocks in the wall, in much the same way as carpenters would join the similar pieces of wood in a table to maintain the flow of ch'i in the grain. When she looked closer, the stone in the wall had a subtle grain that ran through it and in the same direction as the woman's profile was pointing. How curious? That was the way the ch'i ran through the wall and that was what he was showing her.

"What a clever boy." She kissed him on the forehead. He squirmed like all sons do when kissed by their mothers and tried to rub it off. She knew he was pleased both with his discoveries and that he had communicated them to her.

"Well, Ru," she said. "I must have gazed a thousand times at this wall and never noticed the currents of ch'i, let alone which way the currents ran. What a brilliant son I have!"

He broke into a smile that meant more to her than all the riches in the Emperor's treasury. But how strange were these faces in the wall?

CHAPTER 14

General Tiande's Letters

The bird flies high in the sky to avoid being shot by arrows.
The mouse burrows into the earth to escape predators.
Don't you even have as much understanding as these two creatures?
THE BOOK OF CHUANG TZU

The long, disconsolate shadows of dusk accompanied Feng as he followed Qitong through the busy alleys of the Yamen. He had waited until then because he didn't feel safe in broad daylight. He had decided to walk in preference to taking the sedan chair, as everyone would recognise it and it would draw unnecessary attention to his movements.

An old street vendor selling kindling and firewood winked at him with mischievous intent. Did he know him? Or did his father – no, *adoptive father*? Oh, it was so confusing. His new identity was like an ill-fitting garment.

He felt anonymous amongst the heaving market crowds. He turned around and for an awful moment wondered if someone was following him. No, that was absurd. He was nervous and suspicious. Did people know his true identity? That question nagged at his soul like a demon out of the hell of Yama. What difference would it make anyway? He was a member of a branch of the imperial family rebelling against the incumbent Emperor. No one knew that, except him and his mother and... who else?

Either way, he was a high profile, legitimate target for the Emperor. In no way could he afford to be naive about his newfound position. The Shanhaiguan Fortress was the centre of the military might of the Prince of Yan. As soon as the prince turned his considerable forces against his nephew's, everything changed. From private conversations with the prince's vassals, Feng knew that many harboured reservations about supporting their liege lord. Some argued that it was immoral to defy an incumbent Emperor. And what if they were defeated? Their ancestors would pour bad karma on them and their families. Shun had gone to extreme lengths to avoid torture, so Feng was well aware that the Emperor's spies had already infiltrated the garrison. He had to tread on egg shells. Pulling his hat over his head, he followed his house boy through the crowds.

Qitong walked in front of him, holding up a lantern. Feng felt safer in the shadows of the ministry buildings. The streets of the Yamen were bustling with petty officials and their obsequious retainers. Men scuttled by with yokes over their shoulders, balancing heavy loads for their masters and mistresses. Sedan chairs passed this way and that, each more important than the other, jostling for every last morsel of space. A scruffy street vendor was peddling a thick concoction of pumpkin soup and dumplings. The aroma was warming, but he had no appetite. Not for food, anyway.

He wanted Tiande's letters.

As he passed by, a beggar grabbed the hem of his robe and cried, "Cash for a crust, Master. Help an old soldier, would you?"

For fear of catching something nasty, he usually never bothered with vermin. A twinge in the man's tone of voice made him pause and he asked, "Haven't I seen you somewhere before?"

"In a past life?" the man asked, in all sincerity.

"No, not that," Feng said with cold derision. Qitong hurried back with the lantern. In the light, he could see the beggar was a bearded fellow in a tatty black turban. "I know. It was outside the banquet hall the other day."

"The Jinyiwei moved me on," the beggar complained and spat liberally on the ground. Then he added, "You know, your father often helped me."

"Hah! I don't believe you," Feng said and with a gesture of contempt, turned away.

"You're Park's son, aren't you?" The beggar called after him.

"I am," he admitted, swallowing the contradiction. "What's it to do with you?"

"Nothing sir, nothing at all. Just saying. So sorry for your loss. All the beggars are. See, he was good to us, your father."

Maybe what he was saying was true, although Feng had never seen Park stop and talk to beggars.

"You seem to know me, but who are you? What do they call you?"

"I am Kong, Beggar King," the man said, bowing with reverence.

"Left your crown at home?" Feng said.

"No sir, don't wear a crown," Kong replied. "Nor do I have a home."

Feng felt pangs of guilt and delved into his pocket. He dropped a string of bronze cash into Kong's mud-besmirched hands.

"Thank you kindly, sir," he murmured, rubbing his hands around the coins like he'd been given the keys to Heaven. "You're as generous as your father, may his spirit find its way home."

A crowd surged by and jolted Feng out of the conversation. He remembered his purpose. Besides, he had heard enough. Cheered by this odd encounter with a gentleman of the road, he went on his way.

By the time he and Qitong reached the west gate, the night guards were taking over from the day shift. To reach Luli's house, he had to exit the fortress, a rare experience for him. The only occasions he did venture out of the Yamen were to further hone his sword-fighting skills in the military practice yard, or to accompany his father for a ride into the Yanshan Mountains or along the coastal salt marshes.

Luli lived in Shanhai village, barely one li beyond the west gate. At this time of year, every one of the three hundred paces was a mud bath from the persistent rain, churned up by the scores of wagons and carts bringing copious supplies to the fortress. He passed a few folks returning to the fortress, clutching paltry quantities of firewood. Not enough for tinder, let alone for the night.

As dusk settled around them like an ancient pall, he and Qitong approached the old, rickety wooden houses of Shanhai village. A stray dog began barking at Qitong. Others joined in and soon there was a canine cacophony. A black cat scampered out in front of him in pursuit of a rodent. He puffed out his cheeks. Who was more afraid, the mouse or him? He had to pull himself together and he didn't want to be away for long. His mother – no, his *adopted* mother – could pass at any time.

It was dark when they arrived outside the old Po Office. A solitary candle light flickered inside. Feng wondered how karma had transpired to make him sneak through the village like a thief. Was he so scared someone would discover his new identity? A part of him still clung to the belief that he was Park's son and that this was all a macabre joke. As he clutched Park's deathbed instructions, that fantasy left him like a fox chased by hounds.

The clepsydra at the Bell and Drum Tower boomed across the garrison, marking the first night quarter. It dispersed amongst the battlements and towers and the beyond that, the sea, the mountains and the coastal plain.

Qitong, lantern in hand, knocked on the door. Feng heard footsteps and the door opened.

"Who's there? Luli?" he whispered.

No answer. He could only see a shadowy profile. He heard a grunt.

"Ru? Is that you?"

He stepped into a dimly-lit room, bathed in shadows and the strong smell of camphor. His fingers danced on a large wooden box nestling by the entrance where he stood. Someone shuffled across the room towards him.

68

"Who is it? What do you want?" Luli demanded.

"It's me, Feng," he said. "I'm sorry to disturb you."

"Oh, it's you," Luli replied, like she was expecting him. "It's dark – and who's that on the threshold?"

"It's Qitong," Feng said. "He'll stay outside."

"Fine," Luli replied. "Come on in and sit down. Ru will light a fire." Luli delved into her sleeves and gave Ru a borer and a piece of wood. With dextrous hands, Ru enticed fire from the kindling and soon a fire burnt brightly in the hearth. Ru glanced up at him, his moon-face round and friendly. Luli lit another candle stub and held it up, sending light and shadows dancing like ancient ghosts across the room. It was full of objects sacred and profane, lamps, cong, bi, pi, cauldrons, caskets, boxes, shelving and calligraphed sayings, drawings and paintings crowded on the walls. A row of chests lined up against one wall, obedient like parade-ground soldiers.

"Oh, I'm so rude! Ru, make our guest some tea. You'd like some wouldn't you?" Luli asked Feng, inviting him to sit. He nodded.

Luli's face was aglow with a vibrant luminescence and her intense eyes seemed to peer right through him. She appeared younger. Even her movements were lithe and fluid, like a twenty-year-old, not the forty-year-old woman he knew. Either way, the charm of her presence put him at his ease.

"I'm sorry I wasn't able to do more to help your mother," she said.

"You did what you could and I thank you for coming," Feng said, bowing low.

"How is she today?" Luli asked.

"The same. Well, actually, I mean, she's deteriorating," he flushed, embarrassed at mixing up his words. He was in two minds, no mistaking that.

"Boil some of the herbs I left for her and make a tisane. It'll revive her."

"I'll remind Precious," he replied with a respectful bow.

Ru brought the tea and Luli poured him some. He took a sip from a chipped porcelain cup. The tea had a smooth, fragrant aroma. He smiled at Ru and the man-boy slunk behind his mother, coy and shy – nothing new there then.

"What brings you to my door?" she asked. Her concern seemed genuine.

"My mother told me that you... have some letters for me," he said, glancing around as if to make sure no one overheard him.

"Yes, I have. You mean the ones from Tiande?" she asked.

He nodded.

"Ru found them the other day when you mother asked me about them. Ru, can you find General Tiande's letters for us?"

Ru moved by him into the ordered chaos of the main room and sniffed the air like a cat taking bearings. Ru edged towards the line of caskets and stopped at the one nearest the door. Opening the lid, he delved inside and after rustling through some papers, pulled out an envelope with an imperial yellow silk tie. With a triumphant smile, he handed it to Luli.

"Well done, Ru, thank you." She rewarded him with a warm smile and an affectionate pat on the hand.

Outside, a solitary cart trundled up the street, setting off the dogs again.

"Yes, these are they all right," Luli said and passed them to him.

His courtesy name, 'Feng', was written in neat calligraphy on the outside of the envelope. The truth was within his reach. Feverish with possibilities, he ached to know what was inside. Was it information that would defeat the Emperor? Or was it the location of secret plunder from the General's military campaigns? He could do with inheriting a tidy fortune.

He tore it open, only to find… another envelope tucked inside the first.

"That's strange," Luli said.

"It certainly is," he mused. "There are more instructions written on it."

"Read them for us," Luli said, craning her neck. She was as curious as he was.

"'This envelope contains private documents for the eyes of my son, Xu Yingxu. However, they are only to be passed to him in the advent of the death of both his adoptive parents, Magistrate Park and Lady Lan. Signed, General Xu Da, courtesy name Tiande.'"

Feng dropped the documents on the table and clasped his head in his hands. Karma had set another barrier in front of him. The documents must contain vital information; otherwise the general would not have given them to Luli for safe-keeping.

Luli stared him in the eye and asked with defiance, "These letters were left over twenty years ago and as it says, are only to be given to his son. But aren't you Park and Lan's son? I wondered why he had left them for you and why your mother had asked me about them. What's going on? I don't understand. Why do you want them?"

He paused. There was going to be an irrevocable change in his life. He had to admit to the truth of his situation. And he had to trust her. "I am Xu Yingxu, fourth son of my father, General Xu Da, courtesy name Tiande."

There. The world knew.

Luli raised her eyebrows. She hadn't known. With her yin-yang eyes, he had always thought she knew things about other people without anyone ever telling her. Evidently, this was an exception.

"How can I be sure about this?" she asked.

"Because I am telling you." Now he worried she did not believe him.

Luli frowned and shook her head. "Understand that in my situation, Feng, I have to be vigilant. Look around, there are things of great beauty and value here – jade statues, exquisite porcelain vases and precious drawings – all left in my safe-keeping by people who trusted me to pass them on to their rightful soul successor. Alas, a lot of deceitful people come in here and claim to be who they are not. Imposters stand to gain a lot from these bequests and gifts, so I have to exercise caution to make sure I don't give them to the wrong people."

"Look at this then." He handed her Park's deathbed instructions.

She read it over and nodded, "I understand now. I believe you."

He reached across to pick up the General's letters from the table, but she grabbed them before he could.

"I can't let you have them," she said, secreting them in her sleeve.

The bellow of an ox burst into their conversation from outside. That was just about how he felt. "Why not? I've proved to you who I am," he protested.

"Yes, you have, but your father's instructions," she said, pointing to the yellow tie, "specify that I can only release it after the death of *both* your step parents. At the risk of sounding insensitive, your adoptive mother is still alive. May she reside in strength with the Tao."

"I see," he said. Being a young man, the art of waiting was a long way away; somewhere in Tibet, as far as he was concerned. "All right. Thank you for your time and the tea," he said, swallowing his frustration. "I shall go home and look after my adoptive mother."

"Yes, of course," Luli said getting up.

He glanced at her. Her face wore a mask of intense pride and yet, her skin was radiant. She had a strong forehead, jet-black hair tied into a neat bun, high cheek-bones and piercing jade green eyes. All those features were like a declining spring flower. She sensed his intrusive stare and turned away.

"Oh, there's one more thing," he said.

"What's that?" she asked.

"Please keep this conversation secret. As you can appreciate, there are many opponents of my family who would pay dearly to know of the whereabouts of the missing son of the famous General Tiande."

"I understand," she said modestly. "It's safe with me. Don't forget to ask Precious to make that tisane for Lady Lan."

"I will," Feng said, "thank you."

Ru opened the door for him, a dreamy expression on his face. For a moment, Feng was envious of the boy-man's blissful ignorance of the cruel vicissitudes of life. As he stepped over the threshold, he caught another whiff of camphor wood.

Outside, Qitong was waiting for him; as were the dogs, who were yapping at each other.

Feng joined the cacophony and stepped into the shadows of his new life.

CHAPTER 15

The Shadow of Ignominy

Beware the barbarian, they are cunning and deceitful.
When they trade in our markets,
How do we know they don't intend to spy on China?
If we seek a small gain of horses but fail to take precaution against danger,
We stand to suffer great losses.
THE GREAT MING CODE

Luli clasped Ru's hand in hers. On a cold day, the smile in Ru's eyes warmed her heart. She paused to re-wrap his bandanna around his neck. She had never known why, but out of all the scarves he owned, he always chose the yellow bandanna.

The market was bustling with hungry villagers, off-duty soldiers, merchants, shop keepers and servants buying for their households. Luli kept him well away from the wall and its long, grasping shadow.

Granny Dandan was passing and they stopped to talk. Luli noticed that she had about the same down of fluff on her chin as her Ru, which wasn't much. Luli knew her as Precious' mother, but also as a busy-body, gossip and fortune teller, who plied her trade in the market.

Luli asked, "How is the Lady Lan today?"

"Fragile," Granny Dandan replied, in that croaky voice of hers. "I fear for her. She's confined to bed and pining for her poor dead husband. I've seen it before and it doesn't end well. How often does a widow join her deceased husband in Heaven before the elapse of the forty-nine days of mourning? And it's only six days since Park had his life ripped away from him by that monster."

Luli agreed with her and noticed Ru wander off into the market. "Ru, stay close by." He acknowledged with a cursory backward wave and carried on regardless.

"Listen, you'll be interested to hear what Precious told me," Granny Dandan said, her voice softening to a whisper. "Feng recently attended an audience with the Prince and I know what was said."

Luli cocked an interested ear. "Everyone knows Bao was installed as interim magistrate."

"Yes, but do you know who is appointed to the permanent position?"

"Tell us," she said.

"The man is no stranger to Shanhaiguan," Granny said.

"What's the big secret? Who is he?" My, she was drawing this out.

Before Granny Dandan could answer, shouts filled the air like thunderclaps. There was a dispute near to the apothecary's stall where Ru was standing. The crowd dispersed like a flock of birds frightened by a cat. A young man wearing a yellow bandanna emerged out of the crowd. In one hand, he clutched a knapsack. Snatching a backward glance, the man wasn't looking where he was going and was heading straight for Ru. The boy-man was slow to react and the two collided, falling in a heap. By accident, Ru's flailing arm hooked through one of its straps. The young man must have been chased by demons, because he sprung up and hurried off, leaving the knapsack behind. A portly man with a ruddy complexion ran through a gap in the crowd and appeared to be giving chase to the fugitive. Puffing and panting, he shouted,

"Stop! Thief!"

Ru sat up, bemused, the knapsack hanging off his arm and his favourite yellow bandanna sitting lopsided on his head.

The portly man grabbed Ru by the elbow and yelled in triumph, "Got you. This man's a thief. Call the constable."

Ru squirmed at this abrupt and unexpected attention. The crowd congealed around him. People prodded him as if he was a circus exhibit. Luli was by his side in a flash.

"No!" she insisted. "This is a mistake. It wasn't him, it was the other man," she pointed to the direction in which he had run.

"You're wrong," the portly man insisted, wiping his brow with a 'kerchief, his assistants standing behind him and bristling with righteous indignation. "I saw what happened," he continued. "The thief stole twenty taels of silver from my carpet stall. And here it is," he said, yanking the knapsack from the bewildered Ru. "And look, the thief was wearing a yellow bandanna. This is him!"

"No, no, no," Luli said. "This isn't right. Ru's innocent. He's a good boy."

"Not any more, he isn't," the carpet merchant said. "I come here to trade in peace and look what happens. Shanhaiguan was once a safe trading post. Not anymore. Today criminals are running amuck."

The constable arrived, a huge barrel of a man, wielding a heavy flat stick.

"Arrest this man," the merchant said. "This knapsack has all my takings. He stole it."

The crowd were gesticulating at Ru, who was like a beached whale, gawky, helpless and divorced from his natural element.

"There's no use protesting your innocence," the constable insisted. "You'll have to stand up before the new magistrate to do that."

Ru was spouting nonsense. No one seemed to take any notice.

"He's guilty as hell," the merchant shouted, clutching his knapsack to his chest.

"That's evidence, give it to me," the constable said, snatching the knapsack.

"No," the merchant protested. "I need those funds... to feed my family."

"He's right," Granny Dandan chimed. "That's not fair."

"I'll handle this," a man said, pushing through the crowd. It was Bao, the acting magistrate. "I'm afraid, sir," Bao said, "that the constable is right. The knapsack is evidence, I'm sorry, please give it to him. What's your name?"

"Guanting," the merchant said.

"Master Guanting," Bao said, all smiles and peach blossom. "I promise, your knapsack will be returned to you."

"When will that be?" he moaned. "I need those funds. I have important business to transact."

"I'm sure the new magistrate will hear your case as soon as possible," Bao suggested.

"Fine, I'll do that," Guanting said with a grunt.

"Constable, arrest this man," Bao said, pointing an accusatory finger at Ru.

Ru's face was a picture of dread and consternation. The constable grabbed his wrists and hauled him up. Ru clutched his yellow bandanna like a child cradled a favourite doll.

"He only came to the market to steal," Bao suggested, "and from a respectable carpet merchant. Ru has committed a heinous act. He must be punished to rectify the imbalance of the Tao."

Luli bit her lip and let out a low growl. She wanted to rage at the man, but her son was fragile and unpredictable. She put her arm around his shoulder and comforted him with her special mantra, "I'm here with you... right now."

The crowd bayed for Ru's blood. "Thief!"

"Ru," Luli said, firm but yielding. "You have to accompany the constable. I'll come for you. Don't worry."

As the constable led him away, Ru yelled, "Nooo," the shadow of ignominy sitting uncomfortably on his gentle brow.

CHAPTER 16

The Stone Tablet of Laolongtou

Sons, in serving their parents, on the first crowing of the cock,
Should put on their black jackets, knee-covers, girdles and identity tablets.
From their girdle, hang the knife, the whetstone
and the mirror for getting fire from the sun;
As well as an archer's thimble, writing instruments
and a borer for getting fire from wood.
THE ANCIENT CHINESE PATTERN OF THE FAMILY

As the cock crowed, Bolin rose and got ready in traditional fashion. He trudged to work on the wall. For the last three days, he'd been trying to comprehend Dong's verdict that he was not possessed. With every day that passed, he felt like he was entering a deeper trance. There was no one he could turn to. He felt like he had repeatedly returned to the same place in his life and there was no way of burrowing out of it. He was trapped, a feeling made worse by the freezing mists rolling off the slopes of Yanshan Mountains, coating everything in a pall of moisture-laden gloom.

With these anxious thoughts preying on his mind like vultures, he approached the west gate, where a group of men coming the other way started shouting at him.

"What a smell," one of them cried, pinching his nose for effect.

"It's the fish-man," mocked another.

"Hah!" He replied, with a dismissive wave of his hand. He'd suffered these childish taunts at school. Besides, so what if he smelt of fish. His father was a fisherman. What did they expect him to smell like? Roses? He'd had enough of feeling sorry for himself. And he wasn't going to back down. Nor was he going to succumb to these strange visions and a man's voice echoing in the caverns of his soul.

"Get out," another one yelled at him. Did they mean his visions?

"Get out yourself!" He yelled back, making an outward show of bravado.

Stones whizzed past his ear. He ducked out of their way and ran through the west gate. The incident disturbed him and was as unexpected as it was unsavoury. Those men were his peers. They were peasants who bent their backs, used their hands, tilled the soil and worked the land with the beasts of burden. Their lives were filled with heavy toil and forced service. Why had they turned on him? He had never earned their contempt before. He bit down on his lip and hurried through the city. As if his life couldn't get any worse.

He reminded himself that he was a young man with a future. He would serve his parents, his prince and the Zhongguo with ardour and alacrity, despite these initial difficulties.

He raced up the ramp onto the wall road to Wen's morning briefing, which was next to the Stone Tablet of Laolongtou. This was an irregular rectangular stone slab about the height of a man on stilts and the width of his arm. It was not merely a lump of stone. Standing on the threshold of the Laolongtou, its outer face was etched with a powerful inscription invoking the protection of Heaven.

Wen didn't rebuke him this time. "Listen to me," the Master Builder was saying, arms outstretched as if he was summoning a religious power. The Great Wall and the Laolong that lived in it were both sacred, so perhaps he was. "Today, I want you to work on the Laolongtou. Cui, you and Bolin clean the Stone Tablet. Every morning, the mists roll off the mountains and leave a deposit of lichen on its surface. I want it so clean that the gods can see their reflection in it. Now, get scrubbing."

Well, the bad news was that he would have to work near the Laolongtou. Again. He frowned as he felt the headache coming on, stronger than ever. With reluctance, he joined the others. It was all he could do to keep from fainting, as the pain shot through his head like bolts of lightning.

The mists swirled around them, muting all external sounds, as Cui swabbed and scrubbed one side of the Stone Tablet. He grabbed a wet sponge and started removing the lichen, dust and other debris that soiled the inscription on the other side. Soon enough, his hand, the cloth and the water in the bucket, had turned blue. That was unusual. The lichen in the area was yellow, coloured by the sands blown down from the Gobi. Why was it blue today?

He swooned and leaned against the edge of the Stone Guardian. Inside him, a voice spoke.

"Bolin. I'm here. Help me. Free me." It was so clear that he glanced around, but there were only the shadowy profiles of the other workers, shimmering in the mists like ghostly figures.

"Did you hear that?" he asked Cui.

"Hear what?"

"A man's voice, calling my name."

"No, I didn't," Cui snarled. "Careful, Wen is nearby. He'll hear you. Get on with your work."

Bolin wiped the moisture from his forehead and again scraped the sponge over the stubborn lichen, which had deposited strange markings on the stone tablet. Shapes moved in front of his eyes. Why? Was it his pounding head? Was his vision blurred by the mists? Either way, the shape of the lichen changed into the profile of an animal. Now his eyes were playing tricks. Or were they? He stood back for a better look.

"What is it now?" Cui asked in a huff.

"The shape of an animal, here and here," he pointed to the outline.

"Where?" Cui replied. "I don't see it."

"It's there I tell you," he said. "Here's the head, the body and the legs. It's a mountain lion, or some other four-legged creature."

"Hah! It could be anything," Cui said, growing frustrated. "Your yin-yang eyes are seeing things that are just not there. They are blobs of blue lichen. For the last time, get scrubbing. If Master Wen hears you, we'll both be in big trouble."

Bolin scraped his cloth over the surface and the lichen smudged across the stone and lodged inside the engraved script. Soon the lichen was floating on the surface of the water in the bucket and, as the mists cleared, the Stone Tablet was shining like the midday sun.

"Phew, finished just in time. Here's Master Wen, upright as a fence post," Cui hissed.

"Good, that's how I want it," Wen said. "More sweat, less speculation."

As he bowed to Wen and adjusted his hair bun, Bolin heard a voice whisper to him… in his soul. "Save me. Release me. Don't abandon me!"

Bolin pressed his palms into his temples and shouted, "Stop!"

"What's the matter with him?" Wen asked.

"Nothing, Master Wen, nothing at all," Cui said and shook Bolin by the shoulders. That brought him round. Bolin still felt dizzy.

"I hope so," Wen replied, standing in front of him. "There are plenty of other conscripts I can call on. I've no time for indolence."

"No, sir," Cui said, jumping to his defence. "He's a hard worker."

"Mmm, well, this is his last chance!" Wen was curt and stomped off.

"Bolin, pull yourself together!" Cui hissed.

"I'll try, I really will," he said through gritted teeth. The punishment for gross indolence was a tattoo on the face and exile to a distant province, there to grind out a life of serfdom. That was the last thing he needed. The disgrace to his parents would be unconscionable.

Now he was seeing shapes in blue lichen. Whatever next?

CHAPTER 17

The Three Disappearances

There are no waves without wind.
POPULAR CHINESE SAYING

Luli stormed past the constable. "I will see him!" she yelled.

The constable stood at the threshold and fired off a quiver of apologies. "Master Bao, I'm so sorry, she pushed passed me." He rushed over to grab her, but Luli was smart and nimble and nipped behind a man sitting opposite Bao.

"Feng!" Luli stammered. "What are you doing here?"

Feng didn't answer.

"Shall I remove her?" the constable asked, trying to reach her.

"No," Bao said, sitting up in his magistrate's chair. "That won't be necessary. You can leave us."

The constable slunk back to his station outside the large entrance doors of the magistrate's chambers. Luli thought Bao was savouring the sunset of his magisterial power – the new magistrate was due to arrive any day.

"Madam Luli," Bao said, calm as you like. "You've interrupted an important meeting. This had better be good."

"I don't care about your stupid interviews," she was livid. "I want my Ru released."

"That's impossible," Bao replied, equally indignant. "He's been accused of a serious crime and needs to stand trial. If that's all you wanted, you can go back to your pathetic existence. Now, get out of my office!"

She stood on the spot, quaking with a mix of fear and rage.

Behind her, the sound of the drums on the top of the Bell and Drum Tower rang out in rhythmic pulses over the city, consuming it in an envelope of sound, intruding through the windows and beneath the door where the constable stood, in rigid contemplation of his faults. Moments later, the huge nipple gong was stuck thrice, the code for an imperial announcement.

"That's the new magistrate," Bao said. "He's arriving."

"Who is he? He's got to be an improvement of the current incumbent!" she snarled.

"Yes, Bao. What's his name?" Feng asked.

Bao coughed into his hand, "Master Gang."

She gasped. "Gang? It can't be. That lame excuse of a man who was here twenty years ago?"

"Yes, that's the one," Bao said.

"Well I never," Luli tutted. "Just when I thought things couldn't get any worse, karma has frowned on me again."

Feng piped up, "Why? Who is this man Gang?"

"Ssss," Luli hissed. "You'd have just been born when all this happened. Back in those days, Gang was a junior official on General Tiande's staff. Then the east end of the Great Wall terminated in the foothills of the Yanshan Mountains, leaving a thin neck of land to the Bohai Sea. Wing, the Dragon Master, advised the General to construct the fortifications here, to plug the gap. When the building work was finished, the Dragon Master was supposed to consecrate the new iconic eastern end of the wall, the Laolongtou and release the Laolong back into the wall. On the day of the ceremony, Wing never showed."

"What's this got to do with Gang?" Feng asked.

"Gang was reputed to be the last person to see Wing alive," Luli replied.

"And…?"

"Don't you see? That makes him a chief suspect for Wing's murder." Her words cut the air like flashing blades.

"I didn't know Wing had been murdered. I thought—" Feng said.

"No, that's wrong," Bao interrupted. "Wing's body has never been found. Strictly speaking, he's still missing."

"For twenty years! Bao, after all that time, his corpse has rotted. You know that and I know that," she snarled.

Bao stood up and pointed his finger at her. "You listen to me. The prince ordered me to re-investigate this whole matter. If you have anything new to say about what happened in those days, report to me. Above all, do not spread malicious rumours!"

Luli shuffled uncomfortably on her feet and lowered her gaze.

Bao went on, "At the time, Gang was a young official who couldn't hurt a fly. Besides, my investigations point to someone else."

"And who would that be?" she growled.

"General Tiande, if you must know," Bao said. "Wing discovered some dark secret about the General. To cover it up, Tiande had him murdered and disposed of the body."

"That's preposterous, what secret was that?"

"That's what I need to find out."

"Oh, do you?" she said, with an air of sarcasm.

Bao winced, but returned to the offensive. "Don't forget that Tiande was poisoned a few years later, after he'd returned to the imperial court. That was the Emperor's final justice. If he suspected Tiande of malfeasance, why can't I? If anyone was responsible for Wing's disappearance, it was Tiande and that's the report I will make to the new magistrate."

"And the other disappearances?" she asked. She was not going to yield on this matter. "What about Cheng? He also vanished without trace around the same time."

"Who was Cheng?" Feng asked.

"Cheng was the Abbot of the Temple of the Eight Immortals," Luli replied. "Before Dong took the post."

"That's ridiculous," Bao scoffed. "Yes, Cheng disappeared, but so did the Laolong. Neither has been seen since. Are you going to make Gang responsible for them as well as Wing?"

"Yes," she insisted.

"I don't think so," Bao replied. "Neither Wing nor Cheng's disappearance has anything to do with Gang. Tiande was a prestigious general, with an army under his command and the power to make people disappear. Anything could have happened to Cheng. Monks are always leaving their monasteries, lured by the itinerant life. I'll bet he's roaming the Yanshan Mountains, communing with the immortal Tao as we speak."

"I don't think so," Luli replied, gritting her teeth. "Most of all I'm terrified my Ru won't get a fair trial. And I don't trust Gang to give him one."

Bao laughed.

She wondered what he found so amusing when a man's life was at stake. Was it the idea that Ru would receive a fair trial? In short, yes. It was a fundamental legal principle that a criminal could be pronounced guilty only when he or she had confessed to their crime. This permitted the application of legal severities such as the whip, thumb screws and other indiscriminate torture. How could Ru make any kind of confession when he could hardly say his own name? Luli puffed out her cheeks and let the air out slowly.

There was a knock at the door. The constable entered and announced, "The imperial messenger has arrived."

"I must go and greet the new magistrate," Bao said, as he strode out of the room.

"You two – now is the time to leave the chambers," the constable insisted.

She and Feng followed Bao to the Bell and Drum Tower. When she was sure she would not be overheard, she whispered, "Why were you in the magistrate's office? I was afraid they had discovered your true identity."

"No, it was nothing like that," Feng replied, posing a weary smile. Then he added, "They want me to make way for the new magistrate. How can I move out of our house in the Yamen when Park has just died and my mother is so poorly?"

"I'm sorry," she murmured. "If I had the space, you could move in with me."

"You are kind," Feng replied, hanging his head. "But thank you, all the same."

By this time, they had joined a huge crowd gathering in the square. Gang's arrival had stirred the emotions of the citizens of Shanhaiguan. Two runners emerged through the west gate, followed by a procession of wagons, mules and men carrying yokes, piled high with luggage and other paraphernalia. Then came an imperial sedan chair supported by four runners, the silk curtains concealing its occupants from general view.

To the roll of the drum, the curtains were drawn back and a man emerged wearing the black cap and robes of a magistrate. He was short, with broad, burly shoulders, a pointed chin beard and eyes that oozed suspicion. Feng shrugged his shoulders. No, he didn't like the look of him either.

Bao stepped up to him and said, "Welcome to Shanhaiguan, Magistrate Gang."

CHAPTER 18

The Operation of Deception

Every operation involves deception.
Even though you are active, appear to be inactive.
Though effective, appear ineffective.
THE ART OF WAR

Gang had not slept well on his first night in Shanhaiguan. It was not because his guest room in the Temple of the Eight Immortals was sparse and uncomfortable. Nor was it due to some ailment or nocturnal anxiety. No, it was difficult to sleep when you felt like you were floating on a bed of Heavenly ch'i. He had still scarcely grasped the huge opportunity that karma had dropped in his lap – his appointment as Magistrate of Hebei Province. The message from the Prince of Yan requesting him to take up the post had arrived unexpectedly. On the same day, he had accepted it, packed a few essentials and then set off from Beiping with his wife, daughter, chattels and servants. After all these years, he had attained a position of power he could wield without reservation. He was not going to be discouraged by some early morning bell ringing and chanting.

He picked up the book by his bedside. It fell open and he read,

"Every operation involves deception. Even though you are competent, appear to be incompetent. Though effective, appear ineffective."

Perfect! This saying was his lighthouse in the storm. Where would he be without *The Art of War*? He hadn't survived this long inside the imperial carcass without practising Sun Tzu's elevated principles. Deception would enable him to uncover those who were for him and remove those who were against him; those who were for the nephew or for the uncle. There was no bigger rift than a civil war. As magistrate, he was going to exploit it to the full.

Zhu Yuanzhang, the Hongwu Emperor, had led the rebels in their red bandannas against the Mongol incursion. But it wasn't the Mongols who had slaughtered Gang's family, it was Zhu's rebels. Was it accidental? Possibly, but Gang did not care. Zhu Yuanzhang bore responsibility for the heinous act. Now Zhu was dead, his son and grandson still lived. He, Gang, was going to rip out their beating hearts and feed them to the Baku, or die trying. Until that joyous day, he had to play the imperial magistrate to the rabble of Shanhaiguan. To keep them dancing to his tune, he had brought along his own coterie of thugs.

Newly returned to Shanhaiguan, he was wary of everyone, most of all those he had encountered on his previous visit. Twenty years ago, he had ridden the dragon of fortune and there was no guarantee from either the powers of Heaven or of earth that he would be able to do so again. People were fickle and suspicious. He was the same, only more so.

A knock at the door broke his reverie.

"Come in," he ordered.

"Bao, assistant magistrate. At your service, sir," the man introduced himself with an obsequious bow. Gang liked the man's ingratiating manner. It was like his. They were two bricks in a wall.

"Well, Bao, you can start by placing me and my family in proper accommodation. I dislike monks. They're manipulative at the best of times and seditious at the worst."

Bao nodded and raised his eyebrows. Gang took that as agreement.

"Apologies, Master Gang," Bao said. "The family of the previous magistrate has yet to vacate the official residence."

"I'm well aware of that, Bao," he said, rolling his eyes. "If they had vacated, I would not be here, would I?" Oh, was this one a fool as well?

"The ex-magistrate's wife is dying of grief," Bao chimed.

"So? In this temple, I'm constantly distracted by gong striking, monotonous chanting and the stench of incense. I can't work while embroiled in monkish ways."

"I understand, master. I'll see to it as soon as possible."

"Yes, you will," he said, standing up and pacing the floor. "In the meantime, I want to know what legal cases are pending. Start your brief now."

"On the prince's instructions, I've prepared a report on Cheng and Wing, the men missing from twenty years ago," Bao said, passing him a scroll of paper.

The report was as short as it was cursory. "This brings back memories," he smirked. "Tell me, did you find either of them?"

Bao shook his head and said, "After so long, the trails of the investigation are cold. Now you are here, perhaps you can revive them?"

"Of course," he said. "I also want you to show me the layout of the fortress and the rest of the Yamen administrative buildings. It'll refresh my memory."

"Yes, master," Bao said, with another long bow.

Gathering up his long sleeves, he adjusted the ribbon that held his magistrate's identity tablet in place. He wanted it to rest exactly in the middle of his chest.

He sat down in the comfort of the magistrate's plush sedan chair and peeked out of the curtains. Bao had come on horseback and led him out of the temple, over the moat and into the fortress via the north gate.

They passed off-duty soldiers squatting around make-shift tables playing games of chess, dice or backgammon, laughing and jesting in the lead up to the Lantern Festival six days hence. On every street corner were vendors selling fruit pastries, sweet meats, fish cakes and dumplings. Along the way, lowly administrators of the eighth or ninth grade sat with brush-pen, ink slab, ink stone and paper, commissioned by illiterate soldiers to write love letters to send back to their wives.

They were soon by the outer court of the Yamen, which bustled with servants hurrying after their masters, porters carrying mandarins on litters, horses, mules and camels snorting at each other and runners transporting messages to and from the ends of the Empire. The corridors of power were crowded with officials performing the prince's business and administering the law of the land. Or so it appeared.

Gang scrutinised them. He wanted to remain unseen yet see everything around him. They passed the deserted law courts. As soon as he had officially taken up office, they would be busy, exceedingly busy, of that he was sure.

He hardly had time to sit down behind his substantial desk, when a constable entered.

"What is it?" he demanded.

"Your Honour, there's a Master Guanting outside."

"Who? What does he want?"

Before the constable could answer, the doors burst open. "I'll tell you what I want," Guanting thumped his fist on the desk. He was a portly man dressed in a long, flowing silken robe and bob hat. "I want my knapsack back. Bao here told me it was needed for evidence. Without it, I can't conduct my business. I came to Shanhaiguan to buy and sell my carpets and mulberry silk and I was robbed of twenty taels of silver by a little runt."

"I see. That's a lot of cash. What is the boy called?" Gang said, feigning sympathy. He was good at that.

"Ru. His name's Ru," Guanting said, full of bluster. "He's as dumb as a donkey. He either can't or won't speak, I don't know which. But I do know he's a thief. As soon as the case is heard, I want my silver taels released back to me. And there's another delay, well, there would be, wouldn't there? It seems we're waiting for the new magistrate."

"I am the new magistrate," Gang replied, sticking his nose in the air for good measure.

"You are?" Guanting said, waving his arms around, his sleeve rolling back to his elbow. Gang spotted a small but distinctive tattoo on the merchant's forearm. He didn't need a second look: it was a wolf – a Blue Wolf, fangs and claws bared. So... Merchant Guanting was a Mongol sympathiser. He decided to assist the man's case.

He turned to Bao and asked, "When is this man's case scheduled to be heard?"

"Master, it can be heard as soon as you are officially invested," Bao replied.

"Good, that will not be long. I will see to that," he replied. Turning to Guanting, he said, "Theft is a reprehensible crime. I will hear your case as soon as is practicable. The constable will inform you in the usual manner."

"Thank you," Guanting said, adopting a more pleasant tone. "He can find me in the Garrison Inn, on East Street."

As the merchant left, a squat man with a square chin and large forehead walked into the chambers. Hanging from his belt was a variety of spikes, knives and hammers.

"Sheng," Gang said. "Excellent timing, as always."

"At your service," Sheng said with a curt bow. He liked the man. He was his enforcer.

"Sheng, come with me, Bao is going to show us the jail house."

In the cellars across the way from his chambers, Gang found two rows of cells on either side of a gloomy, damp corridor. As he reached for a 'kerchief to quell the stench of human excrement, the guards stood and bowed to him in studied unison. In the background, he could hardly ignore an inmate's piercing screams, who was no doubt being introduced to the delights of cudgels and thumbscrews. A man in a military uniform was berating the guards when Gang arrived in their annex.

"What's the trouble here?" Gang asked.

"Ah, you must be... the new magistrate," the man said, glancing at Gang's identity tablet. "Allow me to introduce myself, I am Major Renshu."

Mmm, what a piece of brittle arrogance, Gang mused to himself. "The honour is mine, Major," he said blithely. "I heard about the awful attempt on the prince's life. Have you caught the conspirators yet?"

"You may well ask," Renshu replied. "My men have apprehended so many suspects, the jail is overflowing."

"Are any of them guilty of Park's murder?" he asked. "After all, what's the point of convicting innocent men? The real conspirators would still be out there, wouldn't they?"

"That's right," Renshu replied, tugging on his chin. "My chief jailor – a man affectionately known as Thousand Cuts Liu – has never yet been known to extract a false confession."

That was unlikely, Gang knew, but instead of expressing his disdain, he said, "Can you show me the cells?"

"My pleasure," the major replied. A guard grabbed a bunch of keys and a wicker torch, before ducking beneath the low ceiling and leading them along a dingy corridor. The guard held the torch against the bars of the first cell.

"This is Suitong. He's as regular as the sun and moon – he keeps returning. This time, he's accused of murder," the major said, the torch casting flickers of light on a man distinguishable by a scruffy skull cap, a long white beard, a single leg and a single hand. By a quirk of karma, the hand that remained was on the same side as the leg. These punishments were inflicted as a result of Suitong's previous brushes with the law. It was clear he could ill afford many more.

Renshu stopped outside the next cell. "This is criminal Ru."

"Ah, yes, I've heard about this one. He's guilty of stealing Guanting's silver. Open the cell," Gang ordered. The guard unlocked the door and thrust the torch into a cradle. Ru cowered at the back of the cell, encumbered by a large cangue, which sat like a stiff board from his neck to his knees. Not only did he have a hole for his head, his wrists were tied to the edges of the device. Unable to feed himself, Ru looked gaunt, emaciated and distraught.

"Kow-tow before the magistrate," Sheng insisted.

In slow, awkward movements, Ru dragged himself to the floor, but not quick enough to satisfy Sheng, who pummelled Ru's back with a heavy baton. Ru collapsed in a heap of limbs on top of the cangue. Time and again, Sheng thumped his baton across Ru's back. The major glanced at Gang, a look that oozed a need for compassion. Gang ignored him, he was enjoying the spectacle. There was something delightfully visceral about human blood: the smell of it, the scent of fear, the sting in the nostrils. Glorious. After a while, Sheng grew bored and stopped.

"Stand up," Gang ordered.

Ru shuffled around in the excrement on the floor, until he righted himself on his knees with a weary, prolonged sigh of pain. There Ru stayed with the base of the cangue on the floor, his head bowed, peering up at him with pleading, hang-dog eyes.

"What is this man's family?" Gang asked.

"He's the son of Luli, the local doctor, geomancer and astrologer," the major replied.

"Ah. I remember her. Her husband fell from the wall. Tragic death," he added with a smirk. He was going to enjoy his work here.

He had seen enough of the cells and decided to return to his chambers. When he got there, he found the oval doors ajar. From the sound of shuffling papers, someone was inside... pilfering.

"Thief!" Gang shouted, as he burst in. Bao and Sheng stood behind him, blocking the exit.

The man nearly leapt out of his skin and yelled back, "I'm no thief."

"Who are you? What are you doing here?" Gang bristled with indignation.

"I'm Feng, the son of Park, the magistrate who's passed over to Heaven. And who, may I ask, are you?"

"I am Gang, the new county magistrate. And you are in *my* chambers, stealing *my* papers."

"I'm collecting my father's personal possessions. There," Feng replied, stuffing a large parchment into a bamboo box. Then he picked up a bronze mirror next to the window opening and headed towards the exit.

"Let me deal with him," Sheng said, with a vicious snarl.

"No," he replied. "That won't be necessary." Then Gang turned to Feng and said, "Master Feng, I can't allow you to remove imperial papers and objects from my chambers." Question was – how was he going to deal with it; the iron hammer or the silk glove?

For once, he decided to wear the glove. "Think," he said, "your mother needs you. Your father's spirit cries out for retribution. Your ancestors call for the proper rites. Go home. Bao will arrange for porters to bring your father's things to you."

"You are kind, though that won't be necessary. When I return home, I will send my boy," Feng protested, nervously fingering one of the boxes.

"Please. It's no problem, Master Feng," he protested mildly, but just enough to get his way. "I will need to assess those papers as they may pertain to active cases. You can understand that."

"Yes... I... Oh, very well," Feng said with obvious reluctance. He plunged his hands in his sleeves, bowed and headed towards the open doors.

Bao stood in Feng's path and said, "And when will you vacate the magistrate's residence please? Magistrate Gang needs to move in as soon as possible."

Feng stopped, taken aback at the request. "My mother is very unwell. I don't have anywhere else to go. I can't..."

Gang was insistent. "I'm a considerate man. You can move today. It's no problem. I can help. Bao will find you another residence. You can have the rooms I occupied last night – in the temple. Bao, despatch runners to help Master Feng move his goods and chattels. Good. That's settled then."

Feng looked like a devil had punched him in the midriff. Bent double with pain, he shuffled out of the chambers.

Gang grabbed the papers that Feng had been so reluctant to release and flicked through them. "They must conceal court secrets," he chimed. "Otherwise our goodly Master Feng would not have been so keen to remove them. Here, study them and see what you can find."

"Of course, Magistrate," Bao replied, taking the wad of papers.

"I want to have a fortunate date for my investiture. Bring me an astrologer. Not Dong," he snapped. "I've had enough of monks for one life-time."

"I agree," Bao smirked. "I will personally go and find you one."

"I have an idea," Gang said, as Bao was leaving. "Bring me Luli. Yes, she will be ideal."

"Yes, master," Bao said and left with Sheng.

Gang sat down at his desk and picked up his well-leafed copy of the Great Ming Legal Code. Protruding from between the pages was a piece of paper – that wasn't there when he left it. Opening the page, he found a note which read:

"The Zhendong Gate: fourth night watch."

That watch was the last one before the dawn. What a time and place!

He glanced around, as if his eyes would miraculously land on the person who left it. There was no one in his chambers, nor in the alley that ran by the window.

When he examined the note, he saw it had on the reverse side the Mongol motif, a leaping Blue Wolf. Hah! He had collaborated with them in the past. So why not again? This message was meant for him. Guanting wore a Blue Wolf tattoo. The merchant must have left it.

In one day, he had allies – a collaborator, an enforcer and a willing assistant. He smiled to himself. This was a rare and beautiful opportunity to wreak further vengeance on the stupid Chinese.

Nothing would stop him.

CHAPTER 19

The Place Where Words are Made

A blind man can't appreciate a scene of beauty.
A deaf man can't enjoy the sounds of drums and bells.
But a man can be blind and deaf in his depth of understanding,
as well as physically.
THE BOOK OF CHUANG TZU

Bolin finished his apprentice duties on the wall early that day. Walking home, he heard a man's plaintive cries in the depths of his soul.

"Help me," the voice pleaded.

He plugged his ears.

The voice spoke again, louder and more anxious. "Release me!"

"Go away," Bolin railed. "Leave me in peace."

"Who are you talking to?" A street urchin laughed at him.

A group of passers-by joined in, mocking his antics. A beggar pointed at him. Ignoring their taunts, he trudged through the churned-up mud, avoiding the wagons bringing supplies through the west gate and entered Shanhai village.

Passing the grocers and the ironmongers, the smell of the sea salt smacked against his nostrils. He glanced disinterestedly at the brocades and vermilion on display at the cloth merchants. Next door, the local wine house was full of fishermen spending their marine profits on the dubious delights of rice wine. His father wasn't amongst them. A drunk fingered a bamboo flute as several intoxicated customers cavorted to his haunting melody.

Luli's Po Office was across the road from his house on Fuyuan Street. Healer, seer and geomancer, her intercession on the Laolongtou, when she had prevented them from harming the gulls, reminded him of just how high her reputation was in these parts.

He found himself walking across Fuyuan Street. What was he doing? Was he really going to seek her help? A magpie hopped along her threshold and then flew off, pursued by his mate. A pair of black and white birds: that was a good sign. He fingered his yin-yang coin charm; the black side with a white dot in the middle and a white side with a black dot in the middle. Yin and yang. The Tao had spoken to him. The magpies were a good omen: he was on the right path.

Luli opened the door, bowed and showed him in. The last time he'd entered her Po Office was when, as a youngster, he had played with Ru. Despite that, the familiar fresh smell of camphor wood wafted over him. Boxes and scrolls in one corner, crates in another, the shop was more or less as he remembered it. The pawned items were neatly labelled in small pigeonholes towards the back of the store. The room emanated a mysterious serenity, a sense of everything in its place and a place for everything. Bolin liked that. In a world of tumult and upheaval, such order, any order, was a welcome restraint.

"Master Bolin," Luli said, wearing a long-sleeved turquoise gown. "You've come. What can I do for you?"

Was she expecting him? She had the foresight of yin-yang eyes, so perhaps she was. "Please, I need your help," he muttered.

"Go on," Luli replied.

"I'm frightened, Luli. It started with headaches, then strange dreams. Now I'm seeing and hearing strange things," he admitted. There, he already felt better.

"What kind of things?"

"Dream visions, terrible things, they are so real, I wake up in a cold sweat. And there's a hand clasped around my throat. I hear a man's voice."

"What does he say?"

"Phrases like 'release me' and 'help me.' I was convinced there was a demon inside me. Dong tried to exorcise it, but when it didn't work, he told me I wasn't possessed."

"Did he?" Luli said, pacing the floor like a tigress. "I think I know what is happening to you."

"You do? What is it? Tell me," he blurted out.

"Can you show me your birthmark?" Luli asked.

"What? Why? I don't understand."

"You know I am the custodian of gifts and bequests left by my deceased customers – the soul donors. Some leave letters for their soul receiver. I've an inkling one of them is for you."

"What's that to do with my birthmark?" he asked, unmasking his exasperation.

"Please," she replied. "Bear with me."

"All right, it's here," he said, standing and lifting the lower part of his robe. "There, that squidgy mark above my right ankle."

"Hah! See! It looks like a reptile; a salamander, possibly a dragon. Let me see if I have a match to it," Luli said, searching the rows of boxes.

"A match? What are you talking about?"

"I'm the keeper of the Po Office, the house of restless souls," she said, as her hands moved with swift dexterity along the rows of boxes and packets. "When a person dies, their Po or soul leaves their body and searches for another body to enter – the body of a baby about to be born. Along with the soul, the birthmark of the deceased also transfers to the newborn. It's the distinguishing mark, the link between the two people, the soul donor and the soul receiver. When the soul donor leaves a gift or envelope for me to pass on to their soul receiver, they draw two things on it: the shape of their birthmark and where it appears on their person."

"Fascinating," he said. Dong had told him of the Taoist belief in the transmigration of souls. But to actually read correspondence from the donor of his soul, that was extraordinary and the last thing he had expected from this visit.

"Hah! Here it is!" Luli cried with an air of triumph and held up an envelope. "Yes. There's a match, both in shape and position. This gives me immense satisfaction. I am a connection between two complete strangers whose lives overlapped simply because they shared the same soul and one of them is standing right in front of me. This letter is written by the hand of the person who donated their soul to you."

"Are you sure?" He could barely believe it. The envelope she handed him felt like the most precious thing he'd ever received. In a way, it was.

"Yes, I am," Luli encouraged him. "And please, you can open it."

Hand shaking, he broke the wax seal.

"Who is it from?" Luli asked.

"How would I know that?" He shrugged.

"Look on the inside of the envelope. The sender should have inscribed his name there."

He looked. It was blank.

"There's no inscription."

"Let me see," Luli said, examining the envelope. "I always insist that the donor mark their name on the inside of the envelope. Oh dear, you're right. There's nothing. Only this note."

"Let me have it," he insisted. Incredible, his soul donor had left him a note. His heart pounding with anticipation and he read:

"To the recipient of this envelope. You are the inheritor of great and marvellous magic powers. Find the Pearl of Wisdom, which waits for you in *the place where words are made.*"

"That's wonderful!" Luli said, clearly excited on his behalf. He was more circumspect.

"No, that's not possible," he replied. "I'm the son of a fisherman and not worthy to receive anything like that."

"Well," Luli said with a mischievous grin, "What about the Pearl of Wisdom? Someone has given it to you."

"Well," he said with a frown. "The note says it must first be found."

Despite that, he shifted on his seat, his breathing shallow. He felt like all the ch'i was being sucked out of him. Yin-yang eyes were difficult enough to accept, but pearls of wisdom were quite another matter.

"Whoever he is, this person is your soul donor," Luli said, brimming with confidence.

"How can you be so sure?"

"Both of you have the same birthmark in the same place on your body. You also have the same gender. Your donor is a man. Same goes to same, that's how the Tao works."

"I don't know about that," he muttered, puffing out his cheeks. "No. This is wrong. Look at me. My clothes are splattered in mud. I don't wear silk gowns or square tile hats. I don't have a sedan chair to take me around town. I'm not a mandarin of the first or second grade who advises the prince. I'm a lowly apprentice working on the Great Wall. How can I inherit special gifts or a Pearl of Wisdom? No, it's preposterous. It must be someone else."

"That's not what the note indicates," Luli protested.

"It doesn't matter. Birthmark or no birthmark, I can't accept it, so please, here, take it back and pass it on to its correct owner. There's been a mistake, a mix-up somewhere. To prove I'm right, I will find this Pearl of Wisdom. I'll find *the place where words are made* and there I'll discover to whom this envelope really belongs."

"No one has ever refused their destiny before," Luli said, hunching her shoulders.

"Well, they have now." Of that, Bolin was certain.

CHAPTER 20

In the Tao, We Trust

Birth is not a beginning; death is not an end.
There is birth, there is death, there is issuing forth, there is entering in.
That through which one passes in and out without seeing its form,
That is the Great Tao.
TAOIST SCRIPTURE

Luli stared blankly at the place where Bolin had squatted during their conversation. How could he refuse his soul donor's envelope? It was unbelievable. Everything happens for a reason, so why? What was going on? If her customers were going to deny their true identities, their true paths in the Tao, what was the point of it all?

She felt like packing her goods and going to stay with her sister in Beiping but that would be like running away. Her son had been unjustly accused and, deep down, she was still enthralled by her role as Po Mistress and all that it entailed. There had to be another explanation to this mystery. And why hadn't the person signed the envelope? She couldn't for the life of her remember who it was, she had so many bequests. Ru would know if he were here.

Bolin's response had made her doubt herself and her role. To counter that, she recalled the many satisfied customers she had introduced to their soul donors. One day, a man had arrived at her door, eyes wide in terror. In terrible nightmares, he imagined himself stumbling around without a head. Luli sat the man down and found an envelope from his soul donor. He discovered that he shared the soul of a man decapitated after being charged with the heinous crime of plotting treason and sedition against the Emperor.

Bolin was stubborn. But she was more so. She would not be beaten. She believed with a passion in the transmigration of souls. Therefore, Bolin *would* inherit great powers, as the message predicted. Heaven had chosen him for a reason and it was her task to fulfil its supreme will.

She picked up the broom, her palms cold against the smoothness of the bamboo handle. She swept the floor, careful to avoid the rows of boxes of envelopes and gifts. Luli found an intrinsic value in cleaning that transcended the simple act itself. It created space, however small, and that allowed the Tao to appear anew. Feeling better, she dusted all of her objects. That was strange, she thought as she picked up a porcelain water dragon, this one had moved. She'd placed it to protect the window. That wasn't the only object that had mysteriously moved on its own accord, which left one explanation. Ru. The little monkey was making mischief. How many times had she told him not to play with the objects? Like the Po letters, each one had its place.

She sighed. It wasn't fair to berate him while he was in prison. She had to get him released and clear his name. In the few days he had been incarcerated, she had seen his spirits deteriorate. He was innocent and vulnerable. So was she, but this was no time to complain. She wiped away a tear.

She startled as a shadow crept over her.

"Bao," she said. "You frightened me. What do you want? Is Ru all right?"

"The new magistrate wants to see you," he murmured.

His lascivious eyes wandered over her body. She could feel them. It made her feel dirty, unclean. Instinctively, she tucked in the lapels of her gown at the neck. She knew his tawdry reputation. All the local women did.

"What about?" she asked with a thin smile.

"Bring your almanacs. He wants advice," he barked.

She was accustomed to receiving such requests from mandarins and commissioners, so this was no surprise. Gathering her tables and almanacs, she put on a headscarf and with reluctance seated herself in Bao's sedan chair. As if she didn't have enough to worry about with Ru's incarceration, now she had to sit near this loathsome creature.

By good fortune, they encountered no delays and they were soon stood outside the magistrate's oval doors, waiting to gain entry to his chambers. From inside, Luli could hear raised voices. Gang was arguing with someone.

"No," Gang yelled. "That is my order. It must be carried out from tonight."

"Why? Explain to me. What's the urgency?"

"Listen, commandant. You've arrested half of Shanhaiguan, yet failed to find any of Shun's conspirators. None of the confessions you've extracted have yielded a single useful lead," Gang was saying. "While you procrastinate, Park's murderers must be found and punished. A man had the audacity to make an attempt on the prince's life. He wasn't acting alone, so the fortress must be swarming with the Emperor's spies. They are vermin, infecting our lives. So, if you please, execute my order and cleanse our city."

"If you insist," the commandant conceded. "Starting tonight?"

"Exactly," Gang repeated.

Luli heard footsteps on the marble floor. Tung burst through the doors and brushed against her shoulder, almost knocking her over.

"How rude," she muttered under her breath, as the commandant stomped off down the labyrinth of corridors.

Bao ushered her into the chambers, saying, "Magistrate, this is Luli, the astrologer."

As she entered, Gang was gazing at a bronze mirror that was perched on the ledge of the window opening. She'd seen it on the many occasions Magistrate Park had called on her divinatory skills.

Gang still seemed flustered by his dispute with Commandant Tung. He stared at her. It looked like he was trying to recall a distant memory.

"Have we met before?" he asked.

She was demure. "We may have met when you were here in the service of General Tiande. We had a mutual friend, namely Dragon Master Wing. Other than that... no, I don't think so." For the most part, that was true. Though everything she knew about him was because Wing had confided in her.

"Whatever," he said, with a dismissive wave of his hand. "I have just inspected the prison cells; you'll have to excuse me if there's any lingering smell of fear and loathing," he added, wiping his forearms and his face with his hands, as if to remove the malodour from his person.

If he's been to the cells, he must have seen Ru. Perhaps he doesn't know that I'm his mother.

"I understand," she said, trying to keep a calm demeanour. "What can I do for you?"

"I want to begin my tenure here with the right auspices. Please, I want you to recommend a favourable date for my investiture. With all the arrests in the city, it's imperative I start work as soon as possible."

"Of course," she replied. Was he asking her to manipulate the signs to his advantage? Surely not. That would be against the will of Heaven.

"You can use the annex to peruse your almanacs," he said, gesturing to the room at the side of the main chambers. "I've had it prepared, there's a silk table cloth and you can smell the incense from here."

Glad of the privacy, she laid out her trusted almanac, a series of scrolls and other tables, full of Taoist sigils, astrological symbols, trigrams from the I Ching and Chinese script aligned to the Ming Dynasty calendar. The characters danced provocatively before her eyes. She blinked. They danced some more. So did the thoughts in her mind. Round and round. Making her dizzy.

Her mind was in turmoil. How to make sense of her situation? Until Gang was invested as magistrate, he was officially unable to hear any legal cases, yielding her the perfect opportunity to delay Ru's case. That would give her valuable time to discover the real culprit.

There was a less attractive side to her predicament. Ru would have to remain even longer in the jail's squalid conditions. He was mute, so couldn't speak or properly defend himself. The other prisoners taunted him. The guards mocked him. His morale was low. If she couldn't unearth any evidence to prove his innocence, or find the real culprit, Gang would pronounce him guilty. That terrified her. Ru would never survive the ordeal of having his hand cut off, or the humiliation of wearing a cangue in public. The trauma would quell his spirit. He'd wither like a flower deprived of light.

She returned her gaze to the almanac. The sigils jumped off the page, delighting in her quandary.

If she manipulated the investiture date, she could ease Ru's plight. Yes, that would work. Then again, that had its own peril. She'd built an enduring trust with the Tao, which in turn had granted her yin-yang eyes, enhanced by the noble gifts of prophecy and clairvoyance. When she was an apprentice, she had learnt of the dangers of betraying that trust.

She remembered hearing about a seer who had received a prophecy, but who had then lied about it. The next day the woman had woken up as blind as a mole. That was karma, the righting of a wrong, the punishment for an abuse of position. Should something like that happen to Luli, what would become of Ru? There were so many imponderables. It was a harrowing choice between her son's possible salvation and her connection to the Tao.

To reason this through, she went back to her foundations, the very things that underpinned her life's creed. She believed the will of Heaven was paramount – in all things. Tempted though she was, she would not manipulate the reading, not for Ru, not for her and certainly not for Gang's benefit.

As soon as she had made that momentous decision, the script started to behave on the page and her hands stopped shaking. To arrive at a propitious date, she had to take account of all possible fortunes and misfortunes. The deliberations were intricate. She checked the tables in the almanac against the prevailing weather. Eight days previously, it had snowed heavily, a definite sign of the yin influence. Since then, it had remained cold and in the freezing weather, the thaw had been sluggish. As long as there remained patches of snow on the ground, an investiture for a magistrate, who was a prominent yang personage, would not be auspicious at all. The pages of the almanac confirmed her theory: the investiture should wait until the sun, the great symbol of yang influence, had melted the snow.

A number leapt off the page. That was it; it was far, yet near. Is that the date she should give? Still undecided, she wrapped the almanac in a silk scroll and re-entered the chambers. Gang eyed her with an air of suspicion. What did that matter? He was suspicious of everyone.

He stood up and invited her over to the window. "Before you tell me your advice, come over here. I want to show you something."

He was playing games now, but she joined him. He moved the bronze mirror out of the way so he could open the shutters. Almost as if he'd arranged it, there was a harrowing scream of pain from the other side of the narrow alley.

She gasped. "What was that?"

"Oh, that's the prison cells," he said, pointing to the basement of the building opposite. Another long, tortuous scream seemed to emanate from the bowels of the earth.

"And do you know what?" Gang asked. He was toying with her, like a cat with an injured bird. "That may well have been your Ru."

It wasn't, but all along Gang had known that Ru was Luli's son. If only she could wipe that smirk off his face. What had he done to her Ru? Her mind was in shreds.

"Well?" he demanded.

"Wh-what are you asking of me?" she stammered, squeezing the almanac in her hand.

"Give me what I want and I will go easy on him."

"And what do you want?" She was choking on her tears, hardly able to breathe, let alone think.

"To be invested at dawn tomorrow."

So soon? She couldn't believe it. In a whirlwind of emotion, she said, "Tomorrow is an ill-fated day." She coughed into her 'kerchief, a stolen moment within which to compose her shattered emotions. "There is still snow on the ground. Wait five days and it will have thawed. That brings us to the day before the moon is round, which is a day of good fortune."

"Hah!" he shouted. "Do you think I care about your yin and yang, your sun and moon, your Heaven and earth? That's for fools. I'm a man of reason, of action, who waits not on the detailed inspection of the yarrow stalks or the tortoise shell," he scoffed. "I *will* have my investiture tomorrow. Sign the decree and I'll keep my promise."

Swirling amidst these intimidations were other currents of intrigue. It was clear Gang wanted his investiture brought forward for a reason that had nothing to do with Ru. But why? His threats made up her mind.

"Well, what are you waiting for? Sign it," he prodded his finger at the investiture decree.

"No, I won't," she said with defiance.

"What? What do you mean you won't?" Gang thumped the table so the brush and ink tablet leapt into the air. She had seen bullies before and she was not going to be intimidated. From her previous acquaintance with him, she knew that in the Chinese zodiac he was a rat – and no doubt one by nature, too. She was a tigress, stalking her prey, fiercely protecting her young. He didn't stand a chance.

"I've told you the most fortunate date for your investiture," she insisted.

"Are you as stupid as your son?" he asked, with lashings of sarcasm.

She took a deep breath and growled, "No, not at all. He's cleverer than I. One day, you'll see for yourself."

"Hah! There's no chance of that ever happening. I'll tell you what I'm going to do. I'll find an astrologer who will give me the date I want and you'll never see your son again. Then we'll see who's clever," he gloated.

To walk away from that ogre was the easiest and hardest thing she'd ever had to do. She had faith she could find a way to keep her integrity and save her son from insanity. Gang might have earthly power, but she had Heavenly power. In the Tao, she trusted.

CHAPTER 21

True Provenance

Conduct the funeral rites of your parents with meticulous care.
Follow the ceremonies of sacrifice even after they are long gone.
Then the virtue of the common people will resume its proper excellence.
THE ANALECTS OF CONFUCIUS

Feng circled his father's coffin, wafting incense from the burner. As the clouds of aromatic smoke dispersed, it revealed the deftly-carved images of the cypress tree on the coffin. His voice was hoarse from intoning prayers and swallowing clouds of incense. He wanted to feel like a proper son ought – a gatekeeper between the world of his ancestors and the world of the living, the world of his father and the world of his father's family. He had placed paper offerings around the coffin. Despite his concerted efforts, he couldn't shake a residual feeling of being an imposter. It was simple. Park was not his father. Nor was Lan his mother; not his biological mother, anyway. He felt like a stranger in his own house. Once-familiar objects felt garish and out of place. Yesterday, he had broken by accident his mother's favourite porcelain vase.

After this morning's awkward confrontation in Gang's chambers, Feng had stubbed his toe on the steps of the Yamen. Then he had plucked up the courage to tell Lan that they had to vacate their home. While he had done it as gently as he could, it had still broken her heart. What was left of it. This was yet another departure. How many more would there be? His life was unravelling like a ball of twine.

He stayed with her. While she dozed in the afternoon, she kept murmuring Park's name. He held her hand, cajoling her, encouraging her to live, to love, to stay until evening, the night, the next morning, until… they moved to their new house, where they could start again. This house held too many memories.

Everywhere, ghosts of old stalked the shadows. Gang was right. It was time to leave.

He left her side for a moment, to cleanse the space around Park's coffin. He wafted the incense burner and enunciated the prayers, but they rose up to Heaven as if on broken wings.

There was a scream from the inner chamber. Precious! What! When it turned into a howl, he knew. He just knew. Lan had drowned in a sea of grief.

Park was poisoned nine days previously, so he'd been expecting it, dreading it. Even so, it still hit him like a thunderclap. Right in the belly. Winding him. Hard. He staggered out of the presence of one corpse, in the gut-wrenching fear that he was about to encounter another. On the way, Precious brushed past him in a flurry of tears and lurched out of the main door. His page, Qitong, was alongside her carrying a lantern. Dusk would fall soon.

"Where's she going?" he asked Strange.

"To fetch the doctor," his manservant replied, his face contorted with angst.

Feng had wanted to say goodbye to his mother before she departed. He took one look at her face and knew it was too late. Her serene features reminded him of a sunset he had once seen in the Gobi Desert. In the stillness, the great red orb sunk into the stark yellow horizon. It was the most humbling experience of his life. Until now. Lan's face wore that look of sublime quiescence. Gone the life etchings of worry and pain. Wiped clean, her skin was smooth, blanched and radiant. He envied her that peace. One day, it would come to him.

Her hand was still warm. He stroked it, trying to keep that last vestige of life, hoping beyond hope that it might defy the Tao and call her back. Then he could say the things he'd always wanted to say but never had the time or inclination, like "Thank you for safeguarding my youth," and "I'm grateful you helped me grow and develop," and "I'd never want for any other mother but you." He'd wipe away a tear and say those three little words, "I love you."

Woven thick in this cocoon of reflection, he barely noticed Precious open the door and let the chill of dusk into the house. Luli followed. He realised his mother's hand had cooled and dropped it so it thudded against the bedside. He flushed with guilt – and at the very moment that he'd let her go, forever.

Luli was at her side. Sitting next to death. Every act was suffused with poignancy: Luli taking his mother's three pulses at the wrist, lifting her lifeless limbs and then closing her eyes. Each act wore a cloak of incontrovertible finality. She could no longer see him, nor he her. She was gone.

"A fine lady," Luli murmured, echoing his innermost thoughts.

Precious, Strange, Granny Dandan and the other servants wailed and beat their chests. The boy, Qitong, filled the sleeve of his robe with tears. The caterwaul was like the dread demons of the underworld. Luli moved like she was walking underwater and had by some miracle acquired the ability to breathe like a baby in the womb. She said something to him. It sounded like, "Come and see me for the letters," but in his present state of mind, the words made no sense.

"Thank you Luli," he mouthed a reply and she was gone, out of the door. Feng's world was leaving with her and with the spirit of his adoptive mother. They were all leaving until he was alone. This was an end, but of what exactly? He cried hot tears for the loss of his father, his mother and now, the loss of who he'd always thought he was. He was someone else, an imposter. That was the greatest shock. He couldn't feel a thing, even if he gripped a hot poker. The outside world didn't exist: it was replaced by an empty, shallow feeling. The servants' wailing was like a soft thrum of rain against the window pane.

In the gathering gloom, he had a vague awareness of lights bobbing around in the inner courtyard of the house. There were uniformed men carrying lanterns. A knock on the door. He froze. He could hear his heart thumping against his chest. What did the knocking want of him? Perhaps, in a moment of compassion, the gods had sent his parents back to him, to nurse him back to health. In this weird dream state, he heard the indistinct sound of the door click open, heard Precious say, "Commandant."

That name stung him into action. Tung? What did he want? What was he doing here? Had Gang sent him to evict them?

Tung must have asked a question because the next thing he heard Precious say was, "Yes, Master Feng is still here. Come in."

That startled him. He smelled a rat. This *was* Gang's doing. The commandant had come to arrest him. *How do I know that?*

The lanterns burst into the house. Heavy footsteps. Swords unsheathed. Shouting, "Where is he?" and "Grab him."

They were the spiders, he, the fly. Thankfully, he knew where to hide. He kissed his mother on the forehead and slid away from her bedside. He swept through the house as silent as a ghost and dived into his hiding place. He would be safer there than in the Purple Forbidden City.

Soldiers scurried past him, opening closets, hatches and wardrobes, moving systematically around the various courts and rooms of the large residence. They looked in the yard and he even heard them searching the well. Cramped and uncomfortable, at least he was away from prying eyes. Nearby, he heard the commandant talking to Precious. Poor dear, she was distraught. How could they conduct a search for him in a house of two corpses? The servants must be delirious at this public intrusion on their private grief.

"We've looked everywhere. So where did he go?" Tung demanded.

"He was here, I tell you," she choked through a veil of tears.

"Well, he's not now," Tung said, as irascible as ever. "I must warn you. Do not venture outside until dawn."

"Why's that?" Precious asked.

"By order of the magistrate, there is a dusk to dawn curfew."

"A curfew?"

"Yes," Tung said. "Listen, the Emperor's spies are everywhere. If you see or hear anything suspicious, let us know, talking of which, thank you for telling me about Feng. What a shock. A charlatan. To think he's been deceiving us for so long. Because of you, the truth is out: the missing son of General Tiande. We need to apprehend Master Feng. I can't tell you everything, but suffice to say, he is a dangerous man. If you see him, do not approach him. He may be one of the co-conspirators, a spy of the Jianwen Emperor."

"So, are you saying… that Feng was complicit… in his father's murder?" Precious asked, between sobs.

If that was what they thought, he was in deep trouble.

"We don't know," the commandant replied. "That's why we need to question him. Don't worry, we'll find and interrogate him."

"I hope so," Precious murmured. "There was mention of a reward."

"Of course, the prince will repay your commendable loyalty," the commandant added, his reply laced with scorn, "Come to the Yamen in the morning for your five taels of silver."

What? Five taels of silver. Was that the tally of all her years of service and loyalty? The ignominy.

He had nowhere to turn. *Think!* Where could he go?

Luli's parting words popped into his mind, *'come and see me about the letters.'* Yes, the letters. There had to be something in his father's letters that could undo these false allegations and prove his innocence. Once the militia had finished their search, he would wait for dusk and sneak out under cover of darkness. He would find refuge at Luli's Po Office. Anywhere to escape this awful place. How could Precious betray him? He felt sick in the stomach.

CHAPTER 22

The Flow of Ch'i

Through the long nights of winter,
Through the long days of summer, shall I be alone.
Long years will pass, and then I myself
Will to my husband's grave wing my way.
THE SHI KING (BOOK OF ODES)

Luli often mused on the late afternoon shadows cast by the snow-capped Yanshan Mountains. They reminded her of who she was – a simple widow – and who she'd lost that dreadful day – her husband, Heng. It brought to mind what might have been, if he had lived. What if there had been the patter of little feet – other than Ru's? Even after all these years she welled up and wiped a tear from her eye.

She had observed the departing shadows of an old and well-respected couple – Park and Lan. They reminded her of Ru and of the suffering he was enduring at the hands of that scoundrel Gang. The prison guards had prevented her from visiting him. She had left them with food for him, but would they give it to him, or scoff it themselves? Ru was fast becoming a shadow of his former self and that was terrifying her.

Despite these disappointments, she'd made her choice. She trusted in Heaven and Heaven had to save her son. It just had to.

Luli wandered into the market, surrounded by the clatter of the stalls closing at the end of the day's trading. In the trees, a flock of small birds gathered, preparing to roost for the night. On the far side of the market square, weary soldiers marched in formation, their leader barking orders. She pulled up her collar against a stiff breeze blowing off the Bohai Sea, picking up the chill from the snow lying in patches on the ground.

Her hands played over the surface of her favourite phoenix-motif fan, a gift long ago from Wing, the old Dragon Master. In one swift movement, she pulled off a strand of cotton that had worked itself loose. As she turned for home, Zetian approached her. She must have appeared disconsolate, because her neighbour asked,

"What's the matter? It's Ru, isn't it? Tell me. How is he bearing up?"

Luli shook her head. "Not well. He's suffering, Zeti," she began in earnest. "The guards beat him and deprive him of food. Worse, they humiliate him. I must prove his innocence – otherwise that awful magistrate will chop off his hand or something worse. It'll drive him over the edge for good."

"I'm so sorry," Zetian said, pressing her hands together in prayer.

"Thank you for your concern."

"Not at all," Zetian replied, "let me know if we can help in any way."

"I will," she said.

From across the market came a clanging sound, followed by a hollow cry. Then a soldier yelled, "By order of the commandant, there's a curfew."

A company of soldiers jogged into the market square, harrying the stallholders who were packing away their goods, pushing and prodding everyone else.

Major Renshu shouted out, "Move on. Everyone, go back to your homes, or else."

The soldiers worked in pockets, singling out small groups of men, who were hauled off by their collars, despite vehement protestations of innocence. Four soldiers were dragging a victim kicking and screaming right by where Luli was standing.

One complained, "Let me go. What have I done to deserve this?"

"We know who you are," the soldier muttered, adding a kick in the ribs for good measure. "You're late for your appointment."

"What? Who with?" The man yelled back.

"Thousand Cuts Liu," the soldier said and then guffawed. That shut the man up.

This was serious. The dusk bell rang out. She couldn't afford to get trapped in this spider's web. She had to leave.

The slow moon was up. Turning for home, she caught a glimpse of the moonbeams reflecting on the Great Wall. In the half-light, she glimpsed a feature in the Great Wall – a face, or rather the profile of a face. She blinked and looked again. There, in the midst of the shadows, she saw women's faces, young and old, frowns and smiles, wrinkled and smooth-skinned. She had seen them before on the wall outside their home, the ones Ru had pointed out to her.

There were more faces, spread out along the Great Wall. With her trained eye, she saw faces high up near the top of the wall, while others were low down, nearer ground level. She was about to turn away when she stopped. It was as if someone tapped her on the shoulder and whispered in her ear, *'You've missed the most important thing, look again.'*

She did. How had she not spotted it the first time? All the faces pointed in the same direction.

Eastwards.

What did it mean?

Since ancient times, the Laolong had transmitted its power through the wall, keeping out the Tartars, Mongols and the other yin barbarians, protecting the yang Emperor and keeping his people safe within the confines of the Zhongguo.

The faces always pointed the same way as the flow of ch'i in the wall – the same direction as the Laolong, the Old Dragon. In ancient times, the flow was eastwards, meaning that the head of the dragon rose in the mountains in the western provinces and his tail sat in the most eastern end point of the wall, which – until twenty years ago – was the Yanshan Mountains. That was when General Tiande extended it to the pale waves of the Bohai Sea.

So, if the flow of ch'i was eastwards – from west to east – why on earth was the new, most eastern end of the wall, named the Old Dragon's *Head*?

If the flow was eastwards, it should have been called the Old Dragon's *Tail*.

But it wasn't.

Why not?

This was a supernatural question and there was only one person she could think of who might know the answer. She rushed off to the Temple of the Eight Immortals.

CHAPTER 23

The Laundry Wagon

Man is born for uprightness.
If a man loses his uprightness and yet lives,
His escape from death is the effect of great good fortune.
THE ANALECTS OF CONFUCIUS

Feng waited for the sound of the first night watch to dissipate, until all he could hear was his own shallow breathing. He lifted the coffin lid and slid it onto the floor. It had been an effective hiding place, but foul and claustrophobic. And not for the squeamish. Squeezed next to his adoptive father's corpse, there was barely room to breathe. Fearful of moving lest he alert those searching for him, his body had almost merged with Park's.

His limbs creaking and groaning, he climbed into the annex and brushed himself down. He mouthed a silent prayer of thanksgiving to Park for helping him one last time.

At least he was free. Keeping to the corners, he crept through the inner courtyard, which was swathed in moon shadows. He trod slowly over a slippery patchwork of snow and ice. With every step nearer the outer gate, another tie to his home in the Yamen loosened and fell away – his bedroom where he grew up, his father's study and his mother's dressing table... he felt light, keen and acute, nearer to the Way, the Tao. He had this ineffable feeling that he was leaving home for the very last time.

Not only did he smell like a dead man, something had died in him, too. He had no family of his own, none that recognised him or knew of his existence. What or who was he then? What did Tung call him? A dangerous spy? A conspirator? No, he was Xu Yingxu, the son of the famous General Xu Da. He had to prove it. He had one hope: his father's letters. How ironic, he was leaving the house of two dead people, only for his life to become dependent on letters written by a third. His ancestors were conspiring against him.

How could he reach Luli's Po Office in the midst of a curfew? The militia were out in force arresting anyone who looked at all suspicious; he, dressed in white mourning robes and smelling like a skunk, was about as conspicuous as a volcanic eruption. The magistrate's residence, in the administrative district of the Yamen, was in the middle of the most fortified garrison in the Zhongguo. As a last thought, he tucked Park's deathbed instructions into a small, sealed lacquer box, which he secreted back in an inner pocket of his robe. He sighed, dismayed that that was all that remained of his parents' memory.

Near the outer doorway, he heard snoring. Huh. Qitong was asleep again. Some gatekeeper he was. Step by step, Feng edged by him. The boy awoke.

"Master," he said, stifling a yawn.

"Shhh!" Feng pressed his finger to the boy's lips. "I have to go. Stay here."

The boy roused himself. With a shake of the head, he whispered, "Master, if you leave, I'll not be welcome here anymore. Let me come with you."

Feng thought a moment. He liked the boy. Qitong reminded him of himself when he was that age: precocious, impulsive and quick-witted. So he replied, "Why not? Come on then, follow me."

The boy nodded and Feng glanced into the street. A rumble of wheels; something was coming around the corner. He hauled Qitong back and they hid behind the gate. A covered wagon trundled into view. Two men sat on a bench seat. One was holding a lantern, while trying not to fall asleep. The other grasped the reins of two grumpy oxen, whose breath smoked in the chilly night air.

The laundry wagon on its nightly round was collecting dirty linen from residences in the Yamen. As it passed by, he and Qitong leapt through the crude curtain at the back of the wagon and dived headlong into a pile of dirty laundry. If the driver had seen them, the wagon would grind to a stop at any moment. He held his breath… and… it rolled on. The back of the wagon was dark and the linen was damp and smelly. What did he care? His escape to the future had begun.

The wagon halted at various places, picking up more soiled linen, which the drivers chucked on top of the pile. The stench was obnoxious. When the oxen started puffing and panting, Feng guessed the wagon was ascending the ramp at the Zhendong Gate. By the time it reached the wall road, the oxen were bellowing and snorting like a couple of demons.

The wagon was ushered through two checkpoints and then headed towards the main laundry situated in Ninghai Fortress, a stone's throw inland from the Laolongtou. Ninghai was the commandant's headquarters, so it was as heavily fortified as the Shanhaiguan Fortress. If this was karma, Feng didn't think it was making it an easier for him to escape.

A stern voice rang out into the night. "Halt. Who goes there?"

Feng recognised the tone: it was Cui. He prayed the old campaigner would pay more attention to his creaking bones than two interlopers in the back of the wagon.

"Who are you guarding? The Emperor?" the driver replied.

"Big ears, don't you know this is the first night of a curfew?" Cui was having none of it. "No, obviously you don't," he added with a sardonic air.

"Listen," the driver replied. "During the day, these grade one Confucian mandarins are as solemn as the Buddha himself. Yet see them after the dusk watch, they're drinking warm wine, entertaining the dancing girls and soiling the bed sheets with the produce of clouds and rain."

"You don't need to tell me," Cui complained. "But I still need to inspect your load. There are dangerous fugitives at large and you never know where they might be hiding."

This was ominous. Cui might be old, but he was clearly no fool. If he searched the wagon, they'd be caught. Feng had to think and act quickly.

"It's dirty linen, not explosives," the driver moaned. "Come on, little emperor, it's late. Let us pass, eh?"

While the drivers argued with the guards, Feng had a moment to think. He prodded Qitong and hissed, "Move. Fast."

"But master…" the boy replied.

"What?" he snapped.

"Your clothes."

"What about…?" he muttered. Then he realised. He was still wearing the white of mourning. He would be conspicuous – even in the moon shadows. "Never mind, I have an idea. Follow me." He slipped out the back of the wagon. Using both hands, he scooped up liberal doses of grease and mud from the wagon's axle and smeared them on his robes.

Cui's heavy footsteps resounded on the stone road, heading towards them.

Quick, think! Protruding gamely above the far side of the wall were several vertical bamboo poles. A scaffold. Heaven had smiled on him. He leapt over the battlements like a cat and crouched on a bamboo platform. Qitong was right behind him.

Hidden behind the wall, Feng listened as Cui opened the back of the wagon and searched through the laundry. It was karma. They'd done it. He hadn't seen them.

From the vantage point of the platform, Feng could see the plain extending beyond the fortress to the land of the Blue Wolf. He might be free, but his predicament had not improved. Luli's Po Office lay in Shanhai village outside the western wall of the fortress. How was he going to go there from where he was, outside the eastern wall? In the near distance to the south, the waxing moon cast a dim light on the waves of the Bohai Sea. Yes, that was it.

"Can you swim?" he asked.

"Like a fish. I was a champion amongst my brothers," Qitong chimed.

"Good, then get your fins on," he muttered.

They could swim round the end of the promontory of the Laolongtou then up the small river estuary to the little port by Shanhai village. It was a long swim and the water was freezing, but there was no other way.

Before he'd reached the deserted beach, the pungent odour of salt, mud and silt reached him. The tide was out so they trudged across the mud in search of deeper waters. From reading coroner's reports, he was painfully aware that many a walker had been sucked out to a watery grave by underestimating the speed and strength of the incoming tides.

And he had to look after Qitong.

"Master," the boy tugged at his robe.

There were noises behind them. And lanterns. There were men on the mud flats. Fisherman? No, it was too early, even for them. He crouched on his haunches and listened. The subtle noises of the dark bay were like a quiet, distant song. The noises grew into shouts. Soldiers. Cui must have spotted them and raised the alarm.

"This way," he said, pointing further out to sea. They had to find water. They could swim under the waves and make their escape. They quickened their pace. He was panting. They ran faster. Oh, his feet were sinking, the cold mud clawing at his ankles. Each step sunk further into the mud. Water was lapping at his calves.

A gunshot rang out. The missile whizzed past his face. Qitong fell headlong into the mud. Feng fell on top of him and turned him over, face up. Thankfully, the boy was only winded. The tide was rushing in. The water was freezing, like a dark mantle spreading over everything. His heart was pounding and his calves ached.

Water washed against the side of his body. He lifted his head to prevent taking gulps of muddy water. There was a whiff of something acrid. At first, he thought it was the mud. It was his sweat, his own fear stalking him.

The soldiers were shouting at each other. A stone's throw away, no more.

"Where is he?"

"I lost sight of him. Lift the lantern."

He daren't move.

"We'll find him," another shouted. "He's a wanted man. There's a reward."

"If we don't catch him, the tide will."

As the soldiers closed in, the waters were rising. Another high wave and they could float off out of sight.

"See him?"

"No. You?"

He slipped off the mud flat and hauled Qitong through the waters, deep enough to crawl along the bottom. They were besmirched with mud. He found a deeper channel. The voices subsided into the distance. Qitong swam alongside him against the onrushing tide.

He glanced back at the coast. Nearby were the lanterns of Laolongtou and, farther away, the Ninghai Fortress glistened in the night. Beyond that, the dark, forbidding battlements of the Shanhaiguan Fortress that was once his home; not anymore.

They drifted with the tide and watched as the soldiers' lanterns bobbed up and down along the beach. They were running, searching for them. Another gunshot pierced the night, but it wasn't close. For the moment, at least, they'd escaped.

The water was so cold, it constricted his breathing. As the tide came in, he swam nearer the coast. Soon they were opposite the Laolongtou, ablaze with torches. The tide was licking at its base, kissing the Old Dragon's nose. He noticed a hole in the sea-facing end of the wall. It was just above the tide line. Sailing often along the coast, he knew every part of the Laolongtou and he'd never seen a gap in the stonework like that before.

The incoming tide allowed him to drift nearer to the strange feature. What was it? Why had it recently appeared? The New Year winter storms must have dislodged bricks from the dragon's 'snout', revealing the mysterious hole. Curious as ever, he made a mental note to investigate it under more amenable circumstances.

Feng swam over to help Qitong, who was struggling to stay afloat. Feng was shivering with the cold, but Qitong's little body was quaking and his teeth were chattering like mad. Brave lad – and not a complaint, to boot. Feng cradled his near-frozen body. A shot rang out, as a puff of powder spat orange-red flame into the night. They had strayed too close to the Laolongtou. He wanted to dive, but Qitong was choking on the salt water and nearly fainting with the cold.

The sea was sucking the life out of them, but the waves hid their escape.

He did not know what to do next.

CHAPTER 24

Amidst the Great Tao

Great Tao has neither form nor substance, yet it fashioned Heaven and earth.
Great Tao has no favours, thus it governs the law and order of the cosmos.
Great Tao has no name, but it gives life to and sustains all beings.
THE TAO TE CHING

The words from the letter echoed around Bolin's head for the umpteenth time. "You are the inheritor of great and marvellous magic powers." They were stuck there. And no matter what he did, neither prayer nor supplication would shift them. They just kept repeating, like a Buddhist mantra.

But how could he, Bolin, a mere fisherman's son, be in receipt of marvellous powers and gifts? It turned the natural order of things upside down. Did Emperors perform guard duty? Did mandarins clean out the latrines? Did scholars collect firewood? No. They did not.

The structure in society reflected the underlying order to the cosmos; the Great Tao, itself. That order had to be maintained, otherwise, well, nothing could function. He knew that. Dong knew that. The Emperor knew that. Why didn't Luli know that?

The more he tried to push these thoughts to the back of his mind, the more they sprang up through the cracks and crevices in his reasoning.

A voice spoke to him in the deeper recesses of soul, "Find the Pearl of Wisdom. Find *the place where words are made*."

"Go away!" He snarled out loud. He must have awoken Zetian in the next-door room, because he heard her rouse and she was soon knocking lightly on his door.

"Son, are you all right?" she asked, entering his room. He pretended to be asleep and started snoring. He felt her tuck in his bedclothes and tip-toe out of the room. As the second night watch sounded at midnight, he fell into an uneasy, restless slumber.

In the deep recesses of his mind, the man awaited him, like a shadowy agent, spying, peering out of the gloom. The darkness was almost palpable, as his dream body floated above his physical body and he found himself looking down on his sleeping self, in his little room, in his little life.

He drifted across the room until he rubbed against the back wall, a strange experience in itself, especially for someone who was particular about where things were and liked them to stay that way. He was not in the habit of 'floating' up against walls. No, in his settled, regular existence, that didn't happen. He felt like his body – *what body was that exactly, since he was looking across at his physical body prostrate on the bed?* – was as light as a wispy cloud and capable of drifting through the wall and coming out the other side.

He was frightened to move either way. If he moved into the wall, would he remain stuck in it forever after? As he fretted, by some miracle he found himself in the outer courtyard. He was quick to notice that, despite the smudges of snow and ice on the ground, he had no sensation of cold. That might have had something to do with the fact that he did not have any skin to speak of.

Either way, he, Bolin, had walked – well, *glided* – through a wall. That was an achievement. In the end, negotiating the realm of the Tao was simple. He liked things to stay the same, like the passing of day and night, the regularity of the seasons and the constant interplay of yin and yang. That included people stubbing their toe when they tried to walk through a wall. That was a definite rule on earth, though not, apparently, in the realm of the Great Tao.

Now he was getting the hang of it, he began to enjoy the sensation of the supreme lightness of being as he rose above his house, above Fuyuan Street, Shanghai village and Shanhaiguan Fortress, with its dark battlements, crenellated towers and massive fortifications. Another part of him experienced the eerie sensation of weightlessness with barely controlled fear. It was a fear that made him concentrate on every little thing, because he'd no idea how to return to his physical body. Was he still 'alive'? His physical body could have died and he could be permanently cut adrift from it! *Is this what death is, then?*

Floating amidst the serene mists of the Great Tao, Bolin drifted over the Ninghai Fortress towards the Laolongtou. This dream travelling was a strange experience. His life had been one long drudge; other than fishing with his father, the occasional visit to the local market town and a trek into the Yanshan Mountains, Bolin had never left the environs of Shanhaiguan. Now, he found himself free to roam at will. Unconstrained by earthly chains, he could move anywhere.

From his elevation, he was able to 'see' the realm of earth, but with an absence of colour. All he could make out were blackened structures and shadowy figures shrouded in clouds of swirling ch'i. Sounds were muffled, like noises heard underwater. Sights were the same – blurred, with no sense of depth and everything in silhouette.

His yin-yang eyes and senses were acute. And with them, he knew someone – or something – was following him. He had a vague awareness of it in the distance, impinging on the fringes of his mind. It rose above him, flapping. Oh, it was a bird with monochrome markings, a gull perhaps. No, it was a magpie; a black and white bird of the Tao. Then it was gone, out of range.

Driven on by the urge to find *the place where words are made*, he hovered over the Laolongtou. A knot of guards warmed themselves around a brazier, keeping off the chill of a winter's night. The magpie shot by him and dived straight through the stone floor of the Laolongtou.

How did it do that?

Bolin himself had moved through a wall, so he could do that; couldn't he? So, he tried and – followed. Passing through bricks and mortar, he emerged into an ante-chamber somewhere beneath the Laolongtou. Why had he never heard of this place? The Tao bird was flapping nearby, trying to tell him something. But what? Then he realised; it was his guide. He followed it through an adjoining wall and into a vault. He felt compressed, his breathing tight. He was choking. It was the same suffocation he had experienced on the Laolongtou and in his dreams.

Inside the vault was an elongated slab, a sort of flat bed, on which were various objects. At the far end of the vault was the silhouette of a long cylinder. With no sense of colour or depth, he couldn't identify these things.

The Tao bird departed and he followed.

Returning to his physical body, he wondered what on earth the vault had to do with *the place where words are made*. He had to find out.

CHAPTER 25

The Lessons of Birth and Death

Going back to the beginnings of things and pursuing them to the end,
We come to know the lessons of birth and of death.
THE TA CHUAN, THE GREAT TREATISE

As the third night watch rang out across the rooftops, Feng struggled across the sand, which clung to his wet feet, pulling him down. At least they had evaded the militia. At one point, he suspected the gods had planted a secret bell on his person that rang every time he moved, alerting the guards to his presence. Wherever he and Qitong hid, soldiers were annoyingly close. The guards even took pot shots at them from the Laolongtou. But they had survived.

Lanterns were flickering in the distance – the militia were as unstoppable as the incoming tide. Feng grabbed Qitong and dived into the long coastal grasses. His heart was beating like a drum as he watched them move inexorably along the beach. But they passed him and Qitong by and when they were gone, he heaved a huge sigh of relief. He kept thinking back to that vault at the base of the Laolongtou. It fired his imagination. It was karma that he had seen it. When he could, he would return there.

When he emerged with the boy, Qitong was shivering, convulsing and unable to stand, let alone walk. His skin had taken on this dreadful bluish hue. The cold of the waters had embraced his little body and wouldn't release him. Feng did what he could to warm him and prayed that Luli had a remedy.

Boy in arms, he staggered around the back of the houses in Shanhai village, looking for Luli's Po Office. He was emotionally and physically exhausted, not only by the death of his two parents, but by the swim, the chase, the boy's parlous state and most of all by his unprecedented fall from grace. His father's letters contained secrets that would allay his and others' fears and restore his rightful position.

This was it. The Po Office. He glanced around the corner of the building into the main street, checking the way was clear. There was not a soul. The boy started whimpering, delirious.

"Shhh!" he said. Having reached this far, he was not going to be caught by the militia.

Qitong lay still in his arms. Feng stumbled around to the entrance gate of the Po Office, looking for signs of life. It was late at night, the sliver of a crescent moon casting no ambient light. There was no sound. Luli wasn't awake.

He laid Qitong on the ground outside the front gate, pushed it open and stepped inside. He turned when he heard a scuffling noise and was hit hard on the head. He crumpled in a heap.

"Argh!" he clutched his head, protecting himself from the next blow which came soon afterwards. "Stop!" He hissed.

"Feng?" A startled woman's voice. "Is that you?"

"Yes," he groaned, holding his head like it was about to burst.

"Oh, Feng," Luli said. "I'm so sorry. Here, let me see to that wound."

"Ouch, that hurts," he moaned, as she touched his head.

"There are many valuables in my shop. I thought you were a thief," Luli said, helping him indoors and onto a stool. His head was spinning and he squealed like a pig. He was ashamed to tell her the truth, that he was on the run and hiding from the militia.

"Don't worry about me, I'll be fine; see to Qitong," he said, pointing outside.

"Qitong?"

"The boy. He's outside, on the ground."

She went out but quickly returned. "He's gone. There's no one there."

"What?" Feng stood up, a move he instantly regretted. He clutched his head and swooned, only prevented from falling over by Luli's helping hand.

"Sit there and I'll tend to you," she insisted, first fixing a bandage around his head before making him a cup of tea. Her warmth and kindness revived the distant strains of humanity in his soul.

"What *have* you been doing? Swimming in a mud bath?"

"I... I came for Tiande's letters," he stammered.

"Of course, I expected that you would; just not in the middle of the night," Luli replied. "First your father and now your mother, I'm so sorry. For both to pass so close to one other; I'm afraid to say this, but you must have upset your ancestors."

He frowned. Sometimes these seers obsessed about ancestors. "The letters?" he pleaded.

"I'll fetch them," Luli said, delving through her piles of scrolls.

She returned moments later with the envelope.

At last, there would be no secrets between him and his father. Until he resolved his past, he could not begin to live in the present and to plan his future. He undid the silk tie and let the scrolls unfold. The calligraphy was neat and tidy, yet elegant and authoritative. He leafed through the papers and the one on the bottom dropped on the floor. Luli stooped to pick it up, glanced at the contents and then handed it back to him.

He thanked her and opened the top one.

"If you are reading this," it said, "my good friends, Magistrate Park and Lady Lan have both joined me in Heaven and you have discovered your true identity."

He sighed. This was his father's hand, his real father. In a moment to cherish, his real father spoke to him from Heaven. This was as close as he had ever been to him.

The first carts of the day rumbled by outside the window. It was getting light. The world awoke from its slumber.

Luli was tidying her shop with a deft touch. So light and free on her feet, she moved like a dancer. Shouts from outside made him jump. Militia. He stuffed the parchments in his sleeve and raced for the door. They were already there, banging on the lintel.

"Open up," someone shouted.

"Come," Luli said to him, "Over here,"

"It's the militia," he snapped. "They're after me."

"Down here!" She lifted up a tattered rug and hauled open a trap door.

"What's that?"

She spoke quickly. "A vertical shaft. When you reach the bottom, turn left into the tunnel. Keep going straight as far as you can until the tunnel makes the first turn. There, you'll find stairs leading up to a hatch. That'll take you to freedom. You'll see where it emerges. Then head for the estuary."

More banging, strident now. "Open the door! Now!"

"Here, take this." She gave him a lantern.

"Thanks, I am in your debt," he said and slipped through the trap door, which slammed shut behind him. He listened to the raised voices in the vestibule and Luli protesting her innocence. She had saved him. He had an escape route. What on earth had happened to Qitong?

He lifted the lantern and descended the ladder. What were these tunnels? Why had he never heard of them before?

CHAPTER 26

The First Pass under Heaven

Tiānxià Dìyī Guān – The First Pass under Heaven
THE WORDS ON THE PLAQUE ABOVE THE ZHENDONG GATE,
SHANHAIGUAN

The sound of the fourth night watch rang out from atop the Drum and Bell Tower. From behind the curtains in his sedan chair, Gang was out of sight, though still able to view everything. Despite the late hour, the militia remained out in force. A knot of soldiers was dragging a man across the square towards the cells. Ignoring his cries for mercy, they beat him with bamboo batons and a choice selection of curses.

Gang smiled to himself. Like putting two starving rats in a cage, it was that easy to foment distrust and suspicion between prince and emperor. How he had delighted in convincing the commandant to enforce a curfew. The jails were already overflowing. Night trade had ground to a halt, arresting the flow of taxes to the imperial coffers. He would have liked to stop and relish the spectacle of confusion and dissent, except he was late for his mysterious rendezvous: '*The Zhendong Gate: fourth night watch.*'

He halted the sedan chair a stone's throw from the gate and sent Sheng and his porters back to the Yamen. He didn't want any witnesses to whatever was going to transpire.

Every time he stood in the dark, damp, yin shadows of the Zhendong Gate, he couldn't help but think of the extraordinary words on the plaque above its outer arch: The First Pass under Heaven. What did that say about the Chinese? That *their* gate was really the first arrival point for *any* Heavenly influence? Did Heaven reserve its finest for the Chinese? It was almost as laughable as the legend associated with the Taoist temple. The Chinese even characterised themselves as 'yang' and everyone else as 'yin'.

What about the Zhongguo? What a startling concept! Was the Middle Kingdom really the centre of civilisation? Had the Lord of Resplendent Heaven chosen the Emperor of China as his supreme representative on earth – to govern all humanity? If it was not so absurd, it would fit neatly into a comic opera!

One day, such hubris would bring the Chinese to their knees, an event he would relish like no other. On that momentous day, the Yellow Emperor himself would kiss the earth before the Great Khan; just like the last time under Gang's great hero, Genghis.

As he marched up to the inner Zhendong Gate, the guards on the battlements rushed to the far side – and out of his line of sight – where they raised a clamour, challenging someone or something outside the gates.

On the ground, the guards bristled at his arrival. One of them shouted, "Halt!"

Another grabbed a lit torch from its cradle and thrust it in his face. An officer stepped out of the shadows and calmed the guard, saying, "I will deal with this." As the guard backed away, the officer bowed to him and said, "Magistrate Gang, an honour to meet you."

Peering at his identity tablet, Gang replied, "And you are…? Ah, Major Renshu."

"At your service," the major replied and threw him a quizzical glance.

Gang guessed he was wondering why a senior official was skulking about in the dead of the night. He muttered by way of excuse, "Couldn't sleep. What's happening here, Major?"

"Riders," the major said, distracted by more shouts from the outer gate. "There are riders outside the gates."

That was intriguing – as was the major's slight Mongolian tinge to his speech. Either way, Gang had expected to meet Guanting, but perhaps the riders were his rendezvous.

"I will see for myself," he said.

A guard grabbed a torch and led him and the major through the inner gates of the Zhendong Gate. Shadows danced on the arched, moisture-laden walls of the tunnel. Soon Gang could hear the conversation between the guards and the riders, conducted through the thick wooden drawbridge.

"Let us in," one of the riders shouted in a thick Mongolian accent. The voice sounded vaguely familiar.

"Who are you? What do you want?" the major asked.

"We're attached to the prince's cavalry," a voice replied. Yes, he had heard that voice somewhere before.

"The prince passed through Shanhaiguan ten days ago. Why didn't you accompany him then?" the major yelled back.

"After the battle, the prince gave us orders to scout the enemy and then report their movements. We're in a hurry to catch the prince, so don't delay us," came the testy reply.

"I won't," the major retorted, "as long as it's true that you act under the prince's orders." Then he stuck a bronze gong, the signal to lower the drawbridge. The winch in the gatehouse creaked and groaned and the drawbridge eased to the ground. On the far side of the moat, three men were slumped over their horses. A damp sweat arose from their exhausted steeds, standing motionless with heads bowed. The men wore the hats and loose garments of the steppes and had deep slanted eyes. Plunged deep into their belts were Mongol sabres.

Gang was nervous. If these were the men with whom he was to meet and they were uncovered as Mongol spies, he might be implicated. He had arrived at the Zhendong Gate at the precise moment of the Mongols' arrival, a coincidence the major would not have missed.

As Renshu marched a contingent of guards across the drawbridge, a guard murmured, "Uh, I can smell the mutton from here," then pinched his nose.

Gang let out a low growl. He hated any snide remark against the Mongols' nomadic lifestyle, that of herding sheep from one end of the steppes to another. What was wrong with that? What about the Chinese, with their sedentary, agricultural lifestyle? They thought they were so superior, so high and mighty, they could rule over everyone. Not if he had his way.

Gang would not forget the insult. He glanced at the man's identity tablet – Corporal Wuzhou. He wouldn't forget the name either.

It did not stop his heart from pounding under his robes. After so many years, he feared his carefully manicured cover was blown. He growled in annoyance. He had so much blood to let to quench his revenge. He let slip a prayer, 'These Mongols better be who they say they are.'

The guards encircled the three riders with sabres and frowns drawn. This was not going to end well. A storm was brewing. The major stared into the Mongols' faces and examined every stroke of every character on their identity tablets, then stood nose to nose with a tall Mongol, whose bearing set him out as their leader.

"And who exactly are you?" The major said in a voice of challenge and provocation.

This was it. Gang fingered his dagger. The soldier next to him was that ogre, Wuzhou. He could slit his throat and make a run for it. He was about to unsheathe it, when, the Mongol replied with inordinate pride, "I... am... Altan."

Altan? Gang knew that name. That was the voice he had recognised. It was Altan – the Mongol shaman – from twenty years ago. Beneath the grime and sweat of the ride, Gang could see the man's canny eyes, flitting about, absorbing every nuance of every movement. Altan was an old fox, shrewd and cunning like no other. The many shared memories came flooding back. If anyone could dupe the Chinese, Altan could. He was a past master at it. Gang felt a flood of confidence flow through his veins.

Then Renshu surprised him, when he said, "Fine, that's all in order. Do you want bedding for the night?"

With that, the guards sheathed their sabres and the tension dissipated into the night.

Gang breathed a huge sigh of relief.

"No, only water and feed for the horses," Altan replied, calm as you like, "we're not stopping. We'll be on our way again at dawn."

The major escorted them to the stables. Gang followed at a distance and waited until Renshu had gone, then joined Altan.

"That was close," Gang blurted out.

"Not so loud," Altan held his finger over his mouth.

"Why didn't the major press you further about your orders?" he asked.

"Never you mind," Altan said with a frown. "There's not much time. Where can we talk?"

"Follow me," he said and took Altan to his chambers.

As soon as they sat down to some wine and dried fruit, he confronted Altan. "Listen, I'm glad to see you again, but you almost landed me in a heap of trouble. I've hidden in the long shadows cast by the Chinese imperial system for over twenty years and I'm not about to waste all that toil. Yet as soon as I return to Shanhaiguan, you show up and at the Zhendong Gate. It's not exactly the best clandestine meeting place. Every Yuan, Wang and Chang has seen us together. Coming here is a huge risk for both of us. You've already aroused suspicions. There are soldiers, villagers and workers still here from twenty years ago. If they remember me, they'll remember you."

"You worry like an old woman," Altan scolded him, taking a slug of wine and wiping his mouth with this sleeve. "I'm a shaman. I deal with Heavenly powers. I will always protect my people. You are still one of my people, aren't you?"

"Of course," Gang replied, feeling the heat of the threat. Adding to his discomfort were the shouts and screams of the inmates in the cells across from the chambers.

"Remember," Altan went on in that hissing kind of voice. "The last time we collaborated, you trusted my supernatural abilities where Abbot Cheng and

120

Dragon Master Wing were concerned. Since then, I have woven my skills with an even finer thread. So, you can trust them again."

Gang paced the floor. Altan had a point. "I believe you. What do you want of me?"

Altan took a deep breath. "Your help. This time, we'll finish off the Chinese once and for all."

"That, I like the sound of. What's your plan?"

"Good," Altan said. "We are blessed with opportunities. With the prince and his cavalry heading south and the yellow lands red with the fires of civil war, now is the perfect time to fan those flames."

"How? I thought the prince defeated the Mongol army?" Gang raised an eyebrow.

"We were beaten, yes, but a rump escaped. The army is small, but fierce and well-equipped. As soon as I leave this place, I will rejoin them."

"Hah! They won't breach the fortress of Shanhaiguan," he scoffed.

"I know that," Altan scowled. "Do not underestimate the Blue Wolf, especially when wounded. The yellow man sits in judgement on the lands and peoples beyond the pale of civilisation, calling us 'barbarians' and 'mutton-eaters'. What arrogance. But I am Altan. And alongside the Mongol forces, I have prepared a spectral army equipped with supernatural powers, one that need never ride a horse nor lift a sword. It is an army that will rend and demolish our foe *without ever taking to the field of battle.*"

Gang puffed out his cheeks. There was no doubt in his mind that Altan was a shaman with a slice of Heaven in his soul and who, twenty years ago, had outwitted both the Dragon Master and the Tao Celestial Master – but to win a battle without a single soldier?

"How is that possible?" he asked.

"With deception and subterfuge, all things are possible," Altan said, beginning to sound like Sun Tzu.

"Tell me more," Gang said, leaning forward.

"You don't need to know it all," Altan said, his eyes narrowing in the light of the lantern. "Don't forget the enduring strength and stealth of the wolf, whose greatest weapon is the element of surprise. You and I have done it before and we can do it again. Still want to collaborate?"

That was the question. As far as he could glean, helping Altan meant trusting in the man's supernatural skills. Well, if that was the only option, he was ready. This was the culmination of his life's work – and Altan's. Together again after twenty years, they could achieve great things. If anyone could make the plan bear fruit, Altan could.

"What do you want me to do?"

"Help the Mongol army breach the Zhendong Gate."

"Is that all?" he replied, rolling his eyes. "How do you intend to achieve that?"

"By blowing it up. There's already a Mongol merchant in town, looking to purchase explosives."

"What's his name?" he asked.

"Master Guanting," Altan said.

"Ai yi yi! I met him," Gang said, standing up in excitement. "This is more than a coincidence. It's an omen. Guanting was in this very chamber, just yesterday," he said and explained the details of their conversation.

"Make sure he gets his knapsack back," Altan said.

"I will. So Guanting left me the note?"

"No, but Guanting and his associate Big Qiang will help you achieve our ultimate goal."

"Who left the note?"

"Major Renshu – an officer in the munitions department."

"Hah, good. I should have realised he was complicit," Gang replied with a knowing nod. "He believed your story too easily."

"We have allies," Altan said. "But Renshu wants to be paid for his services, so Guanting had to raise the funds."

"I see," Gang replied, feeling more confident now.

"There's one more thing," Altan said, clenching his fists. "We must destroy the Laolong, the old dragon."

"How do you do that? It's invisible and moves like the wind."

"It's true, a Heavenly beast can't be killed," Altan said. "But you can disperse its ch'i so widely that it can never again reform as a dragon, like wood smoke in a tempest. Without the Laolong to guard its frontiers and inspire its troops, the Zhongguo will submit to our armies and we shall rekindle the past glories of the Yuan Dynasty."

"Where is the Laolong now?" Gang asked.

"Where we deposited it twenty years ago," Altan said with an air of undisguised triumph, "Trapped in the Jade Chamber, the vault beneath the Laolongtou."

"Why not leave it there?"

"It's too dangerous. I want to splinter its power forever. Now you are here, you can help. I will send word."

Gang liked the plan; he liked any plan to annihilate the Chinese. "How can I help?" he asked.

"We will win the war on earth by first defeating our foe in Heaven. That's why I have seeded the very air around the fortress with the ch'i of the Blue

Wolf. And now you've enforced a curfew, fomenting darkness and fear, we have the precise atmosphere we need. As magistrate, you can wreak havoc under the guise of securing the garrison. In the coming days, I will manipulate the Heavenly ch'i in our favour and you will see opportunities to exploit events. When they come, it will be obvious what you have to do."

"I hope so," he replied. That was clear. As clear as anything could be with a shaman like Altan.

Acting alone, even with all the power he assumed as magistrate, Gang's ability to hurt the huge Chinese imperial machine was small. Whereas collaborating with Altan made his ability to wreak revenge greater than ever. Together they could bring waves of death not only to the Chinese people but perhaps, by means of some national catastrophe, to the Zhongguo, the Chinese nation. The prospect stirred the embers in his vengeful soul.

The sound of the dawn watch resonated across the town's rooftops. The behemoth that was the fortress awoke from its slumber as Altan disappeared into the dim morning vapours.

CHAPTER 27

The Crystal Cave

The Heavens are high above us, the stars are far away.
If we simply investigate their phenomena,
We may calculate the date of a solstice a thousand years hence
Without getting up from our seats.
THE BOOK OF MENCIUS

Luli had knelt down and mouthed a silent prayer after the militia left. They had turned her house upside down, finding nothing and no one. The great clodhoppers had disturbed her papers, her altar, the shelving and the furniture and, last but not least, the Heavenly ch'i that attended her humble abode. She spent an age putting things where they belonged and summoning back the errant strands of ch'i.

At least Feng had escaped. These tunnels were sent by the gods. They had first come to her notice during the original Shanhaiguan construction work. Tiande had come to her Po Office to give her his letters and by accident had left a plan of the fortifications on the table. When seen on the plan, the overlay of the square above-ground fortress on the square tunnels below ground formed an eight-pointed star, which, as every student of the Tao knew, was akin to a huge Bagua charm, hence the name, Bagua tunnels.

She had waited until the curfew was lifted, in the hour before dawn. The room was alive with documents, letters and objects, left by the dead for the living to claim. Just like life, she mused; we inherit the crimes, failings and weaknesses of our ancestors and suffer for them through karma. When would the gods grant her a clean scroll on which to write her life's journey?

At the first slanting rays of dawn, she walked through the fortress gates. With a misty breath, she wrapped her robe around her chest. Jin was at the temple gate.

"Ah, so there you are and about time too," he chided her for her tardiness, even though he couldn't possibly have known that she was coming. "The Abbot told me to escort you to him."

Jin grabbed a lantern and, with determined strides, made his way through the winter gardens, patches of snow still resisting the pale sun. She followed him into the steepled gold and red pagoda at the back of the main temple. She expected him to head up the spiral staircase to the upper floors, but he surprised her by leading her through a hidden door. Where was he taking her?

Down a ramp and along a dark and narrow corridor, they reached a viewing gallery overlooking a cavernous chamber bathed in milky white light.

"What is this place?" she asked, her voice like a breeze through the branches of a tree.

"This is the crystal cave," Jin replied, although that was a mere label and told her little about its function.

The air in the cave was suffused with thousands of cobwebs of ch'i, thin strands looping from one corner to the other. The cave was vibrant, volatile and full of foreboding like the calm before a storm. Her senses quickened; she was excited by this remarkable concentration of power.

Dong must have been below the edge of the gallery where she stood, because he was hidden from her direct line of sight, but she could see him reflected in the crystal walls in front of her. Dressed in purple and silver raiment and a black tile hat, the Abbot ignored her arrival and continued reading from a scroll. His words echoed around the walls, but they were neither Chinese, nor any language she knew. In response to her frown, Jin explained, "he's reading from Taoist Magic Script."

"What magic does the script do?" she whispered.

"Calls up the ancestral spirits," Jin said. "Let's see who he's summoning."

Luli leaned over the railings and breathed in the ch'i. She could sense it flooding into the chamber like water gushing through a breach in a dam. On the far wall, the air shimmered like a mirage. A formless cloud appeared inside the wall and slowly the filaments coalesced into a robed figure wearing a monk's habit. A spectral monk – his face was hidden in the ch'i clouds. Dong bowed and spoke to him, soul to soul, his ethereal words like wisps of sound floating upon the unseen tides of the Tao.

"Great Tao Master," Dong intoned. "Welcome to our time. May your spirit live long and prosper."

"Greetings, Father Dong. I am Abbot Cheng. I come in service strong," the spectre replied.

Dong had called up Cheng's spirit.

"I have tried for many years to contact you and only now the gods have seen fit to allow us to commune," Dong went on, his voice resonating deep in Luli's soul. "We wish to know what happened to you and Dragon Master Wing twenty years ago. On that day, you summoned the Laolong into the confines of the Jade Chamber. The next morning, Wing, the Dragon Master, was supposed to release the Laolong into the Great Wall, marking the dragon's homecoming. The Dragon Master never showed. Then you disappeared. Why? What happened to you both?"

"If that is your wish, I shall tell you." The ghost of Abbot Cheng said. "First, I must warn you that the Zhongguo is under its greatest threat. Only the Dragon Master and his pearl can save it. Find them both. Once they are re-joined, the Laolong will shine like a thousand suns and save the Zhongguo."

"Where shall I find the Dragon Master and pearl?" Dong asked.

"In the Bagua tunnels, there are…" Cheng's voice trailed off and his ghost wavered, then disappeared into the Great Tao, leaving only the ragged edges of silvery white crystals protruding from the cave wall.

Dong beat his gums again, but the air swallowed his words of magic. Several other attempts brought the same abortive outcome, until he rolled up the scroll and departed the chamber. Joining her on the gallery, his shoulders were slumped and his eyes blazed with frustration.

"We were so close," he growled, holding up his forefinger and thumb, a sliver of a gap between them.

"Why did you stop?"

"I didn't stop at all," Dong said. "Someone broke the spell and the interference blocked Cheng's appearance. Now he won't yield to my summons."

"How? Who has the skill to do that?"

"A person well-versed in the mysteries of the Tao. It must be someone nearby and with knowledge of the subtle movement of ch'i."

"There's been one recent arrival of note," Luli said.

"Gang," Dong spat the word out like a mouthful of poison.

"Exactly. I can tell you, he's not who he appears to be."

"Why do you say that?" Dong asked.

"He wanted me to give me a propitious date for his investiture and then told me he wanted it set for the next day. If I refused, he threatened to punish my Ru."

"That's despicable. What did you do?"

"I said no, of course," she said as firm as ever.

"Under such duress, your courage shone though," Dong replied. "Your life, the life of your family and your ancestors, would have suffered terrible karma if you'd have relented."

She wiped a tear from her cheek, "That's why I need your help to free Ru."

"I will pray for his release and help you plead his case."

"Thank you," she said, making a reverent bow.

Dong led her back across to the main temple building. Outside, the sun was rising on a glorious early spring morning; the grass bedewed, the sound of the monks chanting the holy sutras.

Arriving in the cloisters, she turned to him, "I also wanted to tell you about an epiphany. It started with Ru showing me the flow of ch'i in a stone wall."

"Clever boy, that Ru of yours, he's got the gift of yin-yang eyes."

"Sometimes, I'm not sure it's a gift," she said disconsolately.

"What did you see?" he asked.

"Faces... in profile." She scrunched up her face.

Dong raised an eyebrow. "Where did you see these faces?"

"Along the Great Wall," she replied, pointing to it, standing there like some ancient lithic boundary, defying the rays of the morning sun. "Some of the faces were close together, others far apart, some high up on the wall, some near the ground. Together, they made a huge, long tapestry."

Dong's face showed not a flicker of surprise. Instead, he stared her in the eye and said, "Let me tell you about the Laolong. Most bear witness to the dragon's sacred dance through weather patterns; great turbulences of the air, flashes of lightning, peals of thunder. The more subtle traces can only be discerned by those with yin-yang eyes. Those are the patterns that you and Ru have seen on the surfaces of the Great Wall."

"I thought as much," she said. "But the most important thing is that the profile faces all point eastwards, from the western mountains to the sea."

"Mmm," Dong grunted, a frown flitting like a shadow across his face.

"Have I said something wrong?" she asked.

"Not at all; on the contrary, you are correct."

"I knew it," she said, feeling vindicated. "But why? The Laolongtou, the Old Dragon's *Head*, is situated at the east end of the wall. If the dragon's ch'i was flowing from head to tail, the direction of the profile faces should be from the Bohai Sea in the east to the western mountains, that is, westwards. But they're not, they're eastwards."

"You're right, though you must keep this a secret."

"I will, if you explain it to me," she bit her fist. This was worrying.

"Since the Sung Dynasty and beyond, the dragon's ch'i has flowed eastwards from the Tibetan mountains to where the wall used to end, in the Yanshan Mountains. Tiande built the fortress of Shanhaiguan, connecting that old end of the wall to the Bohai Sea. Dragon Master Wing was meant to conduct a ceremony to reverse the flow of ch'i, so the Old Dragon's Head was the real head and not the tail. But Wing never showed up and that is why the head is where the tail should be and the tail is at the Old Dragon's head, the Laolongtou."

"I was there that day twenty years ago," Luli said, "with Cheng, Gang and Tiande. Waiting and waiting for the Dragon Master. Soon after, Abbot Cheng disappeared. It was an awful time of loss when it should have been a time of joy and celebration."

"I heard about it when I arrived from Beiping. Once it was clear Cheng wasn't going to come back, they asked me to replace him as Abbot. Ever since I arrived, I've scoured the temple archives and all I could find was what I have just told you about the flow of ch'i."

"Cheng's ghost has appeared on the crystal wall," she pointed out. "Does that mean he's still alive?"

"I don't know," Dong shrugged. "If the person is dead, the spell summons his ghost. If he's alive, it summons his spirit. It's impossible to tell the two apart."

"Before the spell was interrupted, Cheng mentioned the Bagua tunnels. What do you think he was going to say?" she asked.

Dong shook his head. "I wish I knew the answer to that question. I've always wondered about their purpose."

"As have I," she said. "And I have a nagging feeling it's been staring us in the face."

"I'm going to consult the temple archives again," Dong said. "I've looked before, but I may have missed something. There must be a sacred scroll that mentions the Bagua tunnels."

"Let me know what you find," she said, getting up to leave.

"I will."

CHAPTER 28

A Sign from Heaven

Looking up, we contemplate the signs in Heaven.
Looking down, we examine the lines of the earth.
Thus, we come to know the circumstances of the light and the dark.
THE TA CHUAN, THE GREAT TREATISE

Bolin had seen the vault beneath the Laolongtou in his dreams. But how could he find it? This thought harassed him like those pestilential gulls from the other day.

That morning, a mist rolled off the slopes of the Yanshan Mountains and hung over the fortress like a pall. Drops of moisture ran off his ears and nose, dulling his senses. While they waited for Master Wen, Cui was boasting to everyone how his brother had risked life and limb to chase the dangerous fugitive Feng all around the estuary during the night. He conveniently forgot to mention that they failed to apprehend him.

That left Bolin alone, presenting him with an opportunity too good to miss. He snooped around the floor of the Laolongtou, searching for anything that looked remotely like an entrance to the mysterious vault below. The paving was a yellow-fired brick, except for one section next to the Stone Tablet, which had an incongruous square slab of granite. Speckled in black and white, the slab was large enough for a man to squeeze through. The seal around it appeared as old as the rest of the paving, but he couldn't see how to pry it open.

Cui noticed his antics and asked, "What you looking for?"

"I heard there was a vault beneath the Laolongtou. I thought a man of your knowledge of the fortress might know a thing or two about it." To Cui, flattery was like whale blubber on the hinges of a creaky door.

"Well, you've come to the right man," Cui said, puffing out his chest. "I heard that there are several concealed entrances and hidden chambers in the Laolongtou. So, yes, it's possible."

"What do you make of this?" he asked. Bolin was about to show him the granite slab, when Cui replied, "Quick now, Master Wen's coming."

The apprentices gathered for their morning briefing. By now, the rising sun had burnt off the mist.

"Listen to me!" Master Wen said. "Everything must be auspicious, otherwise Heaven will turn against us and our prince will lose the war. Every detail is important and this morning, this is what matters," he said, pointing to the Stone Tablet.

Once again, the mists had deposited blue lichen on it.

"I want this tablet so clean I can see my face in it. Cui, Bolin, you did a good job last time, so off you go. The others follow me."

He and Cui grabbed a bucket, water, brush and cloth and set about scrubbing both sides. Bolin took one glance at the tablet and took a step back, saying. "This is uncanny."

"What is it now?" Cui said with a tired sigh.

"No, this is something. See for yourself."

"Oh, my goodness, you're right," Cui said, scrunching up his face. "It looks like the profile of... a dog."

"No, it's not a dog," he scoffed. "Can't you see what it is? It's unmistakeable." With his index finger, Bolin traced the profile of the animal, its long snout, bushy tail and lithe body, perfectly represented in blue lichen. "It's a wolf, a Blue Wolf."

"So it is. Master Wen has to see this."

Wen arrived, followed by a knot of guards and an animated crowd of apprentices, who stared at the blue lichen profile with mix of fear and awe. The Master Builder inspected the tablet, rubbed his chin beard and then frowned. Evidently, he did not like what he saw.

"I want three runners," Wen said. "You, call the commandant. You, go to the magistrate. And you, bring Luli. Run like the wind."

While they waited, the crowd was swelled by guards from the wall and soldiers streaming out of the nearby Ninghai Fortress.

Bolin piped up, "I was working on the tablet the other day, when I saw an imprint of a four-legged animal. At the time, I thought that it was strange. This profile is quite clear and there's no mistaking the Blue Wolf."

"It's a sign from Heaven, a terrible sign," someone shouted from the crowd.

"There are malign vapours in the air," said another, coughing into his hand.

"If so, how did they get there?" Master Wen replied.

"I can answer that," a woman's voice said. The crowd parted as Luli strode into their midst. After she'd examined the stone tablet, she said, "Listen to me, everyone, there's only one way the lichen deposit could have formed itself into this shape."

"How is that?" Master Wen asked. Bolin already knew the answer.

"The air itself is volatile with the Blue Wolf." Luli said.

"Volatile'? What does that mean, exactly?" Master Wen scrunched up his face.

"I have to tell you the truth," Luli replied, as the crowd hushed to hear her words. "It's bad tidings. It means that the Mongol is not only close by, he's seeded the very air we breathe."

"The Blue Wolf is chasing the Yellow Dragon," Bolin said, the words gushing out of him before he'd time to censor them. His remark heralded a wave of whispers and alarm, turning an atmosphere of natural curiosity into one of fearful apprehension.

"That's absurd," Cui snapped, ever the pragmatist. "How can that be true? Mongols are people, flesh and bone, not intelligent flecks of blue lichen."

"That may be," Luli said, with an air of authority. "But the Mongols have their shamans just like we do. There's one nearby even as we speak – or at least someone who is working with them."

"Who is that?" Wen demanded to know. "He must be arrested without delay."

Before Luli could reply, the runner sent to call Gang returned.

"Where's the magistrate?" Master Wen asked.

"He's in session," the runner replied. "He's had his investiture and is hearing cases."

Luli hissed, "The scoundrel," and then asked, "Did you see when Ru's case is to be heard?"

"Yes I did, you better get over there, it's scheduled for midday," the runner said.

As Luli ran off to the Yamen, the crowd parted to make way for the commandant.

"Mmm, is this what the fuss is about? A bit of blue fluff," Tung said, in a derogatory tone. "Remove it. This instant."

Cui and Bolin scrubbed it raw and it was gone in a matter of moments. As the Blue Wolf lichen bled into the bucket of water, the spell cast over the crowd was lifted. Tung turned to everyone and with a wagging finger, added, "Listen, we've seen this lichen before. The mists are always rolling down off the mountains. It's natural, not supernatural. Now, get back to your posts."

Tung's pragmatic argument seemed to settle the conscripts, who hurried back to their tasks. Bolin though, did not agree: he believed Luli. He thought they were under attack from an invisible foe. Heaven was turning against them and the Yellow Dragon of China was under threat from the Blue Wolf of the Mongols.

CHAPTER 29

Watch Towers and Guard Moats

To defend the Zhongguo, we establish important posts.
Along the borders, we build watch towers and guard moats,
Connecting the barbarians and the Chinese.
We must construct passes to oppose these violent enemies.
THE GREAT MING CODE

The Bagua tunnels were spacious, but damp and dark. The ambient moisture had frozen into ice on the base of the tunnel, making every step hazardous. Feng managed to stay upright and to protect his father's letters from spoilage. Following Luli's instructions, he emerged out of the tunnels into the grassy, unguarded area between the main Shanhaiguan Fortress and the Ninghai Fortress. He was free and no one had seen him.

Along the shore line, his friends were the long coastal grasses and the undulating dunes which shielded him from prying eyes on the wall. Before the sun rose too high, he re-acquainted himself with the freezing waters of the Bohai Sea, splashing his face, arms and hands. That... was invigorating. With the militia searching for him, he still needed a good place to hide.

His feet dragged through the debris left by the recent storms: pieces of drift wood, fish bones, shells and piles of seaweed lined up along the sea shore. From the other side of the cove, he heard the sound of the buntings flapping in the morning breeze. The harbour was nearby. Then he saw a row of fishing vessels, their nets hung out to dry on the dock. One of the boats would make an excellent hideaway.

When no one was around, he climbed onto the nearest vessel and snuck into a rowing boat and under a tarpaulin, where he covered himself in a blanket and fell asleep like a baby at the breast. The next thing he knew, the boat was pitching and yawing on a heavy swell. The strong smell of the salt in the air rejuvenated him. The men on deck were shouting as they hauled in the nets. He wanted to read his father's letters, but it was too dark under the tarpaulin and he dare not reveal himself.

He heard one of the crew shout, "Where are the fish?"

"Not in our nets, that's for sure," there came the sardonic reply. He recognised the man's hoarse, grainy voice: it was Fuling, Bolin's father. So Fuling was poor and starving, that wasn't news. Fuling had fished these waters his whole life and even Feng knew that the Bohai Sea was as cold and unforgiving as the Emperor was to a disloyal subject.

Feng was in the same boat as Fuling, he thought ruefully; he was poor, starving and soaked to the skin. He had better adapt to his new circumstances and quick, otherwise he would be pulled under by the tides and undercurrents of life and living, where they would swallow him whole and spit him back out.

Abandoning work for the day, Fuling guided the vessel safely back to harbour.

"The gods are against us," he complained. "I've never had such a bad catch."

"I'm growing accustomed to a grumbling stomach," a crew member said.

"You may be but my children aren't," another moaned.

They unloaded their miserable catch and disembarked.

Alone on the boat, Feng lifted the tarpaulin enough to let the rays of the pale winter sun dance on the scroll. The first document wasn't a letter – it was a map entitled: *'Shanhaiguan: Plan of the Fortress.'*

Feng examined it. In the north were the Yanshan Mountains, in the south, the Bohai Sea, with the Great Wall joining them and running east-west. Between the two, the formidable Shanhaiguan fortifications sat in a square. At the centre of the fortress was the imposing Bell and Drum Tower, from which radiated a network of roads connecting its many buildings, towers, battlements and defences. The waters of a moat ran around the north, south and eastern sections of the fortress. The Laolongtou was at the southern section, guarded by the Stone Tablet. To one side of the scroll, Feng noticed a vertical cut-away profile of the Laolongtou showing a doorway leading to a vault.

"There it is," he said with glee, as he prodded the scroll. There was the very structure he'd glimpsed from the water. What was in it? The scroll was as intricately detailed as an almanac and he'd have to study it in depth. One part caught his eye: a section marked 'tunnels'.

From the map, he saw that the tunnel he had used to escape from Luli's was part of a much larger network. They were shaped in a square and the same size as the main fortress above ground, but off-set to it at forty-five degrees, so when looked at it from above, the two structures – the square ground-level fortress overlaid on the square underground tunnels – combined to make an eight-pointed star. They were marked 'Bagua tunnels', the Bagua being a special Taoist eight-pointed star. Why were they built? What purpose did they serve?

The next document was a hand-written letter. The calligraphy was small, compact and precise – his father's writing. His emotions welled up in his chest, as he read:

"Dear son, for that is what you are to me. My courtesy name is Tiande. I am General Xu Da, head of the Xu family. You are Xu Yingxu, courtesy name Feng. That is your true identity.

"When your mother was carrying you, the Hongwu Emperor was conducting a terrible purge of officials and ministers. It was a matter of time before he pursued me and my family. For your own safety, I hid your birth from the imperial court. I left you with Park and Lan, old friends who I know will have loved you no less than I and your mother would have done.

"Alas, if you are reading this missive, it means your honourable adoptive father and mother have passed through the Gates of Heaven. You must move as swiftly as an arrow. Find your brothers and sisters. Take this letter to them. They will weep and welcome you into the Xu family. Go forth my son. You are a dragon amongst men. May Heaven speed your quest. Your father, Tiande."

This was the proof he craved. The transformation was complete. He had inherited a new family. He was now Xu Yingxu. It felt odd to call himself thus, but that was his real name.

Hearing a sound, he peered behind him. Nothing, only his imagination. Even so, from now on, he had to walk silently and breathe quietly. If the Emperor's spies discovered his new identity, they'd have him trussed up like a chicken and beheaded in no time – or use him to obtain a hefty ransom.

He peered out of his hiding place. He was shivering from the cold. Grey clouds scudded across the bleak sky. Gone were the halcyon days of writing romantic poems to imagined love-ones, playing the zither, drinking warm wine, sleeping with the maids and studying The Odes, The Histories and The Annals for the Jinshi exams.

The world had acquired a predatory air. And he was the prey.

CHAPTER 30

The Case against Ru

When Tao is lost, there is benevolence,
and when benevolence is lost, there is righteousness.
When righteousness is lost, there is justice, and when justice is lost, there is ritual.
Now ritual is the beginning of confusion.
THE TAO TE CHING

Luli sat fidgeting in the magistrate's courtroom. With the bitter cold, her hands were like blocks of ice. How was Ru? She was worried sick about him. She had not seen him since the day before, when he looked as white as a snow goose. If the runner had not informed her, she would never have known that Gang had ignored her advice and proceeded with his investiture. She needed all the support she could get, as did Ru, and she had sent a runner to ask Dong to join her. So, until the Abbot arrived, she sat alone in the gallery.

Gang sat behind a long table covered in a red cloth at the far end of the courtroom. On it sat the paraphernalia of writing – brush pen, ink slab, ink stone and paper. Gavel in hand, he directed the constables in that sneering, disdainful way of his. To his right was an oblong piece of hardwood a foot long, and markers for the number of lashes to be applied to the guilty. Luli shuddered at the sight of it. At right angles to the table, two lines of guards, wardens, constables and scribes stood facing each other.

Bao strutted into the court like a peacock. How she would love to ruffle his feathers. Behind him, a big man waddled in and knelt down between the ends of the two lines of guards. It was Guanting. Behind him was his associate, Big Qiang. The court room was packed with citizens, interested officials and a smattering of off-duty soldiers.

Then Sheng, a real rough-neck if ever she saw one, hauled her Ru into the court. He held him under the arm pits and dragged him, Ru's feet scraping on the tiled floor. *Ru, what have they done to you?* The jailors held him up on his knees next to Guanting. Accused and plaintiff faced the full force of the law, or rather Magistrate Gang.

To stop it trembling, Luli bit her lower lip. She felt alone, afraid and scared, which was nothing compared to Ru's predicament. Grime and muck smeared his robe. His hair was dishevelled. A purple bruise marred his face. She had to stay strong for him.

"Ru, I'm here with you... right now," Luli said. "Look at your mother, please."

Ru appeared not to hear her, his head hung low. He was neither aware of his surroundings, nor of what was happening to him. How could he make a satisfactory answer to the charges? Where in this charade was even a thread of justice?

"Merchant Guanting accuses Master Ru of stealing this bag of silver taels." Bao held up the knapsack and rattled it for effect. "And here is the man's signed confession," he added, showing a scroll with Ru's thumbprint on the side. "This is the case we present to the court today."

"No, it's not. I have something to say." As she stood up, Dong hurried into court and sat next to her. At last, some support. The court hushed. "The confession is worthless. He can't speak, let alone read. How can his thumbprint mean anything?"

"I am certain it's him," Guanting said with a sneer.

"When the theft occurred, the market was crowded," Luli replied, her knees shaking with apprehension. "The real thief was wearing a yellow bandanna, as was Ru. Master Guanting mistook Ru for the culprit."

"A convenient explanation," Bao said.

"Ru's innocent. He's a good boy and performs his filial duties." She was insistent.

"Hah!" Bao scoffed. "Then where is the other mysterious person wearing a yellow bandanna?"

"I don't know," Luli sniffed. "I haven't been able to find him. But you must believe me, I'm a mother pleading for mercy. Look at him."

Ru, still kneeling, whistled to himself, but it was out of tune, like he was with the rest of the world. A trickle of saliva dribbled out of the corner of his mouth.

"Everyone in Shanhai village knows he's not responsible for his acts," she said.

"The new magistrate doesn't know that," Bao said, adding another slimy argument.

"Well, he does now. And I can back up my claim," she added, as an unwelcome air of desperation crept into her voice.

"Why bother?" Bao's words were lathered in innuendo. "There are so many other cases to hear today."

Luli took a deep breath. Gang's silent presence loomed large over the proceedings. He sat on his magistrate's chair with a smirk as wide as the Bohai Sea. Luli feared the worst. Her last resort was her stalwart, the Abbot.

"I can vouch for the boy," Dong said. "He would never pluck a flower from a meadow, let alone money from a merchant. When he was five years old, the Tao turned against him and we know about the tragic death of his father. Have some compassion and let his mother care for him. Ru has already paid for some gross misfortune committed in a past life and this new accusation is as unwelcome as it is unjust."

"Unjust?" Gang said, intervening. "That's rich, even more so when monks protect those who rebel against our prince. *That's* more than unjust, that's treasonable."

"I'm not the one on trial here," Dong insisted, in his quietly spoken way.

"That may be," Gang quipped. "But we are watching you. If you are harbouring fugitives, we'll lock you up and close you and your pagodas down in the beat of a drum. Just because your temple is outside the fortress walls, it doesn't mean that the curfew doesn't apply there."

"I would never refuse the decrees of Heaven," Dong said.

"Enough of your impudence," Gang thundered. "You may have the ear of Heaven, but I rule on earth."

How could he say that? That was hubris, which everyone knew the gods abhorred. The courtroom was stunned into an uneasy silence. In this hiatus, Luli spoke quietly but firmly.

"The new magistrate must show more respect for Heavenly matters. I want everyone to know that he asked me to advise him on the most propitious day for his investiture, which I told him was not today. It's obvious that he ignored my advice. This is troubling, because here we have a man who believes he knows better than Heaven."

The audience broke into whispers. How could Gang not follow the auspices? No one had the hubris to countermand them. But Gang had. It was unprecedented.

Then Gang accused her, "Your geomancy was flawed. I obtained a second opinion. The prison cells are over-flowing with dangerous criminals and I have many cases to adjudicate today. That's why this one is now over and done with."

"How can it be finished?" she protested.

"Because I say so," Gang sneered. "I sentence the prisoner to the punishment for serious theft as decreed in the Great Ming Code; to have his right hand severed at the wrist. This will be carried out in two days."

"Nooo!" she wailed and buried her head in her hands. Dong comforted her as Ru was dragged screaming out of the court, his arms reaching out in helpless fashion towards her. Summoning every last morsel of defiance, she cried, "Ru, stay strong. I will save you. Heaven will save you, wait and see."

"Hah! What nonsense." Guanting mocked. "Can I have my money back now?"

Bao exaggerated the act of handing the knapsack to Guanting, who shoved the silver taels into his bag, adjusted his black tile hat and departed wearing a broad smirk.

Dong was undaunted and whispered, "Don't be downhearted. This is not finished yet. There's always a way. The case can be reviewed. Heaven will hear of this injustice."

This verdict was the hardest thing she had ever had to swallow.

"Two days, Abbot. That's all we have to save him."

CHAPTER 31

The Bagua Charm

Therefore, the eight trigrams (the Bagua) succeed one another by turns,
As the firm and the yielding displace each other.
THE TA CHUAN, THE GREAT TREATISE

Bolin wiped the sweat from his brow. It was mid-afternoon and he had been working on the wall road since dawn. The broom handle rubbed against his reddened palms, but at least his work had pleased Master Wen. The wall road was shining like a mirror. Imagine, one day, twenty years ago, this section of the wall only existed as a plan in the General's head. And out of nothing, there was something. *Was the wall always there, in Heaven so to speak, and Tiande and his workers filled it in a brick at a time?* The idea came first, then the realisation caught up. Was that the way of the Tao? Now there was a huge wall and fortress, with wagons rolling in and out of the gates, mule trains carrying supplies, great columns of troops marching across the steppes, all with the promise of spring in the air.

He glanced up the wall road, towards the mountains where the upper reaches of the Yanshan were covered in a faint misty haze. There was somebody on the road. Was it a guard? He looked again. No, it was a group of people and they were not wearing military uniform. Instead, they wore variegated colours, like a sumptuous garden in full bloom. They weren't monks, they were...

"Trespassers!" Bolin shouted, pointing them out to Cui. "Intruders on the wall. Call for reinforcements."

Cui took a quick look and replied, as casual as you like, "No need for that."

"What do you mean?" he stammered. Then the wave of noise arrived. No, it was music, vibrant music. The exquisite strains of the zither, pipe and drum, echoed around the foothills, followed by the sound of singing. Descending like gods from Heaven was a troupe of men and women, playing and singing the most sublime arias.

"Who are they then?" Bolin asked.

"The Great Wall Mummers," Cui said, his face widening in a broad smile.

"So, *they* are the players." Bolin had never set eyes on them. They were a famous troupe of artistes who entertained the villages and garrisons along the length of the wall. Be it music to bring tears to the eyes, masked plays that touched on the very pulse and fabric of life, or the mumming of the great mysteries of the Tao, their performances were legendary.

The acrobats and martial artists wore skimpy suits, while the singers and artists sported regal robes and elaborate caps. At their head was a man famous along the wall, the renowned player, their leader – the Duke. As befitted his nickname, he wore a silken purple robe, with his hair tied in a traditional black bun and a paper-thin Asian Tojo moustache. Bouncing along at the head of this dazzling array of human kind, he reminded Bolin of a naughty sprite, a weaver of mischief and bringer of dreams.

News of their arrival spread like wildfire. The townsfolk gathered at the base of the Zhendong Gate and waved with rampant enthusiasm at the mummers as the latter made their way along the wall road. The players blew kisses to their admirers and dropped flower petals on the crowd, then broke into a spontaneous display. Acrobats turned somersaults, wizards conjured ch'i tigers and shadow boxers performed their silky arts, while martial artists fought each other with lightning speed. A group of origami craftsmen made small intricate paper butterflies, which they released into the breeze; the butterflies fluttered down like so many snowflakes, to the delight of the excited children waiting on the ground to catch them. While striding on stilts, artists juggled balls in the air.

The Duke bustled to the edge of the parapet and spoke to the crowd.

"Although we are always on the move, of all the places on the wall, Shanhai is the one village that actually feels like home," he said, blowing kisses to his legion of female admirers. "The smell of the sea salt is as refreshing as the warmth of your welcome," he added to wild shouts of agreement. "If you'll have us, we'll stay here a while and give our feet a well-earned rest. We'll refresh our connections to the Tao and see what we can draw from its huge repository of arts and skills. We could even perform some dragon mumming. Would you like that?"

The roar of agreement almost shook the Great Wall. "Yes to that," they cried.

Master Wen arrived and said, "Duke. Welcome back."

"Master Wen. Since we were last here twenty years ago, Shanhai has changed but you haven't; the same old grumpy builder, the same meticulous attention to detail." The Duke broke into a huge guffaw.

"If you say so," Wen grunted. "Meet young Bolin, he was born around that time."

"Is that so?" the Duke asked.

"I'm honoured to meet you, sir," he said, making a reverence.

"Mmm, I remember those times, vivid as you like," the Duke admitted, with a sorrowful countenance. "Since then, my players have traversed the Great Wall as far as its most western end and here we are back again. Under normal circumstances, the Dragon Master would accompany us and we've missed his abiding presence. Terrible story that. Did Wing ever turn up?"

Wen shook his head. "We're still searching for him."

"That's awful; his spirit is still roaming the nether world. Let me know if there's anything I can do to help find him," the Duke replied.

"We will," Wen said.

"Talking of twenty years ago," the Duke said, pulling Master Wen to one side, "I've important news to tell you."

"You found a bride?" Wen quipped.

"Not that," the Duke said with a sour face. "No, this is no joking matter. Here, look at this," he added, holding up a weathered bronze medallion about the size of his palm. The Bagua, or eight trigrams of the *Book of Changes*, or *I Ching*, were on one side and arranged as an eight-pointed star. On the other side was a single ornate, Chinese character.

"That's a Bagua charm all right, but I've never seen a character like that before," Wen said, rubbing the medallion between his fingers.

"I believe it's called Taoist Magic Script," the Duke replied. "I found it up there, on a body in the foothills of the Yanshan Mountains. The half-exposed corpse was within sight of the wall road. We guessed that someone had hurriedly tried to cover it, after which the wild animals had opened the shallow grave. Of course, we re-buried the cadaver in a deeper grave, erected a makeshift altar and incensed the area."

"This is bad karma," Wen said.

The Duke nodded. Even Bolin felt a quiver of fear run across his shoulders.

"There's more to say," the Duke added, gritting his teeth. "The body was wearing what remained of what appeared to be a Robe of Descent."

"Wait a moment," Wen said, blowing out a soft whistle. "The Robe of Descent is only worn by monks – specifically by a Celestial Tao Master. It's they who are conversant with the Taoist Magic Script."

After a moment's ominous silence, Wen asked, "How long do you estimate the body had been there?"

There was another long pause, before the Duke uttered the fateful words, "Twenty years."

"Cheng was a Celestial Master, wasn't he?"

"Yes, he was," the Duke said. "A body can only be preserved for that long if he was a holy man. That's why we thought it must be Abbot Cheng. Alas, there are more bad tidings. Whoever buried him wanted to humiliate him."

"Humiliate? How do you know?" Wen asked.

"The Bagua medallion was stuffed into his mouth," the Duke replied.

"So, Cheng was… murdered?" Wen spluttered.

"It looks that way," the Duke said.

"I knew him well," Wen said, his voice quivering with emotion. "He was a man of peace. Why would anyone want to murder – and humiliate – him?"

"That's what I'd like to know," Bolin muttered.

CHAPTER 32

The Mongol Carpet

Apart from our shadows, we have no friends.
THE SECRET HISTORY OF THE MONGOLS

Once Bolin had finished his duty, the late afternoon sun was setting and the shadow of the Great Wall was growing longer and colder. Soon the curfew would chase the people off the streets. With the awful news of the discovery of the murdered body of Abbot Cheng, the coming night seemed darker and more foreboding than before. If a man of the Tao couldn't roam the hills in safety, who could?

Bolin rushed into the market to help his father. They both bemoaned the sad tidings. They packed away the fish stall in studied silence. When they finished, his father said with typical brevity, "It's coming closer."

Did he mean the vault, or the Lantern Festival? Bolin's mind raced with possibilities.

"It's your birthday in two days. Have you forgotten?" His father's voice was as dry as the sands of the Gobi.

"No… No, of course not," he stammered, feeling ashamed of his suspicious mind.

Yes, in two days, he'd have lived twenty years. What had he achieved? A struggle to come to terms with who he was and a stubborn refusal of the opportunity offered in a mysterious letter. He wished he had never crossed Luli's threshold. But the searing headaches, visions and dreams were as real as the three pulses in his wrist. He had to deal with them and what was in that letter. For the moment, he had to get onto the Laolongtou, raise that black and white granite slab by the Stone Tablet and gain entry to the vault beneath.

His father broke his musing, "I saw Luli earlier. She was distraught."

Bolin felt sick. Was it because he refused the letter? He was about to confess, when his father said, "Magistrate Gang found Ru guilty. He's to have his hand severed in the punishment yard in two days."

The news gave him a lump in his throat. How could they do that to Ru? When he was growing up, he and Ru, who was about five or six years older than him, sat together in the little school run by Jin. Ru may have been mute and slow to learn, but he could run as fast as the wind that blew off the steppes. Bolin had fond memories of them stealing apples from the orchard without Jin seeing and galloping round the temple's gardens using branches of trees as make-believe horses.

Sometimes, in rueful moments, Bolin would try and imagine what his friend would be like if his father, Heng, hadn't fallen from the wall. That day, the gods had stolen Ru's wits from him. And now, because of a trumped-up criminal charge, Ru was likely to lose a hand as well.

"I... I wish I could have been there to help," Bolin said. He bent down to stroke a thin black tabby that was sniffing around the fish stall.

"Here's something," his father said and dropped a few scraps of fish on the ground. What a benevolent soul he was. The morsel of fish was immediately surrounded by the local scavenging cats, ribs protruding through roughened fur.

"You're too generous, Father," Bolin said.

His father replied, "'Give and you shall receive', it's written in Heaven. That's the great mystery; the Tao always provides. Look, I'm still here aren't I? And so are you."

There were loud cries from the other side of the market place. At first, Bolin thought it was the arrival of the militia to enforce the curfew, but it turned out to be a dispute near the market stall where the thief in the yellow bandanna had knocked over Ru. Two men were shouting at each other. Guanting was one of them, gesticulating from behind his stall. On it was displayed an array of carpets, from small, intricate mats, to elaborate, tasselled rugs. The finest was a large Mongolian carpet, its snarling Blue Wolf motif, outlined with silver tassels.

The customer was complaining, "Two hundred strings of cash! I wouldn't pay that for a roll of the finest mulberry silk, let alone a roll of one of your Mongol carpets."

In his colourful caftan, Guanting was a bear of a man. He leaned forwards and said in a voice quivering with a surprising degree of emotion, "This, my friend, is the most special Mongolian carpet in the world."

"How is that?" the customer scoffed, a squat man with a pinched look as tight as a closed oyster.

144

Guanting ran the flat of his palm along it and said, "The Great Khan himself once owned this carpet and used it to dispose of any unruly nobles."

"Dispose?"

"Oh," Guanting asked, "you don't know about Mongol carpets?"

The customer shook his head ruefully. Guanting needed no further invitation. "In the Mongol culture, any nobleman who showed disloyalty to the Khan was executed in a way that left no external marks on the cadaver. To achieve this feat of respect, the condemned man was rolled up in the midst of a long carpet, which suffocated him to death."

"Very interesting," the customer sniffed. "But that's nothing to do with the price of rice," and stomped off in a huff.

"Come back," Guanting cried, but the customer had gone, swallowed by the wall's glowering shadows. The soldiers entered and harried the people to leave. The market emptied.

"Pack it away!" Guanting said in a flash of anger. The merchant's servants scampered around like dogs with their tails between their legs and dumped the carpets onto a nearby cart. The last to leave, Guanting grabbed his knapsack and got into his sedan chair, which was soon carried off by his porters, Big Qiang leading the way.

For some reason unbeknownst to him, Bolin decided to follow the merchant's entourage. If he was caught outside after the curfew, it was a night in the cells and a face-to-face with Thousand Cuts, neither of which was appealing. But he knew these streets and alleyways like the back of his hand. Sliding between the shadows, he followed Guanting along Sheepwash Street and down North Way. Soon he was in the seedier part of town, an alley where ribald and revelry run amuck. Guanting lumbered out of the sedan chair and stood beneath the dull light of a lantern. There he waited until a man slunk out of the shadows. At first, they were whispering. Then Guanting raised his voice, "I've brought what you demanded."

The other man looked to see if anyone was around. Bolin caught sight of an officer's uniform and insignia.

Friend or no, the officer growled at Guanting, "It's not enough. Your silver's passed through the hands of the magistrate's office. It's tainted. They'll follow you. At the moment, they're so suspicious that the next thing you know, they'll arrest the moon beams. I'm telling you, this enterprise is riven with danger."

"What are you saying?" Guanting asked.

"I want more. Twenty five taels more. Or the deal's off."

Before Guanting could reply, a knot of soldiers rushed into the alley, shouting, "Curfew. Indoors. Now."

Bolin dived under a covered wagon.

The militia harried the peddlers, vagrants and other loiterers. By the time they had moved everyone along, the alley was as dark as it was deserted.

Bolin had a feeling in his gut. Something wasn't right. Who was that officer? And what exactly was he selling to Guanting?

CHAPTER 33

The Taoist Magic Script

May you live in interesting times.
ANCIENT CHINESE CURSE

Luli closed the shutters of the room, lifted the frayed edge of the carpet and opened the trap door. Under normal circumstances, whenever she made use of the tunnel, Ru would have stood behind her, wearing that terrible look of resignation on his face she knew so well; the one that screamed in silence at her, 'why aren't you taking me with you?' Then he would replace the carpet behind her. But these were anything but normal circumstances. She could close the trap door, but the carpet would have to wait until she returned – if she returned.

How terrible that Cheng had been found, half eaten by animals. The news had shocked her to the core and she was still shaking as she clambered down the vertical steps. What a dreadful time she lived in, her husband dead, her son traumatised and sentenced for a crime he didn't commit. Heaven bled for such injustice.

Her lantern sent flickering shadows along the tunnel wall, intermittent light and dark. The familiar smell of earth hit her nostrils. It always smelled like a grave to her. She headed north along the tunnel, avoiding the mice, moles, worms and other creepy-crawlies. She had known about the tunnels since they were built. Over the years, she'd explored every nook and cranny of the network.

General Tiande had built the Bagua tunnels at the same time as the Shanhaiguan Fortress above ground. Why expend all that effort? She'd never seen any soldiers using them. Its entry and exit points were all outside the fortress walls. Nothing was stored in them and they had no strategic or military value. What was their purpose? Perhaps the Bagua tunnels were to do with the Tao? That was the most likely explanation. She puffed out her cheeks, frustrated that she had yet to tease out the answer.

On occasion, the tunnels took on a life of their own. At certain points, she sensed huge concentrations of supernatural ch'i. That was when it felt like she was wading through a thick cloud of the stuff. Perhaps Dong would discover more from his search of the temple archives.

Climbing up the vertical shaft to the temple, she opened the trap door. The darkness of the night kissed the darkness leeching out of the tunnels. The coast was clear and she sneaked out into a rarely used part of the temple, made her way to the front gate and rang the bell. The gate swung open and a friendly face peered round from the other side.

"Welcome," Jin said, with a broad smile revealing his rotten teeth. He took her to a room with a shrine, where Dong was meditating. When he'd finished, they went to his chambers. Jin served them hot tea.

"We've had a double blow," Dong admitted. "The flow of the Tao is against us; first your son and now Abbot Cheng."

"I knew Cheng twenty years ago. He was kind to me," Luli said proudly. "I can't imagine his body, gnawed by wild animals. It's horrible even to contemplate it." She wiped away a tear; but not her grief.

"I'm going to find out who did that to him." Dong sounded like a demon of vengeance. He got up as quick as you like and a flailing arm knocked one of the lanterns to the floor, snuffing out the candle. Another light extinguished in their lives.

"Heaven will punish the wrongdoer and his family until karma is restored," Dong said, his fist clenched white with rage. "I've sent a monk with one of the Duke's men to the burial site to bless his body and conduct a proper reburial."

"That's good," she murmured. "But the pall of misfortune that hangs over my family won't lift. Ru's punishment is too awful to imagine and I've two days to save him."

"I know," Dong said. "But listen. The tide is turning. Finding Abbot Cheng's body is a breakthrough. You'll see; next, we'll discover who murdered him and what happened to Wing. Then the mystery of the consecration ceremony will unravel."

"I hope so." She wanted to believe him.

"Your family's misfortune will also be resolved. Have faith and believe in the benevolence of the gods."

"I'd like to see some benevolence from humans," she whispered, stifling a tear.

"Listen, I have some good news," he said, rubbing Cheng's Bagua medallion between his palms. "I've found something in the archives." Pointing at two scrolls on the desk, he opened the first. On the title page was a single character;

a calligraphy exemplar of the Taoist Magic Script. "Recognise that?" Next to it, he placed Cheng's Medallion.

"It's the same character," she exclaimed. "Then what's written in this scroll?"

"You may well ask," Dong said, with an air of excitement. "It's nothing less than the text of the ceremony of consecration of the Laolongtou."

"That is an omen," she said, bouncing with joy. "Speak the text out loud and invite the dragon back. That will be some homecoming."

"I wish it were that simple," Dong said. He hesitated long enough for her to believe him.

"Why isn't it?"

"Only the Dragon Master can conduct the ceremony."

"That's all the more reason to find Wing." Luli fingered the scroll like she was touching the sacred bones of a Taoist Immortal. Then she asked, "What's in the other scroll?"

"I'll tell you," Dong murmured. "Jin, please close the door."

He had her full attention.

"Good, I don't want any flapping ears to hear this." He spoke in a soft, intense voice. "The other scroll speaks of an ancient prophecy, which predicted that one day the temple would host a new influence from Heaven, a theme endorsed when the Zhendong Gate was called The First Pass under Heaven. The gate is where spirit energy, high ch'i, enters the world for the first time. It is pristine. That's the legend. That is why the temple was built here in the first place. I believe the term 'Eight Immortals' refers to the eight points of the Bagua tunnels."

"Remarkable," Luli said, nodding with enthusiasm.

"It could go anywhere on earth first, but it arrives here in the Zhongguo. That's why we're the Middle Kingdom, the centre of the world. That's why the Dragon Emperor is the Emperor of all people, not only the Chinese. At the birth of the Ming Dynasty, Abbot Cheng, my predecessor, divined that a pristine influence was on the horizon. It was destined to improve and develop not only the Chinese, but all the peoples on earth. Over the centuries, the gods have tried in many ways to elevate the human race. They've sent philosophers like Confucius, Mencius and Lao Tzu and saviours like the Buddha. Alas, so far they've failed to eradicate man's barbaric ways."

"So, this new influence," she said, not quite believing what she was hearing, "is another attempt by Heaven?"

"I believe so," Dong shrugged. "The seeds of this new influence will gather apace over the centuries to come. The scroll even describes it – it's shaped like a bejewelled sceptre. Here, I'll read you this part, 'The sceptre is covered in shining gems, translucent like gods, where each gem represents a new, previously unknown

149

form of human genius. Its name, whispered in the corridors of Heaven, is the Emperor's Mace.'"

Luli sat in the glow of the revelation. "What does it mean, this Emperor's Mace?" she asked.

"It means that Heaven has not abandoned the human race and that it's still trying to help us. It also refers to the saying, *'May you live in interesting times'*."

"I thought that saying was a blessing," she admitted.

"No, on the contrary." Dong was adamant.

"Why?" she said, scrunching up her face.

"The Emperor's Mace has ushered in a benevolent time of religious quickening," Dong explained. "For hundreds of years before that, there had been no quickening, no supreme ch'i, no elevation – only stasis, inertia, no growth. When nothing was happening spiritually, the best people could hope for was to live in interesting times."

"So that saying is really a curse," Luli said.

"Yes!"

Luli felt her heart beating like a drum. In a few short moments, her life once more bristled with hope. She was not alone. She could save Ru from Gang, the Hammer of Shanhaiguan. And she could help Dong in service to the Emperor's Mace. Imagine – new forms of human genius, never seen before.

She could dedicate her life to that.

CHAPTER 34

Kong, the Beggar King

A happy union with wife and children is like the music of lutes and harps!
When there is concord among brethren, the harmony is delightful and enduring.
Thus, may you regulate your family and enjoy the delights of wife and children!
THE DOCTRINE OF THE MEAN

Squatting with his back against the alley wall, Feng blew hard on his fingers.
He was unsure if that made them colder or warmer, his breath was so misty. The
main source of warmth was the beggar to his right, who stank of rotten fish,
sour wine and encrusted faeces. Unperturbed by these minor inconveniences,
the man was snoring as blithely as the Buddha.

To Feng's left was a row of sleeping beggars, lost, forlorn, their lives inert.
In front of him, another beggar hobbled back and forth down the alley, his rag-
strewn feet crunching the icy ground.

"How long does it stay like this?" Feng muttered, getting up and pacing
alongside him. The beggar wore a look so hollow, it could hold the seas of the
world. Wearing that distinctive tattered black turban, Feng recognised him – it
was Kong, the redoubtable Beggar King. He'd met him six days ago outside the
Yamen. Six days? Six life times more like.

The second night watch rang out, marking the middle of the night. The
howl of a dog was met by the bark of a camel, meaning this was not the only
strange conversation in town.

Kong didn't reply. Feng was convinced his fingers were going to fall off
if he didn't do something quick, so he tried thinking of a warm brazier. It
didn't help. He was still freezing. After another lengthy silence, punctuated
by more nocturnal animal cries, Kong snarled at him, "Well, what do you
want?"

"My family," he replied without hesitation.

"Family?" Kong grunted, then added, more to himself than anyone else, "The Confucian ideal – what more can a man ask of Heaven than a good family?" Kong carried on pacing the night like a wounded tiger.

Feng grunted in agreement.

Kong reached out and rubbed Feng's mud-splattered robe between his dirty fingers. "Mmm, fine material. Silk is it? Now you're serving at my court, you've reached the bottom rung. From here, you can look up and contemplate the arse of the world and try and work out what you've done to upset your ancestors."

"I... I," Feng stammered.

Kong pointed a crooked finger at him and said, "I know you. You're the son of the dead magistrate. The militia are chasing you. Stick by me, boy, I'll protect you and I'll make you rich beyond your wildest dreams. Me, I've got contacts in the Yamen – both the court and the military. It won't be long before I land a big deal. In this time of war and uncertainty, there are plenty of them going down in the shadows of the Great Wall."

"Sounds interesting," Feng said, although his real motive was to explore the vault beneath the Laolongtou. Come to think of it, perhaps Kong *could* help him.

"I like you," Kong decided. "Join me. You've got two things lacking in my associates here," he added, waving a desultory hand at the knot of sleepers.

"What are they?" Feng asked, showing his naivety.

"You've got all your limbs and all your brains. I've got the contacts and the street wisdom. That's a winning combination. Together, we'll go far," Kong fingered his dagger.

One of the sleepers stirred from beneath a threadbare blanket – a young boy, with a dirt-encrusted face and a mucky hat. The lantern flared briefly. It was Qitong, hiding amongst the human detritus. Next to him slept a girl, about the same age. For a moment, they tussled over the ownership of a threadbare blanket, then fell back to sleep, warm in each other's arms. Feng left them alone.

A beggar loomed out of the misty night and came over to talk in animated tones to Kong.

Kong turned to Feng and asked him, "Can you understand the Mongol tongue?"

"Well, yes, I can," Feng said, with wild suspicions running around his mind. Was this a trap – or a ruse?

"Good, then come with me."

"What? Now? There's a curfew, in case you hadn't noticed."

"Hah, don't worry about that. Besides, I know the commandant," Kong said with more than a tinge of arrogance.

Did he now? Kong *did* have contacts in high places. Or was it bravado? The Beggar King kicked two of the sleepers in the back. They stumbled to their feet and seemed to know what was required of them, because without uttering a word, they stood yawning at either end of an open sedan chair. Fixed to the two poles was a chair with wonky armrests, a rickety seat and a backrest made of two vertical planks of wood of differing heights.

Some throne that is, Feng thought. He confined himself to the question, "Where are we going... in the middle of the night?"

"Magistrate Feng, for a man on the street, you ask too many questions," Kong said, as they followed the messenger.

How ironic; the one person who recognised Feng as a magistrate, albeit with a heavy scent of derision, was a lame, conniving, King of the Beggars.

They headed for the seedy part of town where the brothels sat alongside wine bars featuring betting tables, cockfights, arm wrestling and even bear baiting. Every now and again, Feng would think about nipping down a dark alley and hiding amidst the barrels of wine, stacks of frost-laden firewood and bags of rice. At least some folks had it good.

"Not thinking of leaving us, so soon?" Kong said, reaching out from his seat in the sedan chair and thwacking him in the belly. Feng doubled up in pain.

"Me? Never!" Feng said, revelling in the sarcasm.

"Good," Kong said. "Put me down, we're here."

They stopped outside the White Mulberry Inn, One Hand Zhou's wine bar. Kong spoke to the messenger, who disappeared into it and came out moments later.

"They're still in there," the messenger reported, cupping his hand and speaking quietly.

Kong turned to Feng and said, "Follow me and take my lead."

Feng nodded.

The wine bar smelt of a pungent mix of stale alcohol and urine, Feng couldn't decide which was the greater. The bar boasted all of two lanterns, both with a flickering candle near the end of its wick; not unlike himself, Feng mused. The poor ambient light was no doubt to avoid any unwanted attention from the militia, who were conspicuous by their absence. One Hand Zhou served him and Kong. Feng held the beaker in both hands and sipped the mulled wine, letting it trickle down his gullet, warming his insides.

The messenger led him and Kong to a secluded part of the bar. As soon as they sat down, Kong put his finger to his lips and then cupped his ear with his hand. "Listen," he whispered and pointed to the cubicle behind him, separated from theirs by a thin wooden screen. Kong wanted him to overhear the conversation taking place behind it. Feng crooked his neck and soon picked up words in the Mongol tongue.

"The attack is imminent," he heard one man say. "That's why I need the explosives."

Explosives? Attack? What are these Mongols plotting? Feng's ears picked up.

"Fine. It'll be half now, half on delivery. Did you bring the extra cash?" the second man demanded.

"Yes, I made some more sales. It's all here," the first one said.

Feng did not recognise either of their voices. There was silence for a while until Feng heard the second man reply, "Good, that's everything. Collect the goods at dawn. You know where."

"See you then. Don't run away with my cash, or I'll chase your through the halls of hell," the first one snarled.

"Don't worry. You'll get the merchandise – as long as you bring the other half."

The two men stopped talking and Feng assumed they were leaving. Then one of the men – a heavy-set, boulder of a man – passed his cubicle. My, it was Guanting. The carpet merchant shuffled by and appeared not to have noticed them. The other man must have slipped out the back way. Kong despatched the messenger to follow him. Kong's role in this clandestine operation was intriguing, in that he seemed well practiced at the game.

"Now tell me. What did they say?" Kong asked, his eyes glaring like liquid fire.

This was an opportunity for Feng to use what little advantage he had. "I'll tell you, but first I want to know why you are so interested? What's in it for you?"

"Oh, so you think I'm going to reveal my secrets?" Kong snarled. Then he added as an after-thought, "Haven't you heard? There's a huge reward for information leading to the arrest of any traitors. Don't go claiming it before me – otherwise you'll end up swimming with the fishes at the bottom of the Bohai Sea. Hear me?"

Feng took a deep breath and told him the two men's conversation.

"I suspected as much," Kong murmured. "Did they say where they were meeting at dawn?"

"No, they didn't," he replied.

"Pity. But you're certain they spoke about explosives," Kong repeated, pulling on his goatee beard. "Good, you've done well. We'll catch the dog's heads, you'll see."

"Glad to hear it," Feng said with an air of relief. Despite his personal distress, it didn't stop him detesting the Mongols as much as the next man. "Now I've helped you, you can help me."

"All right. What do you want? Revenge on your mother's servant, Precious?"

"How did you know about that? No, Heaven will punish her disloyalty," he murmured. "What I need is to set foot on the Laolongtou."

"That's forbidden. Besides, the place is more heavily guarded than the Emperor's treasury," Kong said, adjusting his black turban.

"You claimed to know the commandant. Then use your influence with him."

"Why do you want to go there?" Kong was the nosy kind.

"I'll tell you… but only after you've got me on there."

CHAPTER 35

The Chrysanthemum

Who knows but me about the Guard at the Gate,
Or where the Magician of the River Bank is,
Or how to find that magistrate, that poet,
Who was as fond as I am of chrysanthemums and wine cups?
A TANG DYNASTY POEM

"Are we there yet, Daddy?" Ju asked, her breath steamy with the cold.

"Soon, darling, soon," Gang replied, pulling up his daughter's collar. "Careful, you'll catch cold," he added, playing the concerned parent. He had reluctantly agreed to bring her along at the last moment.

She wiped her nose with her sleeve.

"Don't do that, your mother would be annoyed if she saw." His reprimand was as sweet as he could make it.

She frowned and scrunched up her nose. Gang peered out of the curtains of the sedan chair, letting in a blast of freezing air. The first rays of dawn were splashed across the horizon, filling it with a glorious pink. He glanced across at Sheng and Big Qiang, who were along for protection.

"Oh, Daddy, close them. Quick!" Ju moaned, burying herself under the blanket. He could have reminded her that it was she who had pestered him to come along, not the other way around, but he refrained. The early hours of the day were not a good time to challenge a strong-minded six-year-old.

Outside the cushioned world of his sedan chair, he noticed a line of soldiers trudging along the street, their head bowed after a weary night's patrol. The barracks must be near and he added with good cheer, "We're nearly there." She smiled and duly reported the good news to her doll.

The porters stopped and lowered the sedan chair onto the ground. They were talking to a gatekeeper, who demanded to know, "Who goes there?"

Gang got out of the sedan chair and was confronted by a large gated house.

"County magistrate Gang," he answered, with lashings of pomposity. He liked the sound of his new title.

The young boy, the gatekeeper, made a deep reverence and asked, "Does my master expect you?"

"Yes and no," Gang replied. "Tell him the merchant couldn't make it, so the magistrate came in his stead."

The boy ran up to the house with the message. When he returned, he pushed his back into the pair of gates, which creaked open with great reluctance.

"Please, honourable magistrate, pass on through," he said by way of a welcome.

Gang's daughter poked her nose out of the curtains.

"Be a good girl and stay in the warm in the sedan chair while I talk to the nice gentleman," he said to her and stepped into the open courtyard.

A man in an officer's uniform strode down the steps of the main house and greeted him with cordial warmth.

"Welcome, magistrate, to my humble abode," the man said. Then he whispered surreptitiously in Gang's ear, "What happened to Guanting?"

"After your meeting last night at the inn," Gang replied, holding his hand to his mouth so only the man could hear him, "he was followed by the Jinyiwei. With the secret police on his trail, he was terrified, so he's gone. He's probably leaving town as we speak."

"And you came in his place," the man said. "I hope they didn't follow you?"

"You don't want to do business with me?" Gang scowled.

"No... Yes... I mean, of course I do."

Ju opened the curtains of the sedan chair, poked out her tongue at him and closed the curtains.

"Ju, you are being naughty," Gang murmured.

"You... brought... your daughter?" the man said, with unabashed surprise.

"Yes? Why not?" He shrugged. It was a risk. She had complained – quite legitimately he felt – that she was confined to the Yamen and hadn't been allowed out to see the town and meet other children. Daughters could be so persuasive. What was more, he had never intended to attend this meeting – until Guanting had placed him in this invidious position. And he calculated that the presence of an innocent child would deflect any unwanted suspicion of him for being out and about on the dawn watch. That was a good enough reason.

As she stepped out of the sedan chair, he made the formal introduction. "Ju. This is Major Renshu."

"Pleased to meet you, Ju," the major said, bowing low.

"And you too," Ju said, curtseying like a true lady. There, she could behave if she wanted.

"Ju, I need to talk to the major. Big Qiang is going to look after you. Aren't you, Qiang?"

Given his bulk and the scars on his face, Big Qiang appeared more accustomed to drinking and whoring than baby-sitting. Little Ju was understandably circumspect about this arrangement.

"Daddy, I want to stay with you," she moaned, hanging on to his leg and glaring daggers at Qiang.

"All right, go back in the sedan chair. Find some paper and play folding and making animal shapes."

"Oh, father, what a good idea, I love origami," Ju replied. As if he didn't know that, he chuckled to himself. Life was all about preparation. Ju ran to the sedan chair.

"Shall we conclude our business then?" the major asked.

"By all means," Gang agreed. He pulled a brocade bag from his inner garments and dangled it in front of the major.

"What's the matter?" the major asked.

"I want to verify the merchandise before parting with this," he said, pointing to the bag. He had just received it from Guanting, who had awoken him in the middle of the night to tell him his predicament. Shoving the bag of money into Gang's hand, the merchant had told him the time and place of the meeting and scuttled off into the night like a frightened rat.

"Well, where is it?" Gang asked with growing impatience.

"It's over there," the major said, pointing to an unattended litter a stone's throw away in the corner of the courtyard. When he looked, someone was exploring the contents of the litter like they were clay toys. By Heavens, it was Ju.

"What the—?" he shouted.

He was interrupted by a furious cry from the major. "Wait! Stop! Get away from there."

Qiang hauled his great bulk over to her as fast as he could, his limp impeding him on every step. But the big man was soon next to the little girl and lifting her up high into the air and away from the litter and its explosive contents.

"What's the matter? What have I done?" the little girl cried, eyes filling with tears.

"Don't worry," Gang said, running across to embrace her. "You haven't done anything wrong. Has she, Major?"

"No, not much," the major growled, his hands on his hips, standing defiantly between Ju and the litter, barring the girl from getting anywhere near it again.

"I told you to stay in the sedan chair and you disobeyed me," he said, smacking the child lightly on the hand. She started crying and her wails filled the morning air with waves of tears. Servants peered through the shutters to see what the fuss was about.

Gang managed to ease his errant daughter back into the sedan chair, leaving her with Qiang and Sheng for company. She'd have to put up with them. What else could he do?

"That was a close call," the major said. "Why did you have to bring her along anyway? Are you mad?"

"I'm going to ignore that remark," Gang snapped.

"We have to finish this," the major was railing at him, "before you, or another member of your family, decide they want to play games with explosives. I have a family too you know and this is my house."

Gang shot him a glance of annoyance. "That's enough," he hissed through gritted teeth.

The major bristled and took a deep breath. "Listen. Give me the money. I want this litter off my courtyard."

"I want the same but you are not making this easy," he said. "Here it is. I hope you're not going to count it out, tael by tael."

"No. Not now, anyway," the major snarled. "And before someone calls the Jinyiwei, please leave my home. And make sure you treat the contents of that litter with extreme caution. Explosives are volatile. Your child could have blown us all to a thousand little pieces."

The return journey got easier with every step. Gang was more than relieved to have left the major's home. Ju was too. Qiang led the way and the runners carried the litter full of explosives in front, Gang and Ju behind and Sheng in the rear.

Ju was upset. He combed her doll's hair and tried singing her a lullaby. He couldn't sing in tune and anyway, she was not interested in the slightest. He wiped a tear from her eye and decided to try charm.

"Do you want to be a good girl for daddy?" he asked.

Her chest still heaving with crying, she nodded pathetically.

"Then look at his," he said and moved the paper around dextrously. She watched with fascination as he folded it this way and that.

"Guess what it is?" he asked, with the shape only half-formed.

"It's got spokes," she said.

"Yes, it has," he encouraged her.

"Oh, they're petals, it's a flower," she concluded, clapping her hands with excitement.

"Can you guess which kind of flower?" he asked.

With nimble fingers, he finished the last twist, "There."

"Is it a rose?"

He shook his head. "Come, it's in your name, so you should know which one it is. Think."

"A chrysanthemum!" she cried, a broad smile lighting up her little face because Ju meant chrysanthemum.

She grabbed it from him and was soon engrossed in smoothing out and tidying the array of petals. Gang breathed a huge sigh of relief. While the experience had been traumatic for them both, it had drawn them closer together. Whether his wife would agree was another matter. For the meantime, he sat back and watched Ju play with the flower, cupping it in her hands and smelling its pretend fragrance with mock delight.

When they arrived home, he instructed Qiang and Sheng where to move the litter. "Take it to the alley between my chambers and the prison cells. No one ever ventures down there and it's out of sight. You'll find a wooden shed, so park it there. Inside you'll see a green tarpaulin, drape it over the litter. We don't want its contents getting wet."

Qiang and Sheng scuttled off and Gang relaxed. Not only had the gods of karma saved him and his daughter, they were on his side, bringing his plans and those of Altan, nearer to fruition.

CHAPTER 36

Dragon Dance

Gems are few, stones many –
That which occurs in great number is not precious.
Dragons are rare, fish numerous –
That which is of rare occurrence is justly deemed divine.
THE LUNHENG (BOOK OF WEIGHINGS)

Bolin stood shoulder to shoulder in a large crowd waiting for the performance to begin. As the excitement grew, he could feel a subtle tingle right through him to the tips of his fingers. The Duke was lining up his players on the stage erected in the shadow of the mighty Bell and Drum Tower.

The excitement was palpable. The Duke strode across the stage, revelling in his fame.

"Dear Shanhaiguan, we are the dragon players," he began, arms high above his head. Eight acrobats somersaulted across the stage, finishing as one and bowing to the audience and the midday sun.

The crowd waved in acclaim.

The Duke continued, "Like the Laolong, our home is the Great Wall of Ten Thousand Li. It takes us ten long years to travel from one end of the wall to the other. Along the way, we are privileged to witness the huge achievements of the Chinese people and the stunning beauty of the land of the Zhongguo. From here, we cross the gaping Yanshan Mountains and then traverse the central plains. We cross the desert, where the sands stretch as far as the eye can see and conjures mirages in the mind. Tigers and bears roam the western mountains whose summits pierce the canopy of Heaven. All along the way, our brave soldiers guard us from marauding bandits and barbarian tribes.

"Amongst the many villages and settlements along the length of the Great

Wall, we have two places we relish performing the most. They are the towns at either end of the wall, the head and the tail of the Laolong. Today, we are back here after twenty years. We hear that the Laolong has not been seen at your New Year's ceremonies since that time, so we are going to perform a special dragon dance and attempt to conjure the dragon from his lair."

"Wait…" a voice thundered. It was Gang, replete in his magistrate's robes. Next to him were his assistant, Bao and his enforcers, Sheng and Big Qiang.

"Magistrate Gang, how pleasant to meet you again, after so long," the Duke said, with a deep bow. Gang though seemed in no mood for niceties.

"Everyone knows the Laolong has been trapped in the Jade Chamber for the last twenty years," Gang said, appealing to the crowd. "And only the Dragon Master, with the Dragon Pearl, can conjure him from his lair… the Dragon Master is still missing."

"We want our dragon back," someone yelled, ignoring his words of caution.

"Laolong! Laolong! Laolong!" The crowd roared, as if trying to summon the lithe beast from the depths of the earth by the elemental power of the human voice.

"People of Shanhaiguan, listen to me," Gang said, through gritted teeth. "What you ask for is dangerous. Before, whenever the dragon players have conjured the dragon from his lair, the Dragon Master has always been in attendance. Who knows what the Laolong will do if freed from its shackles after such a long confinement? What if he were to induce a fierce and prolonged thunderstorm and bring down a terrible flood on us all? Who could stop him tearing down the vault of Heaven upon us in some awful catastrophe? The Duke cannot control the Laolong. The Dragon Master can and to perform the dragon dance in his absence is hazardous in the extreme. I speak as your protector."

People murmured amongst themselves and worried looks flitted from face to face. Bolin yearned for the dragon. Everyone did. Every New Year for twenty long years, the dragon had failed to appear at the annual celebrations. He wondered if, one day, the people would forget about the dragon entirely; believe he was a myth and relegate him to some children's fairy story or a legend in a book of odes. They would no longer expect the Laolong to appear and would be satisfied with a paper dragon, a gigantic origami equivalent. Hah! Bolin was having none of that. Before he could voice his concerns, a shrill voice shattered the morning air.

"No, that's wrong!"

Someone dared to defy the magistrate. The crowd parted and the figure of Luli stepped forward.

"The magistrate is an honourable imperial servant and his word is king on earth, but this is a Heavenly matter," she said, her eyes blazing with the fire of truth. "The Laolong is a sentinel, not a persecutor. He would never harm us, regardless of the presence or absence of the Dragon Master. The Laolong destroys only the enemies of the Zhongguo. I say to the Duke, perform your famous dance. Conjure the Laolong for all to see."

The people celebrated Luli's remarks like they were announcing the birth of an Emperor's new son. The acrobats turned even more extravagant somersaults, this time leaping over Bao and Gang, making them reluctant participants in the festivities. The audience were afraid to laugh openly and show disrespect to the magistrate, but a chuckle or two did ripple through their massed ranks. As Gang slunk away wearing a heavy frown, Bao glared daggers at Luli.

Events unfolded with alacrity. The blaring of trumpets and a crescendo of drums heralded the release of hundreds of balloons and streamers, charging the air with colour and sound. A troupe of stilt walkers strutted onto the stage to the accompaniment of more hand waving. Dancers cavorted and twisted, as the Duke orchestrated a series of elegant movements.

"This is wonderful," Bolin purred. "Are we really going to see the dragon appear?"

"Why, yes of course," Luli replied.

"But how – if he's incarcerated in the Jade Chamber?"

"The dragon is a supernatural entity and is made up of two parts: there's the Great Laolong that occupies the entire wall, but there are many small dragons that exist only in a particular locale. For example, there's a Shanhaiguan dragon, there's a Beiping dragon and so on. Even though the Great Laolong is imprisoned in the Jade Chamber, the Great Wall is still protected by the smaller, local dragons, who are themselves servants to the Great Laolong."

"And the servant dragons are what the Duke and his players will conjure?"

"Yes, that's right and in that instance, the magistrate is correct; only the Dragon Master can summon the Great Laolong."

"Then there is still hope," Bolin muttered.

Next, a line of players each holding up a water dragon face mask, with long, white whiskers and ferocious, red eyes. The dragon players moved across the stage in a synchronised wave. Gyrating like snakes, the dance conjured and enticed the dragon from the Jade Chamber. Would it appear? Everyone looked towards the Laolongtou.

Someone shouted, "Look!"

They were pointing to the east at a huge cloud, as dark as a blacksmith's anvil. A shudder of cold fear went down his spine. This was the true manifestation of the dragon. From in amongst the clouds, lightning bolts flashed across the sky, filling the Heavenly void with ferocious power.

"The dragon. It's free," Bolin yelled.

"The dragon is free." Everyone took up the refrain.

Except Luli – who anxiously shook her head.

Bolin waved enthusiastically at every lightning bolt and thunder crack that rent the earth. The pyrotechnic display was awesome.

Luli was having none of it. "It's not the dragon – not even the local one," she claimed.

"They are its manifestations," he insisted. "The Laolong is there, somewhere inside that black cloud."

"Come, Bolin," she said. "You may not have accepted it yet, but you have the gift of yin-yang eyes and of magic powers, both latent and ready to use. You should know that if it truly was the Laolong, or one of his local servants, it would arise here at the Laolongtou and not many li away in the land of the Blue Wolf."

A chill wind blew in from the south, shunting the storm northwards until it had almost disappeared over the horizon. Not one drop of rain had fallen on the fortress.

He had forgotten about the contents of that letter and its promise of magic powers. It was obvious that Luli still believed the letter was meant for him – and for him alone.

He, though, was adamant. It was not him, it couldn't be. How could he be worthy of it? What did he know of the Five Classics? He hadn't even passed the Jinshi examinations.

He asked, "If it's not the Laolong, then what is it?"

"The cleaving of the sky is a strong and violent portent of war," she murmured in a far-away voice. "The storm arose in the east, which means we can expect an imminent attack from that direction."

"An attack? What are you talking about?" He screwed up his face in a knot.

"I'm just reading the portents," she replied.

"Hah, I don't believe you," Bolin stammered and bounded off to meet Cui.

CHAPTER 37

The Red Kite

Kites in flight will heavenwards go,
Fishes leap in their pools below.
Joyous and free our Prince could be,
How he has raised humanity!
THE SHI KING (BOOK OF ODES)

When Bolin found Cui for an afternoon of kite-flying, the old soldier was already making a show of adjusting his red bandanna.

"I see you're ready to fly," Bolin said.

"This is my special kite," Cui replied, grasping a red box kite, which was about as large as a six-year-old child. Many of the streamers hanging off the base were missing and the remaining ones were tattered. In several places, the canvas had suffered tears during its long tenure. Clumsy attempts to repair them with crude white stitches had added to the general aura of disrepair, none of which bothered Cui in the slightest. On the contrary, they seemed to endear him to his bamboo contraption, rather like a scraggy, but friendly, pet dog.

In the balmy rays of the early afternoon sun, they left the fortress and climbed a low hill just off the west road, where they joined other ardent kite flyers.

"This old fellow is held together by threads," Bolin added.

"A bit like me then," Cui said, with some self-deprecation.

"Very funny, but where did you find 'him'?" he asked.

"Back in the day," Cui began in that tone which said a story was coming, "when I was young and wild, I joined the rebels fighting to free the Zhongguo from the Mongol yoke. Zhu Yuanzhang and Tiande led the guerrilla bands or red bandannas, as they were called for obvious reasons. We wreaked havoc along the Mongol supply lines, raiding along the borders, ghosting through the thick forests and living off the plunder. After one of our raids, I found this kite. Look here; scratched on the handle is a child's drawing of a rat, which is my celestial birth animal. So, I took it as a souvenir."

Cui showed the kite to the wind and an updraft whipped it into the air. Higher and higher it went, as Cui whistled contentedly to himself. The wind played with the kite, a red blur against the background of the ice blue sky. Cui reeled in and then slackened the spool. The kite ducked towards them, almost kissing the ground. At the last moment, Cui tightened the thread and the splash of red swooped up into the sky and flew up like an eagle, almost as high as the cotton-white clouds.

Bolin's attention was diverted from the excitement of the flight to a sedan chair that was racing towards them, which was strange, because its bearers had deviated onto the hill from the west road. Alongside them were runners and a rider on a dappled grey which he recognised as the assistant magistrate, Bao. In which case, Gang was the occupant of the sedan chair. Bolin assumed he was a closet kite fanatic and was heading their way to share their delight.

While the bearers placed the sedan chair down in front of them, Cui taught the kite more of his tricks. The curtain on the sedan chair parted and, sure enough, out stepped Gang. The magistrate planted his hands on his hips and stared alternately at Cui, then at the kite. It was as if the kite had resuscitated a painful memory, because his face was pale as cured, bone white porcelain. Bao dismounted and stood next to his enforcer Sheng and his compatriot, Big Qiang.

Bolin sensed a hidden menace in the air. Cui obviously thought otherwise, because he offered Gang the spool, saying, "Here, the wind is perfect. Want to try?"

Gang grabbed the kite from Cui and stared at the handle. Whatever he saw, galvanised him. An air of intimidation circled the magistrate like a kettle of vultures. What possessed the man? In a terrible frenzy, he turned back and snatched Bao's horsewhip. Cui seemed blithely unaware of this because he took back the pulley and steered the red kite up and away into the pale blue yonder.

With the look of Yama in his eye, Gang smashed the horsewhip across the old soldier's face. More in surprise than pain, Cui fell on his knees clutching his face.

It happened so fast. The horsewhip cracked a second time. Gang hit Cui again, this time on his back. Cui winced and plunged headfirst into the icy ground. The kite spool slid along the ground, pulled by the force of the wind. Bolin grabbed it and tried to intervene. Bao thrust a hand in front of him and with a voice like thunder, yelled, "Lay a hand on an imperial official at your peril."

Terrified and angry at the same time, Bolin was helpless as he watched Gang whip Cui without mercy. Cui was curled into a foetal position. The blows rained down on him like frozen lightning bolts. Bolin prayed for the attack to abate. It didn't. It grew in fury. Lash after lash, Gang was possessed, manic.

Frothing at the mouth, Gang was yelling.

"For mother!"

Then he'd scream, "For father!" and "For brother!" and "For sister!"

Was this a revenge attack? For Gang's family? What had Cui ever done to harm them?

The other kite flyers had gathered around and stood like statues, frozen by the terrifying and seemingly unprovoked assault.

Bolin felt pathetic, doing nothing, watching his friend bleed red blood. When he could stand it no longer, he lurched at Gang, but Sheng and Big Qiang blocked his path, grabbed him by the arms and forced him to watch.

Gang horsewhipped Cui's back, legs and arms as the old soldier cradled his head from the brutal lashes. After every lash, Gang now cried, "The rat! The rat! The rat!"

The magistrate's rage abated, more from exhaustion than anything else. Where once Cui wore a solitary splash of red bandanna, now a steady trickle of crimson oozed out of his every pore. He was like a sack of rice. Gang's face wore Cui's blood spots like trophies of revenge but he seemed as stunned by what he had done as everyone else. The horsewhip hung limply from his bloody hand. He was babbling. Bao escorted him back to the sedan chair as an adult leads a child.

Sheng and Qiang let Bolin go and he rushed to his friend's side. Tenderly, he removed the blood-soaked bandanna and wiped Cui's face. The old soldier was clinging to his life by a slender thread.

Bolin cradled him in his arms and rocked him, crying tears of sadness and grief, the red kite fluttering on the ground, its broken spine stuck in the mud. On the side of the handle was the celestial animal symbol of a rat. What did Gang mean by shouting 'rat'?

Come to think of it, hadn't Luli told him Gang was a 'rat'?

Oh, no.

CHAPTER 38

Army on the Horizon

It is better to preserve a nation than to demolish it,
Better to preserve an army than to demolish it,
And better to preserve a unit than to demolish it.
THE ART OF WAR

Later that day, Bolin was sweeping the road on the section of wall above the Zhendong Gate. He pushed the broom absent-mindedly, sick to the stomach at witnessing Cui's awful beating. How could Gang do such a thing? Did Cui really massacre Gang's family? It didn't make sense.

Bolin gripped the broom handle as if it was his one remaining hold on sanity. He was beginning to think Luli was right – at least about Gang. The man was mad, irascible and must have committed a heinous crime in his previous life, because to beat a man to the edge of death was unforgivable.

Wuzhou came straight up to him and asked, "Is he all right? Have you seen him?"

Bolin reassured him. "Your brother's in the temple infirmary. The monks will care for him there. He's taken a heavy beating, but look, you know him, he's as tough as bamboo. He'll recover – and he's a rat. You think they're dead and they come around, defiant to the last. They're life's great survivors."

"True, but I'm going to sort out that devil Gang, once and for all," he thundered.

"Wait," Bolin said, holding him back. "You can't. Lay a finger on him and they'll lock you up and beat you like they did Cui."

"I don't know," Wuzhou shook his head wearily. "How can he get away with this?"

"I'm afraid he can," Bolin said. "He has all the power here now. He even controls the commandant. We must bide our time. Everyone knows what he did was wrong, intolerable, heinous. We'll find a way to get to him."

"All right, but I'm going to see my brother as soon as I've finished my duty here," Wuzhou said. His eyes wore an angry, empty stare, like an exhausted fighter.

From now on, Bolin thought, things would be different. The beating was an irrevocable act, from which there was no return. Things would never be the same again, not only for Cui and Wuzhou, but also for Gang and for him. The bitter taste in his gullet was exacerbated by an equally bitter north wind blowing off the steppes. He wrapped himself in his hemp winter coat and stooped to pick up more debris from the road.

In the middle of the afternoon, Wuzhou shouted, "Hi. Hi!" Then he pointed to the low rolling hills to the east.

The guards peered into the haze. There was movement on the limits of vision, so it was impossible to discern who it was – Mongol traders, soothsayers, or perhaps mercenaries selling their skilled bow and horsemanship to the highest bidder.

"There they are. I can see something," Wuzhou said.

The guards craned their necks. Some of the low cloud resting on the peaks of the Yanshan Mountains rolled down onto the plain, obscuring their view. The mists drifted, creating odd, ribbed shapes. The winds sculpted the mists into animals, there, the profile of a dog, no, a wolf. The guards pointed at it.

"How can the air form itself into the shape of a wolf?" yelled one, his head clasped in his hands.

Another replied, "Hah! That's no accident. Instead, you should ask 'who has the power to conjure a wolf from mere clouds'?"

And a third shouted, "How can we defeat a foe who commands the very elements?"

The spectre of fear grabbed the guards around the throat, like the Blue Wolf had become incarnate and was about to rip them apart. The wolf was already in the air, usurping the towers of Heaven. Now it left its spoor on the earth.

As quickly as it had appeared, the mists shifted again and the airy wolf was gone. Then, another gust of wind and the play of air and moisture came to a stuttering finale; the grey waves of the Bohai Sea swallowed the mists, leaving a clear view.

On the far distant ridge were hundreds of men, tiny against the huge backdrop of the horizon.

"Who are they?" he asked.

No one wanted to answer that question except Wuzhou, who shouted, "Call the commandant."

It wasn't long before Tung scaled the steps of the watchtower, Major Renshu in tow.

"We've the strongest fortifications in the Zhongguo here, so what's all the fuss about?" he wanted to know, squinting at the distant manoeuvres. "What do you make of it, Major?"

"Too far away to identify the flags," Renshu replied. "Whoever they are, they've taken up a strong position on that ridge. And from that trail of smoke, they're making camp. Could they be ours?"

"Doubt it," Tung said. "If they were a remnant of the prince's army, he would have alerted us to their movements when he passed through here. And why would they make camp, when they are a short march away from a solid roof over their heads? No, it doesn't make sense."

"Then who are they?" the major asked the vital question.

"Until we know otherwise, we treat them as a hostile force under the banner of the Blue Wolf. I want the garrison on a war footing. Station the Han Regiment on the walls and battlements. Equipment checked. Troops battle ready. Officers alert. Got it?"

"Yes, Commandant," the major replied, stiff and correct. Then he added, "Is it the Mongols?"

"Let's find out. Despatch a search party," Tung replied, pacing the road like a restless tiger.

"Wuzhou," the major called him over. "Take five men and report back on the enemy's dispositions."

Wuzhou's chin hit the floor. Bolin could see the man was upset and disappointed not to visit his brother. Bolin grabbed him by the elbow and said, "Don't worry, I'll tell Cui what you are doing. Just come back safe."

Were they Mongols – or not? Wuzhou would find out, one way or another.

If they were a hostile force, then Luli's earlier prediction about an attack from the east was proving correct.

Surely there was nothing to worry about, since whatever the size of the force opposing them, the Chinese possessed an overwhelming superiority and boasted the monumental strength of the Shanhaiguan Fortress? Despite all that, the stench of fear along the ramparts was palpable.

Bolin watched the far-off movements with the wary eyes of a hawk.

There were scores of fires, their smoke snaking up to meet the grey cloud overhead. This had been a grey day all around; the dragon failed to appear, his grey-haired friend suffered at the hands of a maniac and a mysterious host threatened the grey walls of Shanhaiguan.

CHAPTER 39

The Vault

The Tao is profound and invisible, it exists everywhere and anywhere.
This original nature is the eternal law.
To know nature's law is to be enlightened.
THE TAO TE CHING

Since his night-time escapade with Kong, Feng had decided to make himself a disguise, in the form of crutch. To his surprise, it came with an unexpected free gift; a cloak of cultural invisibility. It was as if he was a ghost – because when he limped down the street, no one paid him the slightest attention. From the moment that Precious and Granny Dandan strolled by him without so much as a backward glance, he knew he'd attained the nirvana of a beggar's disguise.

All day long, he had racked his brains. How could he reach the vault below the Laolongtou? The best he could come up with was to spend his last bronze cash on a coil of rope. That was a start.

He had even persuaded Kong to miss the dragon players' performance, so the two of them could hide in the long, salt-laden grasses on the beach and scout the Laolongtou. Though the longer he watched, the more impossible the task appeared. The guards were stationed by the Stone Guardian and around the ramparts. They kept a close watch on all access points, including the dunes. The tide was rushing in and would soon cover the gap he'd seen in the 'nose' of the dragon.

He was about to surrender to the demons of karma when there was a hue and cry further along the wall. And lo and behold! All the guards rushed off towards the main fortress, leaving the Laolongtou unprotected!

"This is karma. Now's our chance," Feng said, making to scale the wall of the Laolongtou.

"You sure?" Kong screwed up his face in anguish. "You know what Master Wen is like. He protects that wall like it was his virgin daughter. If we're arrested for trespassing, he'll hang us up by our thumbs."

"Stop fussing," Feng snapped. "There's no one up there, not even a Blue Wolf."

They stalked across the dunes. Kong lassoed the rope onto the parapet. It gripped first time. *Kong's good at that*, Feng thought. Kong seemed good at a lot of things. With the nimbleness of a monkey, Feng scaled the rope then peered along the ramparts. Not a soul. He gestured for Kong to follow and slid over the parapet.

Finally, he had attained the sacred ground of the Laolongtou. They hadn't long before the gap in the brickwork would be covered by the incoming tide. Feng glanced at his father's plan to confirm the vault's location and moved to the ramparts right above it.

Kong noticed the map and asked, "What you got there? Can I see?"

This was strange. Kong had already spied on a couple of traitors in the wine bar, he was an expert with a rope and now he wanted to look at his map. Who was he? For a beggar, he seemed surprisingly well-informed. Feng was not the only one with secrets. Still, he could trust no one.

"No!" he blurted out, rolling up the scroll and tucking it back in the lacquer box. "If you want to help me, tie the rope round this parapet."

"Why? What are you going to do?" Kong asked. "Oh, I see. You're going to climb down the Old Dragon's snout."

Feng nodded and tied the other end of the rope around his midriff.

"What's down there then?" Kong's said, peering over the parapet.

"If the soldiers return, pull three times on the rope. Can you do that?"

Kong's answer was a scowl and a swift nod.

Feet flat against the stone end of the dragon's head, palms gripping the frozen rope, Feng scaled down the wall. Below him, the waters of the Bohai Sea heaved and swelled and small chunks of ice floated amidst the grey white waves. He descended the outside of the dragon's snout, dangling midway between Heaven and earth.

Kong called out, "Feng, you there?"

"Yes, what is it?" His feet slipped and he hung onto the rope to prevent himself falling into the mire.

"The guards are coming back. I can't get caught here. Sorry, I'm off," Kong shouted.

"Wait, help me," Feng yelled back. No answer. He had abandoned him, like everyone else.

Hanging on to the rope, he lowered himself down the side of the dragon's snout. There were shouts from the battlements. Someone pulled on the end

172

of the rope. Soldiers. He let go of the rope in time and inserted his hands and feet into crevices in the stone work. The rope dropped by him and fell into the churning sea.

He gripped the vertical rock face. The rope was still attached to his waist and the other end was trailing in the cold waves of the Bohai Sea. He felt his hands giving way. A rock whizzed by his head, missing him by a whisker. The soldiers were throwing stones at him. He squirreled down the side of the rock face, grabbed onto a lower ledge, from where he hauled himself into the opening of the vault.

He landed in a heap on the floor. His hands and knees were covered in a slimy mix of mud and seaweed. The vault was swathed in shadows and he waited while his eyes adjusted to the dim light. A wave broke over the rim of the opening, soaking him to the skin. It was a timely reminder – the tide would soon submerge the vault and him along with it. He had to move before the soldiers grappled their way down the outer wall towards him.

The map had shown the location of the Jade Chamber, where the Laolong was supposed to be imprisoned. So where was the entrance to it? He slid his hands along the inner wall of the vault, feeling the rock surface for the outline of a doorway. Eventually, he found it. A deep vertical slit in the wall and another one parallel to it. This was it. This was the 'door' to the Jade Chamber. Hah! It had no handle, so how did it open?

From above, he heard cries. "Feng! You down there!" It was the soldiers.

He pushed hard against the 'door' and all he moved was a piece of seaweed hanging off the rock. There was nothing in the 'door' to hang onto – like his life, really. It was sealed. There had to be a way. The chilling waters lapped at his feet. The tide was encroaching. With the size of the swell, it would fill quickly and he'd drown.

A noise behind him. A rope hung down by the outer vault opening. And another. From above, shouts. "Climb down there."

Feng edged towards the vault opening. With the sea surging in front of him, he peered up at the ramparts. Soldiers were scaling down the dragon's snout. A face appeared over the parapet. Gang.

Damn.

He was so close.

CHAPTER 40

Grappling with Heaven

If wood rubs against wood, flames spring up.
When metal is placed next to fire, it melts.
When yin and yang go awry,
The harmony of Heaven and earth is upset.
THE BOOK OF CHUANG TZU

Gang was well-satisfied with his day's work. Thanks to an unexpected tip-off, he'd arrested the fugitive Feng. Who would have guessed his mother's maid, Precious, would betray him not once, but twice? What a coup. He could use Feng to trade benefits from the prince. Or he could have done with him and sentence him to death. Oh, he did enjoy wielding the mace of imperial power and sprinkling the benevolent embers of his decisions over all and sundry. After beating Cui to a pulp, he had considered halting his quest to emasculate the Chinese imperial machine, a lapse that was only temporary. He did enjoy being the chrysalis of revenge and, well, the Chinese were so accommodating that he felt obliged to wreak as much havoc on them as was possible in a single lifetime. They had wrecked his life. Karma dictated that he should wreck theirs. Perhaps he would come back as an avenging demon and terrorise them again. What a delicious thought!

On his return from arresting Feng, Gang had climbed the ramp up to the Zhendong Tower to gloat at the plight of the guards, who were trembling like leaves in the wind. The crisis that Altan had predicted was bubbling up like lava in a volcano, ready to explode in an eruption of gore and pain. In truth, the timid Chinese guards were right to be afraid. While he had witnessed the spectral horrors that Altan could unleash, they had not. The Mongolian shaman was conjuring spirits and making them dance to his prophetic tune.

Gang taunted the guards, first with false encouragement. "You're so brave. The Mongols will be repulsed by your waves of courage," he said, as the sarcasm floated over them like clouds of sea fog.

No one replied. That was a new development, no doubt arising from him giving Cui a thoroughly-deserved thrashing. The incident had earned him notoriety, a reward he relished.

Because now, no one dared challenge him.

From his sleeve, he plucked his childhood bamboo flute, the one he'd rescued from his burning home many years ago. 'Red bandannas'? Red flames, more like. He would never forget the memory of his father plunging to the ground, an arrow in his back; the terrified screams of his mother and sister as they were raped by the red bandannas, before the house was put to the torch. Who would have thought that old Cui, a wastrel of a soldier, would be delivered up to him on a platter? At last, the gods of revenge were shining on him.

His angry fingers moved over the holes, the flute yielding a reluctant melody. The rage stilled in his heart and a mellifluous tune flared from the embers of his memory. He fiddled on and started to play a jaunty tune. The guards gave him cold frowns and narrowed eyes. Their nervous, disgruntled looks told him his ploy was working as well as sweetmeat.

Again, the guards pointed east. Something caught their febrile attention. He stopped playing to take a look. Waves of ch'i were building around the fortress, infecting both wall and warrior. No, it wasn't another thunderstorm. It was similar to that, an increase in pressure, making the temples pound, the throat tight. Some mighty power was about to burst through Heaven into the earthly realm.

He scanned the horizon for clues. Wisps of smoke rose into the air from the hundreds of fires on the distant ridge. Even the thick-skinned guards sensed an imminent threat. Then one of them yelled, "Get away from me!"

The poor man was as pale as the snows on the peaks of the Yanshan Mountains.

With an air of disbelief, the Commandant Tung asked, "What's the matter?"

"No. Stop! It's attacking me!" the guard cried. Brandishing his sabre, he slashed left and right, like he was fending off a wild animal. There was nothing. He was slashing at thin air.

"What's he seeing that we're not?" Tung asked with a furrowed brow.

"He's terrified," Gang said, with as much composure as he could muster. He guessed this was Altan's work. The master shaman was conducting a superlative performance and he had a front seat.

"Disarm him, before he kills someone," Tung ordered.

The guard swiped at invisible shapes in the air. His face was drawn into a heavy scowl, his body hunched against some omnipotent unseen threat. Cutting the air in two, he swore a well-known protective oath against demons. Everyone recognised it. The man was seeing devils in the air that no one else could.

Gang loved every moment. It was comic; the bewildered officers huddling around their earnest leader, the guards petrified to move against one of their own and yet equally scared to bludgeon the air itself. Besides, how could they? What would they do? Turn into a cloud? Fizzle out? Gang struggled to suppress a smirk.

"Get off me," the guard cried, slashing his sabre into the still afternoon air. He seemed more afraid of the demons than of the guards who closed in a ring around him. With a lunge, he forced the guards back. Again, they edged forwards, he thrust at them and so the dance continued, back and forth. They cornered him, his back to the battlements. His lips were pulled into a demonic grimace.

"There's nothing to be afraid of. Lay down your sword." Tung tried to reason with him.

The guard slashed again at the air, cried out loud and arched back, as if an invisible giant had plucked him off the wall and jettisoned him backwards with the force of ten horses.

Gang watched the guard tumble though the air, twisting and turning, a man unhooked from his element, a fallen being. All the way down, he yelled, one long piercing scream, loud enough to wake the ancestors. His body thumped into the far bank of the moat and laid prostrate, arms akimbo, eyes staring back up at them.

"See if he's alive," Tung snarled.

Gang peered over the battlements, as the soldiers below rushed over the drawbridge to attend the stricken guard. From behind Gang, another guard shouted out in distress. He beat the air with his fists, like he was grappling with Heaven.

Another spectral attack.

"Get away!" the guard screamed. In a terrifying moment, his trousers split from groin to toe, sliced open by an unseen foe wielding an unseen weapon. The injured guard stared at the wound in crazed disbelief. Blood dripped down a deep cut on his thigh, leaving a trail of crimson drops on the pristine stonework.

"Help him!" Tung screamed at the guards. No one moved.

Gang had seen Altan's supernatural work before, but nothing to match this grade of excellence. A moment later, the invisible entity leapt at the injured guard and must have landed on top of him, because the man was fighting the air like a madman, trying to fend off a ferocious attack. He fell on his back, mauled by some kind of wild animal. The invisible beast tore open the guard's throat and a spout

176

of crimson blood spurted into the air. The guard twitched a few times and swiftly bled out, a red pool creeping across the stonework like a malevolent intruder.

The other guards stood in a stunned ring around their dead compatriot. A deathly silence hung over the Zhendong Tower. On it was the infamous saying, The First Pass under Heaven. Gang wondered malevolently if they shouldn't replace it with The First Pass under Hell.

Then a third guard drew his sabre and struck out at an unseen attacker, yelling, shaking his fist at the unruly air.

"What are you fighting?" Tung thundered.

"Can't you see it?" the guard said, beating the wind with his fists.

"No. What is it? Where is it?" Tung bellowed, beside himself with rage.

"A wolf, a Blue Wolf," the guard yelled, his voice hoarse with fear.

Abandoned by Heaven and all that was holy, the guard dropped his weapon and dashed screaming along the road, looking back in mortal fear at the invisible Blue Wolf pursuing him.

"Stop him," Tung ordered the guards. But they stood there like statues, in denial of what they were witnessing.

Tung's next order scythed through their hesitation.

"Kill the deserter."

For Gang, these words were like listening to the crescendo of an exquisite piece of music. Or like the ecstasy of clouds and rain. The Chinese were turning on and rending themselves. He had wondered how Altan would bring about this supernatural war. Now he knew. First, the Chinese had voluntarily brought the Blue Wolf into the garrison on captured banners. Once inside, the wolf had seeded the air, appearing in the blue lichen. A lone Blue Wolf had caused the death of two soldiers and was threatening to destroy the entire garrison – from within.

Altan had promised to attack the Chinese in Heaven and that was precisely what he was doing.

The guards snapped out of their trance, grabbed their bows and unleashed a volley of arrows that thudded into the back of the deserter. The wolf's bloodlust must have been satiated, because the invisible creature attacked no one else.

As a semblance of sanity returned to the wall road, the guards patriotically covered their dead compatriots in red and yellow flags of the Prince of Yan and carried them on stretchers past the terrified citizens. Gang climbed into his sedan chair and followed at a discreet distance. Behind the curtains, his smile was as wide as the wall itself. The people sang a long, slow dirge out of respect for the dead guards.

Gang picked up his bamboo flute and fingered his own favourite tune, a melody from his childhood. Ah, it was so poignant, he could almost cry.

CHAPTER 41

The Plan of Shanhaiguan

Virtue small and office high,
Wisdom small and plans great,
Strength small and burden heavy –
Where such conditions exist, it is seldom that they do not end in evil.
THE TA CHUAN, THE GREAT TREATISE

The jailors threw Feng across the floor like a worthless rag. Skidding across the floor on his backside, he crunched against the wall. The cell door slammed shut. He groaned. Every bone in his body felt hammered. Damn, he had almost got into the Jade Chamber. Notwithstanding the aches and pains, he sat up from his crumpled heap.

The cell was not much bigger than a broom cupboard.

As the dusk watch rang out, he caught a glimpse of the lanterns in the magistrate's chambers in the nearby Yamen. How often he had sat in those very chambers with Park debating the significance of the Emperor's latest missive on the laws of filial piety, the customs of marriage, the importance of ritual worship, the... Oh, what was the point of rekindling those memories? That life was over. He'd swapped the court chambers for a cell. Now that was an unfair exchange. Somewhere, somehow, a cacophony of bad karma had sounded across the caverns of Heaven, dripped into the earthly realms and made it his fate to suffer humiliation, loss and indignity.

Slumped in the corner of the cell, his eyes adjusted to his insalubrious surroundings. So, this was his new prison – with real, not imaginary, bars. His head swam with the smell of faeces and fear. He looked around the cell: four other poor sods wearing cangues. At least he didn't have one of those – yet.

The cangue next to him moaned. He glanced at the man's face, jutting precariously out of the rectangular piece of wood. Oh my, it was Ru. He barely recognised him. He was as thin and gaunt as an old peasant who had poured his life into the rice fields.

"Ru?" Feng murmured.

Ru peered back at him through layers of pain and hurt and let out a soft whimper.

"What have they done to you?" Feng asked, reaching down to offer him solace.

Ru winced, trying to edge his exhausted body further into the darkness of the corner, as if that were possible. Ru and the corner were already married, like a grotesque coupling.

The dusk curfew drums beat out from the Bell and Drum Tower, waves of rolling sound, piercing the gloom of the cell. At that moment, the door burst open. Three shadows lurked outside the cell – Gang, Bao, and Thousand Cuts Liu. Feng had already witnessed first-hand the torturer's legendary skills. When sitting in the Yamen and with the wind blowing in the right direction, he had often heard the screams of horror vomiting out of the underworld, the delightful name bequeathed on Liu's amply-equipped torture chambers. The one thing that Feng liked about Liu was that he had never practiced his skills on Feng. Feng did not want that to change. Not now. Not ever.

He was cold, hungry and tired of running.

"I'm innocent of all charges," he railed. "In fact, what are the charges? Am I guilty of being the son of General Xu Da? I am the brother-in-law of the Prince of Yan. That is not a crime. He will hear of this disgrace."

"You're a clever liar and manipulator," Gang sneered. "The prince, a better judge of men than I, refused to promote you to the post of acting magistrate. It was as well that Bao here witnessed how you abused the aegis of authority, before it was even placed in your hand. Then I caught you rifling through the court's papers. Given the proximity of your father's death, I decided out of compassion not to prosecute you. Then the Lady Lan died in suspicious circumstances. Now I have no leniency left in my heart. You are the most dangerous foe in Shanhaiguan. You are a traitor to your family and to the prince."

Feng was flabbergasted. "Me, the traitor? This… this is preposterous."

"Then why did you run from the commandant? You must have had a reason to hide. What is it? Tell us. You'll feel better for it."

"What?" he cried. "You're mad!"

"Search him," Gang said.

Liu held him in a vice-like grip while Bao dug through his pockets. It was useless to resist. Bao squealed and pulled the lacquer box from Feng's inner sleeve.

"Here's something," Bao cried with an air of triumph.

Gang admired the box, saying, "Mmm, this lacquer is smooth and of the finest quality. Let me see what's inside. Here, bring the lantern closer," he ordered. "There are papers. It's a plan of – oh, yes, this is very interesting. Well, well, well. These are construction plans for the extension of the Great Wall from the Yanshan Mountains to the sea. I'll study them later. Tell me, where did you find them?"

Liu growled and twisted Feng's arm behind his back.

"Luli gave them me."

"Her again?" Bao snarled. "She is mid-wife to every nefarious act in Shanhaiguan."

Gang frowned. "I agree. Bring her in. I'll question her myself. Then I'll deal with that troublesome monk."

Feng slumped into the corner, beaten in both mind and body. Next to him, Ru let out a long sigh.

CHAPTER 42

The Po Office

A famous physician was asked
which of his family of healers was most skilled in the art.
He replied: 'My eldest brother removes the spirit of sickness before it takes hold.
My elder brother cures illness when it is still minute.
As for me, I puncture veins, prescribe potions and massage skin.'
ANCIENT CHINESE FABLE

Luli wiped the moist flannel over the guard's forehead for the twentieth time and turned to Dong.

"It won't come off," she murmured, her voice tinged with desperation. When they'd brought the three dead guards into the temple infirmary, she, Dong and Ju had set about cleansing and preparing the bodies for the sacred rites. One was mangled from a fall, the second was cut to shreds by a wolf's claws and the third had perished from arrows in the back.

They had wiped down the bodies, except for the forehead – where all three had an imprint that would not budge, no matter how hard they tried. It was the image of a rampant Blue Wolf, mouth open, teeth bared, leaping out from the middle of their forehead. If she stared too long at it, it seemed to leap across the space between them and jump into her soul. Even when she glanced away it was there, bounding out at her from behind a table or under a stool.

"It's a stain on their soul," she said with a rueful air.

"No, it's a trick," Dong insisted. "It's a shaman's ruse to make us afraid."

"There's talk of deserters and fugitives and that Shanhaiguan is cursed," Ju added his piece of silver.

Luli wiped once more, then flung the cloth away in frustration. "It's useless. I'm not doing this anymore."

"Then go home," Dong suggested. "Get some sleep and come back in the morning."

He was right. She was exhausted and she missed Ru so badly it ached.

It was night time, so for safety, she returned home through the Bagua tunnels. She climbed down the vertical shaft, the lantern lighting her way. Trudging along, she felt at home in the dark, yin shadows, yielding to the great yang fortress above her. As she edged her way through the still quiescence, she felt pockets of concentrated ch'i. She wondered where this accumulation of high ch'i originated.

This time, she saw in her mind an image, stark and clear and bright. It was a rod of gems, spinning slowly, humming a tune made by the sound of a distant galaxy, serene and powerful. In the moist darkness, that was the cocoon where things gave birth and were born.

Were the tunnels a kind of spiritual womb?

What a strange thought.

She whispered, "What is your name?"

Not expecting a reply, she walked on. Then a voice responded in the depths of her soul. "*What is your name?*"

She stopped. That was not an echo. It had spoken to her. Heaven had spoken to her.

"I am Luli, a Fire Monkey and Custodian of the Po Office," she whispered.

"*I am Luli, a Fire Monkey and Custodian of the Po Office,*" the echo replied. Somehow, at that moment, she knew who she was, what she was doing and where she was going. It all made sense. If only she could hold on to that precious moment of sublime clarity about her life.

There was a noise, a loud voice somewhere above her. It jerked her out of her reverie. She was standing beneath the vertical shaft that led to her house.

What was going on up there?

One slow step at a time, she climbed up the laddered shaft, hearing the voices clearer and louder, the nearer she got to the surface. Several men were shouting. She could hear the sound of things crashing on the ground, breaking. Who were they? What were they…? Oh no!

Filled with dread, she reached the step below the trap door. Through the slit, she could see lights flickering. Soldiers. They were smashing her Po Office to bits. She felt like opening the trap door and giving them a piece of her mind, but they were obviously after her. She would end up imprisoned like Ru and unable to help him.

Think. Who was up there, trashing her precious soul objects and letters? The answer came when she overheard a voice she recognised.

It was Bao, gloating, "Hah! I hope she'll like the alterations we've performed on her home. Free of charge, of course."

Her worst fears crushed the breath out of her body. How could they? That house was her home, her livelihood. Now, she had neither.

A clear image of her room rammed into her febrile mind. The soldiers were trashing the gifts and donations for which she was custodian. The outer door hung off its hinges. There was rubbish strewn outside, dark shadows that were once her carefully-gathered belongings. The place was wrecked, her customer's precious mementoes, in chaos. The letters, scrolls and paper documents were torn to shreds. A small fire burnt in the corner. Elsewhere, precious bequests left by dead relatives, as yet unclaimed, had been opened and ransacked, many stolen, leaving their ruptured envelopes, with nothing left inside. The work of generations, gone, devoured in an orgy of devastation. Their pieces lay sad and unwanted on the floor, trampled into the dirt. It was almost as if the past didn't matter anymore. It was rendered expendable.

She felt violated, hollow and abused.

The Hammer of Shanhaiguan, Gang was the perpetrator of everything bad. But was he the mastermind behind the appearance of the spectral blue wolves? Was he the mysterious shaman? No, he didn't seem capable of that order of supernatural skill. He must have had help – Mongol help.

"Luli, Luli, lovely Luli, come sit on my lap," Bao sang, lascivious to the last. Panic gripped her throat. She daren't move, lest she alert him to her presence.

The soldiers stopped breaking up the place. The noises ceased. She pressed her ear against the trap door. She heard the sound of a stream of water hitting a nearby wall, then another stream and another and a grunt or two. The soldiers were urinating against her walls. Not content with destroying her Po Office, they were defiling it. It was reduced to a soldiers' latrine. A toxic mix of fury and hate rose in her gullet.

Then it hit her like a bolt. The last time she had used the tunnel, she had left the trap door closed but not covered by the carpet. It was exposed and sooner or later... surreptitiously, she began her descent. A step at a time, she edged down the ladder. As she reached the tunnel, the trap door flew open, spilling light into the vertical shaft. For a moment, it backlit a man's head. She scuttled away, hoping beyond hope that she hadn't been seen.

Halfway along the tunnel, she couldn't go on. She stopped to rest, her hands on her thighs. She was stuck by a stark image of broken shards of sculptures and smashed wooden frames of paintings. Preserved for decades, these objects were gone now – forever. Her Po Office was no more. Her head spun and she felt flushed. She dry-retched, then vomited the contents of her stomach.

She heard noises from the vertical shaft. They were coming after her!

Her heart pounding, an acrid taste in her mouth, she raced along the tunnel. Arriving at the base of the temple shaft, a gust of wind blew the lantern out, plunging the tunnel into darkness.

Luli had lost her husband, her son was condemned to lose his hand, her home was defiled and the precious gifts and messages left to her in trust, destroyed – a fitting reflection of how desolate she felt inside. She wondered if that was how god felt about humanity.

CHAPTER 43

The Yin of Life

Death and life have their determined appointment.
Riches and honours depend upon Heaven.
THE ANALECTS OF CONFUCIUS

It was after the second night watch when Gang sat down in the sedan chair. His body eased back into the cushions as his porters carried him though the alleys of the Yamen, stopping only when they reached the base of the Zhendong Gate. Arms folded, foot tapping, Commandant Tung waited for him.

"What's happened?" Gang asked. He was secretly hoping for more bad news – for the Chinese.

"I'm not sure," Tung said. "The guards on the battlements have reported some strange movement outside the gates. I thought you'd want to see for yourself."

"Thank you, yes, I do," Gang said, with evident enthusiasm. "Lead on."

Lantern on a pole, a soldier marched stoically in front of him, Tung and an officer deputation that included Major Renshu. They climbed the ramp, the sound of their footsteps echoing eerily around the tower. As they reached the battlements, a guard challenged them,

"Halt, who goes there?"

"Dolt, what are you doing? It's me, your commandant," Tung snapped, shoving the lance out of the way and slapping the man hard across the cheek. "Pull yourself together. The enemy is out there, not in here."

"S-sorry, Commandant," the guard stammered, bowing low in embarrassment.

Good, Gang thought to himself. *The men are jumpy. Another slice of terror and they'll abandon their posts, if they don't kill each other first.*

"Now, what is there to report?" Tung growled.

"There are some dark shapes just beyond the moat – look, there," the guard pointed at a cluster on the ground.

"What on earth are they?" Gang asked, peering into the shadows.

"We think they're wounded animals," the guard replied.

"Why wounded?" Tung wanted to know.

"There are the moans and groans, like they're in pain."

"Ah, yes. I can hear that too," Gang remarked.

"I smell a trap. Bring an additional unit of swordsmen to the gate and post a unit of archers up here on the wall road," Tung ordered. "Major, see to it."

As he passed him, the major winked at Gang, a wink of quiet collaboration and hidden purpose. The major was no doubt as pleased as Gang was to see yet another Chinese disaster unfolding before their eyes. While the troops assembled, a sedan chair raced up the ramp and out stepped Bao.

"What news?" Gang asked.

"Luli wasn't at home." Bao's reply was curt. "But we wrecked her Po Office. She won't be receiving any more letters from soul donors. We also blocked the entrance to the Bagua tunnels."

"Good, I've had enough of her interfering ways," he said. "But we still need to find her."

"I'm sure she's gone to the temple," Bao replied.

"So am I," he agreed. "Go there. Arrest her. And that dog's head Dong as well. They're two of a kind."

"I'm going," Bao said.

"Wait," Gang called him back and whispered, "I have an idea, let's finish this once and for all."

"I'm listening."

"The monks will all be tucked up in their precious little beds. Take Sheng, Big Qiang and one or two others you can trust along with you. Go and torch the temple. Keep it to yourselves. I wouldn't want to alarm our citizens' religious sensibilities."

"I shall enjoy the fireworks," Bao whispered and slithered off into the night.

Tung appeared not to have heard them and was discussing the incident outside the gate with the guards, when the additional units arrived at the double.

Tung bellowed out his orders. "Major, take a patrol outside to investigate."

The drawbridge was lowered. As Gang peered down from the battlements, the one thing missing from this delicious moment was someone to share it with. Guanting or Altan would relish the opportunity to mock the pathetic Chinese. At least the major was there, he'd be grinning inside.

Leading a large patrol, rapiers at the ready, the major crept across the drawbridge. Soldiers held lanterns on long poles, sending shards of light that flickered on the moat waters. Everyone held their breath, as the major edged ever closer. He prodded his sword at the collection of dark, amorphous shapes.

"Argh," the shape winced.

The major stopped. His men stopped. Even the water seemed to stop flowing for a moment. During the pause, Gang could barely contain himself. It was comic.

"There are bodies down here – humans," the major called up.

"Who are they?" Tung shouted back.

"It's Wuzhou… and the scouting party."

Returned with thanks, Gang mused to himself.

"Bring them inside and lower the drawbridge," Tung yelled.

Gang and Tung descended down the ramp, followed by an air of torpid inevitability. The patrol was hauling in four large sacks.

"Bring them into the duty room and here, untie them," Tung commanded.

Each sack contained a man… or the remains of what once were men. They were a tangle of mutilated limbs, clothed in blood-soaked rags. Three of them had had their necks severed like wild animals. Their heads lolled over their shoulders, there was so little bone and tissue holding the two together. Blood dripped through the bags onto the ground. The stench of death made him want to retch. Even Gang, toughened by a life of unremitting cruelty, felt a twinge of revulsion. Just a twinge.

From the fourth sack came a whimpering sound.

Tung spoke quickly, "This one's still alive. Send for the military physician – and some carts and porters."

"It's Wuzhou, Cui's brother," the major announced. Wuzhou's face was as pale as the white foam of the Bohai Sea. The man was in a pitiful state.

"What's that in his mouth?" Tung asked.

"A slab of meat," Gang murmured. "Mutton, if I'm not mistaken."

"Mutton, what's that for?" A guard asked.

"All four of them have it stuffed in their mouths." Tung was furious. The more he spoke, the redder he got. "They're brave men, not sheep. The Mongols brutalised our men when they lived. Now they're dead, they're trying to humiliate them. Mutton. Hah! The Mongols are mutton. *They're* the shepherds. *They're* the barbarians. My men are brave. I will not allow them to be disgraced. Wash their mouths out. And throw the meat to the rats."

Gang was impressed. Altan had style and his sense of revenge was poignant. He smiled to himself, because it reminded him of Wuzhou's jibe about the Mongols' lifestyle. What was it, 'mutton-eaters'? Who was eating mutton now?

The doctor burst into the room and examined Wuzhou. He pulled the robes from his body, ruby red with blood and took his three pulses. "It's a miracle he's still breathing," he announced.

Wuzhou sat bolt upright, his eyes bulging in their sockets. He opened his mouth and for a moment, Gang thought he was going to utter some profound sentiment, the last words of the leader of a disastrous patrol. That should be interesting. Instead, he surprised everyone and vomited over the doctor, a viscous fluid distinguished by the strange and undeniable fact that it was blue. Blue? Yes, the blue vomit slid effortlessly down the doctor's perfectly clean robes and congealed in an amorphous pool on the floor. The stench was appalling.

The doctor tried wiping it off his robe and admitted, "I've never seen blue vomit."

Gang frowned, but he secretly admired Altan's ingenuity. How did the man do it? This was pure genius.

Tung thought otherwise, "That's disgusting," he murmured, tuning up his nose.

Wuzhou slumped back on the table and then let out a long, slow sigh. The doctor took the three pulses again and said, "He's gone to join his ancestors."

One of the guards screamed, "I can't take it anymore!" and dashed out of the gatehouse.

"Get him," Tung snapped. "And bring him back here."

The other guards hauled the deserter back, kicking and screaming and threw him down in front of Tung like a piece of offal. The man's pale face was white with terror, his chin twitching, his wide eyes scanning left and right for an attack by a pack of invisible blue wolves.

The deserter grovelled at the commandant's feet and claimed, "The blue wolves are in the air and in the sky. They're everywhere."

Well, Gang thought, *I couldn't have put the Chinese predicament more aptly.* To his further delight, Tung turned a deaf ear to the man's excuses.

"You're a coward," Tung scowled. "My men don't run away from blue vomit. Question is, what shall we do with you?"

"Send him out to the Mongols. They can finish him off for us," the major suggested.

"Not that," the deserter pleaded.

"No, I agree, not that," Tung confirmed. "If we let him outside, we'd have to listen to his pathetic moaning all night. "

"Can I make a suggestion?" Gang had a good idea. He was full of them tonight.

"Yes, of course," Tung said.

"There's a punishment spoken of in the Great Ming Code. Tear the skin from his body, then stuff it with straw and make a kind of live mannequin, a facsimile of the man. Now that's a fitting epitaph."

"Excellent," Tung replied.

"Then put the mannequin on the ramparts above the Zhendong Gate, where the guards can see what fate befell this man," Gang chuckled to himself. This was hilarious. The Chinese were doing an excellent job of destroying themselves. He was merely lending them a helping hand. They were so fortunate to have his assistance.

The guards dragged the hysterical deserter from the room. Gang, the major and the commandant were about to follow when the doctor said, "Wait, there's something odd about these men."

"Other than the fact that they've been tortured to death, you mean?" Gang jibed.

"No, not that," the doctor said, a tinge of fear creeping into this voice. Gang realised the doctor was serious. "It was in their eyes," the doctor said.

"What about them?" Gang wanted to know.

"Come and see you yourself. They're blue-eyed," the doctor said.

"Blue... but we're Han Chinese, we're brown-eyed. How...?" Tung pulled on his beard.

"What does it mean?" Gang asked. The simple questions were always the best.

"I don't know. It's like the damned Blue Wolf is roaming around *inside* these men," Tung whispered, as if he feared the guards would overhear him.

Again, Gang appreciated Altan's work. And the shaman wasn't in the room, let alone the fortress. What he, Gang, could achieve with supernatural powers like that!

Gang suppressed a twinge of envy. During the long, dark nights, he had learnt how to thrive in the shadows. He preferred the penumbra, the yin of life and its sinister underbelly. Therein lay his power, deep within the hidden. His desire for revenge had grown, dark moon by dark moon, until it had flowered into an oleander plant, every part as toxic as the rest.

The cold feeling in his heart spread around the rest of his body into a sublime sensation of ecstasy. At that moment, he knew the Mongol forces were going to defeat the Chinese. Yes, revenge would be his.

How he ached to play his bamboo flute.

CHAPTER 44

The Consecration Ceremony

When God created mankind, it was his design that those with knowledge
Should awaken those who were still ignorant.
I am one of God's people who has awakened first.
It is for me to awaken others – for who will do so if I do not?
THE BOOK OF MENCIUS

Luli woke up. Where was she? At home? No, she didn't have one anymore. Bao
and his henchmen had seen to that. The room was dark, other than the one
cast on the wall by a solitary lantern. The cold air made her breath steamy. The
night was thick with sounds, like the hoot of an owl passing overhead. She had
felt like a crepuscular thing, creeping around the Bagua tunnels. Oh, yes, that
was how she had ended up with dirty feet and a mud-stained sarong – running
away from that Bao the ogre.

A man groaned in pain in the corner of the room. That was Cui. She was
meant to be caring for the poor man. It was a miracle he'd survived Gang's
thrashing.

Now she knew where she was – in the temple infirmary. She was squatting,
knees by her chest, back pressed against the wall. Her bones ached. At least she
wasn't outside where the water froze and the rats chased anything that moved
looking for food.

She tucked in the old soldier. If she wasn't mistaken, the man was engaged
in an inner struggle to keep the hounds of death from devouring his soul. Then
there was his brother, Wuzhou. Everyone awaited news of his return – to learn the
identity of the forces gathered on the ridge. Rumours had spread like the sand that
blew in from the Gobi. Mongols – they had to be Mongols. With her yin-yang
eyes, Luli already knew who they were and some of what they were about.

Cui might be near to death but Luli felt not far behind him. Her son was unjustly incarcerated, and now her Po Office was no more, leaving her cast adrift on the currents of life's great ocean. She craved Heavenly purpose. That was her goal. Instead, she felt utterly ashamed of herself – how had she allowed all those bequests to go up in smoke? Perhaps Dong would pity her and take her in.

Lost in these dark forbidding thoughts, another man started snoring. Oh, yes, that was Bolin. He was the shadow in the other corner.

"Ju," Bolin mumbled.

Bolin was talking in his sleep. At least the Baku, the nightmare eaters, hadn't consumed all of *his* dreams. Despite that, they had devoured all of hers, good and bad, except the one that concerned her precious son. She prayed that the dark clouds enshrouding Ru's life should part, that the healing rays of the sun should allow him to recover from his long illness, so that he may feast at the table of life, however tardily. How she clung to that dream!

"Ju." Bolin murmured again.

Were the Baku invading his sleep? No, she wasn't having that. She shook his shoulder.

"What is it?" Bolin murmured, rubbing his eyes. "Is... is he all right?"

"Cui is fine," she said, although in matters of life and death, like in any marriage, it was a protracted negotiation between his will and the will of Heaven.

"Then why...?" He sat up.

"...You were talking in your sleep."

He rubbed his face with his hands and muttered, "I was dreaming of Wing."

"Wing? That's odd." Actually, it was interesting. Maybe she could broach the unresolved matter of the letter she showed him.

He stifled a yawn. "What was I saying?"

"You were talking about 'Ju'."

"Ju, the flower? The golden chrysanthemum?"

"You tell me."

"Ah, now I remember. Wing was leading me towards a door with a golden chrysanthemum emblazoned on it."

"What does that flower mean to you?" she asked.

"It doesn't mean anything," he blurted out.

"Well it should," she said, biting on her anger, "and I'll tell you why, *birthday boy.*"

"What do you mean?" he said, surprised by her abrupt change of tone.

"It's another anniversary, isn't it? And you know which one. But you are in denial."

"I... I don't know what you are talking about," he shrugged.

191

"Yes, you do," she snapped.

"No… I don't. What do you mean?"

"It can't have escaped your notice that today – your birthday – also happens to be the anniversary of the death of the Dragon Master."

"No, I realised that, but it's just a coincidence," Bolin said with a wistful air. Then he added, "Wait, his body was never found. How do you know for certain that he's dead?"

"Don't forget that I have yin-yang eyes too," she vented her feelings. "You've already come to see me and denied who and what you are. Not content with playing the fool once, you're doing it for a second time. You're like a man who's found the keys to Heaven, but prefers to keep them in his pocket, just to make sure he never loses them. Please, accept who you are."

"And who am I?"

The third night watch rang out across the fortress and intruded into their conversation.

Luli heard a clamour, like the sounds of a distant thunderstorm. Men's voices, shouting. The temple bell rang out. Alarm.

"What's happening?" she asked, distracted.

"Let's find out," Bolin said and flung open the door. She and Bolin peered down the corridor. There were raised voices in the outer courtyard.

Someone shouted, "Fire!"

Doors slammed. Donkeys brayed in fear. Owls screeched overhead. There was a roar of fire and yellow flames reached high over the temple roof, licking the blue-white stars. The alarm bell started thudding. There were sounds of men running fast towards them. The footsteps got closer. Around the corner came Dong and a group of monks.

Palms resting on knees, he gasped for breath. "Fire! Run! Save yourselves!"

"How? What's happened?" Luli yelled, frantic.

"The abbey's on fire. I have a very good idea who started it!" Dong said.

From outside the infirmary came the sounds of shouting. Luli peered towards the temple gatehouse. Orange flames hungrily consumed the wooden gates. Monks' cries filled the air.

"Cui," Luli said, shaking his shoulder. "Wake up."

"Leave me be," Cui mumbled. "I deserve to die. This is my time."

"No!" Luli said, "Gang is a monster. I won't leave you for him to finish off like a dog."

"It's karma," Cui said.

"Why? Whose?" she objected.

Cui was adamant. "I'm ashamed to tell you." He seemed to be struggling with himself, wanting to confess and at the same time, reluctant to do so.

192

"I know," Bolin said, "it's to do with the farmstead you said you torched back in the day."

"Mmm," he murmured. "I told you I kept that red kite – with a rat emblem on the handle – after a raid." He was eloquent, as if the fire of truth blazed in him and given him his tongue. "The barbarians were hiding out in local farmsteads. We were ordered to attack one. At the time, we'd no idea we'd received the wrong information. We followed orders and slaughtered the family living there. The rape of the women… that was nothing to do with me. I tried to stop them… somehow, Gang must have witnessed the atrocity and survived. I am so ashamed." Cui buried his head in his hands.

"I wasn't your fault." She pitied the old man. His past had just collided with the present.

Dong was standing at the door, insisting, "We have to leave. The fire's spreading fast, come on!"

"One moment," Luli said, holding out her hand.

Cui spoke with a lump in his throat. "That's why I didn't try to stop him. It was karma. It had caught up with me."

"No!" she said, insistent. "You were following orders. You did not deliberately murder an innocent family. I refuse to leave you behind to the flames."

"You'll have to," Cui said with a weary sigh. "I'm done. I can't move, even I wanted to."

She was not satisfied with that. "I will not see you sacrifice your life on the altar of Gang's ambition. You will live. Bolin, Jin, there's a sedan chair outside. Help move Cui into it."

"We must be quick," Dong said. As they hustled Cui into the sedan chair, the flames were leaping up around them from the gatehouse, spreading across the roof tops and onto the main building. The tremendous heat scorched the wooden rafters. The sounds of terror echoed around the burning cloisters.

Jin and Bolin hurried down the corridor and out the back gate, carrying Cui. The temple was a giant incendiary, lighting up the canopy of Heaven. The pagoda was one huge burning candle. The temple sent shards of flame into the scorched air. Dong's face was screwed into a coil of wrath. The stifling heat chased them across the open meadow towards the back of the temple.

"Where can we go?" Luli asked, wiping the sweat from her brow.

"Through there," Dong pointed to a fissure in the rock. Bobbing up and down with the weight of the sedan chair, they negotiated the twists and turns of the path, climbing into the rocks above the temple.

Dong led them into a cave halfway up the hillside. It was a Taoist grotto – dedicated to the Eight Immortals. A place of sanctuary and healing, it was a perfect place for Cui to recover. From the entrance, Luli peered down with a mix of disgust and awe at the scene of indiscriminate destruction unfolding in the pass. A huge conflagration engulfed the temple: elegant pagodas, cloisters, chambers, smaller temples and the infirmary, rare statues, prayer wheels and spirit tablets, even the beautiful orchard, ornate gardens and the small meadow; all were ablaze.

Dong was livid. "Centuries of toil, decades of prayer and years of good deeds. All gone up in smoke."

"I don't understand. Why?" Luli asked, breathless from the hasty retreat. "With the garrison under threat, who has done this?"

"You don't know?" Dong snapped, lines of fury etched across his face.

It sounded like she should.

"It's Gang's orders," Dong said.

"Yes and I know why," Luli interrupted, "Gang is a very clever and evil man. He wants one thing – revenge. On China."

"I agree," Dong said, his voice as firm as the mountain. "That's why we need this…" he added, reaching into the folds of his gown and pulling out a scroll. "This is what Gang fears the most. It's not the temple he wanted to destroy; it's this. Can you decipher Taoist Magic Script?"

She shook her head.

"Then I'll translate it for you." Dong said. Then with an air of unabashed glee, he read out its title, 'Laolongtou, Consecration Ceremony.'"

"There's another line underneath. What does it say?" Luli asked.

"Only to be read by the Dragon Master, in the presence of the Dragon Pearl."

CHAPTER 45

By the Flute

As the bamboo flute responds to the earthen whistle,
As two half-maces form a whole one,
The enlightenment of the people is very easy.
Therefore, do not present them with perversity.
THE SHI KING (BOOK OF ODES)

Gang emerged onto the roof of the Yamen, Bao in tow. His assistant was turning into a tame puppy and he didn't even require a lead.

The shards and embers of the temple fire were like shooting stars in the night sky, illuminating his path to glory. "You have excelled yourself," he murmured in admiration.

"Thank you. It's a rich sight," Bao replied with a scowl. "I've never liked those monks. When I served under Magistrate Park, Dong always undermined the civil proclamations and then hid behind his 'follow the true path of the Tao' nonsense. The citizens are so gullible; they believe every word he says. Good citizens serve their fief lord, not the priesthood. I pleaded with Magistrate Park to arrest him, but he claimed Dong never quite breached that outright subversion the law needed to detain him."

Well, here was another unexpected boon, Gang mused to himself. He could exploit a man with Bao's toxic enmity and local knowledge. Gang said with a satisfied grunt, "Park was soft as soapstone. I'm a granite mountain. In me, Dong has met his nemesis. If anyone asks, you weren't anywhere near the temple when the fire started."

"It will smoke them out," Bao said with confidence. "I left Sheng and Big Qiang to tie up loose ends. We'll soon have him and luscious Luli in custody."

"Tomorrow I'll take care of her son," Gang said with relish. "Prepare the punishment yard. I want everybody to witness his long, slow dance with a cangue."

As Bao turned to leave, Gang called him back.

"Your mention of Park reminds me," Gang said, "I want to interrogate his son again. Bring Feng to my chambers, right away."

"Yes, Your Honour," Bao said, making a reverence.

"Oh and bring Liu; I might have use of his persuasive arts."

Alone at last, he sighed and sat down cross-legged beneath the flag pole. It was flying the red and black flag that denoted a curfew. The sound of the fourth night watch blessed the fortress and everyone in her.

To Gang, life felt good.

Up above, the stars flickered, like shards of Heaven in the night. Back on earth, the greedy flames consumed the temple. Behind the red-yellow conflagration, the mountains reared up like huge demons, bathed in the eerie light of the fire. His fingers moved without effort across the holes of his bamboo flute. The melody was elegant, simple, with a haunting crescendo. As the flames of the temple rose into the air, he played the tune again.

The higher the pitch on the flute, the higher the embers rose into the night sky. When he lowered the pitch, the flames spread along the ground, like a thousand lithe serpents, then across the temple gardens until they licked the base of the magnificent pagoda.

He could control the fire – he was the fire-bringer.

This was uncanny. Soon he would possess power over all the elements, even the Laolong.

As his playing built to a rousing crescendo, the flames responded in kind, licking the trees like a lover's tongue in the throes of passion.

He grinned. Heaven was shining on his quest for revenge. This was his zenith. He felt ecstatic. The flames snaking up the side of the great pagoda brought back memories of his house and his family, how they'd been consumed by devastating fires. How he had survived those first few days, a child alone in a huge world, he had no idea. He had lived on the road, in the woods, gathering and selling firewood, cleaning the roadside latrines, stealing clothes from the washing line, drinking from puddles and eating berries.

In the end, Heaven rewarded his perseverance. A kind family took him in and gave him an education. A voracious learner, he passed the Jinshi, the imperial examinations. Through his family's influence, he served in the Jinyiwei, the Emperor's secret service. That was how, twenty years ago, he had arrived as a raw recruit in Shanhaiguan to spy on General Tiande. Now he was no longer Jinyiwei. He was the county magistrate.

After a while, he paused and watched the flames lick the sky and bow to the stars. The fire crowned the pagoda; this, a crowning moment in his life.

A little later, he was sitting in his chambers, gazing into the bronze mirror on the window opening and contemplating the interview with Feng. He was desperate to know how much Feng had discovered about the Jade Chamber. Before the memories came flooding back from twenty years ago, four runners hustled Feng in through the oval doors.

Bao said, "Now, cur, kneel before the magistrate!"

Feng's robe was mud-stained and he smelled like he'd washed in a latrine for the last five days; which he probably had. Behind Feng loomed the menacing presence of Thousand Cuts Liu.

"You can have your father's papers back now," Gang said to Feng, waving at a wad of papers by the window.

Feng screwed up his face. He appeared to appreciate neither Gang's generous offer nor his sense of humour. "I don't need them anymore, thank you," Feng spluttered.

"How disappointing. I kept them just for you." He could not resist a chuckle.

"Did you?" Feng reacted. "Is that all you want to talk about, a few insignificant papers?"

Ominously for Feng, Liu rested his huge hands on the prisoner's shoulders.

"Your father's plan of the fortress is a very important document. Imagine if it fell into the wrong hands," Gang said, opening it out in front of him.

"What are you implying?" Feng said, eyes blazing.

"That you planned to hand it over to the Mongols, to assist their attack."

"Are you serious?" Feng asked.

Gang thumped the table, "I didn't bring you here to listen to your inane prattle. You're a part of the Mongol conspiracy and I want to know what their plans are. Either you tell me, or I'll ask our friend Liu here for a little help." It was always a good ruse to bring Liu into the conversation. Once that happened, most people sang like a song bird.

Liu was a meticulous man and placed his special wares on the table opposite. He opened the folds on a leather holder full of knives, neatly secured in pockets of different sizes. Every knife, spike and thumbscrew gleamed in the lantern light.

"Torture," Liu declared, "is a key to Heaven, since it unlocks the truth. The truth greases the wheels of justice. Without torture, the imperial edifice would fail to move. That is why I am its worthy and eager servant."

Gang knew this already, but it was always a pleasure to hear it from the lips of a master practitioner.

Liu plucked a knife from its sheath and thrust it in the air. Then he lovingly ran his index finger along the blade, sighing like a paramour in the midst of foreplay.

"All right," Feng admitted, "I do know…"

"…What do you know?"

There was a long pause. Feng watched Liu running the flat of its blade against his cheek and swooning with pleasure.

"I… I know about the… deal," Feng stammered.

Gang sat back in his chair, fingering the arm rests. "What deal is that?" he asked.

Thousand Cuts was running a long hunter's blade over his forearm, a thread of crimson testament to its incisive sharpness. The malicious smile on Liu's face was quite sufficient to terrify Feng.

"The explosives deal," Feng blurted out. "Don't let him near me," he pleaded. "Please, I'll tell you anything you want to know."

"What explosives deal?" Gang said, hiding his annoyance. How did Feng know about it? This was serious.

"A merchant was arranging to purchase them from another man. I overheard their conversation, translated it for Kong from the Mongol tongue. Kong said he was going to claim the reward."

"Kong, you say…" Gang was caught out. Kong hadn't told him – the viper. He would deal with him later. He pressed on with Feng, "The Mongols, eh? Well, they're camped in the shadow of the wall, they've spies in every wine shop and their army is blotting out the rays of the sun. They've butchered our scouts like animals. And you say there's a traitor in Shanhaiguan selling explosives to that vermin. Tell me the names and quick. Otherwise Liu will demonstrate his considerable range of skills on you."

"If I do, will you mitigate my sentence?" Feng pleaded.

Gang nodded at Liu, who smashed Feng over the head with a truncheon, knocking him to the floor. Groaning, Feng got up, rubbing his head, blood streaming from the wound.

"I'm waiting," Gang sneered. Although of course he already knew the answer to his own question.

"The merchant Guanting," Feng said.

"So in this deal, was he the buyer?"

"I think so," Feng said, still dazed.

"And the other man…?"

"…Was a soldier."

"His name?"

"Honestly, I would tell you if I knew," Feng said, wincing under an anticipated blow that mercifully didn't come.

"Shame," Gang said. He recalled the details of the plot: Guanting had purchased the explosives from the disaffected Major Renshu. Altan arranged that, on a signal to be determined, Guanting was going to blow open the Zhendong Gate, allowing the Mongol army to overrun the Shanhaiguan Fortress and deal a fatal blow to the Prince of Yan's military campaign.

However, Guanting had run off and left Gang to prosecute the plan. The explosives were safely stored away until they were needed. In the end, he needed to know one thing – was Feng telling the truth, or did he really know the soldier's identity?

Gang nodded at Liu again, who whipped out a blade so quickly that Feng didn't see it coming. In a moment, there was a long gash down his cheek, from eye to jowl. Crimson blood oozed from the wound, as it opened its lips to kiss the air. Feng cried out loud and clasped the wound with his hand.

"I. Don't. Know." Feng cursed. "You have to believe me."

There was a long silence. Liu was growing impatient and licked the edge of his blade, scoring his own tongue. He kept glancing at Gang, wanting permission to torture Feng. Gang was thinking. The great elemental powers stirred inside his soul and he heard them whisper, 'He's telling the truth.'

"Fine," Gang said. "I believe you. Woe betide you if I find you have been lying to me. I will set Liu on you and you would wish you'd never been born. Understood?"

"Yes, Your Honour," Feng said, clearly a relieved man.

"Bao," Gang said, snapping his fingers. "Find this military man. Whoever he is, he must have access to munitions and he speaks Mongol. Find those explosives. Search the garrison from top to bottom. And find that merchant," Gang said with a practiced scowl. Of course, he already knew what Bao was about to say next. But he let him say it anyway.

"He was reported leaving the city, yesterday at dawn," Bao said.

Gang feigned surprise and annoyance. He was the magistrate, so he assumed that no one would suspect him of conniving with Guanting. Instead, he thumped the table and shouted at Bao, "Dog's head! You've let him slip through your fingers. Bring him back. Now."

Although Gang reckoned that Guanting must be way out of Bao's reach by now.

He was asserting control over this torrid affair and reeled off a series of commands. "Find that beggar king. He's got questions to answer. Next, send a detachment of troops to the Laolongtou. The dragon is still in the Jade Chamber and needs protecting. Last, but not least, take him back where he belongs," he said, pointing at Feng and holding his nose, "I can't stand the stench of treachery any longer."

CHAPTER 46

The Mark of Shame

When a fish is placed in a pond,
Little there doth it find to please;
Deep down it may dive and lie,
Yet is seen with the greatest ease.
THE SHI KING (BOOK OF ODES)

Today, the chill wind, biting at his ears and fingertips, was a relief. For a while, back at the temple, Bolin feared he would be burnt to a cinder. Once Cui was rescued, he had left Dong, Jin and Luli and headed off on his own. He had to reach the Laolongtou. As he trudged by his village and across the mud flats towards the sea, he felt the thrill of life course through his tired body. It was a new dawn and he never felt closer to finding Wing. He didn't know how, but he was going to set the Dragon Master free. That was what Wing wanted, that was what the prince wanted and that was what everyone wanted.

The 'Ju' chrysanthemum dream and Luli's subsequent challenge had hit him hard. Albeit begrudgingly, he had accepted the significance of what else had happened on the day of his birth, twenty years ago. He had to weigh it all in the balance and decide for himself. What did he want? Who was he? What was he? Could he really be...? The potent thought nagged at the edge of his consciousness, seeking permission to enter.

The land approach to the Laolongtou was not viable, so he had to risk the sea route. He preferred the power of sail. He could still hear Master Wen's threats buzzing in his ear about trespassing on the Laolongtou. That meant Bolin's father would never agree to row him there, so he would have to do it himself. Like most things in life.

He found a rowing boat in the harbour. Over the years, his father had schooled him in the ebb and flow of the tides, the rise and fall of the winds and how to read the yin and yang of the weather. The strong current dragged him out to sea. He glanced back at the cloud of black and white smoke billowing out of the temple. He would have liked to have helped put the fires out, but what he was doing was more important than the temple.

He pulled on the oars, invigorated by the salt spray. Out to sea he was free, at least temporarily, from the stifling pall of conformity that gripped him and his contemporaries. He felt like one of those eunuchs the Emperor employed to guard his concubines. A eunuch was half a man. What good was half of anything to Heaven? Bolin wanted to be a whole man. Then it clicked. Don't settle for less than the full quotient. Be brave and demand your full heritage. That was the message Luli was desperate for him to acknowledge. Now he understood. Find Wing. When he did, he would unravel the tangled mysteries of the past and clear the path for the future, both his and everyone else's.

He tacked against a breeze and edged closer to the Laolongtou. The dawn bled into the new day, as it danced to the eternal song of creation. The pale morning light enabled a cautious approach, one that drew no unwarranted attention from the guards, who appeared intent on looking landward. Besides, the guards were accustomed to seeing fishing vessels and rowing boats cutting back and forth.

He tethered the boat to the snout of the Laolongtou and scrambled across the seaweed encrusted rocks, slipping and getting soaked by the cold waves. Exhausted and shivering, he hauled himself over the lip and into the outer vault. He tried to stand, but his muscles were in spasm and he fell back onto the hard rock. He rolled over into a puddle and waited until the gift of movement was restored.

The dawn rays shed their blistered light onto a door at the back of the vault. There it was. The one he'd seen in his dream. He crawled over to it. The tide was lapping over the lip of the vault, so he had to paddle across towards it. Covered in seaweed, the floor was as slippery as the magistrate himself. All that defined the 'door' were three seams – two vertical and a horizontal – in the rock. Bolin was neither a competent magician nor a sorcerer and had no idea how to open it. He ran his hand around the seal, but there was no way to prize it open.

He heard a shout from above.

"Come out, give yourself up."

The voice sounded familiar. It had a slight Mongolian twinge: Major Renshu. The major shouted, "Whoever you are, there's no escape."

The next thing he knew, a coil of rope hung down from the wall and flapped in the wind against the nose of the dragon. They were coming for him. Damn.

201

Caught trespassing on sacred soil, he would be tattooed on his forehead and exiled to Szechwan or some other remote province. The mark of shame would kill his parents, who would be blamed for his crime. The dreadful consequences unfolded before his eyes. At least Renshu didn't know who he was – for the moment. If only he could open the door of the vault.

He laid his shoulder into it. It didn't move. He heard the sounds of scraping against the rock face above the vault. A foot appeared, wearing a soldier's boot, dangling in the void of the vault opening.

Dawn was bathing the vault in shadows. In his dream, Wing had led him to the vault in shadows and shown him the door to the Jade Chamber with the chrysanthemum emblazoned on it. He examined the door again, expecting to see a 'Ju', a chrysanthemum. Nothing – only the grain in the stone.

Think. Ju. The Golden Chrysanthemum. He whispered the word 'Ju' to himself.

The door shimmered, like vapour rising from the ground on a scorching hot day.

He couldn't believe it. He spoke the word out loud, this time like he knew what he was doing.

"Ju."

Heavenly mists blurred his vision and the next thing he knew, the door had disappeared into thin air. How? Whatever had happened, where the door once sat, there was an opening into the Jade Chamber, itself swathed in darkness.

He edged over the threshold.

In a flash, the door reappeared and 'closed' behind him.

CHAPTER 47

The Wolf Pack

You are better off as grass by the roadside,
Than wife to a soldier at war.
LAMENT OF A CHINESE SOLDIER'S WIFE

Gang did not sleep a wink. After interrogating the imposter Feng, he had returned to the Yamen roof and played his bamboo flute for the rest of the night. Like the sun, the great Yang Master, he had brought light where there was darkness, heat where there was cold and conjured fire from the embers. The scene was like watching a continual funeral pyre, where the corpse was the body of religion. *What glee, what ecstasy, to be me!* He would not want to be anything other than who he was, Gang – no imposter he, but the silent assassin, the stalker, the killer of dreams, a life like no other. It was by the far the best night of his life, with the promise of more to come.

My, he had enjoyed witnessing how Altan pulled on the strings of Heaven. What a marvel of nature. What symphonic glory. What unadulterated delight! How did he do it? The shaman was at the pinnacle of his powers. The dawn or 'breaking yang' watch heralded the ceremonial opening of the city gates. Pointedly, the commandant ordered the Zhendong Gate bolted and the drawbridge left firmly up.

By the time the sun had traversed the celestial sphere, Gang and Altan's plan would reach fruition. Soon, Sheng and Qiang would transport the explosives from the shed in the alley to the Zhendong Gate. Until then, Gang could relax, as he sipped his morning tea and munched on some sweet pastries.

Gang called for his sedan chair and the porters took him to the Zhendong Gate, where Tung was haranguing his beleaguered troops. The commandant looked as pale as the winter snows on the Yanshan Mountains.

"What a night – the temple ablaze," Tung complained. "You know anything about how it started?"

"No, why should I?" Gang said defensively.

"I just wondered. Besides, I've more pressing concerns," Tung murmured, pointing at the Mongol camp fires on the horizon.

"What are their numbers?" Gang asked.

"Thousands," Tung replied. "And it appears they have brought up reinforcements during the night."

The sight of smoke rising from the hundreds of fires into the still dawn air drew from the commandant a weary sigh. That was excellent. The commandant was already exhausted.

Tung explained his dispositions, "Along the east-facing front line, there are five towers of battlements, the Zhendong at the centre. Clustered around each of them, I have posted several hundred armoured soldiers clutching pikes and swords, a unit of archers and various ballistae."

Gang was pleasantly amused. Tung seriously believed that these defences were going to withstand the might of Altan's spectral army.

"Yesterday," Tung said, "my troops were assaulted by invisible blue wolves, fashioned out of thin air. While they fought valiantly, their morale is fractured. They could do with some supernatural help. They prayed that Abbot Dong would provide them with protective amulets. Now that's not possible."

Gang pitied Tung – almost. As far as he was concerned, Tung could station the combined might of the prince's armies there; it wouldn't make any difference to the outcome.

He said with as much sincerity as he could muster, "You are to be commended, commandant. The troops are prepared for battle and we're bound to win."

In his mind, he could hear the haunting flute melody he'd played on the Yamen roof. What a conflagration. The temple fires were still bleeding embers into the day's sombre clouds. Once Altan had weaved his spell and Big Qiang had blown the Zhendong Gate to pieces, the Mongols would swarm into the fortress. The Chinese would capitulate and the Mongol army would re-occupy the Zhongguo. That would be the pinnacle of his life's work. Before that, there were tricks-a-plenty to play.

A guard of the Zhendong Gate shouted, "Ai yi yi!"

Everyone peered over the battlements. Even Gang felt a twinge of fear. It was a hideous sight. They were wolves, a pack thirty or forty strong, racing down the coast road towards the Zhendong Gate. Their bodies seemed translucent in the rays of the pale morning sun,. It was as if they were there, but they weren't there. They were an incandescent, shimmering blue.

They weren't ordinary wolves. They were spectral; half bound in Heaven, half on earth. That was why, Gang assumed, that everyone could see them. While he waited, he suppressed a smirk.

"It's another Blue Wolf attack. Men. Stand firm. Have no fear," Tung said, his eyes loaded with dread.

Gang was going to enjoy the carnage. "So it is," he replied, as he watched the sublime work of the master spell weaver.

They watched in frightened awe as the wolves approached, hell bent on fury. Even Gang expected the rampaging pack to pull up on the edge of the moat and there raise a clamour. That was its purpose – to hold back the enemy and keep the garrison safe from attack. Wasn't it?

"Archers. Take aim," Tung shouted from where they stood on the gantry, his voice hoarse with fright. Their arrows were cocked, their aim steady. Would the spectral wolves succumb to mortal weaponry?

"Unleash the fury!" he yelled.

The bowmen unleashed a volley of arrows, as the wolf pack raced towards their appointment with death.

CHAPTER 48

The Jade Chamber

Go out with awe.
Come back with fear.
THE SHI KING (BOOK OF ODES)

Black. Not a hint of light. Bolin was breathing heavily. Then his head screeched. Ai yi yi, he'd had headaches before, but this was like someone had smashed a hammer against both temples.

He turned around, his hands reaching for the door. What door? It was a wall. In a panic, he'd forgotten it had closed behind him. He banged his fist against the rock. Ouch. This was karma. He had wanted to breach the Jade Chamber and he had succeeded.

There was an odour. My, it was rank. It smelled of decay, pungent and acrid. It was so obnoxious, he almost fainted. This was ten times worse than when he had swilled out the school latrines.

He needed light, any light. From his girdle, he pulled out a candle stub, a piece of wood and a borer. After several attempts at grinding the borer into the wood he gave up; both wood and borer were too damp after the crossing in the rowing boat. They would dry out after a while and so would he.

Until then, all he could do was explore the chamber. He flattened his back and palms against the door and edged sideways to his left, crablike, feeling along the chamber wall. It was smooth as glass. The ceiling was the same. And the colour bottle green with black berry and yew green veins ran through his mind. The floor was composed of the same, dense, smooth stone.

Reaching the first corner, his left foot struck a small, hard object.

"Pick it up," a voice spoke to his soul. It was like a whisper, like when his father would encourage him after he had tripped and fallen. So he wasn't alone in the chamber. Wing was nearby and helping him. He puffed out his cheeks. Stuck in the dark, he obeyed.

As soon as he touched it, his temples started pounding like the drums in the Bell and Drum Tower. He saw images of a man on a horse, charging full pelt at an opposing army, his scimitar cutting them to shreds. He saw more death, the same warrior cutting the heads off a thousand men, stripping the skin from their heads and piling the skulls in a pyramid as high as the Great Pagoda.

Bolin was holding a piece of metal in the shape of a 'u' – a horseshoe and judging from its rusty, uneven surface, an old one at that. As soon as he dropped it, the visions stopped.

Coupling that with the piercing head pains, he guessed it made of was iron. Why was there an iron horseshoe in the Jade Chamber? He had no idea. He carried on exploring the chamber. What was iron to do with? He tried to remember, but his senses were pitching like the rowing boat on the Bohai Sea.

From the first corner of the chamber, he followed the second wall. Now that the initial panic had subsided, he grew accustomed to the livid darkness and his yin-yang senses activated. There was an invisible entity in the chamber that felt imprisoned. As he sensed it, he felt as if it was watching him, which in any other circumstance would have been very strange. Also, it was peculiar that he felt he was with an old friend. Was that Wing? He guessed it must be.

Reaching the second corner, his foot brushed against another horseshoe. The first one wasn't there by chance. He wondered if there were horseshoes in all four corners. Why would someone do that, anyway? If only he could recall what Jin had told him about iron.

He turned again, working his way along the back wall. Then his left ankle touched something on the ground, this time not metallic. He felt along its rough, curved surface. It was made of woven fabric. Pacing it out, it was eight steps in length – a rolled up carpet. Well, he wasn't sure what he expected to find in the Jade Chamber, but two horseshoes and carpet weren't high on the list.

He tried the borer and wood again and this time a small spark leapt out of the ether onto his candle wick. Yes. Light. How light changed everything! Amidst the flickering shadows, he saw the walls were a deep green jade with black serpentine-like veins.

This was the famous Jade Chamber.

In the middle was a rectangular altar. He brushed off a fine layer of dust and discovered a golden candlestick and candle, a glass jar, sealed at the top, a low bowl containing a clod of earth and an empty silver cup. The four objects seemed to glow with an inner light as he picked each one up, cleaning them with his sleeve.

The objects were arranged in a square, with a fifth golden, heart-shaped container in the middle. Its raised centre held a small, spherical object, like a pearl. These must be sacred ceremonial items.

What was the rolled-up carpet doing there? It was more than incongruous, it was suspicious. Unrolling it revealed part of the pattern; there were a shock of greens and browns in the background and on the foreground, some animals claws – a bear or a tiger or a dragon – attached to the end of a leg, a blue animal's leg. Blue.

Wait. There was something solid in the middle of the folds. With his heart pounding, he felt around it. There was silken fabric… a gown. Inside it, an arm… or what remained of one. That was the source of the pungent smell. The limbs were cold, stiff. A body.

He backed away in shock. Vaguely, he could hear Renshu and his men beating against the outer door, trying to gain entry. He felt numb, empty inside. Without looking, he knew it was Wing's body. He had solved the mystery of his disappearance. Why him? Was it karma?

Like dragons dancing on clouds, thoughts flashed through his mind. Now he understood the cries of 'release me' and the feelings of intense compression and bludgeoning suffocation. Dragon Master Wing was talking to him, to Bolin.

He opened the rest of the carpet. The silver claws and blue paw belonged to a Blue Wolf. He should have known. The carpet was full of the beasts; claws bared, mouths wide, leaping out of the fabric like demons out of Yama. So, Wing had had his last breath squeezed out of him by a rampant pack of Mongol blue wolves, albeit embroidered on a carpet. Bolin shed a tear, not for Wing, but for the terrible way in which he'd lost his life.

Bolin had remembered that the Mongols disposed of their nobles by suffocating them in a rolled-up carpet. This was a Mongol mercy killing which left the body intact, with no external marks. Whoever did it twenty years ago was steeped in Mongol ways, yet respected Wing. Who then? Renshu? As far as Bolin knew, the major was only a decade older than he was. That made him too young. The mystery of Wing – and Cheng's – killer remained. But he was closing in on them. He'd bring them to justice. Heaven demanded nothing less of him.

This was… a dragon's lair.

Oh my! The thought struck him hard. He wasn't alone in the chamber – he was with the Laolong. With his yin-yang eyes, why couldn't he see the beast? The candlelight cast a shadow on the corner of the chamber where he found another horseshoe. So there were four. Then he found four more, one each around the corners of the elemental altar. That made eight in all.

Then he remembered. Iron horseshoes warded off the spirit worlds and weakened the power of dragons. This chamber was a prison... for no less a captive than a dragon. The Laolong was present, but dispersed in the spirit worlds, like salt in the ocean.

He was trapped in the Jade Chamber with a dragon and Wing's dead body for company and no way out.

CHAPTER 49

Blue Heaven

In the heat of the attack, words can't be heard – so cymbals and drums are made.
In the smoke of the battle, visibility is poor – so banners and flags are made.
Use cymbals, drums, banners and flags to focus and direct people's ears and eyes.
THE ART OF WAR

Gang could not believe it. Nor could the commandant and the soldiers. The arrows passed straight through the wolves and thudded into the frozen earth behind them. Far from halting or even slowing their rapid advance, the arrows seemed to spur the pack onwards towards the Zhendong Gate. The arrows had failed to pierce raw flesh, leaving not a scratch. How was that possible? He glanced at Tung, whose face was a picture of awe and panic, but mostly panic.

The rabid pack closed on the fortress. The drawbridge was up but that didn't deter them, as they dashed across the empty space over the moat, paws on a bridge of air, and right through the drawbridge. Momentarily, they disappeared from view in the arched tunnel beneath the gate.

The commandant had lined up his bravest troop just inside the inner gate, but they had not been expecting a spectral attack. From the battlements where he and Tung stood above the gate, Tung yelled at them, "Men. Stand firm! The blue wolves are coming!"

There was a strange hiatus in the moments before the pack reappeared on the other side of the tunnel. The men seemed to visibly wilt; shoulders slumped, heads bowed. Some shuffled on their feet, fingering their lances. Many looked to Heaven for mercy. Gang could have sworn that two of them stood in their own pools of urine. It would make no difference to their fate. Altan had conjured these beasts from Heaven – or was it hell?

The macabre pack scudded out of the tunnel and leapt like missiles at the phalanx of soldiers, who slashed at the fiends. Their cuts made a swishing sound as their swords swept right through the spectral beasts. Others stabbed at the ghostly wolves with sharp daggers, their weapons as useless as paper knives.

Snarling and pawing with tooth and claw, the wolves landed on top of the men, throwing them backwards onto the cold stone. The brave soldiers thudded to the ground clutching the terrible beasts, in some horrific lovers' embrace as life danced with death. Arms punching and legs kicking the air, it was the most bizarre sight, like some ghoulish synchronised grovelling.

Neither sword, nor pity, deterred the rampant wolves.

It was as if the air itself wielded subtle knives, cutting the men, slicing legs, arms, hands, ears and noses. The wolves gnawed at the soldiers' throats, blood spurting everywhere, their silver-blue coats stained in the crimson of the victims, rendering them grotesquely visible in the pallid daylight.

It was fierce and deadly. The troop of valiant men lay on their backs, carved into a deathly sculpture of blood and gore. They lay next to their own ghosts.

Even Gang suffered a nervous glance over his shoulder. Would the wolves spare him? He wasn't sure. He trusted that Altan had them under his spell.

Tung was stupefied. Poor man. He couldn't defeat a foe immune to the point of a sabre or the thrust of a halberd. These were killing machines of the highest order. Every guard along the battlements stood frozen with fear. There was no way to fight off these furies.

The panic spread. A terrified soldier standing in reserve behind the slaughtered unit dropped his rapier and ran. Gesticulating wildly, he raced across the Bell and Drum Square, beseeching the gods of mercy. Another from his unit followed, then another and another. As the wolves' attack grew in ferocity, the strength and courage of the troops wavered. The men, raised with a reverence for Heavenly things, were swamped by fears as real as the blood gathering in pools around the dead soldiers. Soon, they all turned and ran, chased by the fiends from hell.

"Archers, stop them! Get them!" Tung yelled. To a man, the archers froze, suspended by the anguish of the moment, their bows hanging useless by their sides. Did Tung mean the deserters or the wolves? Men screamed in anguish as the pack hounded the fugitives through the alleys and byways, leaving a trail of bloody spoor behind them. To Gang, the jarring cacophony of fear and confusion was like listening to the beatific music of the spheres.

There was more to come. The men stationed on the wall stood there like straw dogs, useless, inept, a sacrifice to the demons. No one moved. No one even wanted to move, which was perfect. Having witnessed the deserters running across the square, the archers also raced down the ramp, infected by the same yellow cowardice. This precipitated a further exodus, as all ranks fled for their lives.

To Gang, the scene was better than a comedy.

Only the brave remained.

"This is some dreadful sorcery," Tung muttered, as he strode down the ramp to inspect the carnage. His words hung in the air for what seemed like an eternity, delving into each of the men's souls and examining their fabric for any sign of weakness. Many lesions were found, but none in Gang's mind. He followed Tung. He was enjoying the rich smell of cowardice.

Avoiding the thick, red pools of blood, Tung examined the dead. One man's throat had been ripped out, exposing his innards, a squeamish mess of blood and gore.

"This man has the same eyes as the scouting party." Tung's voice was heavy with defeat.

Gang stooped over the corpse and muttered, "Oh, so he has." Trying not to sound too triumphant, he added, "The eyes are... blue."

That sign was ominous... for the Chinese. Altan had done it. The alchemist had done what he'd promised to do. Without fighting one battle, the Mongols had the Chinese running scared. The blue wolves were pissing on the Chinese from a great height and he loved it.

This was his moment. If he was a painter, he'd have captured this moment on canvas – the impotent arrows of the archers and the blue wolves rampaging at the heels of the deserters. If a poet, or historian, he would have snatched the words from Heaven and described in lyrical detail the beginning of the end of a short-lived and ultimately cruel and abortive Chinese dynasty.

He was in blue Heaven.

CHAPTER 50

The Elemental Altar

Good men are a fence.
The multitudes of people are a wall.
We must not let the Great Wall be destroyed.
Nor let the Prince be solitary and consumed with terrors.
THE SHI KING (BOOK OF ODES)

Bolin thought he heard a hoarse, rasping growl. Was that the dragon? If it was, he sounded ill, like he had a sore throat. *Mind,* Bolin thought *if I had been cooped up for twenty years in a place of little ease, I would be grumpy, too.* Then again, he was not a supernatural entity and he had to find a way out of the Jade Chamber.

Down here in the depths, was he safe, alone with the Laolong? How could he know? What did the Laolong 'eat'? Was he dragon food? He thought not, otherwise Wing's body would be mutilated and it wasn't. Even so, the chamber was cramped and the wick on the candle wouldn't last much longer.

There was a deep, low thud against the outer vault door. Renshu – the major must be trying to batter his way in. Over the years, they had tried many a time to break into the Jade Chamber, but the rock was as thick as the wall at the Zhendong Gate.

He was drawn by the objects on the altar. Hah! Look, a clod of earth, a bottle – for air, a candle – for fire and an empty bowl – for water. Of course, the water had evaporated. What would happen if he completed the four elements again? There was one way to find out.

Where to find water? Easy. His clothes were drenched from the crossing in the rowing boat. Lifting his sleeve above the bowl, he squeezed out a few drops. The salt in the water made it holy enough and able to hold the currents of ch'i.

He lit the candle on the altar, flame kissing yellow flame. He waited and watched. With his yin-yang senses, he listened – ah, he heard a soft, long, exhalation. The dragon's sigh?

What next – an utterance, the words of a spell? He didn't know any spells, so that wasn't going to work. Still, he had a vague idea something was missing. He had earth, air, fire and water, but there was a fifth element in Taoist cosmology – metal. No, it wasn't that, because the bowls were gold and silver. What about the container in the centre? It was designed to hold a small round ball – the Dragon Pearl. Where could he find that?

The smell of Wing's cadaver smacked against his nostrils. He couldn't leave him lying on a half-open carpet. He decided to roll it up and keep Wing like that until he could bring him to the surface. As he bent down to pick up the edge of the carpet, he inadvertently brushed his hand against Wing's neck, tilting his head to one side. Wing's mouth jerked open and a round object fell out of it. He raised the candle to take a closer look. It was a small, lustrous, milky-white marble. No, it wasn't. It was a… pearl.

Ai yi yi! The Dragon Pearl!

What had Wing said in his letter? 'Find the Pearl of Wisdom, which waits for you in *the place where words are made*.' In his mouth, of course. In retrospect, the riddle was simple, like most things in life. If he had not been such a practiced dunderhead, he would have worked it out much quicker.

He placed the Dragon Pearl in the centre of the circle of elements on the altar. The dragon's reaction was a soft thrumming, like the patter of light rain on glass. He wasn't sure what he'd done to help the dragon. But he hoped and prayed that the Laolong had been at least partially released from some long confinement.

This dragon stuff was easy.

He felt a draught on the back of his neck. He glanced around at the back wall of the chamber. There was a door and it was open. It had been integral to the wall, like the one through which he'd entered and he hadn't seen it when he looked earlier. It must have opened when he placed the pearl on the Elemental Altar. It was a way out and a huge relief.

He peered out of the door. There were some steps leading up to the surface, which he guessed opened onto the Laolongtou. Candle in hand, he ascended the steps. He reached a trap door and yes, that was where it opened. At the sea end, a group of soldiers were leaning over the battlements, holding ropes and shouting down to their comrades.

He was determined to remove Wing from this awful tomb and bring him and the truth of his death into the light of day. Returning to the Jade Chamber, he collected the horseshoes. From the folds of his robe, he retrieved a large piece of silken white fabric. He tore in it two and used one half to wrap the horseshoes, depositing all eight of them outside the chamber.

The other half of the white silk cloth, he draped over the carpet and Wing's corpse. That way, he hoped the guards would recognise and respect the fact that he was carrying a corpse.

At that moment, Bolin heard a deep, satisfied purring. That was the Laolong. Pleased he had managed to ease the dragon's plight, he murmured, "Glad to be of assistance."

At one time, he would have thought himself delirious to have spoken to thin air. Not anymore. The Laolong was as real as his hand. He had to admit, he was beginning to enjoy this Dragon Master business. He feared it meant he had accepted who he was, but he hadn't time to think on it.

The carpet was not as heavy as he'd feared, he guessed because Wing's body had dried out. He hauled the long carpet up the narrow steps, emerging into the brisk morning air.

On the Laolongtou, his sudden appearance through the trap door took the soldiers by surprise. The old duty officer came bundling over to him and shouted, "Stop. Who are you? Where did you come from?"

Puffing and panting from the climb, Bolin pointed to the trap door. The officer glanced at it and back at him. Unimpressed, he unsheathed his sword and waved it under Bolin's nose.

"Put that away," a voice boomed out. It was Master Wen accompanied by some new conscripts.

"You'd better answer his question though!" Wen said. The rest of the soldiers stared at Bolin like he was some weird apparition.

For once, Bolin used his wit and said, "You see the white shroud of mourning," he pointed to the fabric draped across the carpet, "There's a body wrapped in its folds. It's Dragon Master Wing's."

"Are you sure about that?" Wen asked, a look of surprise and awe on his face. "He's been missing some twenty years. So you'd better show us."

With the utmost care, Bolin unfolded the rolls of the carpet. On the final roll, the guards and Master Wen let out a collective gasp of amazement.

"His face, his body; it's a miracle!" Wen stammered.

In the clear light of day, Bolin could see Wing's cadaver close up. Although the dead man's face showed some decomposition, the effect of the Jade Chamber had preserved many of his features and a wistful smile played on his pale lips. Wing still wore the trappings of a Dragon Master, a long multi-coloured cloak replete with cosmological symbols girdled by a belt of yellow silk.

"To be so well preserved, he must have led a righteous life," Wen said.

The old officer kow-towed and the apprentices followed suit. Master Wen led them all in a solemn prayer of thanksgiving. Carefully, they placed the carpet on a small hand-drawn cart.

Some distance away, the drums of the Bell and Drum Tower throbbed with alarm. The raucous clash of battle beat out from the fortress. Bolin glanced up to see the world in upheaval. Across the neck of the pass, five or six li from where he stood, he could see the advance of the Mongol van. Beyond the fortress, the temple fire was still ablaze, shrouding the distant mountains in clouds of smoke and blackened fumes.

"What are you going to do with him?" Master Wen asked.

"The commandant must be informed that Wing has been found," Bolin said, sounding mature beyond his years. "In the midst of a brutal assault, Tung will be unable to come and see him here. So, I will take Wing's body to him."

"We will go together," Wen said.

CHAPTER 51

Rosemary and Thyme

Heaven has conferred on man a divine nature.
True accordance with this nature is called the path of duty.
The regulation of this path is called instruction.
THE DOCTRINE OF THE MEAN

Luli had seen Cui right. He was sitting up, smoking his pipe and regaling her with stories of his time in Karakorum, the Mongol capital. That was when he and General Tiande had put the city of wooden huts and circular tents to the torch. What a sight that had been! They had captured a herd of Mongol war ponies, sturdy little things, as hardy as thistles – and with no saddles, just as prickly to ride. The Khan's horse was long dead, but many of its horseshoes had been salvaged. The rumour was that they were kept for some obscure supernatural purpose, though no one knew exactly what. Finally, Cui told her how he had clutched their war lance – which had attached to it either a white pelt for peace or black pelt for war.

Dawn had broken. From the grotto opening, Luli looked down on the chaos unfolding around the Zhendong Gate. She had to enter the fortress and get to the punishment yard, which was where they would take her son, despite the Mongol assault. Today was the day of Ru's punishment and she had to be with him. She would not let him suffer. What mattered was that Ru was saved from the clutches of that devil Gang and pardoned for the crime he never committed.

Now her Po Office was gone, she was close to bitterness. What remained amidst the burnt embers of her life was her trust in Heaven. If that broke, then she would too.

These thoughts buzzed around her head as she set off down the hillside, the huge square fortress straddling the neck of the pass before her. On the wall itself, she could still discern the profile of faces, beautiful in the early spring light. They still faced the same direction, showing the flow of ch'i from the high Tibetan mountains in the west to the Bohai Sea in the east.

She felt sad as she hurried passed the temple grounds. The few surviving monks were scrambling around the rubble trying to salvage anything of value – a holy artefact, a noble sculpture, a rare manuscript or a silk gown, an incense burner or a precious bequest, even a wooden stool or flint. To witness the sorrow on their smoke-stained faces was harrowing.

The pagoda was like a crumbling chimney, a pyre of heat and hot ash, billowing black cloud into the morning air. The main temple was but a few shards of wood, blackened by a man with a beleaguered heart. But there were small mercies amidst this maelstrom – Dong had saved the scroll of the Consecration Ceremony, the homecoming song of the Laolong. When the time came, they would use it to invite the dragon back to his home in the Great Wall.

Until then, there was chaos ahead as she approached the north gate. The garrison's troops were billeted in the north quadrant. This morning they were nowhere near their beds, nor on duty on the wall road. No, they were streaming *out* of the north gate, encumbered not by a back pack and weapons, but by eyes tortured by terrible visions. What on earth had they seen? Many cast furtive glances back over their shoulders, like they were being chased by the hounds of Yama. The crowds prevented her from reaching the gate, so she grabbed a fugitive by the arm to ask what had happened. The man pulled away from her. His face was a dark mirror pitted by inconsolable fear.

Finally, a bedraggled soldier stopped in his flight, "Miss, follow us. Don't go in there."

She winced. His breath stank of rice wine. "What are the soldiers running from?" she asked.

"The blue wolves," he whispered, as if speaking too loudly would summon the dread creatures. "There's a ghostly pack chasing us. Can't you see them?" He didn't wait for her answer.

Peering through her yin-yang eyes, she saw clouds of dirty violet, dark reds and mucky purples, hanging in sheets of ch'i above the fortress, those shades and hues a sure sign of death and frenetic destruction. She spotted a few stragglers – spectral blue wolves. But then she noticed that one had a tail missing, a second had no legs and a third was just a dismembered head. Their spectral shapes were fragmenting, appearing and then reappearing. It made her think that whoever was responsible for creating them was running out of the mental ch'i to sustain them.

Then there was hope for an end to the carnage.

There was nothing she could do to persuade the soldiers to return to their duty, so she squeezed through the north gate and scampered past the main barracks. At this time of day, early to mid-morning, this would normally be a hive of activity, of off-duty soldiers cleaning their kit, to street vendors selling melon seeds or touting vodka and Jinhua wine.

Not today. It was as deserted as the Gobi.

She was determined to catch Ru before he was taken from the cells. She wanted to accompany him to the punishment yard, hold his hand for the last time – before it was dismembered. The thought of it brought tears to her eyes and she welled up. She could not let him see her like that. She had to be strong.

She found the back way to the cells, a narrow alley that ran between the prison and the magistrate's chambers. Before she arrived there, she noticed a donkey cart and a couple of men. They paused on the corner, glanced suspiciously to left and right and trundled off down the alley. They had not spotted her but she had seen them, all right. One was Big Qiang, the other Sheng.

Peering around the corner, she watched them park the cart in front of a wooden shed and then disappear inside. Moments later, they came out carrying a large crate bearing military insignia, which they loaded onto the cart. Soon, they had moved seven or eight of these crates onto the back of the cart.

A steady beat of drums resounded from the direction of the Bell and Drum Tower. This was no ordinary roll, it spelled military alarm. The beating was frantic and the sound amplified as the drummers smashed the drums with heavy bamboo sticks. The Mongol attack was imminent. When she glanced again down the alley, the mules were very upset by the percussive blasts and were not shy in letting their owners know about it.

When the drums stopped, she could just hear Big Qiang telling the donkeys, "Rosemary. Thyme. Will you stop that, please?"

Rosemary was not listening. She snorted and her pretty little nostrils flared in evident disgust. Thyme preferred the more destructive back leg kick, not conducive to anyone seeking a long, healthy life. Sheng dived out of the way of a potential broken limb.

Qiang threw his hands up and yelled some more at Rosemary and Thyme. It made not the slightest difference. He and Sheng should have consulted the almanacs before deciding this was a day for moving heavy loads. Qiang planted his hands on his hips and after a moment of inspiration, rummaged in the cart and pulled out the elixir for mules. Carrots.

While the mules chewed on their meal, Luli noticed six burly men approach from the far end of the alley. She'd seen them hanging around earlier on, rough-looking types, wearing old trousers, coloured waistcoats. The leader wore a tatty black turban.

Keeping out of sight, she watched as the black turban grabbed Big Qiang around the throat and the two tussled in the alley. It took four men to subdue Sheng, who fought like a tiger. Rosemary and Thyme got on with more important things like carrot munching.

Luli could wait no longer. She turned and ran, taking the long way around. Ru needed her more than Rosemary and Thyme.

CHAPTER 52

The Mongol Scourge

Do not stop an army on its way home.
THE ART OF WAR

From atop the Zhendong Gate, the cry rang out, "The Mongols are coming."

Gang was excited, the decisive moment had come. Advancing towards the fortress, hundreds of Blue Wolf banners fluttered in the breeze.

From the top of the Bell and Drum Tower, a series of tumultuous drum rolls announced the enemies' advance to the Chinese army and, Gang hoped, to his associates, Qiang and Sheng. When they had met the day before, Gang had reminded them of the plan, 'Wait for the drum roll signalling the Mongol advance. That's your signal to move the cart of explosives to the Zhendong Gate. Leave it in the middle of the arched tunnel and blow the gate, the tower and the drawbridge to dust. The Mongols must have unrestricted entry to the fortress.'

While he waited for Sheng and Qiang, he watched Commandant Tung gather the scattered remnants of his forces, basically those foolish enough not to have already fled the battlement, the fortress and if they could, the world. Tung positioned the swordsmen along the wall road and the archers in the five towers facing the barbarian foe. He held the cavalry in reserve, as if that would do him any good at all. Besides, they wouldn't hold out for long, not after the Zhendong Gate blew up.

The approach of the Mongol host was slow, giving him ample time to admire the perfection of Altan's timing. The blue wolves' assault had softened up the troops, planting an enduring fear amongst the poor wretches. Now, it was a question of prodding that naked fear with a sustained assault. Altan never failed to impress. The man was in touch with his inner Tao. Not so the guard standing opposite Gang on the ramparts – he was anxiously peering up the coast road, waiting for the final assault.

"The Mongols are strangers to mercy," he whispered in the guard's ear. The man's face went as white as the snows on the peaks of the Yanshan. Well, Gang was just telling him the truth, warning him what was coming his way. The guard didn't see it like that, because his eyes almost popped out of his head and his mouth drew back in terror. The man jettisoned his spear, which clattered into the stone wall, next to Tung's boot. Discarding a weapon was a serious dereliction of duty. The guard knew that. So did Tung. Gang smiled – he'd prompted the desertion quicker than he'd hoped.

The guard ran down the ramp, arms gesticulating and screaming profanities into the unforgiving air. Then another guard threw down his sword and his courage and, shouting curses of hell fire, chased after the first. Scores more deserted their posts, ditching their sabres and their pikes and joining the frenetic race for freedom.

Freedom from what? Gang wondered. From the blue wolves? They hadn't seen one for some time, so perhaps Altan had called them off. From themselves? No. Gang had learnt that people carried their demons with them with tender devotion. From servitude? That depended on Tung's response, which was a sharp retort, "Bowmen. Arrows to the ready."

A detachment of bowmen advanced to the edge of the battlements and took deadly aim at the clutch of fugitives.

"Loose," Tung commanded. The bowmen unleashed their killing arrows, raining death into the backs of the deserters.

Amidst a deathly silence, the commandant yelled across the ramparts, "Clear away the dead. And if anyone else wants to desert; please, go ahead. You know what fate awaits you." No one took him up on his generous offer.

Renshu reported from the Laolongtou.

"Major, I called you back here because we need to prepare for the attack. How many do the Mongols' number?"

"I would estimate ten thousand," the major replied, scratching his chin, "consisting of units of cavalry, infantry and siege machines."

That appeared a gross overestimate and Gang assumed the major was exaggerating the Mongols' strength to undermine Chinese morale.

"That's a strong force," Tung replied, his tone weary and exhausted. "We oppose them with an army low on morale and depleted by desertions. I've sent runners to the prince for reinforcements, which I pray will arrive soon. Until then, we need to augment our forces with as many men as possible."

"What do you have in mind?" the major asked.

"This is what I want you to do…" the commandant replied.

Feng stood in the square by the Drum and Bell Tower. He fingered the long gash down his cheek, which had just begun to grow a scab. But despite the pain, and after so many days cooped up in the darkness, the fresh air, open space and the dim rays of the morning sun felt sublime. Wearing ankle shackles, he was lined up with the other prisoners. He had no idea why. From the resounding drums and the red flag above the Yamen, he did know that the Mongols were advancing.

Opposite them on the square, their ranks were swelled by civilians from all walks of life – shopkeepers, scribes, silk merchants, cooks, waiters, officials, runners and administrators.

With the civilians lined up on one side and Thousand Cuts Liu guarding the prisoners on the other, they were separated by the podium, where the commandant was in deep discussion with Major Renshu and Magistrate Gang.

Feng heard the major ask, "What a rabble. Are you going to rely on these vermin?"

"How dare you question my command? I'll deal with you later," the commandant retorted and strode to the edge of the podium.

"Prisoners," Tung addressed them. "An attack is imminent. Many civilians are going to fight, but we need more brave men. Fight the Mongol today and tomorrow I'll grant you a full pardon."

This was karma all right. Feng was ecstatic. Even Ru broke into a half-smile. The prisoners slapped each other on the back.

"Take a step forward if you agree," Tung said.

That step was lighter than a feather. To a man, they took that small step into a huge freedom. Suitong hobbled in last of all.

"Good," Tung said. "Liu, remove all the shackles."

Feng could finally stretch his legs. No more shuffling along like an old man. What a relief.

"Commandant," the major said to him.

The magistrate piped up with his complaints, "Do you know what you're doing? These reprobates will sooner make a run for it or cut your throat, than fight the Mongols. And this boy Ru. He's due in the punishment yard later today and until then I want him back in prison. Withdraw him from this rash and ill-considered plan of yours, otherwise he'll abscond as sure as night follows day."

Tung glared back at him. "You're worse than the major! Do you want the Zhongguo to fall? Do you want the dark days of the Mongol Dynasty to return? Because your words suggest that you do. So be careful both of you, or I'll arrest you for treason. Is that understood?"

Tung was quaking with anger. To Feng's astonishment, the commandant called for him. Was he going to arrest him as a traitor? Should he try and make a run for it? His mind was buzzing and his legs were so unaccustomed to walking without iron shackles, he stumbled awkwardly over to the podium.

"Yes, Commandant Tung," he stammered.

"You have passed the Jinshi examinations," the commandant said through gritted teeth. This was a surprise, he had not expected compliments.

"I need an educated man like you to keep this mob in order," Tung continued. "I am short of officers. I am going to enlist you as Captain."

"Captain? Are you sure?" He could not believe his ears. His head was spinning so hard his ears nearly flew off. Karma was shining on him, until…

Gang yelled, "Commandant! Stop. You can't do this."

"You again?" the commandant scolded. "What now?"

"This man is a traitor," Gang claimed. "He'll sooner sell you to the Mongols than serve the Zhongguo."

"No, he's not," Tung said. "And I'll prove it to you."

This was an extraordinary confrontation between the most senior civil official and his military counterpart. Tung opened a scroll and announced, "I have a letter here from Tiande, the great General Xu Da."

Feng recognised a copy of the letter which Gang had taken from him. How on earth had the commandant acquired it?

The commandant waved it in the air, saying, "This letter confirms the truth. Warriors of the Zhongguo, I present to you General Xu Da's missing son, who you know as Feng, but who is now Captain Xu Yingxu!"

The commandant raised Feng's hand above his head. The crowd responded with unabashed enthusiasm. Feng had not expected this. He felt as if a heavy burden had been lifted from his shoulders. In a moment, his position was rightfully restored – and more. At last, someone had trusted him.

With a lump in his throat, he said, "Thank you, I am honoured."

"Now, pick up your weapons," Tung thundered. "And fight like dragons."

"Like dragons!" the men responded, piercing the air with halberd, sword and pike.

The recruits hurried to their places. Feng felt a shiver of power course through his veins. For the first time since Park's death, he felt like a man again, helped in no small part by the wave of respect from his peers.

The Mongol attack was heralded by the loud thumping of drums and percussive clashing of cymbals. Feng could barely hear himself think, but then again, that was the purpose of the clamour.

With the noise circling like vultures around the battlements, the Mongols wheeled up their huge catapults and launched burning missiles into the sky. The first incendiary traced a fiery arc over the Zhendong Gate, landing on top of the podium at the base of the Bell and Drum Tower. With One Hand Zhou directing affairs, the dousing teams brought the fire under control. Another incendiary smashed into the upper reaches of the Zhendong Tower itself, spreading fiery embers into the morning air and panic into the bowels of the men. The water teams rushed to douse the flames, as the battle of the elements continued.

Two lines of heavy oxen pulled forward a siege engine, a huge wheeled contraption of tethered bamboo struts, poles and planks, followed by troops carrying ladders, ropes, harnesses and tackle for scaling the walls.

"Make ready to repel the attack," Tung yelled above the blistering noise of battle. Mongol archers sent over a hail of arrows, some of them fire arrows, others no doubt bearing the unwelcome gift of poison. One flew by so close to him that Feng felt it brush past his ear and clatter into the wall behind him. Thank Heavens for karma.

Tung deployed the catapults, launching dragon sticks, ox-bow lances and tiger bombs into the midst of the enemy van, creating havoc with explosions, maiming and wounding the foe.

Risking life and limb, a detachment of Mongols bridged the moat by the Zhendong Gate with thick planks of wood and then wheeled up a great battering ram. Time and again, they smashed it into the drawbridge, which began to buckle under the heavy assault. The Mongol archers protected their precarious position by firing volleys of arrows high into the morning sky that dropped down like killing rain upon the Chinese troops.

Along the length and breadth of the walls the Mongols scaled bamboo ladders like monkeys. In bloody hand-to-hand combat, the fighting breached the top of the wall. Scores of Mongol warriors leapt over the parapet and onto the battlement walkway.

Feng was on the front line, encouraging every last morsel of bravery from both veterans and recruits alike. With his life and reputation intact again, he felt invincible. Fearless for his own safety, he threw himself into the thick of the action, killing the Blue Wolf foe with his captain's rapier. When he lost his weapon, he grabbed a Mongol by the throat and throttled him. The man – no, he was barely a boy – dropped to the floor like a sack of rice. Then Feng kicked a ladder from the battlements, the soldiers on it toppling backwards and crashing into the hard, unforgiving earth.

Bolin and Master Wen made slow progress along the wall road from the Laolongtou. With the battle raging in full view, the guards at the Ninghai City Fortress nervously examined his identity tablet. The captain of the guard prodded the carpet gingerly and muttered,

"Wing's body? Found just like that? After twenty years of searching? That's impossible."

Wen's strong and sturdy presence yielded all the reassurance they needed.

From his position on the wall road, a couple of li from the Shanhaiguan Fortress, Bolin was afforded a natural vantage point overlooking the dispositions of the Mongol forces. By his reckoning, only about a one tenth – about five hundred – were engaged in armed combat, with the remaining nine tenths held in reserve. That seemed like an unusual tactic. He was no military expert, but he thought those numbers ought to have been the other way around.

He took a closer look at the Mongol army. Hundreds of open wagons carrying soldiers facing each other in two rows, clinging on to their lances and pikes, waited to be called into the fray. On the far side of the battlefield, near the foothills of the Yanshan Mountains and beyond the infantry wagons, were several large detachments of Mongol cavalry.

On the exposed wall road, Bolin felt the wind gust in from the west. He rubbed and blew warm air into his hands. Beyond the fortress, in the foothills of the Yanshan, the temple still smouldered, the pagoda pumping black smoke into the air.

Above the Zhendong Gate, Feng and his cohorts were locked in close combat and were leaping around the battlements like they were going to repel the Mongols single-handedly. Feng was the undisputed Captain of the Wall. His hands were covered in sticky, wet blood.

Tung killed one attacker with a rapier thrust to the stomach and ripped off another's head with a single fierce blow.

With his single leg and single arm, Suitong had managed to climb up on the battlements and jump onto the shoulders of a Mongol intruder. While he mashed the mutton eater with his stub hand, Ru helped out by bashing the enemy's head in with the broken half of a halberd.

The fighting was fierce and unrelenting at all of the five towers facing the barbarian. The air was thick with smoke and cries of death. The stench of blood was obnoxious. Crimson rivulets ran down the Zhendong ramp, making it slippery for the soldiers, medical staff and animals going back and forth. There were bodies, limbs, hats, stray footwear, broken swords, discarded rapiers, strewn along the road wall, Chinese and Mongol, dead and wounded.

The battle was in flux; hundreds of men locked in close combat, cries of pain and victory filling the vortices of hot swirling air.

As the Mongol van battered the drawbridge, Gang was fretting.

Where were Sheng and Qiang? The dog's heads were meant to have blown the gate by now. He trudged down the steps of the Zhendong Gate to look for himself. Nothing. Not a cart in sight. He was livid.

And he was still seething about Ru and Captain Feng. Hah! Employing prisoners as soldiers! He had never heard the like of it. And how had the commandant obtained the general's letter? However it had happened, Tung had it now and everyone knew who Feng was. Well, it wouldn't make the slightest bit of difference because he, Gang, could control the elements. He could still take his revenge on that piece of fowl dropping, Feng.

Altan and his makeshift army couldn't sustain the scale of the assault for much longer. They were up against an ancient, monumental opponent – the Great Wall. It would take some breaching. In the attempt, the Mongols were suffering heavy losses. If the drawbridge wasn't blown soon, they would break themselves on the wall.

Sensing the vapours of victory, a Mongol deputation strode up the Zhendong Gate with a message.

In the midst of a lull in the battle, the messenger cried, "Surrender! Open the gates. And we will give you back your lives."

"What are we going to do?" Feng asked. He already knew the answer.

Tung asked the major, "What's your assessment?"

Renshu took a deep breath and said, "The Mongols are swarming over our walls. Though we've repulsed their ladders, many of our veterans have given up their lives. Their battering ram is on the verge of breaching the drawbridge. It's only a matter of time before they run amuck. Then they will deploy their reserves, which are as numerous as the grass on the plain and we'll be hard pressed to keep them out. In short, our situation is volatile and precarious."

"Your recommendation?"

"Accept their terms. Lower the drawbridge and open the inner gate."

"What? Surrender? Never!" Tung scoffed.

"They won't give us another opportunity," Renshu reminded him.

"Do you think I don't know that already?" Tung thundered. "The deceptive feint is their favourite military tactic. If we surrender, they'll murder us all and pile up our skulls in a pyramid outside the gates. No. We fight to the death."

Bolin was passing the Jingbian Tower, the most southerly of the five gates on the Shanhaiguan Fortress. With only one or two more li to the Zhendong, he glanced into the sky and noticed a strange phenomenon – a black cloud of fiery dust and embers blowing over the fortress. It drifted over the battlefield and headed towards where the Mongol reinforcements were drawn up.

Then one hot ember dropped out of the cloud and onto a wagon carrying Mongol troops. Despite being some distance away, Bolin saw it drop onto a soldier's uniform, which caught fire. Next, the man's trousers were ablaze. The strangest thing was that he didn't move. He just sat there, like he expected someone was going to extinguish it. In moments, the flames engulfed the man completely. It was the most unnerving thing Bolin had ever seen. The soldier was burning alive, without as much as a scream. Even more incredible, none of the troops in the same wagon moved one hair's breadth to help him or fetch water.

Soon the wagon load of troops was alight. Not one of them made any attempt to run away, or evade the killing flames. It was supernatural.

A gust of wind blew up, dispersing the black fiery cloud but fanning the hot flames. The fire spread rapidly to the other wagons.

Was it mass suicide? Now, hundreds of troops were alight and scores of wagons were ablaze, sending billowing black fumes into the scalding air.

Bolin scratched his chin and gasped, "That's uncanny."

"Sorcery more like," Wen snapped. "Come on. You don't need yin-yang eyes to see what's really happening."

"Oh-ho!" Bolin stammered. "I may be the new Dragon Master, but I'm struggling to reproduce my predecessor's insight. Please, help me, Master Wen."

"All right," Wen scolded him. "The troops are not real. My guess is they're paper models. I'd wager a roll of the dice that their weapons are as wooden as their courage. The whole thing's a ruse. The Mongols are experts at that," he added with a disparaging air.

"I should have known," Bolin tutted.

"Listen," Master Wen said, puffing and blowing in the ambient heat. "What's the easiest way to take a monumental fortress like Shanhaiguan? Simple, persuade someone on the inside to open the gates. That's the art of war. The show of force of the troops in the wagons was a contrivance. And those camp fires we saw on the horizon? I doubt there was one real soldier next to them. My guess is that they were pure theatre, for our benefit. Dragon Master Wing would have deciphered that on his own and without my help. You've a way to go to catch him up."

Bolin bit his lip and said, "Give me time. I have confidence in my ability to succeed."

Feng was exuberant. The new recruits let out a huge cheer, more of relief than victory. The Mongol infantry reinforcements were no more. The paper soldiers were burnt to a cinder.

"I've never seen the like of it, in all my years campaigning." Tung scoffed, as his guards and soldiers embraced one another.

"It's not over yet," Gang murmured.

"Why's that?" Feng asked.

"Look," Gang jabbed his finger at burnt out wagons, splattered corpses and the bloody detritus and broken dreams of war.

The remaining Mongol reinforcements – their cavalry – were forming up in four lines, each several hundred men long, which stretched like a curtain across the neck of land.

"What are they doing?" Feng blurted out.

Tung scoffed at the manoeuvre, "You watch. I bet they're going to charge."

Feng slapped his thigh. "I've seen some tricks today, but this one takes the prize. A cavalry unit is going to charge a fortress surrounded by a moat? I don't believe it."

The officers were clapping each other on the back, tears of joy streaming down their faces. It was hilarious. Despite that, the cavalry was on the move, a sedentary walk at first.

"Oh, here they come," Tung said, bent double with laughter.

Feng looked again. They were coming.

Ai yi yi! This was ridiculous. Feng couldn't take his eyes off them. Their walk became a trot, then a canter. Soon the Mongol force was heading their way, pennants held high, weapons at the ready, the men seemingly fixed on one last unbridled attack.

"Wait a moment," Tung said, shaking his head. "They can't be, can they?"

The cavalry wore an air of impending menace and the canter had become a charge. The horses snorting and panting, heads down, riders bent low and not a saddle in sight. They were about a li and a half out from the fortress and at full pelt.

"They're doing it," Feng stammered. "They're really going to charge the fortress."

"Don't be absurd," Tung declared, all pompous. "How can horses charge the Great Wall of Ten Thousand Li? It doesn't happen."

"Beg to differ," Gang said, smarmy to the last.

"Wait a moment," Feng said. "Look at the riders' pennants."

"What about them?" Tung snapped.

"They ride like devils, but the pennants are not moving."

"By Heavens," Tung slapped his forehead with his palm. "They're phantoms."

"That's what I was trying to tell you," Gang said, his words as sharp as a Mongol blade.

The horses, now at full gallop, approached the ground about hundred paces from the fortress, where the wagons with their straw soldiers lay in a splendid morass of wooden struts, charcoal wheels and burnt out planks of wood. Normal horses would have become ensnared on the scattered debris, but the Mongol ghost cavalry rode roughshod over it as if it wasn't there.

"You know what this means," Tung grunted. "They're going to ride right through the walls."

"Just like the pack of blue wolves," Feng cried.

From the walkway, pushing the cart carrying Wing's body. Bolin watched the cavalry advance. They were four lines deep. They raced like demons out of hell. With one hand on the reins and the other holding a sword aloft, the riders yelled, "For the Blue Wolf."

Bolin murmured, "Heaven save us!"

As he spoke those prophetic words, the words of a summoning, strands of subtle ch'i oozed out of the Zhendong Gate, forming another wall, this one of yellow spectral energy. The ghostly force spread along the length of the five towers facing the might of the cavalry charge. It thickened into an etheric skin that eventually extended beyond the moat.

Bolin had a benign feeling about this strange mist. The Chinese army, so long hard up against the Mongol attack, stood in awe and wonder as this spectral fog embraced the eastern wall of the fortress in a swathe of golden ch'i.

Time seemed to move slowly.

Below the Zhendong Gate, amidst the carnage outside the drawbridge, a golden tentacle extended out of the mist and formed into… was that an arm? Yes, it was. An arm reached out of the mist towards the battlefield, and it wielded a builder's hoe. Another arm appeared, this one wielding a rake, then another with a shovel. Another appeared holding a whip, then more arms bearing spikes, spades and bolsters for packing the hardened earth, a trowel, shears, plungers. There were hundreds of them. In the next moment, a foot appeared and then a midriff, a torso and finally, the whole man; a peasant wearing a pair of rugged sandals, baggy trousers, a sleeve-less smock and a crude head scarf.

This first ghost, the leader, was a man who held his head at a strange angle. It was as if his head was twisted to the left. To face forward, he stood with his right shoulder to the front. He was followed by thousands of ethereal workers, emerging out of the golden mist. All of them thrust their rakes and spades and trowels into the air, their mouths open in a collective silent roar of defiance.

The leader brandished his hoe, cajoling his makeshift army to fight. Bolin heard a boy's plaintive yell.

"Father!"

Ru's cry of awe and elation echoed around the rooftops of Shanhaiguan, into the sky and around the very caverns of Heaven.

Heng's spectral army prepared to defy the oncoming riders, and wielded their tools and hoes and makeshift weapons above their heads like they were the sharpest sabres in all of the Zhongguo. Ducking down on their haunches, they waited while the hooves thundered towards them. Spectral dust billowed around them, choking their throats. Their enemy's fierce cries of hate filled the fractious air.

Heng delayed until the horses were right on top of them. Together, with a huge effort, the workers simultaneously forced their rudimentary weapons through the horses' exposed undersides, up through their carcasses, until they pierced the riders' hearts and souls.

With fearsome bravery, Heng's peasant army held the line as hundreds of Mongol ghosts perished for the very last time. A pernicious cloud of death filled the air. Carnage abounded and horses were upended. In a fleeting moment, a victory charge had become a prodigious descent into hell.

Bolin, the new Dragon Master, had a strong inkling how this had come about. By removing the horseshoes from the Jade Chamber and by renewing the Elemental Altar, he had allowed remnants of the Laolong to re-occupy a section of the wall by the five towers. The Laolong then did what it did best – repel the barbarian invader.

The Mongol men and pennants and uniforms and pikes and swords and horses, the whole awful phantom edifice, began to evaporate. Like swathes of mist dispersed by the warmth of the sun's rays, soon enough, it was gone, returned to the ether from which it had come.

The ghosts of the dead workers had saved the day. The Zhongguo was safe. The huge cheers along the ramparts reached into the Jasper Pool, the abode of the gods in Heaven.

Heng bowed to his fellow ghost soldiers. Along the entire line of the wall, the victorious peasant workers gathered their tools and re-formed their immaculate infantry lines. Without breaking stride, they followed Heng back into the golden mist from whence they'd come.

When they'd died in the construction of the wall, when they'd sacrificed their lives for the Zhongguo, no one had remembered them.

From that day on, no one would forget them – not Bolin and certainly not Ru.

Luli was frantic now trying to find her son. When she arrived at the prison, the main gate was wide open. With not a guard in sight, she tip-toed down the steps and into the cells. The silence was harrowing, the smell even worse.

The door to Ru's cell was flung open… and he wasn't there. All the cells were empty. The prisoners must have turned on the guards and grabbed the keys. Ru was free! Or had he been caught? Either way, she was petrified for his future.

Back at street level, loud cheer echoed along the ramparts. She ran to the main prison gate, where she found the street crowded with men rushing *towards* the wall.

"What's happening?" She grabbed an old soldier by the arm.

"Ah. We are deserters no more!" the fellow cried, showing more defiance than teeth. "News of our great victory brought us a change of heart, so we're returning to our posts."

"We've beaten the mutton-eaters," another soldier's song filled the air.

Luli was swept along with the heady crowd towards the Zhendong Gate. In the square by the Bell and Drum Tower, people were singing and dancing. The Duke's Mummers performed acrobatics on the stage and the musicians struck up a jaunty, patriotic tune. Stilt walkers strode like giants of old across the square.

So much for the celebrations, but where was Ru?

The returning troops ran up the ramps to the five towers, impressing Feng with their alacrity. There, they rejoined the brave but decimated ranks of the rest of the army. Together, they stood shoulder to shoulder in protection of the Zhongguo.

The sound of a brass trumpet split the battlefield in two. It resonated over the Shanhaiguan Fortress and all the way to the yurts of old Karakorum. The great Mongol general Subutai would have turned in his grave. Kublai would have shed a silent tear. Genghis would have turned away in disgust.

It was the sound of the death knell of the Mongol attack.

"They're retreating," Feng cried, pointing at the Mongols running down the coast road.

"A great victory, but at such a cost," Tung claimed. As he spoke, a Mongol arrow, unleashed by a retreating archer, thudded into the commandant's shoulder, sending him hurtling backwards. He skidded across the walkway and his head hit the other side of the rim of the wall, knocking him out.

"Get him to the infirmary," Feng ordered. A knot of soldiers wheeled up a cart and loaded the commandant onto it.

"In his absence, who is in charge, Captain Feng?" one of the officers asked.

"I am," Renshu said, stepping forward.

"Major," Feng said, "shall I prepare a force to give chase? We are nearly back to our full complement. We can finish off the mutton-eaters once and for all."

The major declined. "No!" He thundered. "Give chase and they'll lead us into a trap. The false retreat is a classic Mongol tactic. Besides, never stop an army on its way home."

"But—," Feng stammered and then held his peace. What a weird decision. The Mongols were a defeated, desultory rabble. Now was the time to destroy them. If it had been the other way around, the Mongols would have shown no mercy.

"You question my command?" Renshu thundered, glaring at Feng.

"No, Major." Feng held his peace. Even so, the major's decision was cowardly and inept.

Across the square by the Bell and Drum Tower, the cries of victory and the persistent drum rolls resounded around the fortress. The musicians strummed and piped the town from the sickness of defeat and desertion to the health of victory and reunion. While folk danced and sang in the streets, Feng felt a hand rest on his shoulder.

"What? Oh, Bao, it's you," he said. "Come to join the celebrations?"

"No. You are to come with us." Bao wore a deep frown and was accompanied by two steely-eyed constables.

Feng grew suspicious. "What's this about? We're free men now."

It was obvious that Bao didn't think so, because he scowled, "Constables, seize him."

They grabbed him by the armpits and lifted him off the ground.

"Put me down. Where are you taking me?"

"To the punishment yard, you are under arrest," Bao snarled, spitting into his face. "You and your other conspirators *will* account for your crimes. By order of the county magistrate."

Across the way, constables were arresting Ru and Suitong.

"Hey, you, stop that!" One Hand objected. "That Tung fellow promised us freedom in return…"

"…Arrest him too," Bao interrupted. They did.

Not only did Feng have a pretty good idea what was going to happen next, he also knew that this was a purge.

CHAPTER 53

The Punishment Yard

How marvellous is the Creator!
What will you be sent back as next?
Will you return as a rat's liver?
Or come back as a fly's wing?
THE BOOK OF CHUANG TZU

Walking into the punishment yard, Gang was at the end of his tether. Altan's master plan had unravelled before his eyes. Sheng and Qiang were to blame. It was their dismal failure to blow up the Zhendong Gate that had led to the Mongols' abject defeat. What had happened to them? Well, it didn't matter anymore. It was too late. The Mongol threat had flared, burned brightly for a while and turned to ash.

One phoenix remained. Revenge – bloody, merciless revenge.

To his immense satisfaction, Gang found that Bao had prepared the punishments with his usual relish and forethought. His assistant had brought several stocks, a selection of very sharp knives and a variety of other torture implements, ready for the infliction of an indecent amount of pain.

A high attendance in the yard showed a keen and dedicated sense of justice amongst the populace. The gods would appreciate that. As soon as the Mongol retreat had sounded, Gang sought to assuage his anger, sending out runners across the length and breadth of Shanhaiguan to promote the event.

This would be a fitting finale to an eventful day – and all because of karma. With almost the last arrow of the battle, the commandant had been removed from the garrison leadership, clearing the way for Gang and Renshu to wreak havoc amidst the ruins.

The seating in the yard was two-thirds full. Aside from the usual coterie of Shanhaiguan lictors and hangers-on, there were the regular thugs and brutes. In the far corner of the yard, he noticed an untidy knot of beggars, thieves and other reprobates, singing loudly and out of tune on last night's wine. Amongst the sea of faces he noticed the Beggar King. Although today he was dressed differently – no tattered black turban.

The remaining seats filled up with more inebriates. Despite, or perhaps because of, the early hour – it was around the middle of the day – they had deigned to vacate their precious stools in the White Mulberry Inn, at least for now. They desired a performance, in which the currency was pain. Who was he to deny them the delightful prospect of freshly-spilt human blood?

The punishment yard was Gang's favourite place – not only in Shanhaiguan, but in the whole of the Zhongguo. He dreamt about it, he revered and idolised it. To participate in and witness acts of gratuitous violence was more than a pleasure; it was a prelude to ecstasy.

"Here they come," a runner announced, bringing his reverie to an abrupt end.

The unmistakeable appearance of Thousand Cuts Liu at the entrance to the punishment yard was greeted with a wave of high acclaim. Behind him, neatly tied to a leash, were three pieces of dog's excrement, their names: Feng, Ru and Suitong. Liu led them past Gang and towards the dock. They each wore this wonderful look of aggrieved injustice mixed with bewilderment.

Liu tugged on the leash to spur them on but just when it was going so swimmingly to plan, Ru sat down and refused to stand up again, despite Liu's best endeavours to drag him along the ground.

"Ru," Feng said with obvious anxiety. "Get up, will you? Or Liu will beat us to pulp."

"What's the matter, little man, lost your toy soldier?" Liu didn't hold back the scorn.

Gang bestowed this pathetic scene a wry, satisfied smile. The darling mother had to turn up eventually. After all, this absurd theatre was partly for her benefit.

"Ru, you dog's breath," Suitong said, elegantly wiping his nose with his sleeve and spitting on the ground. He waved his stub hand in Ru's face, "Don't make it any worse than it already is."

It did occur to Gang that for Ru, it was about to get significantly worse.

Without any prior warning, Thousand Cuts smashed Ru with a truncheon. The mighty blow would have cracked open a piece of granite, let alone Ru's head. The crowd winced.

"Told you," Suitong said, with the air of a person who was often right but equally often ignored.

Gang had to admit – Ru was either mad or just horrendously stubborn, or possibly both. That truncheon blow would have mashed most people's resistance to a pulp. Instead, Ru sat there rocking back and forth in some morbid dance.

A woman's soft voice broke the uneasy silence. "Ru. I'm here with you... right now. Stand up, please."

Ru looked up and there she was; Luli. His mother. Though her hair bun was untidy, it was held with black lacquer pins. She wriggled her way through the people blocking the way and knelt next to him.

"Ru, my darling," she said, wiping away the blood from his forehead with the sleeve of her robe. She kissed him on the cheek, like only a mother can.

"Did you see father?" Ru's voice was weak, but full of pride.

"Did... I... see... *who*?" Luli said, pulling away from her son and staring at him like he was a Taoist Immortal.

"Heng's ghost. He's guarding the wall, protecting us," Ru repeated. "Father's army vanquished the phantom Mongol cavalry. He's a hero."

"He's always been my hero, as have you," Luli said, her voice quivering with emotion.

Ru rubbed the back of his hand on her cheek.

"Ru... you... can... speak," she cried, bursting into tears, her chest heaving. "Thank you." She whispered a prayer. Gang doubted the gods had heard it. They were probably busy elsewhere that day.

Had he a stitch of compassion left in his life's tapestry, Gang, too, might have shed a tear.

As Liu raised the lash above his head, Ru eased himself up and started walking. Liu put the lash down.

"Arrest her!" Bao shouted. Luli surrendered without resistance. The constables confined her in the dock with the others.

"Don't worry," Bao sneered, "we've brought along a spare cangue just for you."

Renshu came into the yard and joined Gang on the podium.

"Major, welcome," Gang said.

"My honour," the major replied. "I came to enjoy the entertainment."

"Good," Gang nodded and then leaned in to ask the major, "Do you know what happened to Sheng and Qiang? And the explosives?"

The major shook his head. "No, I don't. I thought you might."

Bao said with barely disguised glee, "I've a surprise for you."

"A surprise?" Gang replied. "What's that, I wonder? I do like surprises." He licked his lips lasciviously, a subtle act that brought back vivid memories of the last nights' frolicking with the Orchid sisters. He still couldn't decide whether he preferred black or white – or both together. He'd try to decide again tonight and made a mental note to thank Bao for introducing them to him.

"Bring them in," Bao shouted and two runners pulled a rickety cart into the yard. Bao tipped it at an angle and who should slide off the back of it, but a tawdry lump of no good by the name of Cui.

"Oh, good show, Bao," Gang said. "You excel yourself." Gang was beginning to feel his old, thoroughly nasty, self again.

It seemed like Cui was on his last campaign. He seemed only vaguely aware of what was happening. Blood was oozing through the bandages on his face and his back was bent double – not that that was going to induce any pity from him. The runners pushed and shoved Cui into the dock with the others.

Gang stood up, cleared his throat and announced, "You are traitors. I am bringing you to justice for the heinous crimes you have committed."

Captain Feng did not agree. "Is that right? You think you can prosecute us with these trumped-up charges while Tung is injured and otherwise indisposed. Well, you can't."

The crowd hissed. Gang wasn't sure if the disrespect was directed at him or at Feng. Not that he cared; he could control the elements.

"Oh, but I can," he said, his voice dripped with scorn.

Ru decided that, now he had his voice back, he could use it to air his pathetic opinions. Bad mistake. "You, Gang, are a spiteful, small-minded, unforgiving little rat," Ru blurted out.

Why did everyone think that rats were no good? He, Gang, quite enjoyed being one. On his nod, Thousand Cuts gave Ru a good thrashing. That quietened both him and the crowd, many of whom turned away in disgust.

Gang was impressed with Liu. He appreciated his efficient dedication to purpose.

"As I was saying," Gang continued. "You are my prisoners. I have a duty to ensure that the law is upheld. Crimes against Heaven must be corrected in the appropriate manner."

"I want justice!" Suitong complained. "My name was on the prince's New Year's amnesty list. I should be free."

"And how do you know this?" Gang asked.

"Captain Feng told me," Suitong replied.

"Suitong," Gang replied, "you have lived a commendable life and have only committed several murders. Soon you will start a new life, I promise."

"I will?" Suitong turned with glee to Ru and Feng. "I told you he'd listen to my plea."

"Yes," Gang confirmed. "When Liu separates your head from your body, you'll be free to start a brand new life in a new body. Perhaps you'll come back as a scorpion or better still, a viper. Now that would be fitting."

Suitong hung his head low. Gang shared a chuckle with Bao and Renshu. From the podium, Gang looked down on the criminal five. Of his enduring enemies, only the pestilential Abbot was missing.

Bao announced the punishments, "People of Shanhaiguan, Ru is a thief. His right hand is to be severed at the wrist and he will wear a cangue for the period of one moon."

Ru's head was fixed in the stocks and his hand tied onto the platter, horizontal, ready for the amputation. Liu unsheathed a huge sword and ran his finger along its length, an unnerving smile flickering on his face. The crowd were more terrified of Liu than his weapon.

Thousand Cuts swished the sword above his head in a practice blow, before bowing to the podium and lifting the sword high in the air, poised to strike the single blow of amputation. The world paused; Heaven was determining what should happen. The ancestors were inclined one way, the spirits of karma the other. On earth, though, a man at the back of the seating stepped forwards into the middle of the yard.

"Stop this," he ordered.

It was Kong; no longer beggarly, he was wearing a distinctive golden-yellow uniform with an identity tablet slung around his neck, portraying two dragons' mouths holding a pearl.

"That's the uniform of a Jinyiwei," Feng murmured.

"How dare you interfere with the prince's justice," Gang shouted at him.

"Justice!" Kong guffawed at this injunction and said, "Ru's case is a gross injustice. The boy is clearly innocent. I can – and will – intervene."

"That's nonsense." Gang was livid and shook his finger at Kong.

"No, it's not," Feng declared. "I know the law and so do you. The Jinyiwei are invested with the power to overrule local officials, like a county magistrate."

"Thank you, Feng," Kong said. "And if you don't believe my provenance," Kong turned to Gang. "Here's my sword of office." With that, he unsheathed the long, curved blade – such were only granted to members of the Jinyiwei.

Damn! Proof enough. Gang unleashed a scowl, "Is that the best you can muster?"

"All right, then I propose this," Feng protested, his eyes narrow with rage. "We are free to go, because Tung promised us all an amnesty."

"Save your breath," Gang interrupted with an undisguised air of triumph. "Tung is not here and in this court, I alone have jurisdiction. Major Renshu is currently in charge of all military matters. Besides, Tung promised you an amnesty starting tomorrow."

There, that told them.

CHAPTER 54

The Conspiracy

As you sow, so you shall reap.
Nothing slips through the net of Heaven.
ANCIENT CHINESE SAYING

Bolin had guided the cart along the wall road and witnessed the extraordinary spectral battle. So, the Laolong was a compound of the ghosts of all the workers who had died in the wall's construction. What a revelation. And they prolonged their usefulness into the afterlife, which was more than could be said for the mandarins, emperors, princes, consorts and the majority of Chinese officialdom; they all purported to serve the Zhongguo but behind the grand façade of office, they were steeped in greed, corruption and the self-interested abuse of power.

Where was the rotten triumvirate, Renshu, Bao and Gang? The guards at the Zhendong Gate told him. By now, the cortège was a hundred long and composed of people from all walks of life; soldiers, candle makers, iron mongers, horse traders, umbrella makers, street urchins, tea sellers, 'kerchief makers. Genuine people who mourned Wing's death and who cared with a passion about the destiny of the Zhongguo.

As Bolin led them into the entrance to the punishment yard, he saw the Beggar King, Kong, dressed in different clothes to usual and regaling Gang, Renshu and Bao on a podium. Before Bolin could ask Kong why he was wearing an embroidered uniform, Gang strode across the podium, shouting, "What's the meaning of this intrusion?"

With the cortège behind him, Bolin was not going to be intimidated by this petty official. "I have come to put things to rights," he said confidently.

"Hah! Another do-gooder," Gang scoffed. "Methinks this is one of the

Duke's plays, in which the characters are imposters, one and all. Guards, arrest this man."

Bolin ignored the man's ravings and wheeled the cart into the open space in the middle of the yard. He and Master Wen placed the carpet on the ground and started to unroll it.

"Stop that. The Great Ming Code has rules. You cannot bring a corpse here. It's against the funeral rites," Gang ranted, glowering at Bolin from the edge of the podium.

"Why? What's there to fear? It's only a carpet."

"No. You can't." Gang was foaming at the mouth; wild beasts were tearing him apart.

Bolin stopped unrolling the carpet with most of it open but with the cadaver still concealed in the final folds. He wanted the crowd to see the carpet's snarling Blue Wolf motif. Then he declared, "People of Shanhaiguan. This is the moment an enduring mystery of twenty years is solved."

Gang crouched and threw himself at Bolin like a mountain lion. But Kong moved like a jaguar and deflected Gang's attack, wrestled him to the ground, and twisted his arm behind his back.

"Enough," Kong hissed. "Let the man finish what he was saying."

"Thank you, Kong," Bolin said.

Everyone craned their necks.

"Let the gods bear witness..." Bolin cried.

He unrolled the final fold. Wing's body was face up.

"Behold, Dragon Master Wing," a voice said. It was Dong, the Abbot, who had just entered the yard.

The crowd gasped.

Dong knelt down by Wing's side, tidied his robes and laid his arms out to the side.

When the crowd had quietened, Bolin went on, "Today is my birthday and the anniversary of the day Wing disappeared. For many days, he sent me messages from the spirit worlds, trying in desperation to tell me where his body lay. Today, I listened. Along the way, I have found myself. I am his soul successor and his successor as Dragon Master. His body was hidden in the Jade Chamber."

The crowd sucked in a collective gasp.

Bolin narrowed his eyes and said, "No one could enter the chamber because the murderer placed a secret code on it. That code was revealed by the name of a man's daughter and a flower – 'Ju' – chrysanthemum."

"Whose daughter is named 'Ju'?" Dong asked.

"This specimen," Kong said, pointing at Gang.

"Me? No," Gang protested. Kong let him stand up.

Kong called to a runner at the entrance, "Bring the prisoners forward and hand me the knapsack."

From a side entrance, several constables appeared with three men; Sheng, Qiang and Guanting.

"Guanting," Luli cried. "I knew he was a villain. I knew it!"

"These three," Kong continued, "are in cahoots with Gang. They are traitors to the Prince of Yan. When their plan to poison the prince failed, they set out to blow up the Zhendong Gate and let in the Mongols. For that, they needed explosives, which they bought from a man who met with Guanting in the White Mulberry Wine Bar."

"I was there and overheard the deal; who was that other man?" Feng asked.

"This arch traitor," Kong said, turning to the podium and pointing to Major Renshu.

Even in the cold light of day, Renshu was unrepentant. "I did it for the Emperor and for Heaven."

"Hah! Drivel," Kong scoffed at the man. "You weren't driven by loyalty. Greed more like, when you sniffed those taels of silver; I've got them here." Kong tipped up the knapsack and emptied out scores of silver taels onto the ground.

The crowd swooned at the sight of all that traitor's silver.

The major bowed his head.

"Tell us then, who bought the munitions from you?" Kong asked.

The world stopped, as if it had been waiting with impatience for just this question to be asked and now it had, there was the opportunity to unlock the mysteries of the past.

"I sold them to three men," Renshu said. "Two of them are over there." He pointed at Sheng and Qiang.

"Bring them here," Kong said. The constables pushed two men into the arena.

"Please identify the third man," Kong demanded.

Renshu lifted his finger. "I sold them to him – Magistrate Gang."

"How can you believe the lies of an acknowledged traitor?" Gang yelled, pointing a finger at Bolin.

"Me, a traitor?" Bolin guffawed. "It was you who murdered Abbot Cheng in the mountains. It was you who stuffed a Bagua medallion in his mouth. Once a rat, always a rat!"

"Nonsense!"

"Then explain this to me," Bolin said. He was on a roll now.

"What?" Gang sneered at him. "A snivelling recruit like you, how can you possibly add to this fantastical case against me?"

"Listen and I'll tell you. When I first arrived in the punishment yard, just now, how did you know who or what was wrapped in the folds of the carpet? I didn't let on. Yet everyone heard you say 'a corpse'. There's only one way that you could know that – you put it there. Your guilt cried out over the twenty years."

The traitor ducked. With his hands over his head, the crowd pelted him with stones.

"Take them to the cells," Captain Feng ordered.

CHAPTER 55

Retribution of Heaven

Say not that Heaven is so far, so high;
Its servants, it is ever nigh;
And daily are we here within its sight.
THE SHI KING (BOOK OF ODES)

That afternoon wore an air of tumult and triumph: the battle won, the enemy defeated, the traitors exposed. Only the Laolong awaited his full and complete homecoming into the labyrinthine chambers of the Great Wall. This time was special for Bolin, because he enjoyed the adulation due to the one true Dragon Master and keeper of the Dragon Pearl.

In the Ming Dynasty calendar, the fifteen-day period between the new moon at the New Year and the first full moon traditionally culminated in the Lantern Festival; a time dedicated to feasting with friends, cleaning the household and exchanging gifts. This year, the unpopular curfew and the battle had stifled those festivities, so now there was a sense of happiness, release and renewal, with the blooms of spring just around the corner.

To a vigorous roll of the drums and a cascade of cymbals, the flag of victory was raised in triumph above the Yamen. Gusts of a strong breeze stiffened the flag on its mast and helped to disperse the odours of death that lingered on the battlefield.

During the afternoon, the Duke and his players displayed their musical virtuosity and acrobatic skills to the amusement of all. After that, the strengthening wind ushered in dark clouds that towered over the mountains. Bolin's fingers were numb and the tips of his nose and ears were like icicles.

The clouds, heavy with moisture, were gathering with a foreboding that dampened the spirits of the crowd. The first drops fell, turning to snow and covering the landscape with a blanket of white. The mighty wind dislodged the Duke's colourful hat, which he chased unceremoniously down Ox Bow Street. That was when the people took shelter from the coming storm, leaving only the street urchins and beggars outside.

Gang paced his prison cell, trying to stay warm. What inclement weather. The cold filled his bones with frost and his lungs with an icy fog.

Outside the cell, but inside the prison, Thousand Cuts stood braced against the chill.

As dusk approached, Gang heard a woman's voice in the alley by his outer cell window.

"Ru, let me introduce you. This is Rosemary and this is Thyme." It was Luli. What was she talking about?

"They're beautiful donkeys, mother," Ru replied. Her stupid son was there too. The idiot! All that fuss over a few silver taels. Hah! He, Gang, would soon be free. He would have his revenge again. Then they would suffer. If not, he would come back in the next life and start again. He was not some candle that you could just snuff out and never relight; he was forever, revenge was forever and his friends were legion.

"They're hungry Ru, did you bring the carrots?" Luli was saying. "Good, now see these crates on the cart. Take off the tarpaulin and then we're going to put them all back in the shed. We want to keep them nice and dry, now don't we?"

"Yes, mother," Ru said. "What's in them?"

"Fireworks, Ru, a lot of fireworks for the Lantern Festival," Luli replied.

Gang heard a lot of huffing puffing and he imagined they were moving the crates into the shed. After a while, he heard Luli say, "Good, that's all done. They'll be ready for the Lantern Festival. Bring Rosemary and Thyme and let's be on our way home."

"All right, mother," Ru said. "I've got the umbrella here."

He heard them shuffle off with the empty cart and the two mules.

Well, that was lucky. Now Gang knew where the explosives were hidden. "Thank you Luli," he muttered. He would need them – when he was released.

He was counting on the prince's mercy. From prior experience, he knew that princes hated nothing more than being wrong; an affliction that infected everyone. The prince would suffer enduring shame if he was seen to have appointed a traitor to the prestigious post of Country Magistrate. Every nation had their primal fear – for the Chinese it was fear of loss of face.

Gang would emphasise that he had been falsely accused and that instead the blame should be equally distributed on the lecherous Bao, the greedy major, that fool Big Qiang, his enforcer, Sheng and the fat merchant Guanting. The prince would find such a convincing excuse hard to refuse.

Once he was free again, Gang would take up arms against the Chinese. He had unfinished business. Perhaps Altan was still alive. The exhilaration of revenge would be sweeter still – the second time around.

As he moved away from the window opening, he saw Liu manhandling a prisoner to a cell. The prisoner's face was spattered with blood and mud and his cheek bone protruded out of his face. From the light trousers, shirt and bandanna, he was Mongol. The man frowned at Gang as he passed.

Altan!

Hah! They had caught the Mongol ghost rider. Shame. Or was it? Perhaps the arch shaman could weave his magic and spirit them both away from this place of pain and misery.

Bolin was drunk and needed a pee. Legs crossed, he stumbled in near darkness towards the Yamen. There was a latrine at the far end of the alley by the prison cells. By the time Bolin got there, he had almost wet himself. He sighed as he unleashed a full and vigorous flow. A man came and stood next to him. When Bolin finished, he glanced over to see who it was.

"Liu," he murmured. "How are you?"

Liu let out a soft whistle as he did his business.

"Who's guarding the prisoners?" Bolin said, with a mouthful of slur.

"Me," Liu said, garrulous as ever.

The snow storm was strong but short. The black clouds moved away over the long, slow waves of the Bohai Sea. The top layer of the snow froze and the sun appeared in a clearing sky. It bathed the fortress in a late afternoon luminescence. It lit up the Yanshan Mountains in the north, the detritus on the battlefield outside the Zhendong Gate in the east, the high waves of the Bohai Sea in the south and the approaching Prince of Yan's reinforcements in the west.

A gust of wind blew some papers off the magistrate's desk and out of the window. The sun seemed brighter than ever. Its yang-ridden rays bounced off the newly-frozen snow. The whole light of that afternoon sun seemed to concentrate in one place – in the bronze mirror near the window in the magistrate's chambers.

The beam reflected off the mirror and lighted on a piece of paper, with a name written on the bottom. Feng would have recognised that of his father – Magistrate Park. Mote by mote, the rays danced through the air, enriching the darkness with light and warmth, pushing back the void. A thin wisp of smoke snaked up. The paper began to blacken and a tiny flame enriched the paper, bringing light to the darkness, yang to the yin. The paper was soon engulfed and the flame spread across to the next sheet, heading inexorably towards a wooden shed in a little alley that ran alongside the prison cells.

An almighty explosion rocked the fortress to its foundations. It crashed through the prison cell window with the force of a volcanic eruption. A tongue of orange-red flame licked the clouds and then belched forth a cloud of black sulphurous smoke. The report was deafening. The five towers on the Great Wall quaked.

The explosion dislodged decades of accumulated dust in the jail, filling Gang's cell with a cloud of hot, acrid air. Heaven was defiant in refusing him help, because he knew what had caused it. Gang and Altan had incarcerated a huge serpentine supernatural being in a small chamber for twenty years – with only iron horseshoes and a rotting corpse for company.

It was karma – the Laolong's revenge.

The cell, below ground, had a small opening in its upper reaches. Flaming wood and debris flooded his cell in a wave of scorching fire. The same thing was happening to his conspirators; they were frying in their own skin.

The ball of fire rolled towards him.

His skin was bubbling. He belched, as his lungs tried in vain to keep out the blistering heat. His clothes caught fire and his ears popped. Gang barely had time to reflect on his life and its meaning before the fireball melted him; driven by toxic vengeance, he had succeeded in making a dent in the huge imperial façade, so small that it wouldn't even be recorded in the imperial annals.

CHAPTER 56

The Balance of the Tao

Everything returns to the source of its arising.
This is called 'peace'.
Peace means to go back to one's original nature.
THE TAO TE CHING

The waves of the Bohai Sea lapped against the rim of the outer vault, as Luli carried the incense through the chrysanthemum door. She loaded it into the censers, which Jin and the other monks proceeded to waft around the Jade Chamber, smoking out any residual evil lurking in the corners. As soon as they had finished, Abbot Dong called Jin over to him. "Hold on to these," he said, handing him a bunch of eight iron horseshoes.

"What for?" Jin scratched his head. "Iron curtails the ways of Heaven. Let me give them to the ironmonger to melt down."

"Jin," Dong said with a sigh. "The ways of Heaven are high and mighty, the ways of earth low and solid. Sometimes, it's not possible to find a middle way."

"Master, I don't understand," Jin said with a frown.

"I mean that I have a special use for them, so please look after them for me," Dong insisted.

As Jin stored the horseshoes away, Luli thought it was an odd thing for Dong to ask him to do but dismissed it from her mind. Wing's funeral preparations were more important.

She followed the monks up the spiral steps to the Stone Guardian. Perched on top of it was a solitary magpie, waiting to guide Wing's spirit to Heaven. With much solemnity, the procession set off to the shrine the monks had prepared for Wing's corpse. The magpie led the way, cavorting in the joy of its flight.

Waiting for them at the shrine was the Prince of Yan, recently arrived with reinforcements. A large crowd of mourners had gathered, including Master Wen, the Duke and Kong the Jinyiwei. Commandant Tung and Cui stood rigidly to attention, both wearing head bandages that looked more like white turbans. The magpie perched on the shrine, which was constructed of the same rock and stone as the Great Wall. Luli was sure that Wing would have been honoured to be laid to rest in such prestigious circumstances.

Nearby, Captain Feng stood to attention next to the shrines of his adoptive parents. Luli felt glad that he was there to pay his last respects to the couple who had loved him as their own. By his side was the boy Qitong, proudly dressed in the livery of a Captain's manservant.

In a voice rich with emotion, Dong said, "This ceremony is for Wing. After his spirit has endured many years of distress, we give thanks to God and consign his body to rest."

Luli pressed her hand into Ru's. It was warm and no longer reptilian. She smiled – she had her son back.

"We are born alone and die alone," Dong went on. "This simple fact was poignant for Wing. Trussed up in a Mongol carpet, he died a slow, suffocating death. Today we place him in an open sepulchre, so his wayward spirit can breathe the gentle vapours of the broad air, mingle with Heaven's servants and with the magpie's help, find his way back to his ancestors and to the Great Tao. This is a time of peace when everything returns to the source of its arising."

Everyone lowered their head. Luli pulled her lapels close in. It was cold and a light drizzle fell on her cheeks, rain drops mingling with her tears of grief.

"Does anyone have something they wish to say?" Dong asked.

The Prince stepped forward and spoke, as soft as the light rain. "I am grateful to you all and particularly to Commandant Tung for saving the day. To acknowledge his bravery and courage, I appoint him the Duke of Shanhaiguan. As this is a time of reconciliation, I want to extend the hand of kinship to my new brother-in-law. Welcome to my family."

Captain Feng bowed with all reverence before the prince.

"And I restore him to his rightful position as county magistrate of Hebei Province!"

Everyone waved in appreciation at the prince's magnanimous gesture.

"Thank you, Prince," Feng said, with a sombre smile. "I am honoured. I wish my adopted parents could see me now!"

"They both look down on you from above," Luli insisted.

Bolin stepped forward and said, "I am privileged to know Wing in a unique way; sharing his soul's deepest connections. I have received from him

248

an abundance of gifts, skills and abilities. With them, I shall seek to be the best Dragon Master that I can be."

Bolin held up the Dragon Pearl. Even in the drizzly, overcast morning, the pearl was dazzling in its milky brightness.

"The pearl acknowledges you as the one and only true Dragon Master of the Laolong," Dong said. "It has been too long in finding its rightful owner. And as all things come full circle, may we aid Wing's long-delayed journey to re-join his ancestors."

For a moment, a tranquil peace reigned amongst them.

With the ceremony complete, the magpie squawked, opened its wings and flew up and away into the morning air.

Bolin smiled.

The balance of the Tao was restored.

CHAPTER 57

Pacing the Dragon

If you constantly tread on emptiness (i.e. the stars),
Then after three years you will avoid death,
And after four years you will become a terrestrial immortal.
TAOIST SCRIPTURE

Ru was adjusting to normal life. After Wing's last rites, Luli held his hand as they approached the shadow of the wall. Revived by the milk of human kindness, he had accompanied her to help Dong in the final act of the day. The Abbot, Jin and the few surviving monks in their tattered robes passed the Stone Guardian and entered the Laolongtou.

Some parts of the Laolong had eased out of the Jade Chamber and occupied the Shanhaiguan section of the wall. Now it was time to invite the remainder of the Laolong to occupy the whole of the rest of the Great Wall. As Dragon Master, Bolin was to conduct the consecration ceremony, the homecoming.

Dong laid out fourteen pebbles in a specific pattern. "As the Great Wall is a mirror of the Heavens," he explained, "these pebbles are arranged in the shape of the fourteen stars of the constellation of the Yellow Dragon – the head is here, the serpent's body here and the tail here."

"What I do with them?" Bolin asked nervously.

"Each pebble is laid out one step away from the next. I'm going to show you how to pace them out."

Jin approached with a black lacquer box, which was covered with an intricate dragon and phoenix engraving. Dong opened it and took out the cloud shoes, which were made of the bound silk, with jade green and opalescent motifs of the arrangement of the constellation.

"You can rekindle the ch'i energies that Wing created twenty years ago," he said. "Each step evokes the power of the star in that position in the dragon constellation. The great conclave of dragons will hear your petition. The invisible gate will open, allowing the yellow dragon, the Laolong, the faithful servant of Zhongguo, to return to its rightful home in the Great Wall of Ten Thousand Li."

"I am ready," Bolin said.

Jin was in charge of the musicians. "What shall we play, Abbot?"

"Play as you are moved," Dong explained. "We are dragon children. When you hear the music of the dragon in your hearts, play it."

"May I take an instrument?" Luli asked, indicating a flute.

"Of course," Dong said. "We begin."

Luli watched in fascination as Bolin paced out the dragon. In the cloud shoes, he seemed lighter than air, stepping serenely between the pebbles. Each movement was fluid and intricate, simple yet soulful.

Jin played the violin, a gentle rhythmic harmony, coming from afar and augmenting slowly. The other instruments chimed in. Luli started to play. It was as if an invisible power was moving her fingers along the flute holes on their own accord. The music built, as did the power in Bolin's subtle movements. When he stepped around the dragon's head and turned around, he paced out the dragon again until he reached the tail and then paced it out again.

Luli was as lost in the cadences of the music. As the Heavenly ch'i descended on them, so did a light drizzle of rain. She thought no more of it and went back to watching her hands move along the flute without any interruption from her. Why couldn't life be this effortless all the time, lost in the harmonies of the Great Tao?

As the music and dance built, the white fluffy clouds gathered before a blue-grey sky. The rain became heavier, until it was bouncing up off the packed earth of the road.

In torrential rain, Bolin reached the head of the dragon – and stopped. His eyes were distant and drawn into another-worldly gaze, as if he had no idea where he was or what he was doing. A single clap of thunder rent the darkening sky. Then a flash of lightning spiralled down the dragon paths and lit up the top of the Old Dragon's Head in a sheet of awesome azure power.

Ju and Luli stopped playing. The storm passed overhead almost as quickly as it has arrived. There was the sound of the heavy pitter-patter of the rain, hitting the wall road. It softened, yielded to a light drizzle, until eventually that, too, ceased.

Silence reigned, as the wind abated and the elements retreated.

Luli didn't know how, but the wall felt different beneath her feet. The rains had yielded a heavy mist and as she peered back up the wall towards the Yanshan Mountains, her mouth fell open.

At regular intervals along the wall – perhaps every thousand steps – was a golden arch, rising above the wall, then diving into it, disappearing for a section, then rising out of it again, bow after bow, arch after arch.

And it flowed westwards, from east to west.

As she looked to see if the flow in the wall had changed too, Ru called to her. "Mother, come and see."

"What is it?" She still delighted in hearing him speak. It was like having a cherished friend come home after many years travelling away, another homecoming no less.

Ru was pointing at the Great Wall. He was exultant. "The dragon's come back! Look!"

She hardly believed it. She could see the Great Wall twisting and turning around the natural features in the land. She was ecstatic.

"The faces, mother."

"I see them, Ru, I see them." She was emotional. This had been a long journey; for the dragon, for her, for Ru. For the Zhongguo.

"They are pointing the other way. Away from the sea – inland towards the mountains."

"Yes, Ru."

"The faces are different than before," Ru added, with an air of mystery.

"How's that?"

"They're mostly men's faces. And I can see…" He paused. As if taking in the enormity of what he was about to admit.

"What…?"

"There," he pointed to a profile in the wall, "It's father. It's Heng."

"Truly," Luli stammered, "The dragon's come home."

CHAPTER 58

The Emperor's Mace

The eyes of the people are as the eyes of God.
The ears of the people are as the ears of God.
THE BOOK OF MENCIUS

Today was the Lantern Festival, fifteen days since the prince's banquet. Today was a day of looking forward, of welcoming the New Year and of bringing forward the bright yang light of tomorrow and casting out the dim yin shadows of the past. It was a day when the return of the light was celebrated in every home. It was a day to banish the darkness of the previous year and rekindle fresh hopes and aspirations for the new one. More than that – today was a day when the very future of the Zhongguo was held in the balance.

Luli and Ru were standing on the wall road above the Zhendong Gate, waiting to say goodbye to Bolin, who was about to depart with the Duke's Mummers.

"We've a long way to go," the Duke jibed.

"Good luck and may you forever walk alongside the Tao," Luli said.

"With Lord Wing laid to rest," Bolin said, "I can leave Shanhaiguan and follow the path of the Dragon Master. Wing conferred on me the gift of yin-yang eyes and many other skills and abilities, most of which I have no idea what they are or what they do. I intend to learn how to use them in service of the Zhongguo, so the Han people can be of continuing interest to the gods."

"When you return in twenty years, I'm sure we'll see a master of the dragon arts," Luli said, with a sparkle in her eye.

"Why don't you join us?" the Duke asked. "A Mistress of the Yin and Yang, we've always room for someone with your undoubted talents."

"I thank you kindly but, at least for the moment, I think I'll stay here," Luli admitted ruefully. "Heaven answered my prayers to heal my son. Dong has helped me to find the Tao. I intend to ask him if I can help him rebuild the Taoist temple here."

"I hope it works out for you," Bolin said.

Ru said to Bolin, "You were one of the few who were loyal to me in my dark years. After my father's death, I was afraid of life. Now I cherish every moment of it. May Heaven protect you from misfortune."

"Thank you, Ru," he said. "You are the brother I never had."

"We must take our leave," the Duke said. With a flourish of the drum, the troupe set off along the road. As their laughter faded from earshot, Luli and Ru watched them wend their way along the wall road until they climbed up the foothills of the Yanshan Mountains and were just specks on the horizon.

Luli was happy. Ru purred. The wall was glowing, almost phosphorescent; a bright emanation from its walls repulsing the threat of the Mongols.

Down below, the soldiers were puffing and panting as they lowered the drawbridge. Dong and Jin emerged beneath Luli and Ru and stood next to the moat. Jin carried a spade and a heavy bag.

"We've done the north, the south and the west gates, so this is the last one. I need only two more holes," Dong was saying. "Dig one on either side of the arch."

"Yes, Abbot," Jin replied, obedient to the last.

She could hear the sound of the spade kissing the yielding earth. Dong was chastising Jin, "Deeper than that. Imagine you're going to plant a sapling."

Luli was curious. *What are they going to plant in the holes?*

"Good, that's deep enough," Dong said. "Give me one."

Luli craned her neck over the side but couldn't see what they were doing.

"Fill it with earth," Dong ordered. "What are you waiting for? Go on."

By the time they had finished digging the second hole, Luli's curiosity was well and truly piqued.

"Good," Dong said. "That's it. Done."

"But Abbot," Jin sounded like he was in pain. "Why are we burying these dreadful things beneath our sacred arch?"

"Make no mistake," Dong said, in that haughty tone he adopted on occasion. "They're not buried, they're incarcerated, nor will they ever be dug up. There's a spell on them to prevent you – or anyone else – ever finding or retrieving them. And now this is the fourth and last gate where we've buried them, the seal around the Bagua tunnels is complete and can't be broken."

"Why? I still don't understand." Jin was earnest.

"I'll explain." Dong took a deep breath. "You know I told you that the Emperor's Mace is a mysterious and powerful new influence?"

Jin nodded.

Dong went on, "Well, I found a scroll that Abbot Cheng had written, where I discovered why he had the Bagua tunnels built."

"What are they for then?" Jin asked.

"First, the Emperor's Mace heralds a new dawn for the human race, a new template of action and reaction, a new Tao. But Cheng realised that its influence is contrary to the nature of the Chinese people and will be rejected by them."

"Rejected? Why?" Jin was adamant. "We are a zealous, industrious people. We occupy the Middle Kingdom of earth, the Zhongguo."

"That may be," Dong said, "but as a people, we are staid and recalcitrant. We Chinese resist one thing more than anything else and that is change. For us, change is untenable. And the repercussions of the Emperor's Mace will bring change aplenty."

"I see," Jin said.

"No, you don't," Dong chided. "Let me describe the scale of the change that's coming – if we let it. Consider that five or six hundred years ago, life was more or less the same as it is today. Nothing was happening, spiritually speaking. The Emperor's Mace will quicken the pace of change, making human life in five or six hundred years' time unrecognisable to what it is today. It stands to reason that the people more suited to its uptake will be those more adaptable to change, more versatile, less constrained by ritual and custom."

"Oh, you mean like... the Mongols?" Jin stammered.

"Exactly," Dong snapped. "Now do you see why we have to prevent the Emperor's Mace from seeping into the world."

Then Jin replied, "Let me understand this. You're saying that the Bagua tunnels are... a tomb for the *burial* of the Emperor's Mace?"

"Yes. The influence is drawn through The First Pass under Heaven and then confined in the Bagua tunnels."

"Isn't that wrong?" Jin asked. His voice was pained and troubled.

"Why?" Dong replied, his tone like thunder. "Do you want to invite the barbarian back into the sacred land of the Zhongguo?"

"No, of course not." Jin was defensive. "But you don't possess the mandate to manipulate Heavenly matters."

"I don't care, I'm protecting the Zhongguo from inner decay and outward invasion," Dong sounded strident.

"But you've taken those eight horseshoes from the Jade Chamber and buried a pair of them at each of the four gates. In so doing, you're deliberately depriving humanity of Heavenly influence, improvement and potential genius. Instead, you're going to channel the Emperor's Mace into those dark, empty tunnels where it will sit unused for eternity."

"I've made my choice." Dong said and stalked back into the fortress. After a while, Luli heard Jin's footsteps following him and then the gong, announcing the raising of the drawbridge.

She puffed out her cheeks. How could Dong bury those horseshoes under the arch? Here was a man who chose which parts of the Mandate of Heaven to follow and which parts to ignore; a man who preferred parochial advantage to ubiquitous Heavenly glory. There was a new universal birth at play and Dong wanted it stillborn.

Luli shook her head. The Mongol shaman Altan had trapped the Laolong in an enclosed space to profit his own people and deprive the Zhongguo of a supernatural protector. Dong was deliberately imprisoning a pristine Heavenly influence in underground tunnels in order to deprive the world of advancement and protect his own people. Who was the more immoral?

"I can't join *that* temple," Luli said, spitting out the word with disdain. "The Emperor's Mace is the world's destiny. That's what the legend says. Dong must be stopped. Come on, let's tell Bolin. He'll know what to do."

As they set off along the wall road, Ru nodded and said, "I'm here with you... right now."

ACKNOWLEDGEMENTS

A book is the fruition of an original idea and this is the place to give thanks to the many midwives who helped its sometimes difficult and prolonged birth.

First, I owe a great debt of gratitude for her patience to my long-suffering partner, Irene. This novel was born out of a short story about another famous wall, *Vallum Hadriani,* which I wrote for an anthology compiled by North Bristol Writers, so thanks is due to them.

I owe a heartfelt thanks to my beta readers for persisting with the early draft: Chad Legge, Steve Tanner, Janie St. Clair and Eleni Byrnes. Joanne Hall was also as supportive as ever and as always gave me some invaluable editing advice. Warm thanks are due to Frances Woods and Peter Hardie for their specialist Chinese knowledge and advice.

Also, much of the novel was written and edited in the peace and quiet of Buckfast Abbey, Devon in the company of the Benedictine Monks there.

And a last thanks to my parents, may they rest in peace, for instilling in me at an early age an enduring love of books, reading and literature.

Live. Will. Love.